THE SIEGE OF CANDLEBANE HALL

Mike Jefferies was born in Kent but spent his early years in Australia. He attended Goldsmiths' School of Art and then taught art in schools and prisons. A keen rider, he was selected in 1980 to ride for Britain in the Belgian Three Day Event. He now lives in Norfolk with his wife Sheila, working as a full-time writer and illustrator.

CW01082000

Also by Mike Jefferies

LOREMASTERS OF ELUNDIUM

THE ROAD TO UNDERFALL
THE PALACE OF KINGS
SHADOWLIGHT
THE KNIGHTS OF CAWDOR
CITADEL OF SHADOWS

THE HEIRS TO GNARLSMYRE

GLITTERSPIKE HALL
HALL OF WHISPERS

OTHER TITLES

SHADOWS IN THE WATCHGATE
HIDDEN ECHOES
STONE ANGELS
CHILDREN OF THE FLAME

LEARN TO DRAW FANTASY ART

Voyager

MIKE JEFFERIES

The Siege of Candlebane Hall

HarperCollins*Publishers*

Voyager
An Imprint of HarperCollins*Publishers*
77–85 Fulham Palace Road,
Hammersmith, London w6 8jb

The *Voyager* World Wide Web site address is
http://www.harpercollins.co.uk/voyager

A Paperback Original 1998
1 3 5 7 9 8 6 4 2

Copyright © Mike Jefferies 1998

The Author asserts the moral right to
be identified as the author of this work

isbn 0 00 64821 9

Set in Postscript Goudy by
Rowland Phototypesetting Ltd,
Bury St Edmunds, Suffolk

Printed and bound in Great Britain by
Caledonian International Book Manufacturing Ltd, Glasgow

All rights reserved. No part of this publication may be
reproduced, stored in a retrieval system, or transmitted,
in any form or by any means, electronic, mechanical,
photocopying, recording or otherwise, without the prior
permission of the publishers.

This book is sold subject to the condition that it shall not,
by way of trade or otherwise, be lent, re-sold, hired out or
otherwise circulated without the publisher's prior consent
in any form of binding or cover other than that in which it
is published and without a similar condition including this
condition being imposed on the subsequent purchaser.

To my wife, Sheila,
without whose support and encouragement
this siege would never have been broken.

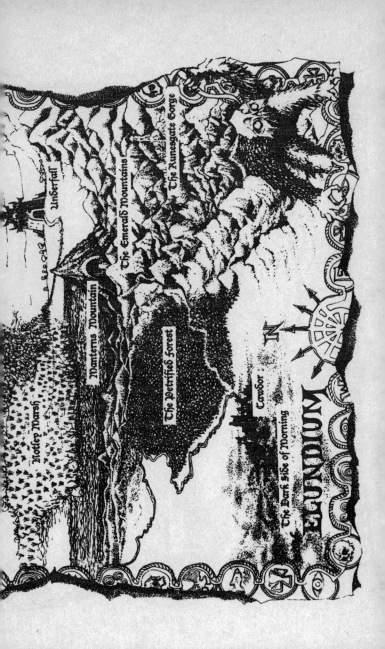

I

An Unwelcome Apparition

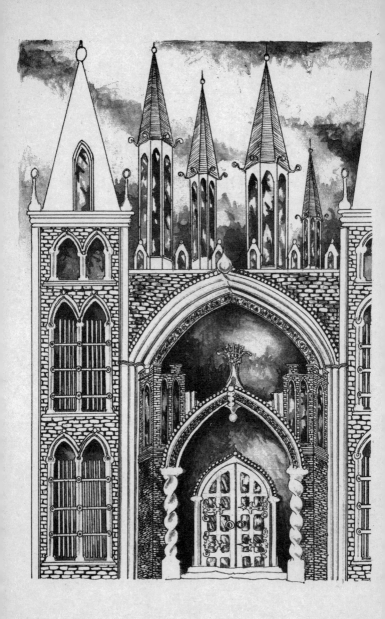

Snatchpurse was possessed by an all consuming black rage he could not shake off. He paced through the ruins of the tower on Stumble Hill with Squark, his white magpie, perched upon his shoulder. The spoils of victory, the pleasure of torturing his captives, everything that he had planned so meticulously had been so cruelly snatched from beneath his nose: those wretched Archers who had defended the tower had unexpectedly broken out and escaped the moment the doors of the tower had been battered down.

'You . . . you . . . you stupid fools! Why did you let that snivelling column of cowards escape? They didn't even have the backbone to stand and fight us and yet you let them go!'

He was snarling at his men who were busy scouring through the debris to find the corpses of any of the Archers who had fallen during the assault so that they could be dragged out and counted.

'This – this should have been our greatest victory, you imbeciles. That miserable Thronestealer's queen, Elionbel, was hiding here, she was right here in the tower! I wanted her captured, I wanted her alive – you fools! I wanted to chop off her hand and send it as a gift to Thanehand.'

Bright bubbles of spittle were beginning to form in the corners of his scaly mouth as he raged, his anger heightening until the pupils of his eyes shrank to murderous pin-points.

'I ought to kill you all!'

He stabbed a vicious claw-like hand at those closest to him as he strode through the archway. His followers knew how unpredictable and violent their leader's moods could be and they cowered away from him as they waited with baited breath to hear his plans.

'Fools! Victory! Fools! Victory!' Squark mocked, imitating his master's voice with a harsh shriek, his head bobbing rapidly up and down.

Snatch was in no mood for it and cursed the bird's insolence with a rough cuff of his hand, sending it tumbling off his shoulder and swooping away from him to fly through the ruins.

Snatch paused beneath the archway that led into the main courtyard and fiercely shook his head, trying to control the anger that flooded through him. Once his purpose had been crystal clear, his one aim was to seize back the power and dignity that the Thronestealer had stolen from his father and the other Chancellors when he had exiled them into Meremire Forest. That was why he had founded the Honourable Company of Murderers. He had only been trying to return the rule of Elundium to its rightful custodians – the Chancellors. The killings, the intrigue and the web of lies and deceptions that he had needed to enmesh and control his followers had merely been the means by which he could achieve his aim. It was all an enjoyable interlude, no more. But since the Eretch – those grave devils they had encountered beneath the eaves of the petrified forest the night before they had attacked Cawdor – had entered them, they had all changed so drastically. Snatchpurse silently cursed his own foolishness for not heeding Loremaster Grout's warning. He had warned them not to meddle with the Eretch. He had told them to wait

4

until he had found out why Krulshards, their creator, had been so quick to abandon them in the ruins. But they had seemed to offer so much. While they waited in that dark, petrified forest the Eretch had promised them victory. Soft, persuading whispers and brief glimpses of the power that they offered could not be resisted. The Eretch had possessed them so easily, they had entered through their eyes and ears, flooded in through the pores of their skin and caused a complete physical metamorphosis. They had fused the rotting Nightbeast armour to their skins, causing the claws and hides they wore as a disguise to become a part of their bodies – giving each one of them a dark power. The sight of his men terrified their enemies and their armoured hide meant that weapons could not harm them. But it had been nothing but beguiling tricks.

The Eretch had set out to ensnare them and persuade them to become willing hosts so that they could escape from their enforced imprisonment at Cawdor. Snatchpurse did not need that snivelling Loremaster to tell him why Krulshards had abandoned them. He now knew only too well what unpredictable, treacherous creatures they could be. One moment they would totally possess a man, urging him to commit all kinds of evil secure in the knowledge that he was invincible and the next, at a blink, they would desert him, leaving him weak and vulnerable. And it was all done without a moment's warning. Whenever the Eretch felt they had found another, better, host they would abandon the first one.

But worse, the Eretch, he had come to realize, were slowing his advance down. They were making his men break off from the march into Elundium and senselessly attack, loot and massacre. They had lost their purpose. The Eretch were dangerous allies but he didn't want to be wholly rid of them, not yet. They gave his men so much power, made them so brave. He didn't want them to go until he had used them to help him to overthrow the Thronestealer and set his severed head upon an iron spike above the gates of the Granite City. He wanted everyone to see the extent of his victory.

Snatchpurse and his most trusted captains, Kush, Thorograsp and Girrolt, who had been with him since the very beginning, had been secretly and carefully watching the way the Eretch possessed their followers and they had schemed for ways to seize back control of them. It was Kush who had first noticed that it was the weaker-willed amongst their men who the Eretch could control most strongly. The ones who had been the easiest to lure into the Honourable Company of Murderers. Often the Eretch would drive them into uncontrollable fits of madness. And it grew much worse when the Eretch had utterly devoured a man's soul and eaten away his mind, feeding on it until he had become nothing but an empty, hollow husk. That was when the Eretch were at their most dangerous. They had noticed that this was when his men were at their most vulnerable: it was when the Eretch would set out to search for a new host.

The Eretch were forced to leave their old host alive and they secured a new body because two grave devils could not occupy the same host, and without a host they vanished in a wailing, haunting cry to become no more substantial than pools of shadows dwelling in a dark corner, watching, waiting for some innocent traveller to pass by. They needed someone they could beguile with their evil whisperings of greed and vengeance. Through this knowledge of the Eretch's weakness Snatch had been quick to realize that there was a way to rid himself of them. One by one as they failed to find a new host and tried to return to the old one, he killed the men. He had no use for those of his followers the Eretch had sucked dry: those men meant nothing to him. Murder in the dark had always been such an enjoyment for him. A speciality of their Honourable Company. He and his few trusted captains had been quick to seize the advantage and they had begun to thin out the Eretch. They had become very good at watching for those of their followers who suddenly showed all the signs of the madness that meant that the Eretch had temporarily deserted them. It was at that moment that they would creep up behind their unsuspecting victim and slip a silent strangle over their heads and brutally jerk it tight. They murdered before the Eretch could get back.

But Snatch had discovered another troubling weakness that everyone suffered from when they were possessed. Their bodies had become strong, clothed in beautiful, scaly armour, with claws, horns and spines, but their shadows had become strangely distorted and they could not bear the pain and discomfort if anyone, friend or foe, should accidentally tread on them. They had become like open wounds and it made them very vulnerable. And this was something Snatch did not know how to stop.

Girrolt saw Snatchpurse pause beneath the archway, muttering, cursing loudly to himself as his rage deepened, and he hurried across towards him. 'Snatch, Snatch, we must celebrate this great victory with a feast!' He shook his leader's arm in an effort to pull him out of this black mood.

Snatchpurse blinked as Girrolt's voice broke into his dark riddling and he turned sharply towards him, his lips tightening into a snarl. 'Victory? You call this a victory?

Do you bring me news that you have found at least one of those wretched Archers still alive?'

Girrolt moved in closer, lowering his voice 'None of us could have known that the Archers would attempt to break out of here, or that they had some of those vile nightflower seeds to throw in our faces. Their thorny tendrils and brilliant flower-heads grew so quickly, we were all blinded and driven back by them. We were powerless to stop them and it was impossible to pursue them once that pack of Border Runners appeared on the greenways' edge. We could do nothing, nothing.'

'I know, I know all about that,' muttered Snatch. There was a lot of truth in what Girrolt had just said but he still could not shake off the cold rage that churned around inside him. Glancing past his captain he caught sight of the corpses of the Archers being dragged into the centre of the courtyard ready for counting. Suddenly he threw back his head and howled with cruel, pitiless laughter. He had just seen a way to use those corpses to their advantage.

He put a friendly arm around Girrolt's shoulder and turned him around to face the courtyard. 'You are right, my friend, we must celebrate this great victory. There shall be a feast in the Archers' banqueting hall this very night but first . . .'

Snatch paused as a gloating smile thinned his lips. 'But while the feast is being prepared I want you, good friend, to hack off the hands from those corpses and stuff them into a sack along with a few other trophies that could only have come from here. Tomorrowlight, after our victory feast, I want you to ride with all haste to the Granite City and deliver that sack of sweetmeats to the Thronestealer. I want you to gloat a little – boast to him of our victories, goad and mock him with our triumphs. Leave him in no doubt that his friends are dead or have fled and that he stands utterly alone upon the brink of defeat.'

Snatch's eyes narrowed into calculating slits as he pulled Girrolt closer to whisper, 'I will sleep easier at night knowing that you have taken charge of the Granite City. Make your headquarters in the Learning Hall, that way you can keep an eye on Loremaster Grout. I don't altogether trust him, he knows too much about our plans and he would betray his own mother if he had the chance to save his own worthless hide. Your presence there will ensure that he doesn't try to sneak into the Candlehall and form some unhealthy, treacherous alliance with the Thronestealer. You can make sure the King stays securely siege-locked in Candlebane Hall at the same time. I want him brought to his knees with starvation by the time we arrive triumphant at the Stumble Gate. Do you understand what you are to do?'

Girrolt grinned and nodded, well pleased to have been entrusted with such an important task. He unsheathed his dagger and spat on the blade lovingly, wetting it with his tongue before dropping onto his knees amongst the litter of corpses and busied himself with defiling the dead.

As they looted and ransacked the ruins of the tower word quickly spread through Snatchpurse's followers that there was to be a victory feast that night in the banqueting hall. A great cheer arose as all thoughts of the escaping Archers were forgotten and the scullions and broth boilers who fed Snatchpurse's army took the meagre sack-fulls of rotting, maggoty meats and mouldy flour they had plundered from the villages they had overrun and swarmed into the deserted kitchens in search of anything edible to swell their provisions. They laughed and shouted, threatening to boil the maggots and cook up a broth fit for

9

heroes as they broke open the cupboards and plundered the larders, dragging everything they could find into the centre of the roasting kitchen. Sacks of flour were roughly torn apart, tall, crystal jars and squat earthenware jugs containing all manner of wholesome sweet and savoury preserves that had been set aside for the coming winter were smashed open and their contents mixed with the flour and handfuls of wild flower seeds to form a sloppy, sticky, fermenting mass which was then thrown into a row of huge, pot-bellied, black, iron cauldrons which had been suspended on trammel hooks above the lighted cooking fires. The scullions scoured the kitchen bins and found crusts of bread, cheese rinds and spoilt forest fruits which they threw haphazardly into the rapidly filling pots. Flagons of ale and barrel dregs were poured in to dilute the evil smelling broth as it began to froth and bubble. Serving trays were piled high with raw, butchered bones, a rare delicacy among Snatchpurse's men, and as the scullions looked around the kitchens they congratulated themselves on their inventiveness. As darkness fell they carried the cauldrons and flagons into the noisy banqueting hall. It was going to be the most lavish, delicious feast that had ever been served in the tower on Stumble Hill.

Snatch belched, well satisfied with the feast, and he sprawled back drunkenly in Lord Kyot's ornately carved chair as he sat amongst his captains at the head of a table set upon a narrow dais in a place of high honour.

'It . . . it . . . it has been our greatest victory,' Thorograsp stuttered through a mouth crammed with food before slowly toppling forwards with glazed, bulging eyes and collapsing across the table in a drunken stupor.

'I'll . . . I'll drink to that . . .' Kush gurgled as he drained his tankard. Froth and ale trickled down his chin as he tried to rise to his feet, only to lose his balance and send his chair crashing to the ground behind him. Shrieks of glee and derision arose from the other revellers.

Snatch opened his mouth to roar with laughter at his captains' antics but he hesitated, his lips thinning into a snarl as he suddenly sensed that something was wrong. The spines on the back of his scaly neck prickled as he rose unsteadily to his feet, clutching at his jug of ale with a clawed hand. His eyes narrowed to murderous slits as he searched the crowded banqueting hall. It felt as though somebody, an unwelcome intruder, had come in and was there, watching him, but no matter how hard he hunted across the heads of the crowd he could see no-one who should not be there. The raucous laughter, the drunken shouts and the sounds of revelry continued unbroken amongst his men as they brawled and squabbled over the mounds of raw bones, eager to seize the tastier strips of flesh, or drank noisily from the upturned barrels and flagons of frothing brews that lined the tables. It was obvious that there was not an intruder at the feast, but who or what was giving him this unpleasant sensation? He just could not shake it off.

Suddenly, whatever it was seemed as though it moved closer to him. He spun around and peered from left to right, searching the leaping smoky shadows cast by the flickering liquid flames of the crude tar-dipped reed torches that had been set to illuminate the feast. Snatchpurse's anger was rising. Surely none of his followers, no matter how drunk they became, would have the audacity to stare at him so openly, to challenge his absolute authority? They all knew how much he hated such insolence. Anger was turning to rage inside him as he stared down across those who had gathered around the base of the raised dais where he stood. His mouth soured into a thin line of distaste as he caught sight of Crimp, the blacksmith's son. He was sitting slightly apart from the others, clutching at the end of the rusty chain that was shackled to the ankle of the ugly little female Tunneller that Snatch had captured during the attack on Cawdor and was keeping alive to torture for his pleasure.

Snatch had long had doubts about Crimp's loyalty. The boy had a suspicious, furtive way about him. It was as though he had something to hide. He would have slit his throat ages ago but Kush and Girrolt insisted that his loyalty could not be faulted so, despite his misgivings, he had given him the task of guarding his prisoner, Sloeberry. Snatchpurse stared down to where the heavy iron fetters snaked into the shadows beneath the dais where she was hiding. It must be her he could feel watching him, staring at him with her bulbous eyes. He had suppressed the impulse to kill her the moment he captured her at Cawdor; instead he decided to use her as a bait to snare that crippled creature, crooked Drib. The boy had escaped with the Tunnellers from the Granite City and he seemed to like the girl. He had wanted so badly to take his revenge, to punish the cripple for daring to loose an arrow strike at him as the Tunnellers were escaping from the cellars. It had wounded him in the chest and the boy would pay for so much pain. He would use the girl to lure him into trying to rescue her. The plan had seemed to work perfectly at Cawdor but the pleasure of his revenge had been cruelly taken from him. He had mortally injured the boy, there could be no doubt about that – he had crushed his skull with a brutal blow from his battle mace. But Drib had escaped, more dead than alive, carried away by his horse, slumped and unconscious in the saddle. He had galloped into the petrified forest where, no doubt, he had died and the wolves would have torn his body limb from limb before the carrion birds pecked his crooked skeleton clean. But the thought of Drib's death brought him little satisfaction. He had wanted to torture the boy, kill him, watch him die but only after he had suffered for inflicting that arrow wound on him which had never completely healed.

Snatchpurse stamped his foot furiously, expecting the sound of it to make the girl cower and look away from him but instead the sense of being watched grew even stronger. 'I'll make her pay,' he hissed.

'What's the matter? What is wrong with you? Why are you stamping your foot?' Girrolt asked in a slow, slurred voice as he struggled to rise from his chair.

'Matter? What's the matter? Can't you feel her staring at me? Can't you see it?' Snatch snapped at his captain.

'Who is staring at you?' Girrolt asked in a bewildered voice, glancing out across the dining hall.

'You'll see!' Snatch turned sharply towards Crimp and snarled, 'Bring that ugly little goblin forwards. Make her dance. Let the entertainment begin. Hurry up, Crimp, jump to it, boy, I'll not ask you twice!' And for good measure he hurled his half-empty ale jug at him.

Crimp leapt to his feet with a startled cry as the earthenware jug struck his shoulder and shattered into pieces, soaking him in ale. He looked up and saw the purple rage that had blackened his leader's face and he made a great show of tugging hard at the heavy iron fetters and cursing loudly at Sloeberry as he pulled her out from where she had hidden beneath the platform.

13

Crimp was not brave by nature, but nor was he as thoroughly evil as he was forced to pretend to be: he was just trying to survive. A knot of panic tightened in his stomach as he saw Snatchpurse towering angrily over him. He lived in daily terror that someone would realize that the evil of the Eretch had barely touched him, that he had resisted their vile whisperings when they had arrived beneath the eaves of the petrified forest the night before the attack on Cawdor. All around him he had seen the others transformed. The disguise they had worn became real horns and claws and armoured skin seemed to become one with them. He feared that at any moment they would turn on him and discover his secret, but to his relief he found that the disguise he wore had loosely fused to his skin though the scales were soft and weak and they would flake off at the slightest touch. He knew he had to be very careful to avoid discovery.

Crimp bitterly regretted running away from his father's forge in the village of Muddle and wished he had never joined this Honourable Company of Murderers. Too late he realized what a stupid fool he had been. Too late he learned there could never be anything honourable in murder. But there was no good crying about that now, he had to try to make amends for the crimes he had committed and now he was secretly doing everything he could to keep Sloeberry alive.

'Hurry, girl, hurry. Get out here and dance for your master.' And then in a lower voice, 'You know that the longer you keep him waiting the more he will beat you and I can do nothing to stop him. Hurry, please hurry.'

He made a great show of rattling the chains noisily and cursing foully as he peered beneath the dais into the shadows.

'Quickly,' he whispered, feeling the crowd watch his every move and resisting the urge to reach out and help her to her feet.

'Dance, goblin, dance!' Snatchpurse snarled amid jeers, taunts and cruel laughter from his macabre army. They picked up the chant and 'dance, goblin, dance' erupted from the drunken mob as the tiny, frail figure of Sloeberry, her face blackened and swollen with bruises, half-stumbled, half-crawled from under the dais and emerged into the dimly-lit hall.

Her wrists and ankles were bloodied from where the heavy chains and shackles had rubbed them raw and her back, arms and legs were a mass of congealed and bloody welts where the whip had cut through the filthy rags that now hung from her emaciated body. Weakly she tried to stand and Snatchpurse sneered at her with impatience.

'What is the matter with you, you ugly little creature? I suppose you think you are too good to entertain the likes of us. I suppose you would rather spend your time daydreaming, pretending that crippled Drib is coming to rescue you?'

Howls of laughter rose as Snatchpurse taunted her.

'Oh he'll come,' she whispered softly to herself, looking up defiantly into the monster's face. 'I know he will come, and when he does he will make you pay for every time you've touched me.'

But Snatchpurse heard her and his mocking sneer turned into a scream of rage. 'The cripple is DEAD – DEAD, do you hear me? Nobody is going to come and rescue somebody as ugly as you, nobody. Now dance. Get up and dance you wretched creature. GET UP!'

He lurched threateningly forwards to the very edge of the dais and grabbed the chain from Crimp's hand, pushing him roughly aside. 'I'll teach you to dance. I'll show you what to expect for answering me back.'

He swayed drunkenly as he gave the chain a brutal jerk and then tossed it aside to reach for the long, iron-tailed lash that lay amongst the greasy, maggoty remains of the feast on the table.

'Now you will dance. You will dance until your feet bleed!' he snarled, raising the lash menacingly above his head ready to strike her.

Roars of encouragement and applause thundered through the hall but he hesitated. The spines on the back of his neck were tingling and prickling as he suddenly became aware of somebody who should not have been there. A body, indistinct, shadowy and standing so close, closer than any of his captains would have dared to stand. He felt fingers, invisible fingers, close around his wrist, preventing him from wielding the lash, and he heard a voice challenging him. It was no more than a whispered echo but it was loud enough to send a cold shiver of recognition through him. He felt the hand that gripped him twist his arm forcefully and pull him off balance. His self-assured leer faltered as he found himself staring into Drib's face, only it was hazy and translucent, barely visible. Snatchpurse's fear tightened around him but he sneered with hate, his eyes narrowing into murderous, glittering slits as he looked right through the apparition.

'I am not afraid of your ghost, you cripple. I don't believe in ghosts. I killed you at Cawdor, you can't hurt me, you can't threaten me: you're not real.'

'Drib! Drib, I knew you would come and save me.' Sloeberry stumbled forwards and reached out towards him as he wrestled to keep hold of her tormentor.

'There's nothing there, you idiot,' Snatchpurse snarled

at her, wrenching his arm free of Drib's grip and lurching forwards, wielding the whip at the boy's elusive shadow as it melted away.

The iron-tipped tails of the lash sang through the air and wrapped themselves around Drib's vanishing forearm. Sloeberry let out a gasp of surprise as she saw him disappear. The tails of the lash momentarily hung in the empty air, outlining the shape of his arm where they had snaked and twisted themselves around it. Snatchpurse felt a sharp tug on the handle of the whip and before he could let go it jerked him off balance. He stumbled forward and, with a frightened cry, he found himself engulfed in a swirling rush of darkness. The feasting hall, the shouts and laughter of his men, everything that was familiar to him disappeared in a flash and became a far away echo. Nightwinds roared and shrieked around him; treetops, bare outcrops of rock and steeply wooded mountain slopes rushed past in a blur of light and shadow. Then the sensation of tumbling, rushing through the starlit darkness, suddenly stopped with a bump. Dizzy and disoriented he found he had come to an abrupt halt in the centre of a shadowy alpine meadow somewhere high up amongst mountains. The sounds of the night were faint and far away. He was still clutching the handle of his whip as he faced the ghostly image of Drib, only now he seemed much too real to be a ghost.

Snatchpurse looked wildly around him. He didn't understand. What was happening to him? What evil tricks, what illusions had drawn him away from the feast at Stumble Hill? But in that instant he found he didn't care. His hatred of the crippled boy consumed him and swelled his rage: his only thought now was to kill him. His only purpose was to be rid of him forever. Looking down he saw that the tail of his lash was still wound around the boy's arm and with a snarl he gave the whip a brutal yank as he reached out with his other, clawed, hand ready to grasp the boy around the throat. But he could not quite reach. It was as though his hand was pushing against a cold, invisible barrier. His snarl of rage turned into a cry of fear as he clawed frantically at the invisible surface, making it ripple and distort Drib's image much as when a stone is dropped into the still surface of a pond. Snatch drew back his hand in fear. At that moment another figure suddenly appeared on the edge of his swirling vision. It appeared to be a body in the shape of a wizened old man dressed in a hessian cloak. Snatch could see him shouting something at the boy, gesticulating as he ran towards him and demanding that he unwind the tail of the whip and free it from his arm. Snatchpurse shrieked. Anger and fury possessed him and he hurled himself forward at the invisible barrier. His one purpose was to strangle the crooked creature and to stop this nightmare.

The barrier shuddered and began to swell where he took hold of it and shook it. Thousands of tiny fractures began to spread across its surface. Snatch pushed hard and then he suddenly felt his scaly face begin to break through. The sweet night scent of heather filled his nostrils and the dark mountains with the star-filled sky began to sharpen into focus. He caught a glimpse of a camp fire and beyond it a huge, ancient wagon covered with a brightly-coloured awning. He continued to smash towards the barrier with his clenched fist and reached out for the crippled boy before he managed to untangle the whip from his arm. He was so intent on grabbing hold of the wretched creature that he did not notice the owl watching him with blinkless eyes from where it was perched on top of the wagon, or see it rise into the air, its talons outstretched, as it stooped silently towards him.

Without warning the dark shape of the owl suddenly blocked out the stars above him as it swooped down towards him. Snatchpurse screamed, throwing back his head, as the bird's talons raked across his scaly face, cutting bloody gouges deep into his cheek. He let go of the handle of his whip and staggered backwards, instinctively reaching up to tear the owl off and protect his face. But the owl vanished as silently as it had appeared. At the instant Snatchpurse let go of the whip he felt that he was being sucked backwards. Drib, the old man, the wagon, everything around him became distorted and blurred and seemed to be far away as he turned over and over, tumbling through the swirling darkness. His face felt as though it was on fire and he howled with the pain. Then the rushing, rolling, tumbling sensation stopped and he landed with a jarring thump amongst the litter of the feast, still upon the dais. The momentum sent him sprawling forwards onto his hands and knees.

For a moment he knelt there, the breath knocked out of him. He was disorientated and confused. The sweet scent of mountain heather, the starlight, the crippled boy and the old man had all vanished and his senses told him he must be back in the Archers' tower on Stumble Hill. The rich aroma of the feast, the acid reek of the tar-dipped reed lamps invaded his nostrils and all around him he could hear the shouts and laughter of his men as though nothing unusual had happened. But surely that wasn't possible? He could not have been the only one to see the crippled boy, could he? Somebody must have seen him disappear.

'You! You, you and you!' he hissed angrily as he leapt to his feet and stabbed his clawed hand at those closest to him on the dais. 'Tell me what you saw. Tell me what happened here a moment ago? That vile cripple was here, wasn't he? How many of you saw me chase him? Who saw me wield a lash at him? Tell me!'

After a moment's confused silence somebody called out. 'We saw nothing, master. We only saw you stumble and fall.'

The mob began to edge nervously away from the dais as Snatchpurse took a threatening step towards them. They knew only too well how obsessed he had been with killing the crippled boy and how unpredictable his murderous moods became whenever he uttered Drib's name.

'Nothing! You dare to say that I was doing nothing? I am never doing nothing. Now tell me exactly what you saw.'

'You . . . you . . . you were about to make that ugly goblin creature dance and entertain us when one of the reed lamps suddenly flared up brightly. It happened at exactly the same moment that you raised the lash and it must have distracted you, master, because you looked around sharply. Then all of a sudden you lost your balance. That is how you came to trip and then stumble. But there wasn't anybody else with you then.' The man spoke and then quickly hid himself in the crowd.

'Oh yes there was!' another voice shouted. 'I swear I saw something. It was shadowy and twisted, a figure appearing right there beside our great lord, and it was hideously deformed. But the lamp flared so brightly that it blinded me momentarily and I couldn't see it any more.'

The men were eager to placate their master before he took his anger out on them and spoilt the rest of the feast.

'Relax, it was nothing,' Girrolt laughed, looking drunkenly across the overturned chair. 'Those fools will say anything if they think it will keep you happy. They'll have you jumping at your own shadow in a moment. They'll have you believing that you saw the ghost of that crippled boy if you let them. All you did was raise your lash to beat the ugly little goblin and make her dance for us and then the lamp flared and you tripped, nothing more. Now come on, enjoy the feast and forget about that cripple, he's been a curse to you for long enough but he is dead. Remember you killed him at Cawdor. He can't bother us any more.'

Snatchpurse spun round angrily and lunged towards Girrolt. How dare he make light of what had happened. But then he paused, frowning. Had he really been the only one to see Drib? He didn't believe in ghosts – or magic for that matter. The cripple had been here in the feasting hall, he was sure of it, he had felt him grab hold of his wrist to prevent him from beating Sloeberry. He had been real enough, the tail of his lash had curled around him and become entangled with his arm, but what had happened immediately after that was a blur, a confusion.

He turned slowly around him and stared down at the wretched little Tunneller. She had sunk back onto her knees and had her head bowed. As he looked at her fragments of what had happened sharpened into clearer focus. The cripple had pulled him out of the hall, he had been dragged through the darkness to somewhere high amongst the mountains, and there had been somebody else with Drib, but who was it? And what else had he seen? What else had happened in that high place? A stab of pain in the side of his face made him express a harsh, ragged breath as he reached up and touched his cheek, wincing as his sharp claws prodded at the sticky, congealing wounds that had been cut deeply into his scaly skin. The memory of the owl attacking him, raking its razor sharp talons across his face, making him let go of Drib and his whip came flooding back. He looked down, searching amongst the debris of the feast for his whip. But it was nowhere to be seen. The absence of the lash, the bloody gouges in his cheek convinced him – there was no doubt in his mind now: he had not dreamt or imagined it, he had not been visited by Drib's ghost. The cripple was alive. He had survived the brutal blow on the back of his head. He was alive, but how? By what evil cunning tricks, by what deception had he slipped past the guards and entered through the locked doors of the hall? How had he visited the very heart of their victory feast without anybody seeing him? Doubt about whether he was dead or alive began to creep into his mind. Perhaps what he had seen was an angry, spectral image invested with supernatural powers.

The sound of Sloeberry's whispering voice broke into his troubled thoughts and he looked down at her. Tears had filled her large, round eyes and were streaming down her dirty face.

'I knew you would find a way to stop him from hurting me. I knew you would come,' she kept repeating, again and again.

Snatchpurse realized that it had to be her fault Drib had appeared. Real or not, he had spoiled their feast. All his hatred and loathing boiled up inside him. He reached back to unhook the strangle that hung from his belt and took one threatening step towards her. He would be rid of her now. He would be rid of her and Drib once and for all. But then he hesitated, his eyes narrowed as he searched the crowded, noisy hall. What if the cripple was still lurking in the shadows, watching, waiting for him to make a move against the goblin before he struck again. There was no knowing how he would attack the next time. Perhaps the owl strike had just been a warning.

He glared down at the girl again and before she could avert her eyes he caught her staring at his bloody cheek. Her tears had gone now and in their place he thought he could glimpse a spark of hope.

'Drib is alive, I know he is now,' he heard her whisper defiantly as she reached up to touch her own cheek with her bruised and blackened fingers.

'Get her out of here! Get her out of my sight!' he hissed at Crimp as he took a violent kick at the end of the chain where it lay on the edge of the dais and returned to his chair.

Snatch sat down heavily in his chair, ignoring the bowls of black, slippery sweetmeats and the frothing jug of ale that had been freshly drawn for him by his eager servers. The crippled boy's unwelcomed appearance had stolen his appetite and soured the feast for him. He could think of nothing else, he had to find out where the creature was hiding. He had to find him and strangle him, be rid of him forever. But how? Where was he to begin to look? The boy had appeared and disappeared so quickly. Squark strutted slowly across the table in front of him, pausing every now and then to search with his sharp, beady eyes amongst the mess of half-eaten food and spilled ale before pecking at a tasty morsel. Snatch cursed the bird irritably and raised his hand to drive it away. He was in no mood for its harsh, shrieking mimicry. But then he stopped his hand. An idea suddenly occurred to him. All the carrion birds of the sky had been gathering around Squark to share the spoils of their triumphant march into Elundium and pick over the corpses they were leaving in their wake. A cunning smile wetted his lips as he reached forwards and fondly caressed the white magpie.

'Go quickly, Squark, go and gather your flocks of pretty friends and fly high through all the mountain passes, search everywhere and find that crooked creature Drib.'

The bird made a shrieking cry and spread his wings. 'Tell them this, tell them that they shall have the bodies of the Archers we found here in the ruins of this tower to pick clean as a reward if they can bring me word of where that cripple is hiding.'

With a whir of his white feathers the magpie soared into the air and Snatch laughed as he shouted to the doorwarden to throw open the doors. Squark flew up into the rafters of the hall and only moments later a rising clamour of harsh cries erupted amongst the other carrion flocks that had roosted there, waiting to plunder the leftovers from the feast. The sound of the beating wings filled the air, making the flames of the reed lamps dance and flicker in the fire baskets as the thousands of birds began to fly out through the open doors and the hundreds of broken windows throughout the tower. They departed in an ominous black cloud low across the treetops towards the distant mountains that fenced Elundium as the first light of morning strengthened in the sky.

Snatch's face split into a sour sneer as he watched the pandemonium and confusion that the birds' noisy departure had created amongst his men. They obviously thought they were under attack: shouts erupted and tables were overturned, the clash of steel rang out as weapons were snatched up. Snatch hammered on the table with his battle mace, smashing plates and jugs as he shouted for order. He was barely able to conceal his anger at them for being so drunk and addle-witted that they had failed to see that the crippled creature had slipped in amongst them.

'Eat, drink, you drunken fools, fill your bellies to bursting while you can because some of you will have a long march and an ambush to set once our feathered friends bring me back news of the whereabouts of that cripple boy. When I know where he is you will run until your feet are blistered and you will bring me back his head in a sack.'

Sloeberry had never given up on the one slender thread of hope that Drib was still alive. She had refused to believe the sneering, mocking voices of her captors who, at every opportunity, relished in describing every gruesome detail of how their Lord and Master, Snatchpurse, had crushed his skull with his battle mace during the rout of Cawdor. They told her how Drib had been so grievously injured that there could be no doubt he was now dead. He had, however, escaped on his mount Sparkfire and she had overheard how the great horse had charged through their swarming ranks with Drib unconscious in the saddle. Somehow she had always believed that he had survived that crushing blow, she felt it deep down in her heart – it was the one thing that had given her the strength and determination to cling onto life for as long as she could. One daylight she would see him riding towards her through the wreath tails of morning mist, the sunlight upon his helm, to rescue her. And now she knew it more than ever.

'Crimp! Crimp!' she whispered urgently, creeping forwards to the edge of her hiding place beneath the dais as quietly as she could. She dare not rattle her chains. Crimp heard her whisper and, after glancing casually around to make sure that nobody was watching him, he moved across and squatted down close to her.

'He is alive, Crimp, I know now that Drib is alive. You saw him appear a few moments ago, you saw him stop that monster from beating me didn't you?'

Crimp frowned and shrugged. There had been some sort of commotion on the dais: he had seen Snatch raise the lash when a peculiar swirl of light and shadow surrounded him, but he had thought it was caused by the lamp suddenly flaring up, nothing more. He knew how much Sloeberry clung on to the forlorn hope that Drib was still alive and that he was coming to rescue her, he knew how she was always searching for a sign and he didn't want to crush that hope. But Drib here in the feasting hall? No, he couldn't believe that, it just could not have happened.

'I don't know, I'm not at all sure what I saw,' he muttered under his breath.

'But look at the bloody cuts on Snatch's face, and why did he send out all those vile birds to search for Drib if he was dead? How do you explain that?' she asked, barely able to contain her excitement.

'Be quiet!' Crimp hissed nervously as he stole a furtive look up at the bloody gouges on Snatchpurse's face. There was certainly nothing on the platform that could have caused cuts like that, but to say that Drib had appeared and clawed at his face was preposterous. There had to be another explanation. But what could have happened? As for sending the birds out searching for the cripple, well, that was easier to explain. Snatchpurse was obsessed with finding and killing Drib and the fouler his temper, the more he seemed to dwell on it.

'I know Drib is going to come and rescue me soon. I am even more sure of it now than I have ever been before.'

Sloeberry smiled at Crimp, reaching out to touch his arm lightly. 'I won't forget how much you have done to try to help me when he comes, and I am going to tell your mother and your father how you have risked your life to keep me alive. They will forgive you for joining those vile murderers, they will be able to see how you have repented for all the bad things they have forced you to do.'

'Will they? I'm not so sure about that.'

Crimp shrugged his shoulders as he moved away from her. He could never expect forgiveness from anyone, not after what he had done.

'We must keep a sharp look out for Drib and be ready,' Sloeberry whispered as she retreated back into the relative safety of the darkness beneath the dais.

'Nothing! They have found nothing, not a single sign of the cripple anywhere! You useless creatures!' Snatchpurse screamed in rage and lunged at Squark, sending the magpie swooping away from him in a whirr of feathers.

'It is impossible, completely impossible! I know he is out there somewhere in one of those high mountain passes. Now tell me what you suggest we do about it?' He snarled as he turned his anger onto his captains. The flocks of tired carrion birds began to settle on the debris of the feast and pick at the bones and scraps or fly up to their roosts high amongst the rafters of the tower.

'Perhaps you saw him in a dream. You know, like an omen that foretold you he would be journeying through the mountains,' Thorograsp suggested.

'Dream? This was no dream, you fool! You don't get owls gouging your face in a dream!'

Snatchpurse turned away from them all in contempt. He could not understand why they did not take Drib's appearance more seriously. He stared out through the broken outer doors of the tower and looked towards the distant, hazy mountains which crowded the horizon line. Suddenly he laughed, a dry sound that could have cracked stone. Of course, Thorograsp must have stumbled on the answer without realizing it. When he had tangled the whip around Drib's arm he had travelled so fast, rushing and tumbling over and over in the air that there was no knowing how far he had been taken. He had assumed that he had landed somewhere amongst the peaks he could now dimly see, but perhaps it had been much further away. Perhaps he had been taken beyond the edge of sight.

An idea began to form. If that was so then the cripple had not even reached those mountains yet. He thought he could find a way to catch that elusive creature, to catch him and kill him once and for all. There may be a hundred or more passes through the Emerald Mountains but as far as he knew they all converged on the one ancient road that led down into Elundium. A cunning smile thinned his lips. He would send one of his most trusted captains with a strong company of men and a flock of carrion birds to patrol the road and keep watch for Drib. From now on nothing would move or crawl along it without him knowing about it. Snatchpurse turned back slowly as the idea crystallized and he searched thoughtfully amongst his captains for someone he could trust with such an important task. His eyes came to rest upon Unsnark and he beckoned him forwards, lowering his voice as he told him the purpose of his mission. He wanted Unsnark to wait at the bottom of the mountains for them to descend; he wanted Drib and any of the Tunnellers or kinglovers who happened to be with him dead. And if he should meet any of the fools who had escaped them when they attacked Cawdor then he should kill them as well. He was in the middle of telling Unsnark how to search every merchant and journeyman meticulously, how to go through their wagons carefully just in case they were hiding amongst their wares, when another thought suddenly struck him. It was an excellent way to control and know the movements and whereabouts of all the people of Elundium.

'You should have no trouble finding that cripple if he tries to hide – his deformed legs will give him away immediately, but more importantly you are to tell those you stop and search that nobody is to travel the greenways without the written permission of the Chancellors. You shall take my seal of authority with you, but use it sparingly, we don't want the greenways clogged with wandering vagabonds. Tell them they are to go nowhere without my permission: anyone who travels must have the mark of my seal or they will suffer instant death. Do you understand? Do this properly, Unsnark, bring me Drib's head and I will make you the permanent Master of the travellers' seal once we have seized Candlebane Hall.'

'Yes, yes, great Lord, I will start out right away.'

Unsnark hurried away and chose those who would accompany him, delighted to have been entrusted with such an important task, but before he had gone three paces Snatchpurse called him back as another, even better, strategy occurred to him.

'You can set up your camp upon the Causeway Fields. Lay siege to the fortress of Underfall while you wait for crooked Drib to appear. Send out the carrion birds and patrols night and day to watch the ancient road. If that boy slips past you I will flay you alive. I know that at least one rider has already managed to break out of that fortress despite the mass of bodies we piled up against the doors of the fortress after the massacre of Marshthistle. I fear it was that rider who somehow got ahead of us on the road through Meremire and warned the Archers of our approach to spoil our advantage of surprise. I don't want it to happen again, do you understand? Siege-lock them in, starve them to death. If they should surrender, kill them. That way we can be certain that they cannot come to the Thronestealer's aid when we march upon the Granite City.'

With a curt wave of his hand Snatchpurse dismissed Unsnark and beckoned forward three more of his captains, ordering them to take three companies of men and follow the Archers into the endless grasslands. 'Burn every village you come across, burn them to the ground if you have to, but find and kill those Archers. Kill them all and bring back their hands as trophies.'

Turning on his heels he started to leave the room when his face tightened into a mask of hatred; he stabbed a clawed hand towards Sloeberry who was crouched down in the dirt and commanded that Crimp come to him.

'I want that ugly goblin watched at all times. Keep her out in the open where we can see her. I'll not be caught unprepared if that cripple dares to show his face around here for a second time.'

II

Siege-Locked

BLACK, RAGGED CARRION BIRDS soared and wheeled lazily on the rising thermals, or hung motionless on outstretched wings in the vault of azure blue, high above the pencil-thin spires, roofs and towers of the Granite City. The flocks of birds had been drawn there by the scent of the city's impending doom and they drifted and spiralled, waiting for the shadow of death to creep relentlessly up across its sheer, castellated walls for their feast to begin.

The hot breath of summer had died to nothing but a whisper amongst the tall, silver-headed ebony trees that stood neglected in the inner courtyards, spreading their leafy shadows across the dry and dusty fountainheads. Bright sunlight scorched the steep, weather-bleached rooftops and cast a forest of irregular shadows from the regiments of chimney pots and the ornamental dragon finials which crept across the maze of narrow streets.

High summer was drawing to an end but it was swelteringly hot in the city. The houses were locked and shuttered, making the streets strangely quiet, devoid of their usual mid-day hubbub. There was no sound of the laughter of children, no rumble of iron-shod wheels over the cobbles; the voices of the cryers as they shouted were silenced and the hustle and bustle of the market place as the merchants and journeymen bartered their wares were as silent as though they had never been. Gone was the haze of noonday woodsmoke from the kitchen fires and the wholesome smells of summer juniper, wild rosemary and the sweet, aromatic spices that usually perfumed the air. In their place there was now the odious stench of overflowing midden ditches and heaps of rotting rubbish that had been left unattended to choke the gutters. But it was not truly silent, for the constant hum and drone of thick clouds of blow flies that hovered over the filth seemed to fill the hot, unsavoury air.

The city seemed shrouded with an unnatural quiet and those who dared to venture out were inclined to huddle conspiratorially together to seek the illusion of safety in their numbers as they glanced furtively up at the Candle-hall. Their talk was full of wild rumour and seethed with speculation about the fate of their king whom they had driven into being siege-locked inside Candlebane Hall. Fear and regret now weighed heavily in their whispers and they rued the day they had allowed themselves to be so easily beguiled, drawn into a treachery they could not deny.

King Thane rested his hands wearily on the sun-warmed stone balustrade of the tall casement window of the Candlehall, wrinkling his nose at the stench of decay that rose up from the streets below. He narrowed his eyes against the harsh glare of the sun as he looked out at the hostile world that now kept him as a helpless prisoner of circumstance. He allowed his gaze to pass down over the thousands of steep rooftops and rows of chimney pots, to flow across the streets and alleyways and travel to the outer, castellated walls that encircled the city and he let it stop on the high archway of the Stumble Gate where once the first step to kingship had been taken. Such a large step from humble candleman's son to king and it seemed so long ago, so far away.

A frown puckered his thin, emaciated face and teardrops glistened before they brimmed over and blurred his sight. His eyes followed the empty, sun-baked greenway bordered on either side with wild, unkempt blackthorn hedges where the road ran out through gently undulating countryside. He allowed his gaze to follow the road as it travelled beneath spreading oaks and elms to vanish into the shimmering heat haze that cloaked the distant eaves of the black forest on the lower slopes of the mountainous horizon line. One question plagued his every waking hour and haunted his dreams: where had it all gone so terribly wrong?

The single blast of a bull horn rose on the hot, stale air. It came from somewhere in the maze of dingy back lanes and dark alleyways behind the Learning Hall, heralding the beginning of the taking. Thanehand caught his breath and gripped the balustrade, his knuckles whitened as the harsh note faded away. Below he saw the few people who had dared to venture out to go about their daily tasks scatter and run for their lives. Blood-curdling shouts and curses rang out, mixed with cruel, pitiless laughter and the sound of the rush of armoured boots as they ran over the cobbles. The Honourable Company of Murderers who had been left by their leader, Snatchpurse the Chancellor's son, to guard the city and keep the King siege-locked, spilled out onto the streets led by Grout, the Loremaster, and Sweepscuttle as his second in command. They were armed to the teeth with knives and cudgels, intent on plundering whatever they wanted, forcing the people into servitude and rampaging through every circle of the city. They battered down doors and overturned carts, dragging out anybody they suspected of hiding or hoarding food, killing them for sport. The terrified towns-people cowered in fear.

'What I would not give at this moment for a company of loyal Gallopers, mounted on the best horses with lances set!' Breakmaster, the ancient keeper of the King's horse cried out angrily as he strode to be by the King's side.

Thane looked round at his old friend and reached out a hand to steady him, a smile of concern touching and softening his eyes. The starvation had reduced Breakmaster to a gaunt shadow and left him weak and breathless but not once in all the long, painful daylights of their deprivation had his loyalty or his courage faltered. When others had slunk away beneath the cloak of darkness to betray him, Breakmaster had stood, steadfast as a rock.

'And then what? Tell me, Breakmaster, tell me what you would do if such a company of horsemen were at your disposal,' Thane asked gently.

The old horseman's watery eyes clouded for an instant as they filled with memories, memories of him mounted once again on Beacon Light standing in the centre of a great battle crescent that stretched away on either side of him as far as the eye could see, filling the Causeway Fields. Above the crescent proud pennants of the owl sewn in blue and gold were flying and standards of the sun embroidered in needlepoint were rising clear of the shadows, rippling in the morning breeze. The dogs of war, the Border Runners, ran at their heels and stoops of Battle Owls wheeled and turned across the sun in readiness for the charge. In his mind's eye he raised his sword and the battle crescent stirred and the sound of horses' hooves became a swift, measured beat. The air was suddenly filled with the roar of thousands of brave voices and the neighing shouts of the horses as they took the bit and swept forwards. Sunlight glinted on the lines of spear blades as they were lowered, and all the glory of the bright morning light reflected from their burnished armour as they gathered speed to bear down on the boiling shadows of Krulshards, the Master of Nightmares, and his foul army as they rode them to ruin.

Breakmaster sighed and blinked as he pushed these memories aside. It had all been so long ago. Now, the stables and the breaking yards in the first circle of the city close to the Stumble Gate were lying empty and desolate. Thankfully the grooms who lived above the stables had had the good sense to throw open the doors of the boxes and had herded the horses out onto the Greenway, giving them their freedom only moments before the city fell. Breakmaster knew in his heart that he would never ride again, never again see his beautiful horses move across the ground with such elastic ease. Those daylights were gone forever.

'Why, Lord, if by some sweep of magic we had a squadron of Gallopers here, saddled and ready in the inner courtyard of Candlebane Hall, we could break these siege locks and issue forth, ride off in line abreast, stirrup pressed against stirrup. We would clear the streets of that evil mob and chase them out of this city in no time at all. Why, we would drive those treacherous Chancellors' sons and all their wretched followers through the gates. They are responsible for bringing about ruin and chaos and they have brought the downfall of everything you have worked so hard to achieve for the people of Elundium. We would drive them back into exile into the depths of Meremire Forest where they belong!'

'If only it were that simple, old friend. We wouldn't be here in this predicament facing defeat if things could be solved so easily.' Thane answered, struggling to control his anger as he watched the villains below rampaging unchecked through the streets. Suddenly they flushed out a wheelwright who was hiding in a doorway. They caught him and, with shouts of delight, they lashed him spread-eagled onto a broken cartwheel in preparation to send him hurling to his death down a steep, winding lane. Thane could hear the man's terrified screams and he turned away helplessly.

'This is my fault, Breakmaster. None of this tragedy would have happened if I had governed the people properly. If only I had listened to wise counsel, if only I had taken Nevian's advice. What a fool I was not to realize how much the people clung to the old ways, how they believed in the structure that controlled the rhythm of their lives. What arrogance I had when I was still heady with the scent of the victory we had just won at the Battle of the Rising.'

Thane sighed and sadly shook his head. 'How blind I was to think that I held the world in the palm of my hand, that one victory gave me the right to make such sweeping changes. What stupidity made me think I could drag the people over the threshold of the new Elundium without one moment's thought to their place in it. How foolish I was to forget that simple old belief that change is always considered to be for the worst amongst the ordinary folk.'

Thane paused, catching the wailing scream of the wheelwright and hearing the rumble of the wheel as it gathered speed. His eyes took on a haunted look as he turned towards the old horseman. 'It was my haste, my blind arrogance, that made the people yearn for the illusion of the security of the old ways. I drove them into Snatchpurse's outstretched arms. It is no wonder that he found it so easy to beguile them with his lies and promises;

they were truly afraid of the new Elundium that I was trying to give them.'

'No, no, no, my Lord, that is not true. They may have misunderstood a little but they have been too easily swayed by that treacherous Loremaster's tongue . . .' Breakmaster tried to protest but the King cut him short.

'It would happen all over again if you try and deny the truth. Don't you see, old friend, even if you had ten thousand Gallopers and strikes of Archers too numerous to count and . . . and . . . and an army of Marchers at your disposal all armed and ready to drive our enemies out, unless you address the truth they would creep back in once your back was turned. If the people do not understand and embrace what we are attempting to do to make their lives better then their doubts and mistrust will only grow again and the yoke of oppression that they were once forced to endure will seem so much better, so much more secure for them than the uncertainty of their freedom. The choices to live their own lives and control their own destinies will hold no promise for them and they will strive to reject it.'

Breakmaster frowned. He didn't understand why the King needed to torment himself with such doubts and recriminations; he would never be able to change the likes of Grout and Sweepscuttle – their greed would always persuade others to follow them. He had done nothing to reproach himself for. Everything he had ever done had been for the common good, even if the people had been slow to realize it. Why, even his own warriors had turned upon his generosity. The old man thought back and realized that it had all started to go wrong at the Battle of the Rising, although at the time it had all seemed quite the opposite. There had been a lot of cheering then; the sounds had echoed like the rolling sound of thunder across the countryside as the King released them all from the pledges that bound them to serve him. And yet, as they were to find out later, barely had the dust of the battle settled and those warriors returned to their homes as free men than the murmurs of dissatisfaction began to frown amongst them. Disloyal, untrue whispers that said that those once proud men who had held loyalty and honour above all things had been betrayed by their king in the hour of their greatest victory. They had been stripped of their rank and abandoned, tossed aside with the hollow promise of being 'free men', a proclamation that left them little better than beggars. Of course this was untrue but that was not the worst of it.

At battle's end on that very same daylight after he had released those ungrateful warriors from their pledges the King had given Lord Willow and his people, the diminutive Tunnellers, with their strange shell-shaped ears and their huge, round eyes, their freedom too. He had also given them the right to roam Elundium as and when they pleased, to garden and mow the greenways as they travelled, and in thanks and payment for their part in the great victory over the shadowlight he had pledged them food and shelter. Who would have thought that anybody would have denied them the joy of feeling the sunlight on their faces or the pleasure of tasting the rain or combing their fingers through the wind after the desperation they had been forced to endure for time beyond counting when they dwelt in Krulshards' prisons deep within the City of Night. The Tunnellers had asked for nothing but their freedom, they sought no payment but the King had insisted that for all the work they did pruning back the wildness that had begun to choke the greenways after years of neglect, they could ask for a bed in the village inns whenever they stopped to rest for the night and the innkeeper would give them a bowl of hot broth to fortify them. Small payment, one might have thought, for a gentle people so cruelly treated. And yet in no time at all it had caused no end of trouble. In all the villages scattered along the greenways edge the Tunnellers were accused of being no better than wandering gypsies, ugly hobgoblins who lived off the backs of honest folk and stole the food from decent people's mouths. They were even accused of awakening the night creatures who had once been their cruel tormentors from the City of Night. The village people had quickly come to believe that the Tunnellers had joined forces with the Nightbeasts who had survived in the depths of Meremire Forest and travelled with them, looting and burning as they went.

Breakmaster felt his indignation boil up. His cheeks flushed with anger. The King was right, of course, the people had turned and twisted all his good intentions with their greed, mistrust and base jealousies.

'The people of Elundium and those so-called loyal warriors don't deserve all the care and tireless effort you have put into trying to make the world a better place for them to live in. And you are right, everything you did, especially giving the Tunnellers their freedom, has all been twisted. Why, I would like to give those villagers a piece of my mind about the way they treated those poor people.'

Thane laughed sadly and shook his head. 'I doubt if it would do one jot of good, old friend. The problems lie too deep for that. You must remember how the Chancellors kept the people steeped in ignorance during the long rule of the Granite Kings because it was the easiest way to control them, narrowing their lives down to a mere existence. It allowed the Chancellors to grow rich and fat from the crippling taxes they imposed. I had forgotten how such ignorance breeds fear and that is a powerful thing if it is allowed to run unchecked. It is hardly surprising that the people feared the Tunnellers; seeing them must have stirred up memories of those old fireside stories the Chancellors had made sure they listened to, stories that had filled them with a mistrust of magic and of the elves and goblins who had once roamed free throughout the forest. It is that ignorance we must seek to change if we ever get the chance now, but it is the very weave and fabric of society, it forms its very structure.'

The dry, slow shuffle of footsteps and shallow coughing in the corridor from the open doorway made Thane pause. He turned his head towards the sound, his thin face tightening into a frown as Arach the Master Mason; Swage the Ironmaster; Prickling from the Honourable Company of Harness Makers; Deckle from the Guild of Parchmenters; and Ghisi the Master Armourer came in followed by Greygoose, the Captain of Archers, with the handful of guards who had remained loyal. They halted, knocked solemnly and what remained of the once great council entered bowing one by one to their king.

'Come, come, dispense with such ridiculous pomp and ceremony: there is no place for that now. Come in and be seated, there are grave matters to debate.'

The members of the council silently crossed to their seats with their heads bowed, avoiding the King's eyes. There had been a terrible commotion at their last meeting the previous daylight when it had been discovered that Warksnare, the over cook and three servers had disappeared and that the kitchens had been plundered. The King had demanded to know how such a thing could have happened but none of them wished to be singled out to explain away such treachery and none of them wished to tell how they had got away with almost all that was left of their meagre supply of food. To make matters worse they had poisoned the only well of drinking water in the Candlehall before disappearing into the night.

'Well, what news have you gleaned by listening at the siege-locked doors of the Candlehall? Are there the beginnings of a whisper that good friends are gathering? Are there allies ready to storm the city and rescue us? Are there growing rumours of disaster amongst the villains who guard the doors? Is there anything being said out there that might give us new heart in these desperate daylights? Breakmaster was just telling me how he would drive our enemies far beyond the Stumble Gate if only he had but one company of loyal Gallopers.'

The King waited for an answer, looking quizzically from face to face, trying to catch and hold their shifting, furtive eyes as the awkward silence expanded. Breakmaster guessed at the council's predicament. To a man they admired the King's honesty and integrity and they each knew of the tireless efforts he had made to create the new Elundium from the ruin and devastation left by the shadowlight, but they also feared him, for he had been touched by magic. He could understand the language of the birds of the air and he could talk to the wild beasts of the forest; the savage dogs of war had run at his stirrups. The old horseman cleared his dry throat and stepped forward.

'I think, my Lord, that the council fears your wrath over Warksnare's treacherous disappearance with all our food and they feel guilty about allowing him to poison our only well. None of them wish to shoulder the burden of it alone.'

Thane turned sharply on the silent council, his lips tight and trembling with anger. 'If you think I would blame you for another base act of treachery then you judge me over-harshly. Why, I thought you were my friends, thrown together by circumstance. Well, I, at least, considered you to be my friends.'

The King broke off and strode through the council to the window and rested his hands on the balustrade, sighing as he looked out across the city. The burden of kingship was at times so difficult to bear. How he wished he had Mulcade, the battle owl, perched upon his shoulder, to feel the prick of his talons through the weave of his cloak and to know that his blinkless eyes were keeping watch. Or to have Esteron, the Lord of Horses, saddled and ready to gallop out of Candlebane Hall to carry him far away from the disasters he had inadvertently created in the name of progress. But, in truth, he knew he could not wish for either. Mulcade was watching over his wife, Queen Elionbel, and her half-brother, the child Krann, on their flight to safety to the tower on Stumble Hill. Esteron he had seen leading all the other horses out of the Stumble Gate only moments before the city fell, and hopefully they were all safe somewhere in the wilds of Meremire Forest or running free across the endless grasslands towards Clatterford and beyond. A smile momentarily touched and softened Thane's eyes. He knew the temptation to escape would have been even greater if Esteron were with him siege-locked in the Candlehall.

Mulcade and Esteron had been with him almost from the very beginning, when he was merely a humble candleman's son. Then he had seen a vision of Nevian, the master of magic, in the Learning Hall and in a heady moment of recklessness he had called out to the Loremaster and demanded that he tell the truth about the Chancellors' tyranny. He had demanded that Loremaster Pinchface reveal the names of the true heroes who, with courage and honesty, had kept back the Nightbeasts during the long reign of the Granite Kings. Pandemonium and uproar had erupted in the Learning Hall as the Loremaster was forced to tell the truth and Thane had had to flee from the howling mob who had glimpsed the magician and who feared all things magical. He had sought refuge with Breakmaster then, knowing him to be his grandfather's one true friend, and he had sheltered in the breaking yards. From that moment on Esteron and Mulcade had protected him on the long road to Kingship and now he missed them. Perhaps, he mused, perhaps if he had known what he now knew he would have followed an altogether different road. But in his heart he knew there could be no other road; fate had chosen to single him out and had tied the footprints of his destiny to the dust of history long before he was born. In the ignorance and recklessness of youth he had found the courage to begin his journey and now he knew he must find the full measure of that courage and, if circumstances demanded it, stand alone and besieged in the Candlehall and follow destiny to its bitter end.

Slowly he turned to face the silent council and said, 'You are all free men whose loyalty and courage I hold in high esteem and I thought you had all chosen to stay here in Candlebane Hall through the bonds of friendship and the love of the freedom we have fought together to preserve, not because you feared me.'

Thane smiled and looked solemnly from face to face. 'I would not hold a single one of you here against your will, or love you less if you wished to flee. Some of you have families hiding in the upper circles of the city and you will want to be with them, and I do not blame you. Nor do I blame any of you for weakness or treachery, though they cannot be easily undone.'

Arach shifted uncomfortably in his chair, 'Lord,' the Master Mason called out, 'we are all answerable to you, we are your eyes and ears, so naturally we feel responsible.'

'And I would not cut off my nose to spite my face,' laughed the King. 'In truth we all are in this terrible predicament together and you must forgive me if I sometimes grow angry or am momentarily consumed with rage because of the hopelessness of our situation. But please remember all of you that my anger is not intentionally directed at you, it is the future, or the apparent lack of it that frets me the most.'

'But, my Lord, it is the future, or our survival to be a part of it, that has consumed all our efforts since Warksnare stole our meagre store of food. Instead of trying to get to the bottom of his disappearance as you ask us.'

'Look what we have found,' Deckle ventured holding up a wicker basket that had three small, curling pieces of fungus with bright orange specks on their outer skin laying on the bottom of it.

Thane peered with curiosity into the basket, wrinkling his nose at the repugnant odour that wafted up to greet him. 'Surely you are not suggesting that something that smells so evil could be edible, are you?' he asked, drawing back.

'We don't know, my Lord, nobody has risked taking a bite to find out yet, and without the knowledge that the cooks possess, or maybe an alchemist, we are reluctant to try. Arach and I only discovered it this morning growing in the lowest, dampest of the cellars beneath the

Candlehall while we were trying to find the most suitable place to dig a new well. We found many different varieties of moss and fungus all growing in abundance – we even found mildew climbing up the mortar between the bricks. There's plenty of it, enough to harvest and keep us alive for some while, if it's all safe enough to eat.'

'I'm not afraid to try it. Necessity has forced me to eat far worse things on the field of battle. I'll tell you soon enough if they're poisonous.' Greygoose interrupted, reaching forwards into the basket to break off a fragment of the slimy, evil-smelling fungus.

'Wait! That's no way to behave. You, of all people, should know better than to do this. You're no good to us dead, are you?' Breakmaster was angry at the Archer's stupidity and struck out at him, hitting Greygoose's wrist so hard that it knocked the fungus out of his fingers and across the chamber. 'You fool, I don't know what's got into you!'

He muttered at the Archer beneath his breath and beckoned him to follow him across the chamber where he retrieved the piece of fungus and he took it to the furthest window to examine it closely. Slowly he turned it over and then spoke again.

'If Nevian, the master of magic, were here, he, in his infinite knowledge, would surely provide us with the answer we seek. But unfortunately he isn't here and the age of magic has sadly long since vanished. We must now resort to the simple but well-tried method used by the apothecaries to decide if this odorous fungus is at all edible. The red spots on its outer skin are nature's way of warning that it is likely to be poisonous – but to whom? That we must endeavour to find out, now watch closely.'

Breakmaster peeled off the outer skin of the fragment

and, pulling down his lower lip, viciously rubbed the fungus backwards and forwards across his gums.

'Nature indeed! I've never heard of such nonsense. I don't see what wiping it across your mouth is supposed to do. It's filling our bellies we should be more concerned about,' Prickling muttered. He had never found the need to give much thought to the whys and wherefores of how the food he ate arrived on his plate. Before the series of calamitous events that had overtaken them and brought them all to the brink of ruin, that had all been left in the capable hands of harvesters, merchants, cooks and servers. He had no more expected people to know the intricacies of saddlery and harness-making than he had expected to know about their part in the greater scheme of things.

'It is rudimentary physics and vital to our survival,' the old horseman answered crossly, catching at the saddler's mutterings. 'If the fungus is poisonous it will make my gums burn and tingle, which, so far, it has not done. However, to be sure it is safe I will leave a piece tucked in between my gums and lip for a while. If it still gives me no discomfort then I would say it is safe for us to eat. Next time, master saddler, you can be the one to decide!'

'Yes, yes, of course, I meant no offence,' Prickling answered, shrinking back in his chair.

Arach rose quickly from his seat and offered a small, battered pewter drinking vessel up to the King. 'I think I have found a new source of water, my Lord. We dug down in the lowest cellar near where we found this fungus and it has yielded enough to fill this cup. But it is pure, pure enough to drink and there will be more, I'm sure, if we dig deeper.'

Thane took the cup carefully from the Master Mason's dusty hands and looked down into the cloudy liquid that filled it to the brim. It didn't look very appetizing but he knew that he had little choice and a glimmer of hope stole through him. They had found the means to survive a little longer. Breakmaster began to chew on the fragment of fungus and with a gulp he swallowed it, wiping his hand across his mouth. After a moment he declared it safe enough to eat although it would possibly be more palatable if they could find something to cook it in and mask its rather strong flavour.

'You have done well, especially you, Arach and Deckle – exceedingly well.' Thane laughed before bringing his cup up to his lips again to drink, savouring the cool, earthy taste of the water before passing it on to Breakmaster, Swage and the rest of the council to share equally.

But the moment's sense of success was brought to a sudden end by the sound of shouts from beyond the siege-locked doors. The sound became a rising mêlée of voices, taunting, demanding that Thanehand, the Thronestealer, show himself.

'How dare they shout such obscenities, such lies and untruths! I'd teach them some manners with the flat of my sword if only I could get my hands on them! I'll show them, just give me the chance!' Breakmaster fumed, his face purpling with anger as he turned to stride purposefully through the frightened council members to shout down at the unruly mob who had gathered below the window and give them a piece of his mind. He had barely taken two steps towards the balustrade before a bulky, coarse hessian sack was hurled up through the open window. It landed on the floor of the chamber at the old horseman's feet with a dull thud.

'Snatchpurse, the High Chancellor and rightful heir of all Elundium, sends you this gift, Thronestealer. Sweetmeats from the tower on Stumble Hill, delicacies for your table, a feast to enjoy!' One of the voices from the crowd jeered loudly and peels of raucous laughter followed.

Thane felt a shiver of dread chill his spine and he feared for Elionbel and Krann's safety as the cruel voice spoke of Stumble Hill and goaded them to open the sack and enjoy its contents. But Breakmaster had a different fear. He already knew that their attackers had somehow found out that the queen and Krann had fled to the safety of Stumble Hill but it was the first time they had used the name of the Archers' tower to fill the King's heart with despair. His initial fear was that they had trapped a venomous dragon snake or caught a nest of spiny vipers and put them in the sack but the old horseman was wilier than that, he prodded the sack firmly with his armoured boot to satisfy himself that there was nothing wriggling inside before he cautiously bent down and picked it up to carry it to the centre of the chamber.

'There can be nothing good or wholesome in that sack, not if you judge by the odorous smell of it!' Swage frowned, covering his nose.

'Everything that Snatchpurse and his murderous friends touch turns to evil,' Deckle added suspiciously.

'There's the reek of death about it and that's for sure,' Breakmaster muttered darkly as he unsheathed his dagger and used it to sever the cord that had been tightly knotted around the throat of the sack.

The jeering crowd outside had subsided into a waiting silence. Everybody except the King and the old horseman gasped for air and hastily retreated as the sack fell open. Prickling, Swage and Deckle, good, steady, honest men, but men who had not yet seen the horror and brutality of war close-up, recoiled and cried out, gagging as the overpowering stench of putrefying decay filled the chamber.

Thane let out a strangled gasp and a wave of revulsion rose from the pit of his stomach and reached the back of his throat. He staggered back from the mass of blackened, severed hands tumbling out of the sack and spilling across the floor to his feet. Breakmaster gripped his arm to steady him and tried to comfort him as best he could.

'We would be fools to believe everything those villains shout at us. Those hands could have been hacked off and then thrown into that sack anywhere. Where is the proof that they really came from Stumble Hill?'

Thane blinked as the old horseman's words cut into the awful image that was beginning to form in his mind. Stumble Hill had fallen. Stumble Hill, defended by his dearest friends, Kyot and his Lady Eventine, lay in ruins; and maybe lying there dead in the rubble, mutilated by beasts, lay their bodies alongside those of Elionbel and Krann.

'Surely there must be a way to tell if those were bowmen's hands. Greygoose, isn't there a way you can help your King?' Breakmaster called out to the Captain of Archers who was hovering in the shadows.

'I . . . I . . . I don't know, my Lord, I have never thought to look for anything that would distinguish us Archers from other warriors – that is apart from the way we dress. But I will look if you wish me to.'

Thane nodded bleakly. 'Yes, please look, and can you tell me if any of these hands are delicate enough to belong to a woman or a child. I need to know if . . . if . . . if they might be . . .' Thane looked away quickly; he couldn't bring himself to utter Elionbel's name.

Greygoose's face paled and he shuddered with revulsion

at what he had been asked to do. He found he was summoning up all his courage to touch the cold, dead flesh. He reached out his hand, but hesitated, suddenly overcome with remorse and the sick realization that the fall of Stumble Hill was all his fault, and the blame for the gruesome, blackened remains that lay on the floor in front of him, if they did, indeed, come from there, could be laid at his door. He had to be to blame for the fall of the tower and each daylight of the siege that they endured he had expected the King to turn on him and curse him for betraying their strategy to Snatchpurse and his murderous company. How else could the Chancellor's sons have known of the tower's importance? How else would they have known that the queen and Krann had fled there, save that either he or Breakmaster had told them – and he knew that the old horseman would rather have died than utter one word of betrayal.

What a fool he had been. What a selfish old fool to have jeopardized everything the very moment that he and Breakmaster had returned from escorting the queen and Krann to the tower in such secrecy. He had never intended it to be such a terrible betrayal: all he had wanted was the Loremaster's reassurance that his son, Eider, would be safe at Cawdor, if indeed he had ever reached that citadel of legends or had travelled as far as the dark side of morning. Perhaps he was still with the Tunnellers who had been responsible for causing all the troubles and had brought about the King's ruin. How blind and naïve he had been, he now realized, to think that Loremaster Grout's loyalty was beyond reproach and he shuddered at the memory of how cleverly Grout had teased the King's secrets out of him with all those hollow promises and reassurances. How the Loremaster had boasted of his integrity while prying out the details of the journey he had just completed and all the while he must have been hiding those treacherous Chancellors' sons in the shadows of his Learning Hall. Greygoose shuddered as he recalled how Grout had pretended to be slightly deaf and had persuaded him to speak a little louder so that they could all overhear his every word. If only he had thought, if only he had realized what was happening. Greygoose so wanted to blurt out the truth of his betrayal and beg the King's forgiveness but the words choked in his throat and entangled him in the silence of despair.

'Can you see anything? Can you see anything that might tell us if they were Archers' hands?' Breakmaster's voice broke through the Archer's misery and he forced himself to pick up and carefully examine each withered hand in turn, smoothing his trembling fingers over the contours of their cold, dead skin.

He paused and frowned. Yes, there was something, something that perhaps a Marcher or a Galloper might have missed. There was a thin ridge of callused skin near the second joint of the first two fingers of each hand, just where a bow string might have been held and repeatedly drawn taut before loosing an arrow. He touched his own hand and found the selfsame callused ridge of skin. He nodded bleakly without looking up. There could be little doubt that these severed hands once belonged to Archers.

'Is there any way of telling if they were the Archers from Stumble Hill?' Thane asked quietly.

Before Greygoose could raise his head to answer or begin to summon up the courage to tell Thane of his guilt of betrayal the mob below the window erupted again into shouts and howls of laughter. Sweepscuttle was giving a particularly ugly villain with a wet, dribbling leer and a patch over one eye a torn remnant of silken gown, now bloodied and dirty and tied around a rock. He hurled it up towards them and it flew through the window, landing on the floor at their feet.

'Snatchpurse, our High Chancellor and rightful Lord of all Elundium, sends you a keepsake, Thronestealer. It comes from the ruins of Stumble Hill. He craves your indulgence and patience to await his triumphant progress into the city and then he will cut off your head and set it upon a spike above the Stumble Gate for all to see,' Grout shouted with an air of authority but a sneer in his voice.

Thane spun round as the rock struck the floor and he gave a cry of recognition. He scrambled after it and tears welled up in his eyes as he unknotted it and clutched it up against his lips, crushing the material as he held it close to his face. He was deaf to the mob, oblivious to the other people in the room with him, as he whispered Elionbel's name over and over.

Shame and anger boiled up in Greygoose's heart as he, too, recognized the bloody fragment of the queen's gown. She had died because of his stupid, thoughtless indiscretions. If only he had not gone to the Learning Hall. His guilt grew, fuelled by Grout's voice beyond the window. He had to silence him, he had to silence that treacherous Loremaster once and for all. Leaping to his feet Greygoose snatched up his bow and quiver, knocking an arrow onto the bow string as he ran to the window. He would avenge the queen's death. He would kill Grout and then throw himself at the King's feet to await whatever punishment he deserved. The bow creaked as he drew back the feathered flight of death to lightly touch his cheek. He looked along the spine, aiming the metal blade at the chest of Grout, who stood slightly in front of the noisy mob.

'No – you fool!' Breakmaster cried angrily. He had watched the Archer rise to his feet and grab his bow and had hardly been able to believe his eyes. What was the man doing? The old horseman threw himself across the chamber and forcibly struck Greygoose's arm a mere second before he loosed the arrow, spoiling his aim and sending the arrow shrieking high and harmless over the rooftops.

'Have you gone completely mad? You know what those villains down there will do to the city folk. They murdered at least ten of them the last time you injured one of our attackers, there's no knowing how many they will butcher if you kill Grout. The King specifically ordered us not to retaliate, no matter how much they provoke us, didn't he?' Breakmaster was hissing as he struggled to control his own anger. He roughly pushed the Archer well away from the window.

'I don't know what has got into you lately, Greygoose. Isn't it bad enough already without making it worse by starting a massacre here in the city? Isn't the King suffering enough? It's up to you and me to hold things together here. Keep clear heads, show a little backbone, we're warriors, we have to set an example to the rest of the council whether we like it or not!'

'But it's all my fault!' Greygoose began gesticulating across the chamber to where the King knelt in helpless despair, clutching at the piece of Elionbel's gown. The Archer let his hand fall to his side, his words trailing away into wretched silence as he realized that Breakmaster was right. It was not the moment to expose his own guilt; it would only compound the King's despair.

'But what can we do? The tower on Stumble Hill has fallen and the queen is dead. Kyot, Eventine, everyone, they must all have perished. There is no denying that is there?'

Breakmaster suddenly gripped the Archer's arm fiercely and he laughed out loud, disturbing the King's grief and causing him to stare from across the room. 'We have all been fools, my Lord. Fools to have swallowed those villains' story about the fall of Stumble Hill so easily.'

'But I have a bloodied fragment of her gown – and what of those severed hands? Are you telling me that my eyes are deceiving me?' Thane retorted angrily.

'No . . . no, my Lord, indeed some terrible tragedy must have befallen the tower on Stumble Hill, but I am not so sure that we have heard a reliable account of what really happened there. For all we know their attack might have been repulsed.'

Thane rose slowly to his feet still clutching at the piece of silk. There was a faint glimmer of hope in his eyes as he asked, 'How so, old friend?'

'Well, we have just jumped to the exact conclusion that Snatchpurse wanted us to.' The old horseman frowned, searching for the words to express his thoughts. 'It's beyond doubt that the bloodied piece of cloth you are holding was once a part of our queen's gown. We all recognize it. But does that necessarily mean that the blood on it is hers, or that she was wearing it when it was torn? Those severed hands undoubtedly belonged to Archers and yet we cannot be sure that they are from Stumble Hill. I counted them as Greygoose examined them and there are barely enough in that sack to account for half a strike of Archers. There are certainly not enough there to lead us to believe that there has been a massacre.'

'So, what are you implying? Are you suggesting that the tower still stands and that Elionbel is alive and safe?' Thane asked.

Breakmaster shook his head slowly. 'I would be a fool to pretend to be sure of anything in these uncertain times, my Lord, but I will hazard a guess and say that yes, I think the queen is alive and that she has, so far, escaped Snatchpurse's clutches. Think for a moment, put cold logic ahead of the fears in your heart. Snatchpurse would, through his base, evil nature, have sent something much more gruesome to convince you that he had either killed or captured Elionbel if he'd had it to send, wouldn't he? I believe he would, and my guess is that . . .'

There was a sudden sound of hoofbeats and the rumble of cartwheels in the streets below followed by a single, harsh blast of the bull's horn before they heard a roaring cheer from the mob. The commotion in the street cut short the horseman's words.

'By all the colours in Nevian's cloak what is happening now?' Thane exclaimed, turning towards the window.

Sweepscuttle's voice rose above the cheering. 'Come to the window, Thronestealer, and bring along all those who skulk and hide in Candlebane Hall with you. Our Lord Snatchpurse has sent somebody for you all to see.'

The jeers and shouts of the crowd shrank abruptly and in their place an awed and frightened silence seemed to rise up from below.

'Yes, come forward, Thronestealer!' another, deeper voice laughed cruelly. The bestial sound sent a chill shiver of apprehension up Thane's spine and struck fear into the heart of everyone in the chamber. Thane overcame his feeling of dread and strode to the window, followed slowly by the rest of his council.

Thane, with Breakmaster close behind him, his hand ready upon the hilt of his sword, walked forwards to the stone balustrade of the tall casement window. They inwardly feared seeing further evidence of Elionbel's death or, perhaps worse, her capture, but neither of them were prepared for what confronted them. They came to an abrupt halt, standing, frozen and unable to utter a word. The horror of what they saw in the street below made their blood run cold in their veins.

Prickling and the other members of the council were drawn by their curiosity and crowded in behind Breakmaster, standing on tiptoe, craning their necks to see what could be in the street below. Deckle was the first to catch a glimpse; it was enough to make him cry out and stagger back, his hands pressed tightly over his eyes. The others simply fled, stumbling against one another, their commotion breaking the frozen silence.

Breakmaster gripped Thane's arm, trying to draw him back away from the open window, and hissed, 'By what unnatural forces of evil is that? Is it man or beast?'

The huge, hideous creature that stood in the back of the cart was wreathed in shadows and as it looked up its scaly mouth split into a sneer.

'I . . . I . . . I know not . . .' Thane answered, tight-lipped and barely standing his ground.

Girrolt, Snatchpurse's most trusted Captain, had travelled with all speed from their victory at Stumble Hill with the specific orders to take charge of the Granite City and to keep Grout firmly in his place while making sure that the Thronestealer was kept siege-locked in the Candlehall, abandoned and alone. He had to bring him to his knees in readiness for Snatchpurse's triumphant arrival in the city. He threw back his hideous head and laughed. It was a cruel, pitiless sound and it pleased him when he saw the fear that his appearance had caused in the faces as they looked down at him from the casement window. Even the King quailed. Snatchpurse had been right, none would have the courage or the strength to stand against them; they were invincible.

Girrolt's laughter lasted but a brief moment; he had a message to deliver. His mouth opened into a menacing snarl revealing jagged, yellowing fangs and purpled gums hanging with drooling strings of sticky, sulphurous slime. His reptilian, hooded eyes shrank into murderous pin-points of glowing light and he raised a clenched, clawed hand to beat it upon his scaly, armoured skin that partially covered his chest and arms. The cart he was standing upon swayed and shook wildly as the horse between its shafts reared and plunged in terror, fear of the unnatural creature overcoming its exhaustion. Girrolt cursed the animal and felled it with one blow across the top of its head.

'See me, Thanehand! See me, Candlecur, Throne-stealer. Look at me – Girrolt, the Chancellor's son, who once you dared to banish into exile. See what I have become. Look! Look at me, Thronestealer, look and know that you are staring into the face of your impending defeat.'

Girrolt saw the speechless look of horror on the King's face and it goaded him to touch and caress the sharp, livid indigo spines and the bony ridges that ran protect-ively across the top of his head and down across his shoulders. He laughed. 'Our great leader, Lord Snatch-purse and the Honourable Company of Murderers – yes, every single one of us – all those you once banished and all our followers, who are many, have been invested with the dark power of the Eretch. That power, for years beyond counting, has waited in the shadows on the dark side of morning, waited for a company such as ours to be its host. You have no idea, Thronestealer, of the power that pulses through our veins. It is beyond your wildest dreams. Your weapons cannot harm us and there is no fortress in all Elundium strong enough to withstand us.'

Girrolt continued in a sneering voice. 'I see doubt in your eyes, Candlecur. Tell that Archer who is strutting in the shadows behind you to loose an arrow at me. If you do not believe what I say then kill me! The Archers of Stumble Hill could not stop our advance. Storm after storm of arrows bounced off our skins as we broke down the doors of that wretched tower and smashed it all into ruin.'

Thane lifted his hand to beckon Greygoose forwards only to find that his Captain of Archers was already at his elbow, an arrow knocked onto his bow string. Greygoose didn't wait for the king to give him the signal, his rage and shame at his own betrayal overtook his caution and the knotted muscles of his bow arm released the arrow. It shrieked through the air and struck the creature square in the centre of its chest, throwing up a bright blaze of sparks that made the mob, who had crept in close around the cart to watch the spectacle, gasp in dismay.

Girrolt swayed slightly, letting out a shallow breath as the arrow impacted, and then he laughed. Catching at the broken shaft he plucked the shattered steel blade from amongst his armoured scales and held it up triumphantly for all to see.

'You see, Thronestealer, nothing can hurt me – nothing! You cannot harm me: I am touched by the power of the Eretch. Go on, if you still harbour doubts about my invincibility tell that fool of an Archer to loose his whole quiver. No, wait, I have a better idea, let him use these trinkets I have brought for you from the ruins of the tower on Stumble Hill.'

Girrolt reached down into the cart and then hurled a long bow of black ebony and two arrows wrapped in a muddy, torn piece of a blue and yellow cloak through the window of Candlebane Hall.

'I would know that bow anywhere!' Greygoose cried as it clattered to the ground at his feet. The two arrows, wrought from the purest silver, fell out of the torn cloak and he stooped to gather them up reverently, feeling the sticky oil from the bow on his fingers.

'It is the Bow of Orm!' he whispered to the others, 'Kyot, Archerorm's son, put it in his father's hand when he laid him to rest and he wrapped both the arrows and the bow in the cloak of blue and gold. I saw him put it into his grave niche beside the outer doors of the tower on Stumble Hill. The armourers of the tower hammered silver arrows into the walls around him so that he would not go into Death unarmed. The bow and these arrows have been taken from Archerorm's grave.'

Thane gripped the balustrade, white-faced in anger as the awful implications of what the Archer had said about the bow struck home. There could be no doubt now, the tower must have fallen. Kyot would never have allowed anybody to defile his father's grave niche, not while he had the strength to prevent it. But what of Elionbel? What of Krann, Eventine and all the other Archer families? Had any of them managed to escape?

A howl of laughter harsher than a hyena's bark, rent the air, spilling out of Girrolt's drooling jowls. 'It's no good fretting, Thronestealer, they are all dead, all trampled into the dirt. Nobody escaped from Stumble Hill, nobody at all. We don't take prisoners, not unless we're hungry!'

Girrolt paused and slowly wiped his claws across his mouth making a revolting, swallowing noise as he allowed what he had just said to sink in before delivering the next cruel barb exactly as Snatchpurse had instructed. 'The power of the Eretch that makes us so strong and beautiful became ours thanks to the ugly little goblins – those Tunnellers you are so fond of. That's right, look surprised, Candlecur, but we would never have found the Eretch if we had not pursued those Tunnellers all the way to Cawdor after making sure you were all helplessly siege-locked in the Candlehall.'

Girrolt's laughter became a gloating sneer. 'Just think about it, Thronestealer, we would never have known where those Tunnellers had fled to if you hadn't gone running to the Loremaster the moment they escaped with that stupid old horseman – yes, that one, the one who is standing there right beside you. You had to ask about those myths and legends, you had to ask about Cawdor and where it might lie and if there was still a road that led to it. Not that going to Cawdor did those ugly little goblins any good, no, nor their friends. The Eretch shunned them just like everybody else with any sense has ever done. It was the easiest day's work we have ever done, most enjoyable. It was the first time we had fought after joining with the Eretch and we massacred everybody. We burned Cawdor to the ground. That great impenetrable fortress of Underfall, yes even that has fallen beneath our shadow. The tower on Stumble Hill lays in ruins; nothing can stop us now. You are all alone, Candlecur, your friends are dead, dead or scattered, your hope has shrivelled. All your tomorrows lie in ashes and dawn hasn't even broken yet!'

Girrolt gloated, well satisfied with the shocked look of horror and despair that his words had engraved on the Thronestealer's face. He laughed and jumped lightly to the ground while being surrounded by the cheers and shouts of the mob as he hurried away towards the Learning Hall with Loremaster Grout and Sweepscuttle running to keep up with him.

For a moment Thane stared silently at them, overwhelmed by the hopelessness that the speech had carried to him. Cawdor, Underfall, the tower on Stumble Hill, they had all fallen – everything was lost. His last, fragile flame of hope had been extinguished. Breakmaster had brought back a wild story of meeting a ragged hoard on the greenways when he had escorted Elionbel and Krann to Stumble Hill – he had told him how they had been journeying to Cawdor through all the adversity of deepest winter and how their leader was a blacksmith. This blacksmith had told Breakmaster how Nevian had appeared before him in a vision in his forge and told him to gather all those who were still loyal to the King and to take them to Cawdor where the fate of Elundium would be decided on the dark side of morning. Thane had clung to this slender hope, the thought that all those loyal kingsmen and the Tunnellers who should have already been in Cawdor, would come to his aid. He had dared to hope that Thunderstone, the Keeper of Underfall, would somehow rally enough true men at arms and would join forces with Kyot's strikes of Archers to march upon the city and break the siege. But now he realized that this hope was futile, they were alone, truly alone, and he knew they must act quickly. Turning, he strode into the centre of the chamber and beckoned Breakmaster and Greygoose to him with all the members of the council.

'I will not crouch here like a trapped animal any longer, not now, not now I know that all hope is extinguished. No! I will throw open the siege-locked doors and stride out onto the steps of this once great Candlehall and make my last stand with the light of the new sun shining on my face. But I would not ask for your deaths, I will not demand that your blood stain these hallowed steps, my good and loyal friends. You who have stayed steadfast and true through such adversity have already sacrificed enough. I release you from your pledges of loyalty and I urge you to escape while you can. Slip away the moment darkness falls, follow the passageways that Warksnare used to get out of the Candlehall unseen, melt into the swirling shadows of nightshapes and go to your homes. Do whatever you can in the short time that is left before Snatchpurse and his monstrous army reach the city gate. Protect your families, if you can. Go, go quietly, and make ready to escape. Go with all honour before it is too late.'

Prickling shuffled uncomfortably as he glanced at the door of the chamber. He had never in his life felt such an urge to run, but he didn't want to be the first to go.

Breakmaster drew his sword, his face mottled purple with anger as he offered it, hilt first, to the King. 'There may be no dishonour for the likes of Deckle and Arach slipping away beneath the cover of darkness but I am a warrior. My pledges were not made lightly. I will not be so easily pushed aside to creep like a traitor in Warksnare's footsteps. My place will be at your side, my Lord, until the last breath.'

'And so will mine, Lord, until my quiver is empty and my bow lies broken and silent!' Greygoose cried in a voice full of anguish and despair. There was no doubt in the Archer's mind that his son, Eider, had died in the massacre at Cawdor and with his death there was nothing for him to live for.

Thane suddenly laughed, heartened to have such friends standing by him, and he gripped both Greygoose's and Breakmaster's arms. 'Then together we shall build around us such a wall of our enemy's dead that songs will be sung about us and the tale will be woven into fireside stories for years to come.'

'Lord, forgive me a moment,' Greygoose whispered, turning away quickly to look out of the window in an effort to hide the tears of grief that had welled up in his eyes. He had loved Eider so much and now he knew that he would never have the chance to throw his arms around him and tell him. He would make up for betraying the King's confidence, he would buy back his honour with his life, but he could not tell of his indiscretion now, it would only make the pain worse.

Blindly staring across the city he let his gaze travel past the weather-bleached rooftops and out across the summer-scorched fields with the shady hedgerows. He looked past the rolling hills and over the dense canopies of the dark forest, following the dusty, meandering ribbon of the empty Greenway as it threaded its way towards the hazy horizon line which was broken by the sheer, shimmering walls and cold peaks of the Emerald Mountains. Somewhere out there, somewhere beyond that distant mountain fence, lost forever, lay his son's body. A movement upon the very edge of his sight, a fast-moving dot, momentarily appeared and then vanished. He picked it out again as it slowly, steadily approached across the countryside.

'My Lord, wait, there is somebody, a messenger perhaps. I can see a person approaching the city,' Greygoose hissed, hastily stepping back away from the window and wiping away his tears. Raising his hand to shield his eyes from the fierce glare of the sun he used his phenomenal Archer's gift of sight that had been passed down through generations.

'Messenger? Is he friend or foe?' Breakmaster demanded, turning to stride over to the window, but Thane restrained him.

'Keep back out of sight, there is no way of knowing how many prying eyes are watching us. We do not want to give our enemies a clue that a rider approaches.'

'It is a horseman, my Lord, and he is riding hard. From the way he is avoiding using the road and is keeping to the shelter of the hedgerows and the overgrown ditches to cross every stretch of open country, and from the way he is keeping to the shadows beneath the eaves of the forest I would say he has to be a friend.'

'Where is he? Let me see!' Thane exclaimed as he rummaged for King Holbian's glass amongst the mass of scrolls and maps of Elundium on top of the ancient wooden chest.

The glass was an ancient, slender, cylinder of black ebony and brass that cleverly held two polished lenses of the purest crystal at either end. Thane carefully lifted the heavy tube with both hands and put it to his eye to search across the countryside in the direction that Greygoose indicated and at last he found the small, fast-moving horseman.

'Errant! It is Errant and he is riding Dawnrise!' he cried, adjusting the glass and bringing the horseman clearly into focus just a moment before both man and horse vanished from sight behind a dense stand of blackthorn.

Slowly Thane lowered the glass, his face lined with concern. Dawnrise was stumbling with exhaustion and even from this distance he could see that the horse's flanks were white-lathered with sweat, and Errant looked in no better shape as he hunched wearily, swaying in the saddle and urging the horse forwards.

'Errant cannot possibly know that the city has fallen into the hands of Snatchpurse's murderous villains or that we are siege-locked here in the Candlehall. Somehow we have to get warning to him and stop him from venturing too close.' Breakmaster frowned as Errant reappeared and then vanished behind another hedgerow.

'He must know something is wrong to be proceeding with such caution, but you are right, we have to warn him. But how will we do it? We are trapped in here tighter than rats in a barrel,' Thane answered, slowly sweeping the glass across the fields and hedgerows closer to the city and finding two roving bands of Snatchpurse's men looting and burning the scattered hamlets along the Greenway's edge.

'I could warn Errant, my Lord. I could slip out of here the way Warksnare did,' Arach, the Master Mason offered. 'The city is riddled with secret passageways and disused alleys and I need not use the city's gates if I can find the entrance to one of the old culverts that pass beneath the outer walls.'

At that moment there was a sound of footsteps in the corridor outside the chamber and two very frightened faces appeared in the doorway. 'Lord, we used all that noise and confusion to slip into the Candlehall by an old forgotten entrance. We are sick of the Chancellors and want to join you if you will let us.'

Between them they held out a shabby woven blanket

full of wrinkled apples. 'There are more who want to join you, if you'll let them,' one of the men ventured.

'You are all welcome, we will find a place for every one who wants to see an end to these Chancellors,' Thane cried, embracing them.

Arach laughed softly to himself. 'We rebuilt the city from the rubble that was left after the great battle with the Nightbeasts: there is nobody who knows what lies beneath the reconstruction better than I do. I could lead all those who seek sanctuary by secret ways into this Candlehall.' The Master Mason suddenly hesitated. 'But there is a problem, my Lord: I never leave the city and I will be hopelessly lost in the countryside. When I get outside the walls I will not know how to find Errant.'

'You bring the people into the Candlehall, Arach. After you have led me beyond the outer walls, I will find him, have no fear of that!' Thane urged, turning towards the door of the chamber and pulling his cloak about his shoulders.

'No, my Lord, you cannot go, it would be far too dangerous. Let me go instead. There is not a blade of grass or a bush in the hedgerow that I am not familiar with,' Greygoose intervened, shouldering his bow.

Anger flashed in the King's eyes. He had spent too long skulking in the shadows, if Errant had news he wanted to hear it immediately.

'Greygoose is right, my Lord, you must stay here and give strength to the people who join us,' Breakmaster interrupted. 'And another thing, if you go and Girrolt comes back demanding your presence at the window, threatening to murder more city folk if you don't comply, how am I to explain your absence? If for one moment he suspects that you have slipped out of the Candlehall, if he for one moment thinks you can escape, he will send everyone he commands to scour the countryside.'

Thane saw the sense in the old horseman's argument and with a sigh of frustration he unbuckled his cloak and threw it aside. 'Oh, very well, I will stay here and allow Greygoose to go in my place.'

He gripped the Archer's arms tightly. 'Take good care of Arach and don't either of you get caught, do you hear? Bring Errant to me with all speed.'

Thane told the council to make ready to receive all those who would come to seek safety in the Candlehall and then he dismissed them, keeping only Breakmaster by his side. Waiting until the door of the chamber had finally clicked shut he turned sharply on the old horseman.

'Well? What do you make of it? What do you understand from what Girrolt said – how much of it was truth and how much a lie? Who are these Eretch? What dark power do they command that they can mutate a man into such a monster?'

Breakmaster frowned and shook his head. 'I know not what to think, my Lord, I have never heard of these Eretch before but we do know that those Chancellors' sons have blackened souls, diseased by greed and treachery. I doubt that it would take very much to create monsters out of them. Sadly it is clear that Stumble Hill has fallen but as to how much of Girrolt's talk was lies and how much the truth I cannot say. I will say, however, that I do not believe that it was all true. I believe it was calculated to throw us into despair. Perhaps Errant will enlighten us. Have patience, my Lord, it will be a short wait and in that time rekindle the fragile flame of hope.'

III

A Circus of Deceptions

DRIB CROUCHED, his back arched, his crooked feet braced hard against the front board of the heavily laden circus wagon. The reins were as taut as bow strings in his hands. Nevian, the Master of Magic, sat wrapped up in his ragged hessian cloak of deceptions, lost in his thoughts and seemingly oblivious to the swaying creak of the wagon as its wheels jolted and bumped over the steep forest track. Drib's arms ached from constantly hauling on the brake lever and it juddered so violently that his teeth almost rattled loose in his head each time the brake blocks bit against the huge iron rims of the wheels, sending up shrieking sprays of bright hot sparks as they checked their precarious descent. The reins were cutting raw, red weals across his hands. He struggled to keep the horses straight and prevent the wagon from slewing sideways and tipping them all over the crumbling edge of the narrow, uneven track that twisted and snaked its way purposefully down through the pine trees and dense undergrowth covering the steep slopes of the Emerald Mountains.

Somewhere down there, somewhere along the meandering track lay the fortress of Underfall, concealed in the shadow below. Suddenly the track dipped and seemed to vanish. The cart lurched forwards and gathered speed. The suddenness of it tipped Drib off balance before he had the chance to grab at the brake lever and throw his weight against it. Equestrius, the Lord of Horses, and

Sparkfire, Drib's smaller mount who Nevian had persuaded into the harness both threw up their heads and snorted in alarm as the breaching straps began to cut into them and the weight of the wagon suddenly propelled them forwards. Their hooves started to skid and slip, churning up loose earth and rocks as they fought to stop the wagon. Drib somehow managed to grab the brake lever and pulled at it, forcing it back with both hands. The cart lurched and swayed before coming to a grinding halt.

Its rear wheel was resting on the very brink of the gully. In the sudden silence Drib heard the clatter of an avalanche of small stones, broken branches and clumps of earth that the wheels of the wagon had swept over the edge into the valley below. He let out a frightened breath of relief as he eased the reins, and wiped away the dirt and sweat that was trickling into his eyes before glancing sideways to his passenger. The magician was still deep in thought, muttering and mumbling to himself as though nothing untoward had happened. He was no doubt planning acts, performances of deception, that would beguile their enemies into believing that they were watching a real circus. Drib was still not convinced that it would work – he could not believe that they would be allowed to travel undetected into the heart of Snatchpurse's camp.

Nevian had made Drib his apprentice and had taught him much magic. He had made him practise his skills as an acrobat and perfect the art of invisibility, but he was still sure that somebody would notice his crooked legs. Somebody would recognize him before he had the chance to rescue Sloeberry. Drib had fallen hopelessly in love with the small Tunneller ever since they had all been held prisoners in the cellar beneath Candlebane Hall, and the terror he felt about her being Snatchpurse's captive seemed to grow inside him daily. It caused him to doubt that Nevian's plan would ever work or that he would ever be able to tumble convincingly. It caused him to suspect that everyone would see through Umm's disguise as the circus strong man. He was such a gentle creature, very large and for sure strong but so timid: the slightest disturbance would send him cowering beneath the cart . . . and surely someone would notice that he had seven fingers. Drib had dressed him up to make him appear fierce and had tried to make him understand that he should act wild but he was just too gentle, too caring.

And who in the world would believe that Equestrius or even Sparkfire were ordinary carthorses? They had a few burs clinging to their manes and tales and mud had been liberally plastered all over them but it could not conceal their power or majesty. And what of the ancient warriors? What of the ones who vanished into the forest an age ago when they felt betrayed by their King?

Nevian had asked the Border Runners and the Battle Owls to spread the word throughout all the wild places and tell of their circus, tell every loyal citizen that the King had great need of them now. With each daylight since their perilous descent from the high passes over the Emerald Mountains their ranks had been swelling and the Kindred Spirit was now almost a small army. The ancient warriors silently appeared from the undergrowth and fell into step behind their circus wagon. Nevian had done what he could to disguise them, to hide their true appearance from the flocks of evil birds that now patrolled the skies, but they still didn't quite look like clowns or jugglers, travelling hawkers and tumbling men. But this circus of deception had to work. They had to rescue Sloeberry and the future of Elundium depended on them. If he had learned anything during his recuperation at the magician's tower perched high above the Runesgate Gorge it was that anything was possible. Anything could be achieved if you wanted it badly enough.

Drib grinned to himself as he gathered up the reins and prepared to move on down the steep track. Who would believe all the things that had happened to him? Who would believe the fantastic adventures that he had been caught up in? And it had all started that daylight when the King had come upon him lying in the gutter outside the Learning Hall. It was all because of his love for horses. He had suffered such cruel jibes and hurtful remarks then about his wild dreams which did not befit a crippled boy but they were all such distant echoes now. He had proved them all wrong. Not that it mattered much any more, if the magician was right about Elundium standing on the brink of ruin. If they allowed Snatchpurse to seize power then it was all over. But none of his adventures would have happened if the King had not stopped on that morning and lifted him up out of the dirt and shown him such great kindness. It was the first time anyone had looked gently upon him since his father's death. The King had sat him upon Esteron, the Lord of Warhorses and let him ride him to the end of the lane and back, but more importantly he had told him that nobody, not even a crippled boy, should be denied his dreams. Drib sighed as he reached down for the brake lever; it all seemed so long ago now.

Silkstone, the owl who had befriended Drib and had been with him since his adventures had begun, and Orundus, the aged Lord of Owls whose home was amongst the high rafter beams of the magician's tower, both suddenly stooped down through the pine trees that grew beside the track. Silkstone shrieked a shrill warning as he flew to Drib's shoulder, urging him that they should all hide. Orundus startled Nevian out of his scheming, telling him that flocks of carrion birds were amassing above the tree tops in the valleys below. At the same moment Umm, who Nevian had sent ahead to use his forest skills and find them a safe and secret way down out of the mountains, suddenly appeared. He burst through a clump of undergrowth that arched over the steep track just below where the wagon had stopped; he had Grannog close at his heels.

'Rocks – you threw rocks – they upset the birds. All the bad birds are coming. Hide! Hide! You must hide!'

His breath came in gasps as he gesticulated wildly and pointed with his long arms down into the valley below. Nevian could just make out harsh shrieking cries and he rose anxiously to his feet, gripping onto the high side of the wagon as he leaned out to see below. The black mass of birds were flying up from the trees, wheeling and turning together. The shadow from their ever-increasing flock was relentlessly swallowing up the mountain side as they slowly rose, soaring on the warm thermal updraughts as they searched below them.

Stealth and secrecy were the element of surprise and the magician knew that these would be their greatest allies. Once already, by accident, they had almost squandered that element and alerted Snatchpurse to their presence in the Emerald Mountains when he had allowed Drib to look into the Eye of Arabra, the far-seeing crystal orb. Unfortunately Drib had touched the surface of the crystal and had been drawn into it, transported in a rush of darkness into the feasting hall of the ruined Archers' tower on Stumble Hill. He had appeared in the midst of the Chancellors' sons while they were celebrating their victory and the boy, no more than a shadowy wraith, had found himself standing upon a raised dais close enough to Snatchpurse to be lashed by the whip that he was about to use to beat Sloeberry with, hooking it over Drib's wrist. It transpired that the fusion of wraith and solid matter momentarily drew the Chancellor's son back through the eye of the crystal into their camp in the high pass of the Emerald Mountains. Silkstone, in anger, had flown down and raked his talons over the half-man half-beast and caused him to drop the lash and be drawn back into the swirling darkness, but not before he had glimpsed the magician and their circus wagon with Umm crouching in the shadows.

The whip had stayed with them; it was at that moment still in the back of their wagon, and this bothered the magician. It had been a dangerous incident – how much had Snatchpurse seen? How much had he remembered? If the whip was still with them then the bloody gouges that Silkstone had torn through his face must still be evident and the wound would cause him to remember. Nevian felt it was no coincidence that the carrion birds spent so much time scouring the steep, inhospitable passes that led down through the Emerald Mountains. Were they, he wondered, searching for that ghastly image that had interrupted their victory feast, scarred Snatchpurse's face and stolen his whip?

Fear of discovery and the ruination of all their plans galvanized the magician into action. He called out to all the warriors on the road behind them ordering them to cover all traces of their wheel marks and then get safely out of sight.

'Quickly, boy, drive the wagon into the nearest clump

of undergrowth – look, there's a good place up ahead!' he urged, snatching up the driving whip and cracking it in the air above the horses' heads.

The reins jerked and became taut in Drib's hand. Before he had the chance to warn Nevian that the slope was too steep, the horses surged forwards, veering off the track and charging up the steep mountain side. Drib gave a cry of alarm and clutched onto the seat as the wheels rode up over hidden rocks and glanced off fallen trees. For one moment the wagon threatened to topple over onto its side. Equestrius and Sparkfire had seen the approaching danger and had thrown their weight into the harness. With necks outstretched, ears pricked and nostrils flared they pulled the leaning wagon over the rough ground and up the steep slope, ploughing headlong into the dense thicket. Drib and Nevian had to throw their arms up to shield their faces as they were carried through the almost impenetrable barrier of thorny brambles and overhanging silver spikes that blocked their path. Suddenly the horses came to a halt, blowing hard, with steam rising from their sweating flanks. Umm and the rest of the company crowded in around the sides of the wagon, crouching, hiding themselves in small spaces as the sound of the birds and their engulfing shadow drew ever closer.

The dense undergrowth swayed. The leaves and flowerheads rustled and sprang back into place and then were still. Silence enfolded them as the clack, clack of the carrion birds' wings darkened the air and their harsh, shrieking cries passed slowly overhead. Nevian waited with drawn breath, listening intently until all traces of the birds had vanished before he signalled to the Kindred Spirit to proceed, but with caution. He warned them all to be on their guard even more vigilantly than before.

'We should be at the doors of the fortress of Underfall before nightfall but remember,' he hissed, 'once we leave the cover of the forest we must all become the travelling circus.'

A tight-lipped, apprehensive silence broken only by the soft jingle and creak of the horses' harness and the slow, measured rumble of the wagon's wheels fell over the Kindred Spirit as the late afternoon wore on and their shadows lengthened on their long, steep, winding descent. There was a bitter, acrid smell – the scent of decay and desolation hanging in the air that was growing stronger with every footstep. The once beautiful forests of the lower slopes, the ebonies, oaks, larches and elms that fenced the causeway fields and arched high across the road abruptly stopped and gave way to gaunt, charred stumps that stood bare and broken amongst a sea of choking ash. Ahead, beyond the burnt skeletons of the trees, the great fortress of Underfall rose, grim and grey. Its huge iron-studded doors appeared to be securely locked and bolted, its rising galleries and towering battlements were thinly shrouded in evening mist. The fortress had a deserted appearance and its hundreds of narrow, iron-spiked windows stared out blindly across the blackened, burnt-out ruins of the hamlet of Marshthistle, that in better daylights had grown up in the shadows of the citadel along the brink of the wide drainage ditch beside the raised causeway leading up to the great doors.

'It looks as though we have come too late. There is nothing here but a burnt-out shell. Underfall has fallen and now stands empty and abandoned.' One of the warriors muttered darkly, shading his eyes as he walked beside the wagon.

'We must journey on without stopping.' Nevian sighed.

He had so hoped that it would be otherwise. He had depended upon Underfall withstanding the Chancellors' onslaught.

'No, wait!' Drib cried, jumping up onto the seat of the wagon. 'I think I saw a movement in the ruins of those houses. And look, there's an encampment of tents, or something, close to them. I can see camp fires being lit and look – there are lights being lit in the highest gallery of the fortress. People must have survived Snatchpurse's attack. Come on, let's hurry, somebody might have seen Sloeberry and be able to tell us news.'

'Wait – hold hard, Drib!' Nevian interrupted, catching the boy's sleeve. 'Those people down there could well be Snatchpurse's men laying siege to the fortress. We must proceed with caution. It would be madness to rush head-long into their midst now wouldn't it?'

Nevian let go of Drib's arm and quickly began to organize the Kindred Spirit into the long, colourful circus procession that it was meant to be. Drums, pipes and whistles were held in readiness, bright flowing banners were un-furled.

Drib's shoulders sagged slightly as he nodded reluctantly. Of course the magician was right but Drib was afraid, deeply afraid, that for all their carefully laid plans they would arrive too late to rescue her. That one, brief, stolen glimpse that he'd had of Sloeberry through the Eye of Arabra would be his last. It would stay engraved on his heart forever: her beautiful slender face had been black-ened and swollen with bruises, the silken strands of her fine, dark hair had been hanging in knots. She had looked so pitifully thin and emaciated as she was dragged forwards into the shifting, lurid lamplight of that grotesque feast. A mass of bloody weals across her back and shoulders and her arms and legs had shown clearly the marks from the repeated lashings of the whip that she had been forced to endure. She had been dressed in such filthy rags that no mark of the beatings lay hidden. Tears welled up in Drib's eyes. She had been the first person in his life who had not looked down at his crooked legs with disgust, the first not to have given him that cold glance of dismissal, and he could not imagine the rest of his life without her.

'Standing there staring into space, Drib, is not going to get your Sloeberry rescued now is it? Look sharp! There are two very special kites to fly if I'm not mistaken and then I want you to go to the head of the procession and start tumbling and turning somersaults. Take stock of everything you can see and hear; stay alert.'

The old man paused, beckoning to Drib and making him stand closer. 'I also want to see just how good you have become at being invisible. Slip inside those tents, count their weapons, find out everything you can and then, if the opportunity arises, try and get inside the fortress. Find Thunderstone or Errant, if they are there, and tell them I need to see them urgently.'

Nevian understood the boy's misery far better than he realized and there was a softness and a gentleness in his voice as he prompted him into action. He had his own doubts about the chances of reaching Sloeberry while she was still alive – not that he would ever reveal those thoughts to Drib.

Drib blinked and wiped away his tears. Nevian was right, standing there worrying was not going to achieve anything. 'Yes, I'm sorry, I'll prepare the kites right away. I can do that while we are on the move if the wagons keep to the smoothest part of the road . . .' He hesitated. 'I met Errant once. He was there when the king picked me up out of the gutter, but what does Thunderstone look like?'

Nevian laughed. 'The Keeper of the last lamp at World's End needs no description, Drib. You'll know him immediately you set your eyes on him. Now, quickly get to work on those kites, we'll be in sight of Underfall shortly.'

Drib scrambled beneath the awning of the wagon and called out to the owls to come to him: the dark spectre of his worst fears was quickly pushed into the background. The idea of the kites had come to him quite suddenly on the morning they were leaving the Runesgate. They had just finished loading the wagon when he had noticed Silkstone hovering, motionless, above the treetops of the gorge, hunting for his breakfast. That was when the idea of disguising the two owls as kites had occurred to him. After he had experimented with a little paint and cut out pieces of parchment he'd had Silkstone hovering in the shape of a dragon kite that would fool even the sharpest-eyed enemy.

Rummaging in the depths of the swaying wagon he gathered together the pieces of parchment that he had already cut and glued into the long, snapping jaws of two dragon heads and, taking care not to ruffle their feathers, he fitted them over the owls' heads. The masks cleverly concealed their faces and yet allowed them to see through the cut-out eye holes. With a paint brush dipped into a pot of bright vermilion paint and another into a pot of bilious yellow he painted the bold design of a flying dragon across both of the owls' bodies and outstretched wings, trying hard to ignore their disgruntled looks.

'You will be our eyes in the sky,' he whispered. He fixed soft pieces of parchment which he had fashioned into scaly dragons' tails securely to the headpieces of the kites and held them in place with thin eider twigs. Finally he knotted a long length of strong, silken thread to each of the owls and, taking them forward, released them and then carefully tied the two strings to the side board close to where Nevian sat.

The two owls rose effortlessly into the evening sky to hover motionless above the wagon. 'It is quite extraordinary! Such an ingenious way to disguise the owls. I am sure that nobody will give them a second glance as they keep a good look out.'

The old man lifted his hand to wave at the old owl but Drib saw some of the black, ragged carrion birds rising from the ruins of Marshthistle and he hissed a warning, stopping him.

'Get out of sight, Drib, and change into your acrobat's costume before they spot you. Do it as fast as you can. Musicians – play, clowns and jugglers begin your routines. It is time for the circus.'

Drib ducked back beneath the awning just in time before the first shadow of the birds darkened the sky above them. With harsh cries they circled the kites curiously, pecking at the parchment, jostling and pushing at them with their wings, making them dip and sway, and then suddenly as abruptly as they had appeared, they lost interest and swooped down low across the circus procession. The clowns and jugglers, drummers and whistle players, instinctively ducked and for an instant the music faltered. Umm gave a wailing cry as the birds raked their talons through his bright orange hair. Nevian called out, rallying the marchers as they closed in tightly around Umm to give him courage while the birds twisted and turned, flying amongst them, searching with their sharp, prying eyes but finding nothing but a ragged bunch of circus performers.

In no time they returned to their roosts, their curiosity satisfied.

During the commotion Drib pulled on the tight breeches, soft slender deerskin shoes and the narrow-waisted, bottle green acrobat's jacket that Nevian had found for him amongst the discarded court costumes in the Tower. But his face grew pale and serious and his fingers fumbled slightly with nervousness as he buttoned up the twenty tiny, silver buttons and hooks from the high collar of his jacket to his belt buckle.

'What is keeping you, boy? Those birds have spread confusion amongst the tumblers and Umm has become very frightened. We have almost reached the edge of that encampment where there is a crowd beginning to gather. I need you here in the front of the procession doing those spectacular somersaults you have been practising. You have to lead the circus right up to the fortress – as close as you can get. Now hurry up!' Nevian called out urgently.

Drib jammed on his three-cornered acrobat's hat to complete his disguise, and then he reached for the flap that covered the back of the wagon, but fear paralysed him and stole his courage. What if some of those evil creatures who had attacked Cawdor were in the crowd? What if they were there watching the circus procession approach? Surely they would know him instantly, no matter how clever his disguise. It was one thing talking about the acrobatics, even practising the magic art of invisibility in the safety of the magician's tower, but what if he accidentally mistimed a somersault? What if he became distracted and took one false step?

The lights of the camp fires cast huge, moving shadows across the awning of the wagon. Drib looked at the ominous shapes and the weight of the responsibility that rested on his shoulders bore down on him. He knew that one single unguarded movement in front of so many watching eyes would reveal who they really were. If that happened they would never get the chance to rescue Sloeberry. As the thought registered, the clear sound of her voice welled up in his memory. He took a deep breath, steeling his courage and dispelling any doubts. It was now or never. He thrust aside the canvas flap and leapt to the ground, bending his crippled legs to spring high and gracefully into the air. His series of nimble cartwheels took him past the wagon and out amongst the procession. Voices from the watching crowd began to rise in murmurs of approval as he leapt and jumped, turning in slow, graceful somersaults above the upturned heads of the crowd. Drib kept a sharp look out for a place to set up the circus as close as they dared go to the fortress. Then he saw it, a grassy spot close to the raised causeway less than sixty paces from the great door.

'Give us time to set up our tent, good people,' he called out in a clear voice, 'and then gather round. The Kindred Spirit will perform for you as soon as we are ready. Our clowns and tumbling men will make you laugh, our jugglers and acrobats will perform feats of daring. Fortunes will be told and there are many wonderful mysteries for you all to see. Gather round, gather round.'

'Excellent, excellent. Well done everybody,' Nevian whispered as he brought his wagon to a halt in the shadow of the raised causeway. But his words of congratulations were short-lived and hardly out of the magician's mouth before somebody spotted the likely leader of the encampment. He was surrounded by a dozen or more of his henchmen and they were all armed to the teeth and striding purposefully towards them.

The shouts of the gathering people swelled as the ugly, half-human creature who appeared to be their leader, demanded to know who the strange company were. Drib heard the ring of steal as weapons were unsheathed.

'We are but poor travelling folk, a circus, come to entertain you,' Nevian called out, and with suspicious muttering the crowd split apart to let them through as the leader of the group beckoned them forward.

Drib spun around and let out a frightened gasp. 'He's got to be one of Snatchpurse's men! Look at him! He's covered in those same armoured scales – and just look at that vile ridge of bone and spines that is growing across the top of his head. Oh dear look, his hands are clawed. He's one of the creatures I saw feasting in the ruins of the tower on Stumble Hill when I went through the Eye of Arabra. I'm sure he is. And he must have spotted me. He must have seen through my disguise.' Drib felt faint with fear.

'No, not necessarily, boy, but be quick, make yourself scarce. Make yourself invisible just to be on the safe side.' Nevian frowned as he watched the approaching figures. Only their leader appeared to be clothed in that foul, scaly armour and that struck him as odd.

'Drib, where are you, boy?' he whispered to the surrounding shadows as he caught sight of a faint, elusive shape. 'Go and see if you can't find out how many more of Snatchpurse's men there are around. Count how many others you see who have been possessed by the Eretch.'

Turning quickly to the rest of the company who had gathered around the wagon he whispered urgently, 'Look busy. You all know what to do, do what we have practised on our journey through the Emerald Mountains. Remember, you are now the Kindred Spirit.'

Without another word the company set about erecting the brightly coloured circus booths around the wagon as they began to prepare for their first performance, trying to make it seem as though they had been doing it all their lives. Nevian shrank down into his own disguise to become a wizened old man, a humble soothsayer and teller of small fortunes dressed in a tattered hessian cloak. The shadow of the advancing party fell across him.

'Who gave this untidy, disorderly rabble permission to journey here to Underfall? By whose authority do you think you can pitch these tents here, right beside the causeway? Which one of you is in charge? You tell me, old man, yes, you. Do you want me to flog the skin off your back for having the audacity to drive that wagon straight through our camp?' Unsnark snarled, grabbing at the collar of Nevian's cloak.

Unsnark's sharp claws tore through the tattered weave of the cloak to pull him closer. Snatchpurse had warned Unsnark to be vigilant when he had sent him to guard and seize the fortress of Underfall. He had warned him to keep a special lookout for Kinglovers while he kept the inhabitants of the citadel trapped inside. Were these turncoats? Were these people traitors who might, by clever subterfuge, try to smuggle food into the fortress or be foolish enough to try and slip through its door to swell their miserable ranks?

Nevian feigned surprise as he replied in the most conciliatory voice he could muster, pointing up towards the grim fortress. 'Forgive us, great and noble lord, but did you say this was Underfall? Is this the great fortress that stands at World's End? Well that is a surprise – who would have thought that the road through that grim wood that borders the western edge of Notley Marsh would have led us here.'

'I've never heard of such a road through the wood . . .' Unsnark growled, his suspicions sharpening as his grip increased on Nevian's collar.

'Oh yes, my Lord,' Nevian protested, 'there is a road through the wood. It is wild, and in parts almost completely overgrown through lack of use since the good Chancellors have ceased to rule us, but it is still a road and we have been journeying on it as we crossed the far-flung western meadows from the margins of the restless sea. We have been stopping in the villages along the way to set up our circus. We had no idea that the road would lead us here or that we would need permission to show our skills. The Kindred Spirit are but a simple, wandering group, my Lord: nobody actually leads us, we rather let the road be our guide and we live by performing for our supper wherever we stop. And since fate has brought us here, please let us entertain you. It would be a great honour for our humble company to have such an illustrious audience. It will just be for one night. Please, let me apologize now for driving our wagon through the centre of your camp. I meant no offence, but my eyes, you see, have become dim with age. In truth I see little of what we pass these daylights, I see little upon the road . . .'

Nevian paused. He sensed the ugly brute's hostility had wavered slightly from the moment he mentioned the good Chancellors. Now he knew he must press home the idea that the Kindred Spirit were none too fond of the King. He chose his next words with careful consideration. 'Mind you, the less any of us see these daylights, the better it is I don't wonder, what with all the calamities and misfortunes this

King has brought raining down upon our heads. If it wasn't bad enough him banishing the Chancellors into exile, now he's gone and caused us no end of troubles by trying to change things. You would have thought he would have known better. Change is always for the worse you see, even I – a simple teller of fortunes – could have told him that he would come to no good by changing things.'

Nevian let his voice trail away into a shallow, crackling wheeze, ensuring that the mob who towered over him saw him as no more than a shrivelled, weak old man. But his quick, hooded eyes watched them all to gauge their reactions.

Unsnark's clawed hand twitched hesitantly. He had never intended to let this ragtail band of gypsies enter the Causeway Fields let alone camp so close to the fortress but the sound of their music, the colour and pageantry of the jugglers and clowns had all hypnotized him. He felt angry that they had beguiled him and he intended to chase them off, and none too gently. But suddenly he found himself in a quandary: if the old man was to be believed then this wandering band were loyal supporters of the Chancellors. Surely it would be better to let them rest for the night and reward their loyalty, show them that it was well founded rather than send them roughly on their way. Still, he couldn't make his mind up. Snatch-purse had expressly forbid any trespassers while they sieged the fortress and brought about its final destruction.

'Our circus could be ready to perform for your pleasure in no time, no time at all, my Lord, and I would consider it an honour to cast your fortune, and those of every man who comes to my booth.'

Nevian's gentle persuasive voice cut through Unsnark's indecision. Surely, he reasoned, if he let them stay for just one night they couldn't possibly get up to any mischief, especially if they were kept busy performing their circus acts until late into the grey hours. He could always double the guards on the causeway and put a couple on the doors of the fortress. But there was one thing that still bothered him and cast suspicion over their sudden and unexpected arrival. He had never heard of a road through the wood and he wanted to know if it really existed before he made his decision about letting them stay. If he found out they had lied then he would kill them on the spot. Keeping a firm hold on the old man's collar he turned sharply on his men, demanding to know if any of them had heard of the road that skirted Notley Marsh.

Unsnark's men were not true warriors in any sense of the word, they were ordinary village folk – blacksmiths, victuallers, coopers, goat herders, saddlers and the like who had been rounded up and press-ganged by Snatchpurse into the Honourable Company of Murderers as they overran each and every village in Elundium. The men shuffled uncomfortably and stepped quickly out of Unsnark's way to avoid his ruthless gaze as he turned on them. They were all terrified of him and all the other half-human, half-beast creatures who were wreathed in shadows and invaded their villages in the name of the Chancellors. If things had not been so bad as they struggled to survive on the black edge of ruin and starvation then they would not be here. But the Honourable Company had looted and burned as they pleased and they had murdered anybody foolish enough to try and stand in their way. Secretly, many of the people hated what they were now forced to do in the name of the Chancellors, but all too late they had come to realize that they had played no small part in aiding their grab for power. Now they knew how wise King Thane had been to banish them to try to change their corrupt, tyrannical governments. But there was little, if anything, they could do now but endure the cruel yoke of oppression and hope for better daylights.

Drib felt a surge of panic as he listened intently to everything that was going on from his place in the shadows. From the way the monster had hold of Nevian by the collar, and from the way he kept on questioning him and his henchmen about the road through the wood, Drib guessed that the safety, the very lives, of the Kindred Spirit depended on the answers. Unobserved, Drib thought he had caught glimpses in the men's eyes of a distant dislike, even hatred, of Unsnark that they shrouded the moment anyone looked directly at them.

'Well, you miserable rabble, has somebody bitten off your tongues? Does such a road exist – yes or no?' Unsnark snarled impatiently.

Drib knew he had to do something quickly and so took a desperate chance. Using his cloak of invisibility he slipped in amongst Unsnark's men, picking and choosing only those whose eyes had revealed their inner, hidden dislike of their leader. He lightly touched them on their arms and whispered to them softly:

'If you want to see an end to the Chancellors' black tyranny and a return of the King's freedom then you must say that you know of the road through the wood.'

Unsnark barely seemed to notice the slight ripple that passed through the ranks of his men but Nevian's sharp eyes saw it, and he noted the puzzled look on their faces. He wondered what Drib was up to. Surely there was nothing he could do to save the situation. That ripple was no more than a gentle sway left by a summer breeze combing its fingers through ripening corn but for those it touched it left the faintest whispering promise of freedom in the night air: if only they would speak and say that the road really did exist. Drib's voice had stirred up the answer that Nevian and the Kindred Spirit so badly needed them to utter.

Unsnark did not listen for more than a minute to his men's account of the validity of the road through the woods before his grip on Nevian's collar was released. Perhaps the old man hadn't lied after all. 'Your circus had better be worth all the trouble I could get into for allowing you to stay here for the night. You are to be gone at first light and you will go directly to the tower on Stumble Hill and report to our victorious leader, Snatchpurse. He will not be so pleased to hear of your trespassing here but I am sure he will be most interested to hear about your travels beyond the western edges of Notley Marsh and the villages you stopped in along the way. Yes, he will be pleased to hear news of them, most pleased.'

Unsnark turned on his heel and picked out a dozen men to stand guard upon the tents, ordering them to be extra vigilant and not allow any of the Kindred Spirit to venture one step upon the Causeway or anywhere near the doors of the fortress.

'And don't be fooled or distracted by any of the circus tricks. I will cut off your heads at the first sign of trouble,' he warned as he strode back to the encampment.

'Drib, Drib, where are you? What did you say to make those men give credence to the road?' Nevian hissed as soon as the scaly creature and his henchmen were out of earshot.

Drib reappeared beside the magician but kept safely within the shadows as he laughed softly into Nevian's ear.

'That is excellent, my boy, and if we had the time I

would have you speak more of the whisper of freedom and take the rumour throughout the camp – but it is more important that you somehow try to get through those siege-locked doors of the fortress and alert Thunderstone and Errant to our presence. It is vital that I meet with them, no matter how briefly, before the sun rises across the Causeway Fields.'

One of the whistle players interrupted the magician to warn him that their audience was already gathering.

'I'll do my best,' Drib whispered, and vanished before the groups of figures, drifting across from the encampment, caught sight of him.

With a dry snap of his fingers and whispered words of magic Drib abruptly disappeared. Instantly the texture and colours of the night air intensified around him. The soft, swirling nightshapes that had carried the darkness from beneath the silent eaves of the forest and up out of the deep drainage ditches to creep across the Causeway Fields changed from gentle violets and azure blues into hues of the deepest indigo. Drib's senses sharpened until he could hear even the faintest scratch and scrape of insects burrowing into the ground beneath his feet and the slow crack and groan of the stones in the massive wall of the fortress that overshadowed them as it settled onto its ancient foundations.

Unseen, he slipped through the gathering crowds, passed the guards that had been set upon the Causeway and ran silently into the shadows of the great iron-studded doors of Underfall. Drib's ability to use the power of magic had come on in leaps and bounds from those first disastrous fumblings in the magician's tower, but he was at a loss as to how it could help him now. He pushed against the aged, thundercracked, ironwood doors. They barely moved. They hardly rocked against their sturdy locks. He raised himself on tip-toe, pressed his ear against the thick, grainy wood and listened for a long moment. Gradually he found it possible to pick out the distant, muffled and measured tread of the guards who patrolled the galleries and battlements: they were much too far away to hear him if he called out, and anyway he would probably alert the whole of Unsnark's men if he did anything that stupid. Drib sank down onto his haunches, completely at a loss. There had to be a way. He wouldn't give up so easily. Climbing to his feet he slowly felt his way along the base of the sheer, impenetrable fortress. He stared up at the overhanging galleries that had been edged with twisted iron spikes and the battlements above them which were etched in silhouette against the star-strewn sky. He touched and searched for the slightest chink or handhold and a sign of any way to scale the walls but found that the hard, grey granite was as smooth and slippery as glass to high up beyond his reach.

A dark, silent shape stirred the cool night air close to Drib's face and momentarily blotted out the stars above his head. Before he could utter a startled gasp of surprise and raise his hands to protect himself, Silkstone stooped and alighted onto his shoulder. 'What are you doing flying around? You are supposed to be hiding in the back of the wagon if you're not wearing that disguise I made for you,' Drib hissed in alarm.

'Something has made Unsnark suspicious. He is having second thoughts about letting us stay here for the whole night. He has ordered our tents and the wagon to be searched thoroughly before he will allow the circus to start. Nevian sent Orundus and me out to seek safer perches until the search was over.'

The owl hooted so softly that Drib had to tilt his head and press his ear close to his beak to catch everything he said. The boy looked back anxiously to where he could see the tops of the tents beyond the Causeway. He could clearly hear raised voices and angry words. He took an uncertain step and reached beneath his acrobat's jacket for the hilt of the dagger that he had hidden in its lining. Surely his place was at Nevian's side defending him, not fruitlessly wasting time trying to get himself inside the fortress. A sudden slow drum roll and the shrill, high notes of the whistles sounded. Drib heard the angry voices subside as the bright, colourful flare of freshly lit reed lamps illuminated the tents and sent up the leaping, twisting shadows of the tumblers: Unsnark must have finished his search and had satisfied his doubts enough to allow the circus performance to commence. The small boy gave a sigh of relief and returned his attention to the sheer, smooth walls of the fortress.

'You and Orundus had better find yourselves somewhere safe to hide. The last thing we need is those evil birds or one of Unsnark's guards to catch sight of you,' he whispered to the owl.

Silkstone bobbed his head backwards and forwards as he hooted softly into the boy's ear, 'The birds will never hear a sound even if I was to fly close to their roosts. And remember they cannot see one peck in front of their beaks in the dark. As for those guards – if any of them were sharp witted enough to catch sight of me they would take it as an omen that something good was about to happen. Remember, you have already sown the seeds of doubt with a whisper in the dark about the King's freedom. You saw how much some of them hate their leader. They are not going to give us away are they?'

Silkstone spread his wings and rose silently before he stopped and hovered. 'You had better hurry up and climb that wall. You haven't got all night to waste!'

'It's all right for you, you have wings. You can fly as high as you like. I have searched and searched and I can't see a way up. The walls are so smooth, without the smallest toe or finger hold,' he muttered helplessly.

'Yes there are. If you look above the reach of giants the walls are rough and almost as pitted as the cliffs of Cawdor. You can easily jump that high. I'll hover to show you exactly where the best places are.'

'But that's ridiculous. I'll never be able to reach that height!' Drib muttered dubiously as the owl searched and then hovered quietly. But then he began to take measured backward paces. He quickly recited some words of magic, hoping that they might help him to jump higher and then he raised himself on tip-toe. After a moment of contemplation he sprang forward onto his hands, pushed and turned high in the air, landed lightly and then sprang up again even higher. The third turn brought him close to the exact place that he had wanted to be, right in the shadow of the wall. Bending his arms as his hands touched the cold earth for the last time he gave a mighty thrust and as he turned he felt himself soar high into the air. The sparkling canopy of stars above Drib's head seemed to draw closer as he reached the pinnacle of the jump and he seemed to hang motionless in the air for a long moment beside the owl. Instantly he reached out and as he started to fall back he found his fingers jamming into a maze of small cracks and fissures that time, wind and weather had scoured out of the sheer, hard granite surface. Scrabbling frantically with his feet while he still had the strength in his fingers he found a narrow purchase and for a long, thankful moment he clung there, breathing raggedly, limpet-tight against the wall. He had got this far and he wasn't going to let go now.

Silkstone fluttered around his head urging Drib to climb, and carefully, with the owl guiding him with hushed, hooted whispers, he began to edge his way up. It was very different from scrambling up chimneys and considerably more difficult than the time he had climbed down the cliffs at Cawdor in search of food during their long, hungry winter there. Soon his fingers were sore and bleeding and the toes of his soft, deerskin shoes were scuffed from the rough stone; the muscles in his arms and legs throbbed and ached, but he had no intention of giving up. Gritting his teeth he slowly climbed, often reaching up blindly to find the tiniest handhold, straining every nerve and sinew as he searched for somewhere to grip precariously with his toes. But the real test of his nerve came when he had reached the underside of the lowest gallery. Inch by tortuous inch he traversed it, hanging upside down, only to find his way up past the narrow-waisted windows blocked by a mass of twisted razor-sharp iron spikes which had been set there to keep out all the foul creatures of the night. With bated breath and infinite care he squeezed and worked his way over the spikes. Twice he almost slipped and lost his tenuous hold which would have sent him down to impale himself on their bitter points. By the time he had reached the underside of the second gallery his arms were growing numb with exhaustion and cold beads of perspiration were beginning to trickle down his forehead and find their way into the corners of his eyes. It still seemed impossibly far to the battlements.

But luck was with him. Reaching up and pulling himself

level with the mass of interwoven spikes that guarded the windows of that long, dark, empty gallery he discovered to his relief that they were set slightly further apart than the one below. 'I think I may just be able to get through here. I am going to give it a try,' he called out softly to the owl.

After a lot of wriggling and careful turning and twisting between the barbed tines he inched himself forward and managed to squeeze through. With a gasp of relief he dropped down rather noisily onto the wooden floorboards of the gallery. During the long, exhausting climb he had unwittingly let his cloak of invisibility slip and dissolve away leaving him clearly visible and casting a slight shadow in the starlight.

'Silkstone, I've done it – I'm inside . . .' he began to whisper as he scrambled to his feet, only to give a startled cry as he felt strong hands grab hold of his arms with a vice-like, inescapable grip. A lantern flared in Drib's face and momentarily blinded him as he was lifted up from the ground. Blinking and looking frantically from left to right his heart pounded as he saw that he was surrounded by three large, grim-faced warriors, all with their swords unsheathed and with two of them pointed at his heart.

One of the men reached out and grabbed hold of his hair, jerking his head back and turning it, none too gently from left to right. 'Now let us see what kind of evil little creature we have caught.'

'I'll bet he has claws or suckers instead of hands to have been able to scuttle up those sheer walls,' the warrior on the right growled, snatching at Drib's wrists to examine his hands.

'I say we should slit his throat and throw him back down. That will show the vile monsters that they can't break in here so easily,' the third man added as he raised his sword towards Drib's throat.

'No, no, please don't kill me. I am not one of those evil creatures, I have come to help you,' Drib cried, desperately trying to break free. He could feel the cold, keen edge of the blade pressing against his throat and he knew he dared not even swallow.

'Nevian, the Master of Magic, sent me,' he said in a small, faltering voice. 'He told me to get inside the fortress in any way I could and then find Thunderstone or Errant. I am to tell them that Nevian must meet with them before dawn breaks. It's really important for me to get that message to them: the future of Elundium depends on it. He won't get another opportunity to talk to them because those villains surrounding the fortress are making us move on at first light. Please, it really is urgent, please take me to Thunderstone or Errant. I am not one of your enemies, I am part of the Kindred Spirit, a part of the circus that arrived just before darkness fell.'

Drib felt a slight hesitation in the men who surrounded him and he suddenly thought of a way he could make them believe him. 'My name is Drib but everybody in the Granite City called me Crooked Drib because of my legs. Errant will remember me, I'm sure he will, if you just ask him. He was riding with the King and Breakmaster on the daylight that they brought that beautiful pony into the city. They came upon me lying in the dirt – I was hurt in the gutter outside the Learning Hall. Ask him, he'll tell you, the King sat me upon Esteron's saddle – go on, ask him.'

The warrior holding the sword against his throat stepped back a pace and lowered the blade slightly, but he didn't resheath it. He vaguely remembered something

Errant once said on his return from the Granite City, something about such an incident. But Errant was not there, he wasn't in the fortress, he couldn't verify the boy's story or even to say whether this was the same boy. Errant had ridden out in a desperate bid to reach Stumble Hill ahead of the evil hoards who had suddenly appeared from out of the Emerald Mountains and attacked them. They had burnt Marshthistle to the ground and had massacred all the inhabitants – Errant had taken advantage of all the confusion and had ridden out to take the rarely-used and dangerous road through Notley Marsh. He hoped to be able to warn Kyot and Eventine that their enemy was advancing in a black tide along the greenways through Meremire Forest. But what if Errant had been captured? What if the story of the boy lying injured in the gutter had been tortured out of him? The boy's hands looked quite normal apart from the fact they were bleeding and sore from the climb, but his feet were very crooked. He may be telling the truth.

'We had better take him down to Thunderstone,' the guard muttered. 'We'll let him decide what to do about him.'

Drib breathed a silent sigh of relief but still he wished he had Silkstone with him. The guards marched him along the gallery and took him down a series of steep, winding stone stairways and through damp, echoing vaults and passageways. From there they travelled out into a maze of courtyards and keeps and eventually he guessed that they must have reached the outer keep. Suddenly, less than twenty paces ahead of them he saw the huge, siege-locked doors of the fortress.

Drib paused and took the chance to look up at the night sky for a moment before one of the guards hurried him away through a low archway to their right. He could hear voices beyond the arch and could just hear his name being mentioned. Light suddenly streamed through the archway, illuminating the courtyard. There was a crunch of footsteps that made Drib turn his head towards the open door to see the fiercest, oldest warrior he could ever imagine approaching him with giant strides. The man wore no armour save a closely woven mail shirt of the finest silver links that shimmered in the lamplight as softly as watered silk. Over this he wore a simple, cornflower blue cloak that was drawn together beneath his beard with a golden clasp wrought in the shape of an owl. His leggings were of leather and his knee-length boots of pale calf skin. There was no doubt in Drib's mind that this warrior was Thunderstone, the Keeper of the great lamp of Underfall. He had sat in the Learning Hall and listened in awe at Loremaster Grout's feet to so many stories of Thunderstone's battles to keep the lamp burning against all the swarms of Nightbeasts who issued out of the gate of Night, threatening to overwhelm the fortress. The old man's face was stern and firmly etched with carelines and yet there was a glint of something, a strange undiminished light that burnt in his piercing gaze. It was a light that time and weariness and being the last Lampmaster in a troubled world had not extinguished.

Thunderstone was not the least bit pleased that their defences had been breached and he strode beneath the archway full of anger. But before he'd had a moment to study the small, crippled boy dressed in old-fashioned court clothes two owls stooped out of the dark, starlit sky and flew into the courtyard. The larger and more majestic of the two alighted on the keystone of a nearby archway while the other, smaller owl, settled on the boy's shoulder.

Both owls sat poised, their wings slightly spread, their talons flexed with their beaks open wide as they watched the warriors of Underfall with their blinkless eyes. They were ready to attack at a moment's notice.

Without hesitation Thunderstone lifted his open, outstretched hands in a gesture of welcome as he greeted the two battle owls. He listened and yet he understood little of their muted hoots and whispers save that, if necessary, they would defend the boy with beak and claw. 'Rest assured that no harm will come to him while he is here in the fortress of Underfall, you have my word on it.'

He motioned to his men to resheath their weapons and release the boy. When he returned his attention to Drib a smile seemed to have softened his piercing gaze and pulled at the corners of his mouth. 'You keep illustrious company, young Drib. It proves to me that beyond doubt you are who you say you are. But need must have driven you hard to force you to scale these impenetrable walls. Nobody, my lad, has ever achieved such a feat before.'

Thunderstone paused and a troubled look clouded his eyes. 'You told my guards that Nevian urgently needs to speak with me before the new daylight dawns; you say it concerns the fate of all Elundium, but I don't understand. Why did he need to send you with this message? Why has he not just appeared here in the fortress? Locks and doors, brick and stone are not impassable obstacles to the Master of Magic are they? They certainly never used to be.'

'Nevian's magic has changed, my Lord, he doesn't seem to be able to do half the magical things that the Loremaster used to tell us about in the Learning Hall.' Drib hesitated, glancing at the huge, siege-locked doors. Talking about the magician's failing powers seemed like a betrayal, but he had to make Thunderstone open the doors to let Nevian into the fortress. They had to carry on with their plan to save Sloeberry. Everything Nevian had said depended upon rallying everyone they could to fight against Snatchpurse. Drib felt he had no other choice so, lowering his voice, he continued.

'I have been Nevian's apprentice for a little while now. I live in the Runesgate Tower with him and I have often heard him complain that the real magic faded with the last of the Granite Kings. He has become very forgetful and I am forever running to fetch him his books so that he can look up spells and refresh his memory. Sometimes he has to do that with just the simplest of charms. But that doesn't mean he isn't working as hard as he can to save Elundium. He is trying to save all of us from the Chancellors' black evil.'

Without pausing for breath the boy told Thunderstone all about their circus of deceptions and how already many warriors who had once abandoned their King at the end of the Battle of the Rising and vanished into the forests had joined their ranks and become members of the Kind-red Spirit.

'Please, please, you must open the doors, just a little, just wide enough to let Nevian inside. It really is very important.'

Thunderstone stood undecided. He would dearly love the benefit of the magician's council and wisdom, even if his powers of magic were somewhat diminished. They had all been siege-locked, trapped for too long, but could he risk breaking the siege doors? Could the few loyal warriors who had remained with him guarding this fortress at World's End withstand the sudden onslaught of the hordes who even now encircled them and would know immediately the doors were unlocked?

'Could you just open the doors a tiny crack? They wouldn't have to be open far to let Nevian through.' Drib's voice broke into Thunderstone's indecision. He blinked to look down at the small, crippled boy with the owl perched on his shoulder and forgotten memories of another youth came flooding back. He remembered how once, against all adversity, he had fought outside these very doors with only a broken blade and a shattered helm to guard against a wall of evil Nightbeasts long after all hope had fled. In those days he had refused to accept defeat and had fought on desperately until, at battle's end, he had knelt, too exhausted to see the strengthening daylight. He remembered now the words that Nevian had spoken to him as clearly as they had come to him in the silence of victory.

'Great deeds have set the measure of this victory, and your part in it, child, shall not go unforgotten nor unrewarded, for when all hope had perished it was you alone who held this Causeway.'

Thunderstone suddenly felt very ashamed that he had left the burden of the fate of Elundium on the shoulders of an old wizard and a young boy, that he had even for one moment hesitated to unlock the doors and welcome Nevian in with open arms.

'It shall be done immediately, but we will have no more of this secret subterfuge. It is time for action. My warriors will form a flying column and charge out and surround Nevian and bring him safely into the citadel. Yes, the time for skulking here is over. We will fly the King's standard once again on the Causeway Fields . . .'

'No, no, no,' Drib cried in panic. That was the last

thing Nevian wanted. He must explain, and quickly, that their strength lay in secrecy.

'But how can we keep it secret? If I open the doors even the tiniest crack and let you slip out to bring the magician here can you both get past the ring of guards that have been set outside? There are so many sharp eyes watching this fortress.'

'Oh, that's the easy part, just you watch!' Drib laughed, and with a whisper of magic and a snap of his fingers, and a small somersault for good measure, he vanished.

'Where? What's happened? Where are you?' Thunderstone frowned, looking about him uneasily and searching all the shadows.

'I'm right here, beside you,' Drib whispered, touching his arm and making Thunderstone jump.

'But you have disappeared, I can't see you. Even your shadow has gone.'

'It's only simple magic, Nevian has been teaching me all sorts of things while I have been in the Runesgate Tower. That is how I got past the guards to scale the wall.'

'He has indeed taught you much. But from what I can remember, Errant told me that you are quite an extraordinary boy and you have come a long way from your beginnings in the Granite City.'

The old warrior laughed as he directed the door wardens to quietly undo the siege locks and draw back the bolts and beams and open the doors just wide enough to allow the boy to slip through. Drib drew his breath and without a sound he squeezed through the narrow gap between the heavy doors. He hurried back across the Causeway to find the circus tents full of noise and activity which was keeping the audience enthralled. The jugglers and the clowns had columns of plates spiralling in the air and the tumbling men were leaping and dancing, creating a kaleidoscope of comic foolery in the lamplight. It took Drib a moment or two to find Nevian who was hunched and huddled in a small booth telling the fortune of a large, coarse-featured fellow who, as the magician spoke to him, looked ill at ease, as though the old man had touched upon hidden secrets. It made him keep glancing anxiously over his shoulder and out into the darkness lest someone was eavesdropping.

Drib, unseen, crept back into the booth and crouched down behind the magician, suppressing a grin as he listened to Nevian adopt a frail, crackly voice as he teased out the man's secret doubts and dislikes of the Chancellors. He was getting him to utter thoughts he would never have dared to voice openly in the company of Unsnark's men. Nevian's once great powers may have been reduced to little more than small magic with the passing of the last Granite King but his second sight and intuition were still crystal clear. Clear enough to see into the souls of ordinary men and to gauge their strengths and weaknesses and know the measure of their integrity.

'I could do nothing, nothing, none of us could. When Snatchpurse's men invaded our village they took everything we had and forced us into serving them. We are worse off now than we have ever been,' the man was muttering wretchedly, wringing his hands together.

'Would you wish to turn against them?' Nevian whispered.

'What's the good of that? Except as a sure way to get myself murdered. I may hate this tyranny but I can't do anything about it. Nobody can. Anyway, we have already committed the worst treason we can by turning our backs on the King and allowing the Chancellors to seize power. We are doomed.'

'You are not alone in your hatred of the Chancellors, I can reveal that much to you,' Nevian murmured.

The man's eyes showed a sudden interest and he leaned closer. 'Who are the others? What can I do to join them? How will I know them?' he hissed, gripping the old man's wrist in his excitement.

'Take heart, the time will come soon enough. You will find each other and your password will be "King's freedom". Mark my words, the King will give back the freedom that the Chancellors have stolen from you, he will give it to all those who rally beneath his standard. Be ready when the word comes and remember – "King's freedom".'

Drib touched Nevian's arm lightly to warn him of his presence. The old man's eyebrows rose slightly.

'Go, go quickly, and remember – "King's freedom",' he urged and sent the man on his way before closing the flap of his booth.

'Well, did you succeed? Did you find Thunderstone and Errant? What happened, you've been gone for a long time, I was getting very worried. Where are you, boy? Show yourself!'

Nevian was becoming impatient and the moment the man was safely out of earshot he began to search the shadows of his small tent. Drib reappeared in a muted flash of blue-white light and grinned, nodding, well-pleased with his success. He told the magician about how Thunderstone would be leaving the door of the fortress ajar, just a crack, until the first finger of dawn light touched the sky.

'Come on, come on then, there isn't a moment to lose. We have so many strategies to plot and plans to formulate.'

Nevian gathered up the hems of his cloak and began to mutter the word of a spell which would render him invisible, but then he hesitated and glanced down. He frowned, irritated that his ragged sleeves were still plain to see. He tried again, but to no effect. Then he hurriedly rummaged through the voluminous pockets of his under cloak in search for the book of rudimentary magic that he had taken to keeping with him at all times.

'It's no good,' he muttered, turning to Drib, 'I . . . I . . . I er seem to have mislaid my spell-binder. You couldn't be so good as to recite the spell to make both of us invisible could you? Only I seem to have forgotten the words – just temporarily of course.'

Drib smiled and reached up to take the old man's hand as he whispered the words of magic. Abruptly, he vanished and then, bit by bit, starting with the hand he was holding, the image of the magician faded and melted into nothing beside him.

It didn't take Drib long to realize as he sat listening to Nevian and Thunderstone talk of the enormity of the task that confronted them that it was going to take a lot more than a Kindred Spirit if they were to stand the slightest chance of rescuing Sloeberry and defeating the Chancellors. Gradually, as the talk stretched through the long hours of the night and the lamps burned down, a battle plan was forged. It was agreed that their strength lay in secrecy and hence they must move with extreme caution, shrouding their purpose until all those who had kept their loyalties to the King hidden during the rise of the Chancellors had been found and gathered into mighty battle crescents.

'A clash of arms is not the only issue here. Victory might well lie in discovering the nature of the dark evil of the Eretch and why it has found itself a host in the black souls of the Chancellors' families. We dare not reveal ourselves until we have found a way to destroy this blackness,' Nevian warned.

'The Eretch! Is that the name of those monstrous creatures who attacked us?' Thunderstone asked.

Nevian shook his head. 'That's only a part of it. Perhaps you will understand more if Drib describes the rout of Cawdor to you and repeats the words that Snatchpurse, Chancellor Ironpurse's son, taunted him with moments before he managed to escape on Sparkfire.'

A cold shiver ran up Drib's spine and his face paled as he told of the hideous black, boiling shadows filled with half-human, half-beast shapes that swarmed out of the petrified forest to envelop Cawdor. 'We were out hunting and we galloped back the moment it happened and yet we could do nothing to stop them. Our weapons were of little use. Snatchpurse captured Sloeberry and he was holding her unconscious body up to taunt me as I fought my way into the inner courtyard. He howled at me, saying "Your King is siege-locked, starving to death in his Granite City and that magician who was once so fond of helping him steal what rightfully belonged to others has faded to nothing. All your friends will soon be dead." And then he said something about how Elundium would soon be his.' Drib let his voice fade away to nothing and rubbed at the tears that had begun to brim in his eyes as he remembered that dreadful daylight and how he had seen that inhuman monster shake Sloeberry so violently before he had cast her limp, blood-stained body onto the cobbles at his feet.

'Those same hideous creatures attacked here after burning Marshthistle to the ground and massacring the inhabitants, but it happened a little differently.' Thunderstone frowned as he remembered. 'One minute they were swarming towards us beneath a forest of black banners, pouring across the Causeway Fields, and then, quite unexpectedly, they stopped. They were just out of range of the Archers but certainly still close enough for us to be able to see their vile armoured scales and the spines and bony ridges that grew across the tops of their heads.'

Thunderstone paused and shook his head. 'You said that these creatures were once the Chancellors' sons? Well they have certainly changed, and not for the better.'

'You will find this next bit difficult to believe,' he continued, lowering his voice, 'but the air above these monsters began to darken and eerie shadows – wraiths, ghostly figures – began to rise out of them and then the darkness advanced towards us, swallowing up the daylight. It was the strangest sensation as the blackness boiled up against the doors and began to spread out and up across the sheer walls of the fortress. There was nothing we could do to stop it as it poured in through every crack and gap and culvert. The sunlight in the long galleries suddenly faded and then we were all isolated, trapped and surrounded by our own fears. The air seemed to be stifling and it was so full of wailing, whispering voices that we could hardly breathe. It felt as though hundreds of cold fingers were touching us in the dark and trying to find a way to get inside, to get under our skins . . .'

'You mean they were trying to possess your souls,' Nevian interrupted sharply. It confirmed the report that Umm had given him when he had secretly watched the Eretch possess Snatchpurse and his murderous followers the night before they had attacked Cawdor.

'Yes, that's right, it did feel as though they were trying to take us but I shouted out to my warriors and tried to drown out their persuasive whisperings. I knew that no goodness could possibly come from such evil, ugly creatures such as the ones who had burned Marshthistle to the ground. The moment my men started to resist, to deny them, the ghostly shapes became frantic and they seethed with rage, clawing violently and leaving raw, red weals. And then, as suddenly as they had come, they melted away. The sunlight streamed back into the fortress and the wraith-like figures glided back across the Causeway to vanish back into those monstrous creatures that they had first appeared from.'

'So then did Snatchpurse attack?' Nevian asked.

'Well no, that is the strangest thing, he didn't, although he must have known that those ghostly figures had left us untouched. No, they left us alone but defiled the dead of Marshthistle, piling up their corpses against the doors of Underfall. I am sure it was an attempt to prevent us from getting out to warn anyone of the invasion. They set light to everything that would burn and they marched towards Meremire Forest. It took us two daylights to clear away the dead and open the doors wide enough for Errant to gallop out and try to warn Kyot and Eventine in the tower on Stumble Hill. The creatures that now surround us are under the command of one of those evil half-human creatures. They arrived the day after Errant rode out.'

Nevian frowned thoughtfully and as Thunderstone paused for breath Drib burst in. 'Did you happen to see Sloeberry? Did you catch a glimpse of her? She would have been bound in chains . . .' Thunderstone shook his head: there had been too much noise, too much confusion with the fire and the smoke for any of them to have been able to see clearly inside Snatchpurse's camp.

One of the guards who had been set to watch for the approaching dawn suddenly hurried forward to report that the grey hours were beginning to lighten the sky and that the Kindred Spirit were breaking camp. Nevian rose quickly to his feet.

'There is still so much to discuss, so many strategies to form, but there is no time. Tell me, did you see any weaknesses? Was there anything at all in those half-human creatures that we can use to our advantage?' The old man asked as they hurried through the inner courtyards and made their way towards the outer keep.

'No, there is nothing. Wait! No, I'm wrong, there *was* something very odd about their shadows. They would at times suddenly change shape, especially if somebody accidentally touched or trod on them. It seemed to make their owners very agitated,' Thunderstone replied.

'Now that is very interesting!' Nevian's bushy eyebrows rose. 'It leaves little doubt in my mind that the Eretch must once have been a part of Krulshard's dark evil. He always hated having his shadow touched and Kruel, his vile offspring, was shadowless until King Thane sewed one into his footprints at the Battle of the Rising, and when that happened it reduced him to an innocent baby, devoid of all evil.'

Pausing by the gap between the outer doors of the fortress Nevian gripped Thunderstone's arm in parting. 'Remember,' he whispered, 'Drib and I have done what we could in the little time we have had here to sow the seeds of discontent amongst Unsnark's men. Be ready to welcome them back beneath the King's standard. Leave the doors slightly ajar each night and they will come to you in ones and twos. Begin your march on the Granite City when the summer leaves turn to gold in the high pastures. Travel in secret by way of Grimly Wood, there was once a road that skirted the western reaches of Notley Marsh in better daylights. You must find it and gather all those you can beneath the King's standard. We will meet again before the doors of Candlebane Hall and then we will rescue the King and rid the world of the Chancellors' black evil for ever. Be there on mid-winter's daylight. Do not be late!'

'The circus is almost ready to leave. We must hurry.'

Drib grasped the magician's hand and quickly shouted the spell. As the magician began to fade he called out to Thunderstone, 'I nearly forgot – keep a sharp look-out for Marcher Berioss and the Tunnellers, and all the folk I led over the high passes of the Emerald Mountains last winter. Most of them fled into the petrified forest during the rout of Cawdor but Berioss has promised to find them and take them to the Granite City. Yes, there is a chance you might come across young Eider too, he is with the huntsmen of Largg and they may well be on the road. Tell them of our battle plans, tell them to meet us at the doors of Candlebane Hall on mid-winter's day . . .'

'Wait, who is this Largg? Can he be trusted? And Eider? Is this Greygoose's son?' Thunderstone began, but the magician had vanished.

IV

Deep in the Petrified Forest

DAWN BROKE slowly across the petrified forest and the new sun rose to show itself blood-red across the Emerald Mountains. Shafts of misty sunlight filtered down through the dense, silent canopy of leaves to dapple the forest floor and warm the masses of hanging orchids, causing their flowerheads to open and spill a heady fragrance into the air, brightening the gloomy, verdant colours of night with their large, fragile petals of azure, cadmium, primrose and saffron hues. Insects hummed and danced with shimmering, iridescent wings fluttering in the pools of light, doves cooed and blackbirds burst into song in the thick undergrowth while squirrels leapt from branch to branch and bullfrogs croaked as the forest slowly came to life.

Beside a still, silent pool in the depths of the forest Marcher Berioss stood resting, alone and forlorn, trapped by the forgotten threads of Nevian's magic and forced into the shape of an ancient, gnarled tree. Nevian had impressed upon Berioss the importance of finding everyone who had survived the rout of Cawdor and bringing them to the doors of Candlebane Hall on mid-winter's day. The old Marcher had searched through the petrified forest in his effort to gather them together. He had strode away from the ruins of Cawdor full of hope only to have these hopes eroded away by his fruitless search: he could not find a single one of them no matter where he looked.

Luckily for the old Marcher, traces of the spell that the

magician had once cast in haste and anger over all the warriors who had refused to pledge loyalty to their new King had clung to him and had lately saved his life. He had not always believed the magic to be lucky: sometimes it had made his skin itch and feel as rough as bark and his knuckles had often swollen painfully to grow like knobbly twigs. His joints had creaked and groaned with the sound of the wind rubbing amongst the branches of a tree and at times moving had been slow and full of pain. The spell had become a part of him. He thought it had been left there deliberately as a reminder, a punishment, for once abandoning his King, but he had been wrong in this assumption. Nevian had been unaware that the spell had endured for so long, he had thought that the magic that had once bound the spell would dissipate into the wind once it had been used and was complete but it was those forgotten threads that had saved the warrior when he was driven over the cliff edge at Cawdor by Snatchpurse's murdering hordes. He would have plunged to his death on the rocks far below had he not cried out in despair and felt the magic stir within him and come back to life. His armoured boots had swollen and split apart and his toes had spread out into a mass of grasping, clinging roots that burrowed into the fissures and storm rills of those sheer, black marble cliffs and had broken his descent. His breast plate had shattered to reveal the sturdy trunk of ancient, weatherworn bark, his riven helm had broken apart and his head, hair and beard had become a tangled garland of vines and creepers whilst his arms and fingers had grown, twisting and dividing into a gnarled, sparse canopy of branches. Perilously he had clung to a narrow ledge half way down that cliff face and despair and desolation had overwhelmed him. He could do nothing to defend Drib, Eider or the Tunnellers who he had sworn to protect on their long journey to the dark side of morning. Nor could he halt the final destruction of Cawdor.

And this is how it was when Nevian found him many daylights later after he had slowly and laboriously clambered back up to the top of the cliffs to begin his search for any survivors of the attack. Unfortunately the old magician could do little to change him back into his former shape: he could only remember a handful of the words that he would need to break such a strong and enduring spell. He had tried, with some disastrous results to begin with. First he had made the tree grow so rapidly that it almost choked poor Berioss inside it as the buds swelled and opened into new leaves and the mass of trailing vines that clothed the trunk burst into flower, obscuring his sight. But by trial and error Nevian gradually shrunk him as much as he dared until he was only about twice his normal height: a giant of a man, but his face had partly reappeared through the foliage and the strips of bark had softened to allow his mouth to split open and now he could breath normally once again. Two of the stoutest branches had established themselves as his arms, complete with large, knobbly hands and gnarled fingers and a long, irregular crack had appeared in the lower part of the trunk that had widened to release his legs and the mass of roots that burrowed themselves into the ground whenever he stopped had now shrunk back into long, knobbly toes.

Berioss could still easily be mistaken for a gnarled, old beech tree if he stood perfectly still. But it was the best that Nevian could do in the circumstances, and he had promised Berioss that once the King had been rescued from Candlebane Hall and the Chancellors' black evil had been put to an end he would take the old Marcher back to the tower at the Runesgate Gorge. He hoped that if he could search through his books he would find exactly the right words to break the spell forever.

The tree swayed and creaked slightly, a shiver rippled across its age-scarred bark, rustling its leaves. Berioss stirred and awoke to the new daylight. Stretching his arms and flexing his stiff, twig-like fingers he breathed a deep sigh of resignation as he thought of the long, fruitless day of searching that he was sure lay ahead of him. He reached out with his long, knobbly toes and parted the wet knapweed and woundwort that grew on the edge of the pool and touched the liquid reflection of the sky that was mirrored in its still surface. Gentle ripples spread out in slow, widening circles across the pool, disturbing the silent shoals of swordtails and rainbow fish, making them wheel and turn as they vanished in flashes of bright colours amongst the tangled weed that covered the bottom of the pool. Berioss was about to bend and drink his fill when the dense undergrowth on the far side of the pond began to move. Berioss stood very still and watched, the fingers of his right hand tightening around the shaft of a crude spear that Nevian had made for him in the ruins of Cawdor. A strong odour of wet earth and leaf mould began to fill the air as the undergrowth rustled and parted and two huge creatures covered in sparse tufts of orange hair approached the water's edge cautiously. One of them seemed uneasy and kept lifting his head to scent the air, but eventually they seemed satisfied and both squatted down at the water's edge to drink. Berioss had never before seen such strange looking beings in all his marching days, and yet there was something about them that stirred his memory as he watched them reach down with their long arms and cup their broad hands together to scoop at the water. He studied them, stared at their leathery, wrinkled faces, their deep-set but gentle black eyes and flattened nostrils and watched as they noisily gurgled the water with their large, loose-lipped mouths. He wondered what it was about them that made them appear so familiar.

One of the creatures raised his hands high above his head and emitted a deep, musical, laughing sound and then shook his hands fiercely in the air as though he was trying to shake them dry. That was the moment that Berioss saw that he had seven fingers on each hand. There was something about the creature having seven fingers that struck a chord in his memory and he looked down quickly at their feet which were only partly hidden in the lush grass. They had two extra toes. Berioss remembered then the morning that Snatchpurse attacked Cawdor. He had taken a company of Tunnellers hunting in the forest. They had not ridden far when Oaktangle and Eider had discovered a mass of seven-toed footprints in the soft earth all around a fallen oak in a clearing quite close to the eaves of the forest. Silkstone's warning shriek about the attack on the fortress had put an end to any further speculation about who the footprints had belonged to, but now he knew.

Berioss looked warily across the pool towards the strong, hairy, muscular bodies as another memory came to him. They fitted perfectly the description that Drib and Eider had given of the creatures who had attacked them when they were struggling to get the carcass of the Nightboar back to the citadel on the crude sledge they had made on that first day at Cawdor. Then he remembered something that Nevian had told him. It had been one of those creatures who had saved Drib's life; he had called him Umm and had said that he was one of the Yerrak, a shy, nomadic people who lived in the forests. He remembered Nevian

telling how Drib had been found deep in the forest, unconscious and gravely injured, still lying on Sparkfire's back.
The Yerrak had led the horse out of the forest high up in
the Emerald Mountains and had taken him all the way
to the tower in the Runesgate Gorge for the magician to
heal him. It made Berioss wonder if perhaps these Yerrak
were not so savage or dangerous after all. Perhaps they
had seen something of the Tunnellers?

The old Marcher pushed the end of his spear into the
soft earth and leaned forward as silently as he could with
barely a rustle of leaf or the creak of bark. He let his long
arms trail out over the pond, his fingertips almost touching
the surface of the water. He hoped that he might be able
to understand something of their speech as they made
slow, deliberate gestures to one another. He could hear
their voices rising and falling in soft, melodic tones that
at times were no louder than the murmur of the wind
amongst the leaves, or the sigh and babble of clear water
running over the pebbles. The warrior's interest suddenly
sharpened as he caught the sound of Drib's name very
distinctly. He could understand parts of their speech and
he turned his head to listen intently. One of them seemed
to be talking about how they had found the small boy
almost dead on the horse's back and how Umm had taken
the long and dangerous journey to search for the magician's tower.

'He was so cruelly injured I am sure he'll die,' said one
as he wailed and covered his head with his hands.

'No, no, by leaf and branch there was magic in the boy.
We all saw how he had the power to grow another hand
when Umm had torn his own off. He will survive. Umm
will find the magician's tower.'

'Magic indeed!' Berioss was barely able to suppress a

ripple of laughter from stirring his branches and making his leaves rustle as he heard them describe Drib as magical.

The boy certainly had something unusual about him: an almost bottomless well of optimism, considering his disabilities, and he was very likeable, except for his irritating habit of continually chatting and using ten words when one would do, but there was definitely nothing magical about him. Berioss remembered quite clearly the incident that the Yerrak were discussing. One of them had torn off the boy's glove when they had attacked the sledge with the Nightboar's carcass on it. Berioss chuckled again at the thought that these simple creatures thought that the glove was the boy's hand.

The two Yerrak jumped to their feet as the leaves of the tree directly across the water rustled. 'It must be the small people of Cawdor, the ones we promised Umm we would watch over, they must be coming. They must be following us.'

They shrunk back, silently parting the undergrowth to vanish from sight.

'These people – the Tunnellers and their horses – they make so much noise as they move about that we would have surely heard them if they were following us. Anyway we would have smelled them. It cannot be them, it must be the morning breeze stirring the leaves of that old tree. There is nothing to fear.'

They hesitated and stared at Berioss, scratching their foreheads.

'But that tree – it wasn't there the last time we stopped here to have a drink. I don't like it. Let us get away from here as quickly as we can.'

'It must have been. This forest doesn't have enchanted trees – they can't move about.'

Still they stood staring uncertainly at Berioss. They thought they knew every tree in the petrified forest, every rock and bush, all the secrets from the high, inaccessible passes of the Emerald Mountains down to the restless surf that thundered and boiled along the dark margin of their world beyond the eaves of the forest. They were sure that the tree had not been there before.

'Come on, let us touch its bark, let it talk to us and then we will remember it.'

They very hesitantly crept around the edges of the pond. Berioss froze. He had never meant to give himself away. From what he had overheard, they had seen the Tunnellers, and only yesterlight: they couldn't be very far away, but in which direction? He had to find out. From what he could remember Nevian telling him about the Yerrak they were very shy and he didn't want to frighten them away by revealing himself too quickly.

Berioss held his breath, his eyes almost closed in case they caught sight of them. He waited. The two Yerrak approached very stealthily and he felt the soft touch of their hands on his rough bark as they reassured themselves. With a quick, shaking movement Berioss made a grasp and caught hold of the Yerrak's arms, trapping and holding onto them tightly, preventing them from escaping. The two Yerrak wailed and shrieked in real terror: never before in all their travels through the forest had a tree attacked their people. They fought to break free from the tangle of branches, but the more they struggled the tighter they were held.

For the first time since Berioss had been trapped within the shape of a tree he silently thanked the magician for at least making him twice his normal size and with the strength to match, because he certainly needed it now.

The Yerrak began pulling so hard in different directions that they were beginning to rock him from foot to foot. He feared that at any moment he would find himself tumbling backwards. He had to do something quickly, he had to try and make them understand that he meant them no harm.

'Be still, be still both of you and listen to me. I mean you no harm. I come in peace.'

He talked to them in his deep, marching voice, the same voice of authority that so often, long ago, he had used to cry above the roar and clash of battle and to rally men and steel their hearts as the black shadows of the Nightbeasts had swarmed towards them, shutting out the daylight. The Yerrak stared at the tree, searching to see where the sound of a human voice could possibly have come from.

'Nevian, the Master of Magic, the one whom Umm sought has sent me to tell you that Umm has found the magician's tower in the Runesgate Gorge and the boy he took there lives.'

When they heard this the Yerrak stopped struggling slightly and repeated Umm's name to each other.

'Yes, that's right, I said Umm. Umm found the tower and the boy is well; the magician healed him,' Berioss repeated quickly. The Yerrak might have stopped struggling but their terror still burned in their eyes and their bodies were trembling. It was a lot to ask them to accept talking trees that could move.

Berioss arms were beginning to ache and he knew he couldn't hold onto them for much longer. 'I come in peace – peace, do you understand? I will not harm you.'

He spoke slowly, twisting his bark-covered face from one to the other of the frightened Yerrak. He realized that there was little chance of making them understand that he was not really a tree or that Elundium teetered on the brink of ruin if the Chancellors were allowed to seize power. He doubted if they even knew about the world beyond the margins of the mountains and the forest they inhabited.

'Peace, you come in peace.' One of them frowned.

'Yes, that's right, in peace.' Berioss smiled. At last he seemed to be getting somewhere. He took a chance. He released his grip on them completely, telling them as simply as he could that he wanted nothing more of them other than their help to find all the people who had survived the rout of Cawdor and had fled to the forest to escape the massacre.

'Umm would want you to help me, I know he would.'

The two Yerrak crept backwards out of reach of his arms, but they did not turn and run. They drew together and whispered in such soft, musical tones that Berioss could hardly hear them, all the while darting anxious looks up at him.

'Small people, you want us to show you where they are? They are in the forest,' one of them gesticulated towards the undergrowth beyond the far side of the pond.

Berioss caught at the words and he nodded vigorously. 'Yes, yes, that's right, I am looking for the small people, the Tunnellers, Oaktangle, Mistletoe ... I need to find all of them as quickly as I can. Will you show me?'

The Yerrak huddled together momentarily and then gestured to him to follow them. Before Berioss could blink they had vanished into a tangle of bushes away to his right leaving only a rustling of leaves and a swaying of the hanging flowerheads as a clue to the direction they had taken. He grabbed his spear and strode after them, clearing a broad path through the undergrowth as he moved. The Yerrak left barely a footprint or a broken twig and all day he struggled to keep their elusive shapes in sight, catching only an occasional glimpse of their bright orange, tufted hair in the shafts of sunlight that filtered down to dapple the forest floor. The Yerrak led him deep into a part of the forest where he had never before ventured, constantly pausing and turning to call out with their undulating, musical voices to make sure he didn't lose his way, yet they never stopped for a moment and he never managed to catch up with them. The ground became broken and rocky as it began to rise beneath the old Marcher's knobbly feet. Steep hills and narrow valleys rose before him, thickly wooded with tall, black ebonies that soared above his head as straight, sturdy and smooth as castle columns and gnarled and twisted ironwoods, interspersed with silverspikes whose spread out branches blocked his path. Thick undisturbed leaf mould and hidden mossy rocks made the ground slippery and treacherous underfoot. Berioss puffed out his cheeks as he gasped for breath: he was finding it a struggle to keep going. The sun was beginning to set and nightshapes were gathering the shadows together, weaving them into the colour of night as twilight deepened into silence across the seemingly endless wooded valleys of the petrified forest. At last he came upon the Yerrak as they waited for him in a small clearing.

'Listen – small people are just ahead,' one of them whispered, sweeping his seven-fingered hand vaguely across the darkening undergrowth.

Berioss stared into the thickening gloom and listened, but all he could hear was the faint roar of a waterfall tumbling and cascading over rocks, plunging into some hidden valley in the distance. Somewhere far off he thought he heard a dog bark but the sound faded before he could be sure. He sniffed the heady scent of water jasmine, wild rosemary and nightblossom. 'I can't hear anybody,' he frowned, turning back to find that he was alone: the Yerrak had silently vanished into thin air.

For a moment anger flashed in the old Marcher's eyes and he looked wildly around the clearing, calling out loudly and cursing the Yerrak for deserting him, but he was too weary to hold onto his anger and too exhausted to try and find out where they had gone. The sound of a distant waterfall seemed to grow louder as the night silence intensified and it made him realize how thirsty he had become during the long day's march through the forest. He licked at his parched and cracked lips and took a step towards the sound of the cascading water and then hesitated. He wasn't afraid of the dark, but with his cumbersome shape he needed to see his footing, otherwise he might well stumble and fall over some unseen obstacle, and once fallen he would never be able to rise.

'Tomorrowlight, I'll drink my fill tomorrowlight,' he sighed, resigned to spending the night in the clearing where the Yerrak had deserted him.

Settling down he spread out his long toes, pressing them into the soft earth to balance himself. Perhaps the Yerrak had not abandoned him at all. Perhaps, in truth, they had fulfilled their promise and he would find the Tunnellers near the waterfall in the morning. His eyelids started to close and his arms dropped to his sides as sleep began to steal upon him. Pale, silvery moonlight shone down into the clearing, casting soft, velvet moonshadows around the tree.

A faint noise, the rustle of undergrowth, made Berioss

stir and murmur in his sleep. The sharp snap and crack of a twig breaking underfoot in the darkness suddenly awoke the old Marcher and his eyes sprang open, but before his hand could reach out for the spear that he had pushed into the ground beside him, dozens of huge, shadowy shapes with luminous, pale amber eyes broke cover all around the edges of the clearing and bounded towards him. A cold, wet nose brushed against his hand and all around he heard soft growls of welcome.

'Magadus – is that you? Have you come with your Border Runners?' he called out with relief as he felt the weight of an enormous dog stand up on its hind legs and sniff at the rough bark on his trunk. The dog barked and Berioss knew without a doubt that there were others with him. He rubbed his hand through the dog's broken coat, laughing as he made a fuss of his old friend. Obviously the Border Runners were not the least bit troubled that he was trapped within the shape of a tree but then perhaps they recognized that he was still the man he had always been. But then neither was he the least afraid that they were savage hunting dogs: they had so often fought beside one another in the great battle crescents against Krulshards' dark evil. But, he realized as he glanced across at the large, ferocious pack who were milling about in the moonlit clearing, the Yerrak might view their presence quite differently. Perhaps they had caught the scent of the approaching pack and that was why they had vanished so abruptly without so much as a farewell.

'Magadus, I have been searching for the Tunnellers in the forest for many daylights without much success. The people you helped on their long journey to Cawdor. It is really important that I find them. You don't know where they are do you?'

The dog barked and rubbed himself against the old Marcher and then bit softly on the old man's arm as though to lead him towards the dark undergrowth on the edge of the clearing. He seemed to be going in the same direction that the Yerrak had indicated before they had disappeared.

'Not too fast, old friend,' Berioss called out. 'I can't see a hand in front of my face and I find travelling in the dark rather difficult of late.' The dogs crowded around him and began to shepherd him into the undergrowth.

Unseen branches thwacked against his trunk, hanging vines and creepers snagged around his head and neck, threatening to choke him. He constantly tripped and stumbled over hidden tree roots. But slowly, step by ponderous step, he and the dogs forced a path through the thorny undergrowth and he found himself climbing up a long, steep slope. The trees gradually thinned out as he reached the top. Below him lay a deep valley as featureless as the one he had just climbed out of, and beyond that for as far as he could see in the moonlight, lay other wooded hills and valleys, while above, cold and distant, the sky was carpeted with millions of bright stars.

'I thought you were leading me to the Tunnellers!' he gasped, searching for breath as he leaned heavily on his spear.

Magadus growled softly and gently pulled at his arm, turning him towards the head of the valley where the moonlight shone on the waterfall, silvering the shimmering plumes of spray as the roaring water plunged into the dark depths of the valley below.

'I can't go down there,' cried Berioss, shaking his head and making the leaves rustle around his ears. And then amongst the perfumed scent of the night blossoms he caught the vaguest scent of woodsmoke.

'Wait a moment,' he frowned, trying to hurry further along the ridge towards the waterfall and peer down through the trees. Yes, far below he could see what looked like the glowing embers and flickering light of what must be camp fires – not one or two, but dozens of them. With a laugh of relief he knew then that he must have found the Tunnellers. Magadus barked, urging him to go down into the valley and then, surrounded by the pack of Border Runners, he quickly vanished back into the sparse pine trees that grew just below the ridge.

'It's easy for you with four legs!' Berioss muttered to himself as he chose what looked like the easiest way to follow them. But no matter how cautiously he moved, his large, cumbersome feet would create a small avalanche of loose stones, fallen pine cones and soft crumbly earth. He frequently stumbled, and to save himself from toppling forward onto his face he had to cling onto the stronger trees as he stumbled his way down the scree. Gradually as the stars turned and paled in the sky above his head he descended the steep, treacherous slope. The tall, whispering pines gave way to rowan trees, ironweeds, oaks and elms beneath whose spreading canopy of branches everything grew darker while thick leaf mould muffled his footsteps. All was silent as he approached the sleeping encampment save for the rumbling, soothing roar of the waterfall. His head filled with the sweet, heady scent of the night blossoms that grew and flourished in the misty, wet air beside the water.

The old Marcher frowned as he drew closer: where were the guards? They should have set guards to watch during the night – surely they hadn't forgotten everything he had taught them during their long, hard winter at Cawdor. Had not the rout and utter destruction of the citadel been lesson enough? He passed unchallenged between their cooking fires and saw that they had allowed it to dwindle into glowing heaps of ash ringed by blackened cooling stones. The strengthening dawnlight brightened and he could see the low houses that they had built for themselves. He stood, admiring their distinctive curved roofs of tightly-woven saplings, smoothed with moss and earth to seal and make them completely weathertight before being covered with larger tufts of grass and layers of growing moss. He knew from the nights he had spent in such shelters that they were snug and warm on even the coldest night. Amongst the Tunnellers' small dwellings he could also see there were much larger huts. Berioss had intended to wake the Tunnellers the moment he arrived in their camp – there was so much he wanted to ask them, and he had so much to tell; but he hesitated. His eyes felt heavy and sore with tiredness and he was stifling a yawn as his body ached and creaked with weariness from the long, arduous night's journey through the forest.

A few paces beyond the encampment, he caught the glint of the waterfall as it cascaded into a deep pool. It was surrounded by lush undergrowth, giant cream lilies, fragrant tunsole and purple fluted brambleheads that hung down to trail across the rippling surface of the water. He ran his tongue over his dry lips remembering how parched he was and he could feel himself being drawn with slow footsteps towards the water.

'Perhaps I'll just refresh myself first. I will just have a moment's rest and close my eyes while I wash away the tiredness,' he murmured to himself as he found a way around the pool. He stood close enough to the rushing wall of water to be in its drifting curtain of spray. With a contented sigh he lifted his arms and tilted back his head, closing his eyes as he opened his mouth to let the drifting water envelop him and soak away his many aches and pains. The water splashed and ran down his face, darkening the texture of the bark. It tasted so deliciously clean and felt soothingly cool.

'I will wake everybody in a moment or two,' he murmured, spreading out his tired toes amongst the lily roots but immediately he fell into a deep, dreamless sleep.

The sun had risen high above the rim of the valley, the rays warming his rough bark as it dried, before Berioss began to stir. Somewhere, far away on the edge of consciousness, he could hear the tumbling rush of water and what sounded like whispering, anxious but familiar voices. He blinked and for a moment he was unsure where he was. But then he started awake and found himself standing beside a waterfall surrounded by a circle of curious faces. His memory of the previous day flooded back to him.

'Oaktangle! Mistletoe, Damask! At last, I've found you all!' he cried, taking a step towards them, only to see them all scatter away from him in confusion.

Oaktangle, the leader of the Tunnellers, wasn't sure if he had eaten something at supper to give him strange dreams or if his sleep really had been disturbed during the night by the eerie, rustling, creaking sound of a gnarled old tree moving slowly through their encampment in the moonlight. Had he really peeped out through the closely woven saplings and seen it or had it all been a dream? Logic told him that it must have been a dream: trees could not move on their own unless they had been enchanted, and he was pretty sure there was no magician within leagues who had the power to make a tree walk. He had just about convinced himself that it must have been a dream when he hurried through the sleeping camp in the first light of dawn to plunge his head into the cold water, only to come to a startled halt in front of the tree. It was the one from his dream. Open-mouthed he stared at it, his heart pounding. The hairs on the back of his neck started to prickle. There it stood, towering over him, close to the waterfall. Glistening droplets of water were dripping from its arched branches and running down between the cracks in the rough, ancient bark. The surface of its trunk appeared to rise and fall slightly and from somewhere inside the tree Oaktangle could hear a low, rumbling noise that reminded him of snoring. He could remember another time when he used to hear snoring. Berioss the old Marcher who had protected them on their long journey to Cawdor and had given up his life for them during the citadel's destruction used to snore.

Oaktangle had retreated away from the tree without making a sound and when he was far enough away he turned and ran back to wake everyone in their encampment. Slowly, silently all the survivors of Cawdor gathered in a circle around the old tree. Quencher, the blacksmith, had armed himself with a heavy, forging hammer and Flock, the saddler, gripped a razor-sharp, half-moon saddler's knife in his hand whilst the fishermen, masons, ironmasters, Tunnellers and everybody else who had gathered to watch stood waiting to see what would happen.

'Look, isn't that a spear laying against the tree's trunk? Should we do something quickly before it wakes up? It might stab one of us.' A fisherman stepped forwards and brandished an axe at the tree.

'No, no, wait! It might not mean us any harm. Trees are such beautiful things,' Mistletoe called out and stepped in front of the man who then reluctantly lowered his axe.

Other voices rose in protest and fear. 'Perhaps it is one

of the trees that Nevian once cast his spell over. Perhaps it has been wandering alone in the forest,' Damask suggested.

'No, all those warriors that Nevian once turned into trees were changed back at the Battle of the Rising. It can't be one of those,' Blackthorn disagreed.

'Trees don't move of their own accord, it's just not natural,' a weaver muttered darkly.

It was at this point that Berioss stirred and woke up, but it took him quite a while to convince them who he really was.

'It's Berioss, Marcher Berioss!' Quencher finally cried, striding towards the old warrior to clasp at his twig-like hands in startled surprise, laughing with relief.

'You mean to say that Nevian's magic endured for all that time? It lay hidden inside you? You must come and tell us everything – it seems so incredible. But first you must eat,' Oaktangle cried with delight. Berioss was led into the centre of their camp and made as comfortable as possible before a celebration feast was prepared.

'You can still eat the same food as us, can't you?' Damask asked, gently touching the rough bark. Berioss laughed, nodding as he inhaled deeply to savour the wholesome smell drifting up from the bubbling, black-bellied cauldron that had been suspended over newly-lit cooking fires.

'It must be very difficult moving about,' Mistletoe remarked sitting at Berioss' feet and looking up across his broad trunk. 'Will you ever be able to change back into your proper shape?'

Berioss smiled as he nodded. 'Oh, yes, Nevian has promised that once we have rid Elundium of the Chancellors' dark shadows he will search through his books and find the exact right spell to break this enchantment. He will change me back but . . .'

Mistletoe noticed his hesitation and saw the doubt in the old Marcher's eyes, but he was quick to disguise it with a laugh. 'Of course at times it is extremely hot and uncomfortable trapped in here but I can probably still stride a lot faster than any of you. Anyway I mustn't complain too much: if it hadn't been for the forgotten threads of that spell I would have been killed when those monstrous villains drove me over that cliff edge.'

As Berioss spoke, everyone from the encampment gathered around him, eager to hear everything that had happened to him since the fall of Cawdor.

'So it was the Chancellors who were behind all those terrible things that we were blamed for.'

Voices on every side besieged Berioss with questions, leaving him little time to swallow but a mouthful of the welcome food that Mistletoe had brought to him.

'You said Drib is in the magician's tower – but do you know what has happened to Eider?' somebody asked, while another urged that they do something to rescue Sloeberry immediately.

'Will those Chancellors attack us here in the forest? How safe are we?' Malthera, Quencher's wife, asked anxiously, clutching her hands together. She had not told anybody, not even her husband, that it had been their son, Crimp, who had loomed out of those terrifying, boiling shadows when the citadel was attacked. She had not even admitted to herself that he had made a wild stab at her. She had glimpsed the look of horror on his face, the remorse in his eyes as he realized what he had been about to do and the blade had turned and merely grazed her. The next moment a strange swirl of rainbow colours and light had engulfed the shadows in the courtyard where she had been attacked and in the confusion she had lost sight of Crimp and had found herself running, swept along amongst everybody else as they tried to escape.

'Wait! Wait a moment and let me try and answer your questions one at a time,' Berioss cried, raising his hand and waiting for silence before he continued. 'Firstly let me tell you that Nevian and Drib are going to attempt to rescue Sloeberry the moment the boy has recovered from his injuries, but how they are going to do it I just don't know. As for Eider I rather hoped I would find him here with you people. As for your safety, Malthera, I don't believe we can be sure of anything,' he frowned as he turned towards her. 'No matter where anybody tries to hide we cannot be sure they will be safe. The black evil of the Chancellors will stretch out and find us all, mark my words. If they are allowed to carry on unchallenged then in time they will kill King Thane and seize power and then their tyranny will touch every one of us.'

'Then we are doomed. There is nothing we can do to stop them,' a weaver cried out. 'It's hopeless. I broke a good axe on the scaly armour of one of those monsters who attacked us at Cawdor. They are invincible, there is nothing we can do to stop them.'

Voices began to cry out with fear from all around but Berioss searched out the man who had started this panic and held his gaze with his steady, sea-grey eyes, channelling the fear he saw within him.

'That, my friend, is where you are wrong.' Berioss paused as he allowed the people to fall silent. 'They may have appeared as invincible to us then – half-human creatures, covered in armoured skin – and it is true that they have won a battle against us, but victory is not theirs, not while we still have the spirit and the will to fight back.'

Berioss laughed softly as he looked from face to face. 'The Chancellors can never triumph, not if everyone in Elundium who is loyal to the King stands up against them. Yes, that is right!' he cried, sweeping his hand across the doubting crowd. 'If every one of us who cherishes honesty and integrity and who has a love of freedom joins together to repel this yoke of oppression, then the tyranny these Chancellors would lay so heavily upon our shoulders can be broken. We can throw it off!'

The old Marcher suddenly reached down to where he had laid his spear and lifted it up, brandishing it for them all to see. 'The power to rescue Elundium from the brink of disaster lies within you all. Every one of us standing here has a part to play.'

'But . . . but . . . how? How are we to help? We are not warriors like you, we are craftsmen, journeymen – what can we possibly do against those vile creatures?' Quencher asked, and a low murmur of uncertainty spread through the listening crowd.

With a rustle of leaves Berioss turned sharply towards the blacksmith. 'Surely you, of all people, have not forgotten Nevian's words when he appeared to you in your forge? Well let me remind you, and all the rest of you, that the Master of Magic foretold that the fate of Elundium would be decided by the few people who were still loyal to King Thane, far away from the Granite City. It would be decided here on the dark side of morning. Have you forgotten that it was those very words that made you all journey through the depths of winter to Cawdor? Much has changed since then, but our cause is still the same.'

Berioss' face softened beneath its thin covering of flaky bark. 'I know you have the courage in your hearts. Your strength to endure has already been tested and it has not been found wanting: the time to fulfil Nevian's prophecy has come. Quencher, that forging hammer you hold in your hands must become a battle mace. Flock, it is time to wield that saddler's knife for a very different purpose. I promised Nevian that I would search for you in the forest until I found you and from the ashes of our defeat I will make a mighty army. We will bring tears of joy to our beleaguered King's eyes when he sees us approach the Granite City.'

Berioss lowered his voice. 'Remember how mighty oak trees grow from tiny acorns. So shall our battle crescent grow from strength to strength as we gather on our travels all those who, through necessity, have had to hide their loyalty to the King and have kept their love of freedom from the murderous darkness of the Chancellors.'

'Berioss is right, we have hidden ourselves away in the forest for long enough. We must set out right away!'

The people, fired up by Berioss' words, called out, eager for the journey to begin.

'No! No! Not so fast!' Berioss held up his hands for silence. 'Armies never march on empty stomachs nor do they fight with their bare hands. We have to plan, to organize ourselves. We will need to find a source of iron so that we can forge weapons and armour. We will need warm clothes and stout leather boots, and we must have plenty of provisions. We will be no better than the Chancellors if we have to plunder every village and farm along our way. There is much to do; it is a very long journey from here to the doors of Candlebane Hall, and we must not be late. I have given Nevian my word that we will be there by mid-winter's day.'

'We have not been sitting around doing nothing since the citadel was destroyed,' Blackthorn exclaimed indignantly, his hands on his hips. 'Go on, take a good look, you will see we have been working very hard. We couldn't do anything else but watch helplessly from the safety of the forest as Cawdor burnt to the ground, but the moment those evil creatures had marched away and the ashes were cool enough, we crept back into the ruins and silently salvaged everything that we could. It was amazing how much had not been destroyed.'

'I wish we had known that you were clinging to that ledge half way down the cliff. We would have come and rescued you,' Mistletoe added.

'It is of no matter. In fact, in the circumstances, it was better that you did not know that I was there. If you had pulled me up I would not have met the magician, and then where would we be?' The old Marcher laughed as he looked over the heads of his friends.

It was true what Blackthorn had said – they had certainly not been idle. He caught the glint of metal in what he thought must be the blacksmith's forge amidst the clutter of long handled tongs, swages and strikers, bellows and oaken anvils partly hidden beneath a shady tree. Through the open doorways of some of the larger dwellings he glimpsed much of what had been achieved at Cawdor during their long, hard winter and now it all looked new and clean. There were weavers' looms, spinning wheels and cobblers' lasts; larders stocked full of the fruits of the forest and rows of hanging smoked and salted fish and meats.

'Such industry, such industry,' he exclaimed as he caught sight of wagons and handcarts lined up to the right of the trees. His hopes soared. Their long march could start much earlier than he had first thought possible, and as for making warriors out of them, well he had already taught the Tunnellers much of the skill of arms and they could teach the others as they travelled.

'How soon can we start? What do you think?' Damask pressed impatiently.

'By the look of it we can start as soon as everything is packed up and loaded onto the carts and the horses are harnessed. But . . .' Berioss' face grew grave, 'we must travel in secrecy and with extreme caution: it would be disastrous if Snatchpurse or any of his murderous followers got wind of what we intend to do. Nevian warned me to move with stealth and not to squander the advantage of surprise.'

Berioss looked around the camp. 'The first thing that we need to do is to organize a guard. Last night I walked into this camp completely unchallenged. I thought I had taught you the importance of setting a watch. What would have happened if I had been a company of Chancellors?'

'But there is no need for us to set a watch,' Oaktangle laughed. 'The Border Runners have been doing it for us. They have been keeping very close to us ever since Cawdor was destroyed. In fact it was them who found us scattered and hiding in the forest. They gathered us all together and led us to this hidden valley. I bet you they showed you the way here last night. We would probably have starved in the beginning if they had not brought us hares and rabbits to eat. If anybody wants to attack us they have to get past them first, and that would be no easy matter!'

Berioss smiled. He had to agree. The Yerrak had brought him quite close, but it was Magadus and the pack of Border Runners who had actually shown him the hidden valley. Without their help he might have been wandering fruit-lessly amongst the surrounding forest: he would never have found them.

'Well let us hope that they come with us on the long

march. We could certainly do with their help,' he murmured, glancing up the steep wooded sides of the valley for a glimpse of them.

'They will, I know they will, they love their freedom as much as we do,' Mistletoe replied as the company split up and began to prepare to break camp.

V

The Tower of Largg

THE STARS TURNED and paled before fading as the grey hours lightened the sky, heralding the new morning. The cold, clear colours of dawn edged across the frozen turquoise waters of the lake and over the thickly wooded mountain walls that hemmed in the tower of Largg, the huntsman. The tower stood, wrapped in silence, a solitary eyrie high up amongst the nest of eagles in the inaccessible peaks of the Emerald Mountains, majestically wreathed in shadows as the daybreak strengthened.

Eidergoose stirred restlessly in his tiny sleeping chamber within the tower, troubled by persistent, dark dreams of regret, before being awoken by the clatter and bustle of the kitchen below as the voices of the cooks and quarrelsome scullions mingled with the barking of the hearth dogs before the tower came to life. But Eider had no appetite for life and dreaded the shout that he knew would come at any moment, summoning him down to break his fast before the day's hunting began.

'Why oh why was I such a gutless coward?' he muttered bitterly as he threw back his heavy sleeping rug and got up.

He avoided seeing his own thin, haunted reflection in the still surface of his earthenware wash bowl as he plunged his face into its icy coldness. He was overwhelmed with remorse, consumed by guilt, devastated to remember that he had deserted his friends in their moment of greatest need. He was so ashamed by the fear that had so suddenly and unexpectedly gripped him as he had galloped abreast of the others at breakneck speed, out of the petrified forest and down across the windswept headland towards the citadel, following Silkstone's shrill warning that Cawdor was under attack. The strangling fear that had seized him when his courage had failed, the sensation of his fingers freezing with terror on the bowstring as he sighted those hideous half-beast, half-human creatures who swarmed and filled the gate arch of the citadel, would forever be etched in his memories. Waking or sleeping, wherever he looked they haunted the shadows and spoiled the sunlight. He had disgraced his family and made a mockery of his father's proud name. He was the Captain of the King's Archers. But in one, cowardly moment Eider had squandered this honour by allowing his horse, Nightshade, to be infected by his fear and by letting it rear up and spin around to bolt away and carry him out across the Causeway, through the fleeing people and into the safety of the forest. All the while Drib, the little crippled boy, and the Tunnellers, who were so much smaller than him, had shown their courage, the bravery that he lacked, and they had ploughed on defiantly forward across the Causeway into those monstrous creatures. Why oh *why*? The thoughts plagued him. Why had he not torn at the reins and turned his bolting horse instead of clinging there, hunched, with his eyes tightly shut until, in exhaustion, Nightshade had run himself to a standstill in the shadows of the Emerald Mountains.

Eider dismounted and looked back, overwhelmed by the shame of what he had done. He cast aside his bow and threw himself onto the ground, covering his head as he wept. He would have lain there in despair until death claimed him and the carrion birds picked his bones clean. But quite by chance Ayeshe, Largg's daughter, was out hunting mountain hares close by. She heard his cries of anguish and found him collapsed upon the ground beside the exhausted horse. At first, although she could see no evidence of a wound, she had thought him gravely injured and had ordered her father's huntsmen to carry him home to their tower. When he had arrived there her father's healers had examined him and had applied every poultice, drench and cure they could but nothing would draw him out of the black despair that consumed him. He would not eat unless forced, nor talk coherently, but sat alone, staring out across the frozen lake, repeatedly muttering to himself. Everybody tried to get to the bottom of his misery but all they understood was that he had deserted his friends in the hour of their greatest need. Then, quite suddenly, just as dusk was falling after he had been in the tower for five daylights, he had leapt to his feet and insisted that he be shown the road to Cawdor saying that nothing else mattered: he must now make amends for the dreadful thing he had done and ride back and rescue any who had survived the attack.

Word quickly spread through the tower that Cawdor had been attacked and Largg, deeply troubled by what he had heard, summoned Eider to his private chamber. Vague and troubling rumours had been reaching Largg. He had heard that Elundium teetered on the brink of ruin through internal strife and he had received reports that a small company of refugees, people loyal to the King of Elundium, had managed to find a way over the high passes of the Emerald Mountain in the depths of winter and had settled at Cawdor. Largg had no quarrel with Elundium or any of its kings, and he cared little if a handful of its people settled peacefully in the ruins of Cawdor. It was a haunted place and his people never ventured near it but if what the young Archer had said was true then an attack on Cawdor was too close to home to ignore. He would have to get to the bottom of it. With the care and infinite patience that befitted such a wise and skilful huntsman, Largg encouraged Eider to confide in him and tell him the cause of his misery, and to explain why he insisted on returning to Cawdor immediately.

Largg's anxiety for the safety of his own people deepened by what he learned from the young Archer. He sent out scouts to watch the eaves of the petrified forest and set extra watches on the pathways that led up to the tower. He warned his people to arm themselves and be ready for war just in case those half-human creatures who had invaded Cawdor should turn towards them and find a way to breach their defences. Courage, he had counselled Eider as he put a fatherly arm around the boy's shoulders, was an elusive thing that could desert even the bravest warrior – at times when they least expected it. It did not mean that deep down the bravery was not still there. He would find it, he assured him; he could see in his eyes that beneath the pain and wretchedness there was no coward lurking. It would be foolhardy, he said, to return to Cawdor until his courage was strong: he refused to allow it, even though Eider tried to protest and begged to be shown a way down through the maze of steep mountain passes and ravines that guarded the approaches of Largg's tower. But Largg stood firm and reminded him that if the story he had told was true, that he had faced an enraged Nightboar on his first daylight at Cawdor, killing the beast with one carefully-aimed arrow strike, then he had courage, he had plenty of courage, and if he stayed willingly as a guest and rode to hounds, hunting with his huntsmen, taking on even the most ferocious beast without flinching, when he was strong again then he would know the very moment he was ready to return. And when that time came he would organize a hunting party to search for his friends. Largg gave his oath. The older man did not doubt for one moment that the boy would rediscover his courage: he had steady, sure eyes and the makings of a very good Archer, but somewhere inside his tortured soul the pain was in control and he needed time.

Eider lost count of the days. The shame of abandoning his friends, of running away in the height of battle and not knowing if the people who had been with him were alive or dead continued to overshadow his every waking moment and he could think of nothing else. He shunned Ayeshe's kindness and turned away the friendship of the people of the tower, refusing food unless forced and he spoke to no one. His face became gaunt and his body bone-thin as he sank deeper into dark misery. He rode with the hunt but he had no heart for the chase and he took to saddling Nightshade and riding alone to the farthest reaches of the steep heather meadows and the terraced gardens that surrounded the tower as he searched for a way to escape. But there was none. He followed the edge of the lake to where it plunged in thundering waterfalls, its hidden gorges shrouded in mist and spray, and there he sat, allowing the mist and despair to engulf him as he stared out across the sheer precipices and the maze of gullies and ravines that kept him a prisoner. He looked out towards the distant, hazy horizon where he knew Cawdor must lay, so far, far away, beyond his reach.

When Ayeshe could stand his black despair no longer she rode out upon Maelstrom, carrying Eider's bow and quiver and confronted him, thrusting the bow into his hands.

'Do you think that starving yourself or refusing the help you are being offered will rescue your friends? Do you really believe that you are so different from everyone else?'

'What do you mean? What do you know?'

'You are wallowing in self-pity because you feel you are a coward but don't you realize that everyone is afraid? Why should you punish yourself for merely feeling the fear that every man feels? Maybe, in truth, you are braver than most men and this was the first time you felt this beast inside you and it made you run, but we all have that beast. Most people have lived with it long enough to know how to control it but for you it was your first meeting. You will not be so afraid of it again, but you will be afraid; everyone is.'

Ayeshe's words shocked Eider and jolted him out of the mood that he had sunk into and in one awful moment he realized how much he had indulged his feelings since that dreadful day, how much he had inflicted upon these kind people who had taken him in and cared for him. He blinked away his tears and for the first time since Ayeshe had found him, a ghost of a bitter smile touched his lips and lightened the shadows that shrouded his eyes. He didn't know whether she was right, but allowing himself to sink into a morass of black despair was not going to rescue his friends or do anybody any good. He allowed Ayeshe to lead him back to the tower as dusk fell and he felt shame when he thought of the way he had been behaving. For the first time since he had arrived he took his place at the table without prompting and he ate of the food that was placed before him.

Largg saw the change in the youth and he smiled, catching his daughter's eyes. The healing had begun. Long after the meal was over and everybody had taken to their beds Eider and Ayeshe sat beside the dying embers of the fire, surrounded by the snores and grumbles of the hearth dogs and they talked late into the night. For Eider it was as though she had touched at a hidden spring as his innermost feelings welled up. Her smile, her soft voice coaxed out his pent-up agonies and as the silent grains of sand slipped unnoticed through the hour glass, through the night he found himself telling her things – secret, private, personal things – that he would never have dared to utter openly to anyone else. He told her of the frustration of growing up in his father's shadow, always afraid of failing, always aware of the impossibility of ever being such a great Archer. He told her how he had always doubted that he had courage but had hidden his fears beneath a whole catalogue of recklessness at home and in the Learning Hall. It had always been easy for him to make his friends and fellow pupils applaud his bravery but all the while he knew deep inside himself that it was all a sham. Each reckless act had led to another and he had been drawn deeper and deeper into the fear that when he had the need for real courage and cold-blooded bravery it would not be there. He had always believed that one day his own weakness would find him out, and so it had happened.

Ayeshe did not laugh at or scorn his inner demons. She understood only too well the root causes of his despair for like the young Archer who sat so close beside her, as Largg's only child and mistress of the tower, much was expected of her also. There were moments in the flickering firelight when reaching deep inside for the hard truth had brought tears to Eider's eyes but she had reached out and taken his hands into hers. She had looked at him, holding his gaze with her gentle, dark eyes and had told him that if the truth be known, there were probably many times when both of their fathers had found their courage deserting them. To fail, she had smiled, was only too human, but to strive to master the fear, to pull it out into the light and know it, that took real courage.

As Eider listened to her gentle voice and looked into her eyes with the flames licking the redness in her thick, black hair he saw for the first time how beautiful she was and he found his breath had been stolen from him. He realized then that he could find his courage, but not alone.

'Will you help me? I don't have the strength.'

Ayeshe laughed softly, looking up to where the pale light of dawn was touching the vaulted window. 'I don't know if I can. I will try, but only if we ride together, stirrup to stirrup, and you show me how to fell a Nightboar with a single arrow strike.'

The turquoise lake thawed and during the warmth of the summer days Eider rode with Ayeshe and they both threw their energies wholeheartedly into the chase, often riding far ahead of the other huntsmen in their impatience and as they closed in around the most ferocious beasts Eider was eager to show that his courage had returned. He would spur Nightshade forward, slipping the reins and reaching back into his quiver for an arrow, and yet as he knocked it onto the bow string there were so many times when his hand trembled and he would be unable to fell the beast with a clean, well-aimed arrow strike. Disappointment haunted him. Inside he knew he could do it, but the harder he tried the worse it became. To make matters worse he felt that he was failing in Ayeshe's eyes. He had known from that night together that he wanted, more than anything else, to be a hero for her. He wanted to have her riding close by his side, to watch her talk at the table, to hear the music in her laughter and to see the sunlight and shadow fall across her beautiful face. She made his heart quicken, and he sensed that she felt something for him too. There was a warmth in her eyes, a lingering moment when their hands would touch accidentally and then freeze. They shared secrets so willingly in the candlelight and there was a fast-growing intimacy between them. But doubt made him hesitate. Was he mistaking kindness for love? He had seen love blossom between Drib and Sloeberry while they were in Cawdor but he had never experienced such feelings himself and he was both excited and confused by them. Sometimes they made him feel afraid – they seemed to extend to the very depths of his soul. Secretly he had promised himself that he would declare his love for Ayeshe the day that her father said he was ready to ride in search of his friends. But that day still seemed so far away.

Eider had been worrying so much, trying so hard, that he failed to realize that both his courage and his confidence were returning fast but Ayeshe and the huntsmen saw it. One evening Largg took his daughter aside and told her that the young man would soon be ready to leave their tower. He saw a shadow of sadness cloud her eyes.

'Eider is not our prisoner, child. You have helped him to grow strong again and you, even more than any of us, know how much he yearns to find his friends. Surely you would not have me keep him here against his will?'

'No, no, of course not father, but I have come to feel . . .' Ayeshe's words faltered as they trailed away into silence.

She quickly turned her face away as she blinked back the sudden tears that filled her eyes. Inwardly she had always known that the day for Eider to ride away would arrive and yet she had hidden from that stark truth as they had grown ever closer. They had shared so many wonderful moments, so many dreams. Secretly she had begun to hope that he no longer wished to leave, that he might stay forever.

'A caged bird will always mourn the loss of the sky, and it dies quickly. You know that, Ayeshe, and you would not wish it upon him. The birds who have their freedom return when the lake thaws and they fill our terraces and orchards with their sweet music. Eider may come back to you but first he must be allowed his freedom. He must be allowed to search for those he feels that he has abandoned, though first you must let him go, Ayeshe. Make him glad to be free and happy to be strong and whole again.'

Largg spoke softly but the words, no matter how gently they were uttered, could not blunt the emptiness that she felt was already drawing in around her. As Ayeshe paced her room high in the tower overlooking the lake she realized that her father was right and as the hollow toll of the bell summoned everyone to evenfare she resolved to hide her true feelings and keep the pain locked inside herself. She would fill every moment they could still share with joy and laughter, and perhaps, she hoped, he would enjoy her company so much that it would mean that one day he would return to her. Tears of sorrow would not wet her cheeks until he rode away.

'Tomorrowlight,' she whispered to Eider, squeezing his arm and looking deep into his eyes as they left the long banqueting table, 'tomorrowlight I will take you to a very secret place that no one here has ever seen. It is on the very roof of the world.'

Ayeshe kept her promise and the moment they had broken their fast she took Eider into the stable to saddle up the horses. As the sun climbed into the cloudless morning sky they cantered, side by side, around the lake to its furthest margin. The ground became marshy and they were forced to rein in their horses to a walk; Ayeshe cautiously led them between clumps of marsh grass and seemed to follow an almost invisible path into the quickmire. Treacherous pools of sticky, green mud and stagnant water bubbled on either side of them as Eider followed her uneasily, keeping as close as he dared, but even then Nightshade sank above his fetlocks at times and had to stumble out of the oozing mud to regain the path.

Ayeshe slowed her mount and looked anxiously into the thick undergrowth on their left as they rode closer to the dense banks of giant bracken fronds and thickets of silverspikes that could very easily pierce armour. Tall bulrushes blocked their way ahead. 'There is a hidden entrance somewhere near here, the trouble is the undergrowth grows over it so quickly.'

She edged Maelstrom along the narrow bog path ahead. 'Here it is!' she called out, beckoning Eider to follow as, with a turn of her spurs, she urged her horse off the path.

Maelstrom snorted, the whites of his eyes showing and his ears flattening against the sides of his head before he splashed through the mud and abruptly vanished into the undergrowth. Eider had to follow quickly before the path vanished. He held his hand up to shield his face as they forced a way through the bracken and brambles: thorns scratched at his hands and snagged in his cloak but in less than six strides they were through the dense shrubs and the ground suddenly began to rise sharply out of the marshes. In no time he found himself on a rocky track that was clear to follow as it zig-zagged up through the pine trees that grew on the steep mountainside.

It was hot and gloomy beneath the trees. The sound of the horses' hoofbeats was deadened by the thick carpet of pine needles and the noonday silence broken only by the creak and jingle of their harnesses, their labouring breaths as they climbed, and the soft, persistent whisper of the wind combing its fingers through the branches high above their heads. Shafts of sunlight filtered down through the trees, dappling the livid patches of moss and lichen that speckled the bark and covered the rocks nestling amongst the roots of the trees. Whichever way Eider turned his head he could hear the rush and gurgle of water running over stones, cascading into a multitude of secret pools as it found its way down from the snows that perpetually cloaked the peaks of the surrounding mountains. Gradually, as they climbed higher, it became lighter as the trees began to thin out and the sparse mountain grass gave way to bare, broken rock and the debris of winter avalanches that had come to rest amongst the trees.

'It's not much further now. Keep Nightshade close to the mountainside,' Ayeshe called back to him as she rode out beyond the last of the trees and up onto a narrow ledge of rock.

Eider rode out from the shadow of the trees and the bright sunlight momentarily blinded him. Loose shale disturbed by his horse's hooves clattered and rolled away, causing Nightshade to snort in alarm and scramble to keep his footing. Eider clutched at the reins and cried out in dismay as he looked out. There was nothing below him. The mountainside had dropped away and far below them he could see the glint of sunlight on the still, turquoise surface of the lake and beyond that the roofs of Largg's tower. The banqueting hall and the stables looked no larger than toys. A wave of dizziness swept over him, he felt sick and light-headed.

'Don't look down, Eider. Lighten your hold on Nightshade's reins, give him his head and he will find his own way up onto the ledge. Just shut your eyes, you will find it easier.' Ayeshe's voice seemed to come from somewhere above him.

Eider shuddered as he tore his gaze away from the sheer drop and forced his eyes shut. He felt Nightshade surge and stretch as he hung onto the pommel of the saddle while the horse scrambled up onto the narrow ledge and followed Maelstrom.

'It's safe to look now,' Ayeshe laughed as she dismounted.

Eider blinked his eyes open slowly. He gasped. She had not exaggerated when she had promised to take him to the roof of the world. 'It's just so beautiful . . . it's' – he was lost for words to describe the sight that spread out below him. He dismounted and let his gaze travel across the vast landscape of mountains, thick, wooded hills and valleys, brooding forests, steep, alpine meadows already carpeted with summer flowers and swift rivers that became sparkling waterfalls before falling into still lakes. It all lay spread out far below them wherever he looked until it gradually vanished into the purpled haze of the distant horizon line.

Starting with the tower, Ayeshe began to name all the things they could see below. 'That is where I found you, over there close to the eaves of the petrified forest near the shady pool.'

She touched his arm and pointed to the place, smiling to herself as she did so. They could just see the hidden pond on the edge of the forest before it formed a dark, unbroken line that climbed up over the hills and descended through countless valleys until it vanished into the heat haze. Eider shaded his eyes from the harsh glare of the sun and searched across the sombre trees. After a moment he thought he had picked out the ancient road that they had first travelled along through the forest on their way to Cawdor and, far, far away to the very edge of his sight he thought he caught the faint glimmer of the sun upon the sea and the black, broken silhouette of the citadel. An immense sense of longing and empty despair welled up inside him.

'That must be Cawdor.'

The words seemed to spring to his lips and he had to turn away quickly, but not before Ayeshe saw the pain fill his eyes.

'Eider, I did not mean to hurt you. I did not bring you here just to remind you . . .' she began, but he raised his hand to stop the words.

'How do you know of this place? Who showed it to you?'

'Why nobody.' She was surprised at the urgency of the question and hurt by the anger in his voice. 'I first found the hidden path in the marshes many winters ago when the bogs were frozen and it was easy to follow the path up here to the summit. Father forbids the huntsmen to come up here, he says the mountain belongs to the eagles and they believe that dragma beasts live here. But that is just a silly tale, my grandfather killed the last of those creatures long before I was . . .'

A sudden low, snarling growl, deeper and more menacing than anything she had ever heard before shook the ground beneath her feet and she was enveloped in a vile, decaying stench. For the first time in her life Ayeshe felt real, paralysing fear. In a daze she turned around and stepped backwards as the snow-covered ground directly in front of her collapsed and a cavernous black opening appeared. Something was moving in the darkness. Something was coming towards them. She could do nothing – fear had stolen her will. She stood and waited for the creature to appear. With a bellowing roar a monstrous, scaly beast, far larger than the most ferocious Nightboar, slowly emerged from its black lair. It snarled, blinking its small, red, reptilian eyes and exposing rows of razor sharp fangs as it belched out choking, yellow fumes and tongues of livid fire sprang from its gaping jaws. Its elongated body was ridged with armoured spines along its back and its bilious yellow scales glistened and rattled as it reared up. Its long, forked tail thrashed at the snow and made it boil as it turned to steam. Slowly it advanced towards her but she could do nothing. As it towered over her it reached out with snapping claws. Both horses snorted and neighed wildly, filled with terror. But Eider moved quickly. He reached out and managed to grab at his bow from Nightshade's saddle just before the horse shied away.

'Stay very still,' he hissed at Ayeshe as he reached back into his quiver with quick fingers, selected an arrow and nocked it onto his bow string. Cold beads of sweat broke out on his forehead but his heartbeats were very slow as he searched for a place to aim. Slowly, deliberately he drew back the bow string until it was taut. The vile reek of the creature filled his nostrils and its hideous shape blocked out the sunlight. Doubt tightened a knot around Eider's stomach and he remembered the fear that had overwhelmed him at Cawdor. The dark spectre of his panic seemed to grow before his eyes.

'No! You will not visit me a second time,' he muttered through gritted teeth.

He looked up with his steady, Archer's eye and examined the creature's towering body for its most vulnerable spot. Courage flooded through him. There was a gap, a tiny soft spot between the armoured scales where, he guessed, its heart must lay. He stood, statue-still, his legs set slightly apart as he held the arrow in place – its feathered flight brushing lightly against his cheek. As the dragma beast lurched forward the ground shook, it opened its claws and swept them down towards Ayeshe. Time was frozen. Then Eider saw the chink, a pale patch of skin between its scales. It was all he needed. With a triumphant shout he released his arrow, sending it singing through the air before it struck its target. With a loud thwack it pierced the skin and sheered through muscle and sinew, splintering bone and scything through flesh before it struck deep into the creature's heart. The force of the arrow strike halted the creature instantly and for a moment it towered over Ayeshe, its outstretched claws twitching. Then it gave out a howling scream and shuddered. Its scales rattled as it shook its head violently, tossing it from side to side as it started to flounder and topple towards her.

Eider flung his bow aside and in one frantic rush he grabbed at Ayeshe's arm and pulled her clear seconds before the huge beast buckled. It staggered and fell, snarling and bellowing, but with each cry it grew weaker until its hind legs buckled and it fell slowly forwards. It twitched as it convulsed and then it lay still, the blood from its fatal wound spreading out across the ground beneath it. For a moment Eider held Ayeshe tightly in his arms. She was trembling and he could feel the pounding of her heart against his chest.

'It's all right, the thing is dead. It won't hurt you now,' he whispered gently, stroking the silken strands of her hair and catching the scent of her perfume. He had never held a woman before, she felt so soft, so warm. He wanted the moment to last forever.

'I have never . . . never felt so afraid. I never knew what real terror felt like before,' she sobbed, suddenly pulling away from him and looking up into his face.

Their eyes met and Eider's heart missed a beat as it pounded the blood around his veins. Tears had misted her eyes and some were escaping to trickle, unnoticed, down her cheeks. She looked so vulnerable, so beautiful: he just wanted to hold her in his arms again and kiss away the tears. He wanted her to know how much he loved her but he hesitated, tongue-tied and awkward.

'Ayeshe . . .' he began, but the moment was lost – she had turned away and was looking down at the huge creature that lay sprawled on the ground less than two paces from where they stood.

'In all the old stories, in all the fireside tales, nobody has ever killed a dragma beast with a single arrow!'

She prodded the animal's thick armoured scales cautiously with her feet as Eider stood, silently cursing his hesitation. But holding her so close had simply strengthened his resolve to tell her how he felt.

'It was just a lucky shot,' he grinned, knowing how untrue those words would sound.

The clatter of the horses' hooves caught his attention and he realized that they had moved dangerously close to the edge of the precipice in their fright. He turned away to calm them, picketing them securely before he returned to Ayeshe's side.

'I have never seen such a beast. It must be at least as

long as your father's banqueting hall and it looks like a fat, giant lizard. Look at that long forked tail and those loose pieces of skin that hang down on either side of its shoulders. They almost look like small sails.'

'Long ago dragma beasts could fly – well that is what the legends say – that is why there are all those spikes set in the roof of the towers and the banqueting hall, they are meant to stop them from swooping down and perching on the rooftops. They breathe fire and twice they have set the tower alight, killing the horses and taking them away in their jaws. But the one my grandfather slew could not fly. From the stories I heard his huntsmen tracked it through the forest for seven daylights before they finally managed to corner it in a deep gully.'

'This one obviously couldn't fly with wings like that,' Eider murmured as he bent to examine the beast, moving slowly around it and inspecting it from every angle. 'It must have been very old. Look how its scales have rotted along its back, they have fallen away and its skin is all wrinkled and hanging off its bones.'

Suddenly Eider didn't feel too good about killing the beast – perhaps it was the last of its kind. Ayeshe sensed his troubled thoughts and squeezed his arm. 'You had no choice: the dragma beast would have devoured us both if you had not felled it. But it will live on in our fireside stories if we take home a trophy, and we must or nobody will believe that the beast even existed, let alone listen when we tell them how you stood your ground and killed it with one arrow. Come on, help me cut off one of its enormous claws – that should convince them.'

It was late in the afternoon and a hard, white frost was already beginning to form across the dead beast's huge scaly body as they remounted, their trophy safely stowed in a blood-stained sack and hanging from the pommel of Nightshade's saddle. Ayeshe brought Maelstrom to a halt on the rim of the plateau just above the narrow ledge that would take them down into the trees and she looked back at the creature in silence. There would be nobody who would not hear of Eider's courage.

'My father will be so proud of you,' she smiled as they set off home.

It was late and dusk had cast deep purple shadows beneath the trees. The nightshapes twisted and danced in swirling haloes around the bright, flickering pools of light that were cast by the staysafe lanterns that Eider and Ayeshe carried as they rode out of the trees and down through the last of the steep heather meadows towards the tower.

Eider listened to the fading toll of the bell summoning him to the feast, but he hung back shyly, hiding in the shadows outside the crowded banqueting hall. Looking in he saw soft firelight flickering in the vast, soot-blackened chimney at the far end, illuminating the long trestle tables which were piled high with the feast that had been set in his honour. The flames in the hearth hissed and flared up as the hot fat from the carcasses of the two wild boars turning over the fire dripped into them. Everybody was dressed in their finest clothes. The huntsmen were clothed in soft, knee-length leather boots with silken trousers and high-buttoned doublets with long sable cloaks thrown back across their shoulders that swept all the way to the ground. The womenfolk wore short, ermine capes with shawls of the finest lace over long, flowing gowns of shimmering satin which had been richly embroidered with needled stories of the chase.

The firelight reflected around the room from the hundreds of mounted hunting trophies that filled the walls of the hall, sending shadows leaping up above the heads of the crowd and into the rafters. Children laughed and ran through the throng as they played hide-and-seek beneath the tables while they waited impatiently for the feast to begin. From where Eider stood he could see that there were at least a dozen or more large, broken-coated hunting dogs lying sprawled on the flagstones close to the fire, basking in its warmth as they too, waited for the scraps to fall to the floor when the carcass of the wild boar was carved. Everywhere in the hall the talk was of nothing else but Eider's cold-blooded courage in standing his ground to slay the dragma beast with only one arrow strike and thus saving Ayeshe's life. Suddenly he heard soft laughter at his elbow and he felt Ayeshe's hand upon his arm. He turned to look into her face and caught his breath; she looked so beautiful. Her face was framed by her long, dark hair that now fell gracefully onto her bare shoulders. She was robed in a long gown of the finest ermine and wore a silver necklace of the most intricate design around her slender neck.

'Come on,' she smiled, entwining her fingers with his and gently pulling him forward. 'My father and all the people await you, they wish to honour your bravery. You showed great courage out there today.'

She squeezed his hand in hers as the crowds opened up to let them through and began to cheer. But Eider hesitated. His cheeks were flushed hot with embarrassment; he was reluctant to enter the hall.

'But I do not deserve all this. It just doesn't seem right that your father is holding such a feast in my honour. Surely he hasn't forgotten how I deserted my friends in their moment of greatest need. Surely he can't have forgotten how I turned tail and . . .'

'No, no of course he hasn't forgotten,' she laughed softly, holding his gaze and pulling him close to her. 'Nor have all the people gathered here tonight forgotten. They are all huntsmen and huntswomen and each one of them knows what courage it must have taken for you to have stood your ground to face that beast today. They are all familiar with the spectre of fear that can loom up unexpectedly out of the shadows and they know how difficult it can be to master that fear. Your courage was truly tested today and it was not found wanting. Come on, eat, and receive the honour due to you. Look, my father beckons you forward and I wouldn't be at all surprised if he doesn't organize that hunting party that he promised you when you first arrived, the one that will help you search for your friends. Come on, walk in with me.'

Feeling very conspicuous, knowing that everyone's eyes were upon him, Eider allowed her to lead him forward through the doors of the hall. The cheering reached a thunderous roar and at each step strong hands reached out to grasp his arms in congratulations as they walked the entire length of the banqueting hall. Largg rose smiling from his ornately carved chair and embraced Eider, calling out to his people in a loud voice. 'Welcome, bravest of all the huntsmen, welcome to my tower. Welcome, dragma beast slayer, and let the feast begin.'

He called out Eider's name and raised his silver goblet to his lips as a signal and throughout the hall crystal cups, pewter mugs, goblets and tankards were lifted in toast and Eider's name was shouted to the rafters. Largg clapped his hands for silence as a minstrel stepped forward and began to sing the ballad of how he had slain the beast.

'It is our custom that the honoured guest must carve the first slice,' Ayeshe whispered to him. 'Nobody can begin to eat until you have done that. It doesn't matter how you do it, I'll give you the signal.' She led him to the head of the main table close to the fire hearth and placed a long, curved, razor-sharp carving knife into his hand and then stepped quickly back.

Eider was alone now and out of the corner of his eye he could see the two, huge, roasted boars being carried forwards by their spit, supported by four strong scullions. The blackened skin of the carcasses hissed and crackled as they were lifted and set securely upon a studded iron carving rack on the table in front of him. Eider swallowed nervously and tightened his grip on the bone handle of the carver. He had never been to a feast where anything quite like this had been carved and he didn't want to make a fool of himself. The minstrel's voice and the sweet music of the lutes gradually died away and the noise and bustle of the waiting crowd fell into anticipatory silence. He knew that every eye was upon him as he slowly raised the carver.

'Kill the beast . . . kill the beast . . . let the feast begin!' Ayeshe called out from behind him and with a sudden, stamping of feet every voice in the hall joined in with the chant.

Eider realized that Ayeshe's cry must have been the signal and with a shout that was lost amongst the roar of the voices around him he plunged the blade down hard into the blackened, prickly skin of one of the carcasses. Shouts of encouragement and laughter erupted all around him as the hot fat splattered up over his knuckles and the smell of roast meat filled his nostrils. The crowd surged forward around the long trestle tables to fill their empty platters. He felt Ayeshe's hand on his arm, gently pulling him back, and he let the crowd push in ahead of him.

'Leave the carving to the cooks and scullions and let us go somewhere a little quieter. Look, there's a seat in that alcove near where my father is sitting. The servers will make sure your plate is full throughout the feast.'

Eider followed her as quickly as he could, though the crush of people meant that he was constantly being stopped and offered things to eat as an excuse to engage him in conversation and find out every detail about how he had felled the beast. Eventually he reached her side, clutching a heavy earthenware bowl piled high with a rich variety of forest fruits that had been given to him along the way. He found a place for it on the chest beside the seat.

'Have you ever been to such a wonderful feast as this?' she asked him, smiling and choosing the ripest purple fruit from the bowl.

'Oh no, no I have not been to anything like this,' he grinned, but the laughter faded from his lips as he glanced around the crowded, hazy, smoky hall. He couldn't help noticing how different it all was. Their strange clothes, all the animal skins with the silks and satins, their voices, their customs – everything, he realized, was so different from all that he knew. So different to the people he had grown up amongst in the Granite City. Elundium and the life he had known seemed suddenly so remote, so far away from the noise and the laughter that was going on all around him at this moment. He felt an ache of loneliness, an overwhelming sense of regret for what he had lost by running away from his family with the Tunnellers. And now he had even abandoned them at Cawdor. He felt so alone. His face grew drawn and serious as he turned back to her.

'Do you really think that your father will let me leave soon?'

As he began to ask Ayeshe the question the words froze and he stared, open-mouthed at the strange, translucent, ghostly figure that began to appear just in front of him. Cold beads of sweat prickled at his skin and an icy shiver ran up his spine. The noise and bustle of the hall faded into insignificance as he realized who the figure was.

'Drib . . . Drib . . . I'm so sorry I ran away . . . I am so ashamed of myself . . .' he stuttered, the colour draining from his face as he reached out his hand and took an uncertain step towards him. Ayeshe gave a startled cry and shrank back, dropping the fruit to the floor as she saw the ghostly figure appear in front of her.

Largg had been watching Eider and his daughter out of the corner of his eye and he was waiting for the right moment to beckon them to him. A party of outriders that he had sent to Cawdor in search of Eider's friends had arrived only moments before the feast began with news that he feared would envelop Eider in black despair. The men had found the ruins to be deserted and they could find no sign of life anywhere near. He was afraid that the announcement he was about to make would not sound well coming after such bad news, but he had made a promise to the young Archer and he would honour it. There could be no doubt now that the full measure of Eider's courage had returned. He had proved that quite conclusively. He had sworn that Eider would be shown the hidden road out of their mountain fastness and given a hunting party to accompany him once his courage had returned: now it was time to honour that pledge. But where he would begin to search for his friends was now in serious doubt.

He was about to summon the two of them to him when the ghostly apparition began to appear. Largg inhaled a shallow, fearful breath and half rose from his chair, knocking over his goblet and spilling its contents across the table. Ghosts were the sacred carriers of omens, both good and bad. They were restless spirits that dwelt in the half light, shrouded in mystery, and it was dangerous to dabble in the magic needed to summon them without good reason. In this realm none could do it without Largg's permission.

'Who has dared to call you to this happy feast?' Largg asked in a whisper, expecting the barely visible wraith to turn and drift towards him with the omens it carried, but, to his surprise, it moved towards the young Archer and he distinctly heard it speak the boy's name.

'Eider,' it said, 'Eider, you look so unhappy. What has happened to you? Eider, you must not worry, it's all right, I'm not dead. It's me, Drib, I'm really alive. All of us . . . most of us . . . survived that attack on Cawdor. Sloeberry was captured and we are going to try and rescue her. I'm with Nevian now. The Chancellors have the King seige-locked in Candlebane Hall and everybody's going to try and march on the Granite City and get there by mid-winter's daylight to set him free . . .'

'Drib! Drib!' Eider cried in confusion. 'What do you mean? Who has taken Sloeberry prisoner? Where are you? Don't go!'

Eider reached out to try to catch hold of the faint, translucent image of his friend but the moment his fingers touched it the image vanished, leaving him standing alone and confused. He didn't know how it had happened or where the boy had suddenly appeared from but there were a thousand questions he wanted to ask him. It was all over so quickly. One moment Drib was there, the next he was gone. Only Ayeshe and her father, and perhaps a handful of people standing close to Eider, saw the apparition appear and a low murmur of uneasiness and suspicious whispers arose around him as people began to edge away from him.

Largg realized that the spectre had nothing to do with him. Perhaps, he wondered as it vanished, it was one of the young Archer's friends come to haunt him from Cawdor. But there was something about it, an urgency in its voice, a substance about its shape that made him doubt that it was a ghost. But what was it? He could see that whispers were growing amongst his huntsmen and he rose to quell them quickly before they could take root and spread. He laughed as he reassured them, persuading them that they had seen nothing more sinister than a shadow, a trick of the light cast by the flames from the fire. He called for the minstrels and clowns to entertain and the moment of doubt was immediately dispelled. Then he walked over to take Eider and Ayeshe by the arm and guided them away from the throng into the back of his alcove.

'Now tell me what you just saw,' he demanded, his face becoming very serious.

'I . . . I . . . I thought I just saw the ghost of Drib, my friend, only I'm not sure whether he was a ghost or not, I'm not sure what it was. He looked so different, he was dressed in strange clothes.'

Eider found he was excited rather than afraid and he turned from Largg to Ayeshe who looked too shaken by the experience to say a word.

'Keep your voice down, Eider, and concentrate. All three of us saw something, that's for sure. Now let us get to the bottom of it: I don't like mysteries and apparitions appearing in my hall to cast a shadow over such a happy feast. Take a deep breath, boy, and repeat everything that the ghost said.'

Eider closed his eyes and breathed deeply. After a moment's thought a smile softened his face and he answered Largg. 'That was not Drib's ghost. Drib is the best friend I have ever had and I just know he isn't dead. Somehow, I don't know how, he has ended up with Nevian the magician – that is exactly the sort of thing that is always happening to him. It wouldn't surprise me if he didn't get the Master of Magic to cast a spell so that he could appear here . . . so that he could tell us about the King being siege-locked and get other people to join their march on the Granite City.'

Largg's face grew grave as Eider related everything that Drib had told him. It had all happened so fast that the young Archer had not fully understood a half of what had been said, but he repeated it all word for word. From the reports that Largg's outriders had gathered along their unfenced borders, his concerns for the safety of his small kingdom had been growing steadily, and if what the ghostly figure had said to Eider was true, it confirmed his suspicions that the disgraced Chancellors had arisen from their exile in the depths of Meremire Forest and were on the brink of seizing Elundium. His scouts had brought back word of ruin and chaos from everywhere in the countryside of Elundium; they had seen law and order break down over recent times, and now there was little resistance to stop the Chancellors' slow, relentless advance. His men had brought back stories of disquiet and fear of huge, hideous, half-human creatures who led the Chancellors' army, but who or what they were none could tell save that nothing could stand before them.

But there was something else that bothered Largg as he listened to the young Archer. It brought the stories of the troubles of Elundium far closer to home than made him comfortable. He'd had his suspicions that it was the Chancellors who had attacked and destroyed Cawdor – the attack had all the markings of their brutality – but the question that had kept on niggling at Largg was why those murderous villains had travelled all the way through the Emerald Mountains to massacre Drib and his friends? Surely they couldn't really pose a threat to their treacherous plans? It was a mystery and it worried Largg, because if they had made the journey once there was nothing to stop them from coming back and invading his kingdom again, when they had secured the throne of Elundium. He knew he had to do something, but what? He had no army to send to King Thane's aid.

'I have to get back to Cawdor.' Eider's voice broke into Largg's thoughts. 'I have to find the others, it's really important. If I am to get to the Granite City and help rescue the King I will have to leave now.'

Largg frowned as he looked at the young Archer and he sadly shook his head. 'I am sorry, Eider, but you must steel yourself for what I am about to tell you. Black news has come to me from Cawdor: it lays in ruins, it has been utterly destroyed and is empty.'

'But how do you know that, father? Why have you waited until now, at the very feast that is being held to honour Eider's bravery, why are you telling him such things now?'

Ayeshe was angry and her eyes brimmed with tears.

She had always admired her father's honesty and had set much store by it in their dealings with their people but now she discovered that he had hidden this truth and she felt shamed by it.

'I could not tell him before this, my child, because I did not know myself until tonight. Now please let me finish. I was concerned for the safety of your friends after the fierceness of the attack you had described and I sent out a small party of our best trackers the day after you told me what had happened. I dispatched them with all haste and they rode to Cawdor to search for your friends. Their orders were that if they should find them, they should bring them here. Those riders did indeed search long and hard, scouring the forest league after league and combing that desolate fortress in the hope of finding some clues as to the whereabouts of your friends, but sadly there were none. That is why they were so long in their journey – they only arrived back as darkness was falling tonight. I met them only moments before the feast began. I am so sorry but I fear that all your friends must be dead.'

'No, no, you are wrong,' Eider cried, breaking free from Largg's grip. 'They are not dead. Did I not just tell you that Drib said that most of them had survived. They are not at Cawdor because they have begun their long march through the forest and over the mountains towards the Granite City.'

Eider paused, looking from Ayeshe to her father and for the first time since he had arrived there he had laughter in his eyes. 'I must find them and join them. I am one of the Knights of Cawdor and I must take my place in their ranks. I will be with them at the Granite City, I must. Now I understand why Marcher Berioss took so much trouble training us to be warriors. He always used to say that if every single one of us stood up to fight for what we believe is right we will form a mighty battle crescent. That is why Nevian brought all those ordinary people who were loyal to the King through the mountains in the depths of winter. They are to form part of our battle crescent. I must set out to find them right away.'

'Patience, Eider, patience. You have my promise that you shall set out as the new dawn breaks and you will have fifty of my best huntsmen mounted on our swiftest horses with you. They should help swell the ranks of your battle crescent. But come with me now, both of you, we have a long night of planning ahead of us. There are weapons and provisions to organize and maps to study. Finding your friends while they are on the march through that wilderness will be no easy matter, there are so many roads that they could be taking through the mountains and they all lead down into Elundium.'

Largg put his arms around their shoulders and led them towards his council chambers, calling out to his most trusted captains to meet with him immediately. He paused as they stood on the threshold of the chamber and chuckled as he suddenly realized why the Chancellors had been forced to journey all the way to Cawdor to try and massacre all the people who had fled there. It was Elundium's hidden strength, all those ordinary people fighting for the King. It was their very decency, their honesty, that the Chancellors feared and it would rise up against them. Nevian had struck right at the heart of it when he had taken them to Cawdor. They certainly were a force to be reckoned with. And the Chancellors had failed to destroy that force. Another way to help the King of Elundium suddenly occurred to Largg as he waited for his captains to gather around him. The Chancellors may have brought

Elundium to the brink of ruin and starvation but he could send aid. He turned quickly to Eider.

'Tell your King and Marcher Berioss, or whoever commands the battle crescent that once you have overthrown the Chancellors we will send all the food and clothing he needs to help his people. We will send as much as our pack horses can carry through the mountains.'

Eider fell silent as he gripped Largg's hand in thanks. Then he caught sight of Ayeshe standing slightly behind her father and saw that her eyes were full of a sadness she could no longer disguise. Instantly he knew the cause of that sadness: he would be leaving as soon as the new dawn broke. Suddenly it was as though he had seen his own reflection, and everything she was feeling welled up inside him. The strength of the emotion took him by surprise and at that moment nothing else seemed to matter except Ayeshe. More than anything he wanted to hold her while he told her how he felt but it was too late. The huntsmen who would ride with him were filling the room and he felt as though they were to be separated forever. He tried to force a path through to her but the men were closing in around him, their eager voices drowning out any words of his. Hands seemed to pull at his sleeve as they tried to attract his attention and questions were being asked about the length of their journey. Distractions from every side overtook him until he could no longer see her and then Largg unrolled a large, parchment map onto the table and demanded that he concentrate while he pointed out dozens of the passes that his friends might have taken to cross the Emerald Mountains. By the time they had studied their route and questions had been asked and answered, she had gone. There was no sign of her. He was desolate.

Eider stood there, alone in the centre of a crowded room, fearing that he had just missed the only chance he might get to tell Ayeshe how he felt about her. He feared that he had lost her even before he had left her father's house. The joy and excitement about setting out in search of his friends, the only thing he had wanted for so long, seemed dulled, tarnished. He was confused by the conflict of feelings that seemed to be waging a war inside him. How could things change so quickly? How could he feel so miserable when he had just been given the chance to achieve his dream?

'Eider – come over here, tell us what the village folk in Elundium are likely to think about us. Will they be hostile or friendly?' one of the huntsmen called out to him.

'What's the matter with you, Eider? We thought you would be overjoyed at leaving at first light, you look miserable. Isn't this what you have wanted to do ever since Ayeshe brought you here?'

Eider nodded bleakly, and did his best to force a smile as he busied himself with the preparations for their departure but during the long night his eyes were constantly straying towards the door in the vain hope that Ayeshe might reappear. But as the grey hours paled the stars and the huntsmen finished getting things ready and then dispersed to saddle their horses, Eider realized that she would not be coming back: he shivered despite the warmth of his fur-lined cloak. He walked out forlornly into the morning to mount Nightshade at the head of the company of horsemen just beyond the great doors of the tower ready for the beginning of their journey. They waited, silently, watching the strengthening light of dawn fill the sky, painting the fresh new colours of morning across the snow-capped peaks as it spread slowly down the steep, darkly wooded mountain slopes and through the purpled heather meadows. The first rays of morning touched the pinnacle of the tower and melted the crackling layers of hoar frost that had gathered on the weather-bleached rooftops during the night, turning it golden. The hot sun opened the flowerheads that grew thickly on the terraces surrounding the tower and burnt away the thin, wispy wreath tails of mist that clung to the still surface of the turquoise lake. It was going to be a beautiful morning. Eagles were already on the wing, soaring high above the tower in a cloudless sky and blackbirds and song thrushes in the brambles and briars that grew on the lower slopes were beginning to burst into song as they heralded the new daylight. A breath of wind stirred the tall mountain grasses, tugging restlessly at the riders' cloaks and lightly fingering the horses' manes. It was time for the road.

The moment the sunlight touched the doors of the tower they were thrown open and Largg, accompanied by his minstrels, emerged with all his people to see the company of warriors leave. There was music, singing, tears and laughter mingling around them as garlands of shepherds' rod and silver weed were strewn across the beginning of the path to ward off evil spirits. Sprigs of freshly cut, dewy heather, bound by silver thread were given to each rider who accompanied Eider to remind them of their mountain fastness and to bring them safely home. The horses began to fidget as the crowds surged around them. They stamped their feet and snorted, showing the whites of their eyes in their impatience as they tossed their heads to set the bit rings jingling. They were eager to set their feet on the road.

Eider felt heavy, alone and untouched by the tears and

laughter and the embrace of so many farewells. He stood up in the saddle, pressing the balls of his feet against the stirrups as he searched across the heads of the crowd in the forlorn hope that Ayeshe would come out to see him off. But she was not there. Largg saw the haunted look in Eider's eyes and he hurried over to his side, gripping his hand in farewell as he handed a small bunch of heather to him. He had grown to like the boy and would miss him sorely. He reached inside his cloak to give him a letter, sealed with his own crest and addressed to the King of Elundium and bid him a safe journey. Before he stepped away he offered Eider a quiver, crafted from thin inlaid strips of black ebony that had been covered with the finest deer skin and bound together with a delicate tracery of hammered silver. The quiver was full of the very best arrows that his chief fletcher could produce, each one tipped with a newly-forged steel arrow-head that could pierce the thickest armoured hide.

'You have been so generous already, my Lord, this is too much,' Eider protested.

'This gift is worth nothing if you don't use it well. But if I am a judge of men then you will make every arrow strike count. These arrow heads will find their way to the very hearts of your enemies. Now ride, Eider, ride with all speed and find your friends. Rescue your beleaguered King and come swiftly back to us, for there will always be a welcome here for you.'

Tears of sadness and regret brimmed in Eider's eyes as he prepared to leave. He would have given anything at that moment just to see Ayeshe once more, to hear the music and laughter in her voice but instead his face was grim as he thanked her father for his gift. The crowds fell silent as he raised his hand in a last farewell and gathered up the reins. He turned to take one last, long look at the tower before turning Nightshade to face along the road and prepared to lead the men out. Suddenly the sound of iron-shod hooves rang out beyond the open archway that led into the stableyard and he could hear his name being called. The company came to an abrupt halt and Eider felt his heart miss a beat as he pirouetted Nightshade to see Ayeshe mounted upon Maelstrom, dressed and armed as though ready for a long journey. She was riding out to meet him, a guard by her side. His cloak tails flew as he spurred his horse forwards and they met upon the green-sward in front of the tower. The people in the crowd seemed to hold their breath collectively as they watched, waiting.

'Ayeshe, I couldn't find you. I searched everywhere.'

'I nearly didn't come. To say goodbye to you now would be so painful I didn't know whether I could bear it.'

'But why are you dressed like this? You surely can't come with us?'

Ayeshe laughed softly. 'No I can't come with you, well, not all the way, but if I had not come to see you go how could I know whether you would come back?'

Eider was confused, but as he looked down into her eyes he was sure of her feelings and his own and his heart felt less heavy. Then he felt a hand upon his arm and looked down to see her father standing beside them holding a great hunting bow, freshly oiled and newly strung. He pressed it into Eider's hand.

'Guard my daughter well, Eider. Ayeshe spoke with me late last night. I was against her coming with you at all but she has persuaded me. She is my only child, her life is here, but I have agreed that she ride with you far enough to show you the path through the mountains. She knows the secret ways better than any other in my kingdom and I know she wants you to be sure of the way back. Go with my blessings and be sure of a welcome here when you have fought your battles.'

If ever Eider had doubted his feelings for Ayeshe there were no doubts now. Clearly she felt the same for him and his heart was too full to consider the perils of the journey. Already he was looking forward to returning. The crowd seemed to catch the excitement of the moment and began to surge forward as Ayeshe bent down and kissed her father on the cheek. Then she turned to wave to the people and they cheered as, side by side, Eider and Ayeshe cantered out, leading the great company of huntsmen towards the distant eaves of the petrified forest and the high pass that would take them into Elundium.

VI

Deluge in the Grasslands

NIGHTSHAPES were beginning to spread their muted colours of dusk and draw long indigo shadows across the gentle undulating swell of the endless, empty grasslands that stretched away into the distance in every direction. The first pale evening stars were beginning to speckle the sky before Lord Kyot and his wife, the Lady Eventine breasted the small, grassy knoll crowned by a wind-riven ring of stunted blackthorn trees and interwoven silverspike, and reined in their weary, sweating mounts after their hard ride, stirrup to stirrup across the open plains. The two swiftest Border Runners left the pack and scented the ground, moving silently in and out amongst the tangled roots of the blackthorn, searching for danger but finding none as the rest of the pack, who had run with them tirelessly all daylight, reached their leaders and sank down onto their haunches, panting with exhaustion.

'Is this the ancient fortress, the ring of thorns we have been searching for?' Kyot asked as he stiffly dismounted and eased Spirit's girths.

'Yes, this is the place called Thorny Hill. From up here we'll be able to see if those monsters are following us long before they come within bowshot. My father once told me that this hill used to be a fortified place, and there was water fed by a secret spring with a deep ditch to keep out the Nightbeasts, but it is clear that the ditch has long since vanished and the defences have fallen into dereliction. No matter, we should be safe enough here for the night and if I am not mistaken there is still water here. Look, I can see the reflection of the sky on that still pool of crystal clear water right in the centre of the crown of thorns.'

Eventine jumped to the ground, removed the bridle and stripped Tanglecrown's saddle from his back, allowing him to stride forward and drink deeply from the pool. Kyot untacked Sprint who, surrounded by the dogs, followed the stag to the water.

Kyot turned to look out across the rolling grasslands and anxiously searched for the rest of their company. Eventine raised her hand to shield her eyes against the glare of the low setting sun and looked back across the undulating land for any sign on the horizon of their compatriots. She could just make out the gloomy smudge of Meremire Forest, brooding beneath the black pall of smoke that hung over it and beyond that the hazy, indistinct mountain peaks that rose sheer and seemed to march away to the edge of sight.

'I can see them, look, over there!' She pointed away into the distance.

Kyot shielded his eyes and followed her hand but it took him a moment to pick out the glint of the setting sun reflecting on the helms and spear tips of the long, straggling column of Archers with their families as they briefly appeared and disappeared in the lie of the land, gradually drawing closer with each footstep.

'How many times must I tell our men to keep the column closer together. They must keep in tight battle order. They are so vulnerable to attack strung out like that, especially if those evil flocks of carrion birds suddenly swoop down on them.' Kyot frowned anxiously as he searched the darkening sky behind them.

Eventine turned towards him, her weary, travel-stained and dusty face softening into a smile. The blaze of the setting sun momentarily haloed and illuminated her fire-gold hair as she took his hand, entwining her fingers with his. 'We have seen nothing of those vile birds for three daylights now. Perhaps they have given up pursuing us.'

'They are out there somewhere, I have caught glimpses of them every now and again. They know where we are.'

'But we must slow down a little,' Eventine warned softly. 'Our Archers' families are doing their best to keep up, but they are not used to keeping such a fast pace – especially the children. Remember we have barely stopped to gather breath since we broke out of the tower. Let them rest here for a day or two and recover, let them get their strength back. We still have a long way to go: there must be at least fifteen daylights before we see the spires of my father's house. I fear if we press on without stopping many of the younger ones will perish from exhaustion and hunger long before we reach the safety of Clatterford.'

Kyot hesitated before reluctantly agreeing to her wishes as he looked out across the empty plains that surrounded them. Time was their enemy: they had to get to Clatterford and re-arm, forge new arrowheads and gather all those loyal to the King as quickly as possible. They had to search all those grassland villages, collect all those who valued their freedom and persuade them to join his army and travel with all haste to the Granite City to join the warriors defending the King. They had barely enough arrows left between his Archers to fill two quivers; their swords were notched, their shields riven and their spears blunted and splintered from fighting their way out of the tower. They would be very vulnerable to attack if they stopped to rest, and yet he knew that Eventine was right – they could not carry on at this breakneck pace. But dare they risk stopping for as long as one, let alone two daylights, out here, in the open? It was not only their vulnerability to attack that bothered him: there had been no time to gather together more than a meagre handful of provisions. They had only some pieces of waycake and stale crusts for their long journey to Clatterford. They had been lucky to escape with their lives as their attackers had battered down the doors of Stumble Hill and they had left with only the clothes they stood up in. They would never have broken through the seething hoards without the precious pouch of nightflower seeds that Queen Elionbel had kept with her since the Battle of the Rising. The seeds had instantly taken root as soon as they had hit the ground, bursting into brilliant, white, scented blossoms that their attackers could not abide. And there, upon the greenways' edge had crouched the Border Runners, ready to spring to their defence. Luck had indeed been with them then but as they rode deeper and deeper into the grasslands it had seemed to desert them. The vast, undulating grasses seemed to be devoid of life, and hunger was forcing them to buckle their belts ever tighter. With each new daylight they were growing weaker. Even the Border Runners were beginning to look gaunt and exhausted.

'In the old grassland legends it was told that fortune always smiled on those whose need drove them to seek refuge here,' Eventine whispered, drawing her cloak tightly about her shoulders as the mournful evening wind rustled through the blackthorn leaves and made her shiver.

'Well we have little choice now. Yes, we will make camp here and we will rest for two daylights. Perhaps if there is some truth in those old legends fate will smile upon us: we certainly need it. At first light tomorrow I will take out our best Archers and we will hunt for something to eat.'

Kyot tried to laugh lightly but there was little conviction or real hope in the sound as he realized that they had little chance of finding anything to eat in that barren, empty wilderness. At that moment Sprint snorted and lifted his head, his ears pricked, and Tanglecrown tossed his huge, crystal-tipped stand of antlers and roared.

'What is it? What have they seen?'

Kyot grabbed his bow and reached back into his quiver for one of his last, precious arrows only to give a cry of delight as Rockspray, the Battle Owl who had befriended him once, long, long ago, stooped down with shrill cry of greeting and let fall a large grassland hare from his bloodied talons before alighting upon Kyot's shoulder.

'Look, Kyot, look, true friends have come to our aid, they've brought us all the food we'll need to survive, and more. Look, the legends are true, this is indeed a hallowed place.'

There was joy and relief in Eventine's voice as she laughed and lifted her arms as more and more owls silently appeared out of the thickening dusk. Each one let a freshly killed hare or rabbit drop from their talons before carefully perching amongst the thorny branches in the ring of stunted, wind-riven trees.

'How, how did you find us? How did you know we were starving?' Kyot was bewildered as he looked into Rockspray's unblinking eyes.

The owl ruffled his feathers and Kyot smiled as he smoothed Rockspray's chest and remembered those last, desperate moments when the monstrous horde had assaulted the tower, battering the doors and swarming up their siege ladders. The evening sky had darkened as those evil carrion birds had risen out of the surrounding treetops forming a menacing, shadowy black cloud that had wheeled towards them, shutting out the light. The King had sent Mulcade, chief Loftmaster Owl, to protect Queen Elionbel and her half brother, Krann, when they had fled to the tower. Kyot and known then that the owl would have fought until his last breath but he had sent him away, urged him to escape while he could, telling him that he would be able to do far more good raising the alarm amongst the other Battle Owls and Warhorses, warning everyone who would listen that Elundium had been invaded, than in staying and fighting to the death.

'Was it Mulcade who told you of the fall of Stumble Hill?'

Rockspray nodded his head rapidly, moving it backwards and forwards as he communicated with Kyot.

'Mulcade will warn everyone who will listen. We have flown far and wide, we have searched everywhere for you but we only found your trail through the grasslands yester-light. It was immediately clear to see how hard need has driven you so we hunted for your supper.'

'And it will be appreciated. We will set to and prepare the food immediately. This banquet will be roasting over a fire before the rest of the company even arrives here,' Kyot laughed as Rockspray lifted from his shoulders and flew to perch amongst the other Battle Owls.

'But should we be lighting fires? If we light one big enough to cook such a feast it will be visible for leagues, it will tell our enemies exactly where we are.' Eventine was concerned but Rockspray interrupted her with a shrill hoot and spread his wings.

'We will fly high and wide. We will keep watch throughout the long, dark hours of the night. No harm will come to you on Thorny Hill.'

The owls lifted up into the starlit darkness and vanished as silently as they had arrived. Kyot watched as they disappeared and then murmured to Eventine.

'You were certainly right about fortune smiling on those whose need drives them to seek refuge here. Who would have thought the owls would have found us in this wilderness.'

'Oh it was no coincidence, I am sure of it. We had better hurry if we are to get that feast cooking.' Eventine smiled, glad that there was still some power in the old legends despite the ruination and neglect that time and weather had caused to the ancient fortress.

'I noticed the remains of what looks like some shallow fire pits. I'll cut some wood and have a fire going in no time. It will act as a beacon for the others to guide them here now that darkness has fallen.'

Kyot unsheathed his sword but Eventine called out a warning: 'No! Do not cut any living wood from the crown of thorns. Remember this is a hallowed mound and there is no knowing what misfortunes will befall us if you defile it.'

Kyot hesitated and glanced anxiously around him, feeling the hairs on the nape of his neck prickle with foreboding. She was right, this was no ordinary hill. He let his sword slip back into its scabbard and delved into his pocket to pull out a spark, crackling it alight between his fingers and dropping onto his knees, searching the ground around the base of the trees to find wind-blown branches. He soon had more than enough kindling to set a fire going and before long had both the disused fire pits full of hot embers. Eventine used her dagger to gut and skin the hares and very quickly they had them roasting over the embers. Ribbons of bright sparks and the delicious smell of roast game rose into the still night air, filling the nostrils of the weary Archers and their families, giving them new hope and strength to hurry forwards in the darkness.

'It's a miracle! Where did all this food come from so suddenly?' awed voices asked Kyot as they climbed up the hill. One by one the Archers released their mounts to drink and graze before they found themselves places around the fires and began to eat. Elionbel, who had been riding in the centre of the column to keep Fairlight and Krann safe, arrived leading the two ponies as both children had fallen to sleep in their saddles.

'Are we there yet?' Fairlight asked sleepily as her father, Kyot, lifted her to the ground.

'What's that lovely smell? Are we going to have a feast?' Krann asked, yawning as one of the Archers helped him to dismount.

'Yes, we are going to have a feast. The owls have been here and brought us all this lovely game and now it is ready to eat.' Eventine laughed as she led Elionbel and the children across to a place that had been left for them close to the fire.

'I saw the owls fly over us as dusk was gathering. Tell me, did they bring news of Thane? Did they tell you how things are in the Granite City!' Elionbel asked anxiously once the children were busy eating.

Eventine grasped Elionbel's hand in hers and shook her head sadly. After a moment of sadness there seemed to be an unspoken agreement between them to push away despair and dark thoughts, at least during the night hours, and they moved over to sit with their children.

*　　*　　*

It was early in the evening of their second daylight at Thorny Hill, and the company were just settling down to rest after eating as they talked of the journey that lay ahead of them when Eventine noticed a faint, acrid smell of burning on the fresh evening breezes. Before she'd had time to ask Kyot if he had smelled it the horses became restless in their picket lines and the Border Runners guarding the hill started barking furiously. Kyot barely had the time to scramble to his feet in the rising mêlée of noise and movement before the Battle Owls reappeared, flying low and fast. Rockspray stooped directly to his shoulder shrieking an urgent warning: they must run for their lives before many of the creatures who had attacked Stumble Hill with their carrion flock came too close – they were advancing rapidly through the grasslands towards them, burning everything that lay in their path.

Kyot snatched up his bow and quiver and ran with Eventine and many of their people to the top of the grassy knoll. Eventine uttered a cry of dismay as she peered out into the gathering dusk and looked back towards the Emerald Mountains. The mountains were obscured and as she looked along the distant horizon line for as far as she could see in either direction she saw a mass of flickering pinpoints of light. A cold knot of dread tightened in her stomach. The one thing the grassland people feared above all else was fire sweeping unchecked through the prairies in the summer. They knew only too well that it would destroy and kill everything that lay in its path and nothing but a deluge could stop it.

'What is that strange noise?' Fairlight asked as she stood on tiptoe and tried to see what the people around her were pointing at.

Elionbel called out for everyone to be silent and in the

quiet they all heard, very faintly and from far away, the dull roar of the greedy flames eating through the tinder dry grasses. It was racing towards them, jumping across small ditches and dew ponds, driven by the strengthening evening wind. It was devouring everything it came across and sending up a dense, choking pall of grey-white smoke that blotted out the pale stars.

'What is going to happen? Are we going to get burnt in that fire?' Krann asked in a small, frightened voice as he pointed out towards the distant wall of advancing flames.

'No, no of course not,' Elionbel replied but she couldn't disguise the fear in her voice as she grasped both the children's hands in hers.

Eventine stood tall and held up a wetted finger into the wind. It was as she feared, the weather was driving the fire directly towards them, and at great speed. Without revealing her concern she smiled down at the two children to reassure them. 'We are going to ride through the night as fast as we can. We will ride towards Clatterford and cross the Weir Pike Fords as quickly as possible. That will be quite an adventure in the dark won't it? Now you must make sure that neither of you fall off, come on.'

In a whisper she urged Elionbel to get all the Archers' children mounted and ready to leave in a moment and then she turned to Kyot who was mesmerized by the advancing flames. In a quiet voice he warned her that the wind was getting stronger and it was driving the fire straight towards them. Then he blinked and turned to her. 'We must saddle the horses and ride, we must ride faster than the wind if we are to reach the Fallen Fold River before the fire overtakes us.'

'No, wait,' she cried, catching hold of his sleeve. 'We

can't just run and save ourselves – there are hundreds of people in the grassland villages who are completely unaware of the danger they are in. We must try to warn them. We must tell them to make for the Weir Pike Fords and seek shelter at Clatterford until the fire has burned itself out.'

Kyot hesitated and shook his head. 'No, that would be impossible. The villages are scattered in every direction – we couldn't possibly reach all of them, not unless the company splits up. But we can't do that. Few, if any, of our Archers have ever ventured this far into the grasslands before and they would be lost in no time. We must keep together. We will do our best to warn those villages we pass and the others . . .'

'The owls will guide your Archers. They will take them to the villages and bring them safely to the Weir Pike Fords.' Rockspray hooted softly.

Without wasting another moment in debate, save to tell each man in which direction he was to ride, the Archers mounted after hurried farewells and cantered away on the swiftest horses, disappearing into the darkness as they followed the hoots and calls of the owls who would guide them to raise the alarm throughout the grassland villages. Kyot and Eventine quickly gathered together what remained of their company, impressing on them that they must keep close together or they would become lost. Girths and buckles were checked and securely tightened and with the Border Runners on either side of them they set out, keeping as fast a pace as they dare across the undulating, night-dark countryside as they followed Rockspray's distinctive calls in a westerly direction towards the Weir Pike Fords.

All night they rode without slackening the pace. The

horses were breathing hard, with sweat streaking their necks and labouring flanks long before Kyot brought the company to a halt beside a still dew pond to rest for a moment while the grey hours lightened the sky and dawn broke. Eventine reined in Tanglecrown, dismounted and hurried across to where Kyot was making sure the girths on the children's mounts were properly eased and that they didn't let them drink too much water from the pond too quickly. She silently caught his attention and, drawing him away from the others, she pointed back the way they had just come, to where the new sun was rising, still partially hidden by a haze of blood-red clouds. They looked out over the grasslands, wreathed in billowing, unrelenting smoke and fire. Far behind them Thorny Hill rose, a gaunt and blackened silhouette, its crown of stunted, wind-riven blackthorns now a blazing beacon of crackling flames.

'I think the fires are gaining on us. No matter how fast we ride we can't keep ahead of them.' She whispered softly to Kyot, making sure none of the others could hear her. Kyot was silent as he roughly measured the leagues they had covered in the strengthening daylight. He nodded: there was no doubt, the line of advancing flames was closer to them now than when they had left Thorny Hill.

'How much further is it to the river crossing?' he asked, gravely.

Eventine looked carefully around her to get her bearings and frowned. The dew pond, the lay of the land, were both unfamiliar to her and she realized that in the darkness they must have veered away from the path she knew would have taken them to the river. 'I'm not sure exactly where we are except that with the rising sun behind us we must still be travelling in a westerly direction. We will have to trust that Rockspray is taking us directly by the shortest route possible, but my guess is that if we can keep going at something like this pace we will probably reach the crossing some time tonight, probably just as night falls.'

Kyot looked back to the advancing wall of fire. The crackling roar was definitely louder now. He realized that even if the horses could gallop tirelessly all daylight, which was impossible, they still would never make it. They probably would not even get to see the river before the fires overtook them. He glanced across to where the company was drinking from the pond and talking to one another in low, anxious voices. He moved closer to Eventine.

'Don't let the others know – especially the children – but I fear there is little hope of us reaching the safety of the river before the fire catches up with us. Our only chance is to hope the wind drops or even changes direction, but there seems little chance of that happening: if anything, the wind is getting stronger.'

'Look mother, look! The sky has turned all red and is on fire now as well as the grassland. The sun looks very angry doesn't it.' Fairlight was running across to them from the pond.

Eventine picked up her daughter and held her tightly as she looked up to the sky and saw that the wispy clouds that veiled the sun had indeed turned deep red. 'Tell me,' she asked Fairlight, with laughter in her eyes, 'has your tutor taught you how to read the weather yet? Has he told you about looking at the sky and knowing what the weather will be?'

'No,' Fairlight thought for a moment, shaking her head, 'but he made us learn a funny rhyme about the clouds that goes like this: "red before bed your sheep are well led; red in the morning take this as a warning." But we don't understand what he means.'

'The red sky is a warning to the shepherd that the weather is about to change very quickly. Now go and tell the others to get mounted up, we still have a hard day's ride ahead of us.'

'Come on, Kyot, we must ride as fast as the wind and hope that the weather breaks before the fires overtake us. We must try, come on!'

Tanglecrown came trotting to her side and she leapt into his saddle as Rockspray rose into the air from where he had been resting on a rock beside the pool. The dogs fanned out around the company as Eventine spurred the Lord of Stags forward to follow the owl, with Kyot following gravely along behind her. He had little faith in those quaint, old-fashioned folk sayings about the weather, feeling that they were wrong as often as not, and he looked up at the reddish veil of wispy clouds that was beginning to thicken and partially obscure the sun as he tightened Sprint's girth and vaulted into the saddle. He hoped that for once the shepherd's warning that was now so visible in the clouds did indeed forecast a change in the weather – and a change to their advantage.

All morning Eventine kept the company together and led them as fast as she could across the undulating grasslands. Often she caught sight of groups of villagers and the Archers who had gone to warn them of the fires as they fled, all travelling in the same direction, towards the river crossing that still lay far away ahead of them. Rockspray seemed to lead them with more urgency as he saw how close to them the fires were burning. The dogs began barking and the horses sensed the tension around them and stretched their necks, with manes streaming out and nostrils flared as their speed increased. The bit rings jangled madly as they galloped through the tall, tinder-dry grasses in a desperate attempt to keep ahead of the flames that were drawing relentlessly closer.

It gradually became darker. Kyot didn't know whether it was the storm clouds which were piling up in the sky overhead or the smoke from the fires that were now sweeping over them, threatening to block out the light. Day seemed to turn into a stifling, choking night and the crackle of the flames became deafeningly loud. As he turned to look behind him hope shrivelled as he saw twisting ribbons of bright sparks stirred up by the force of the wind being lifted high into the air and carried far forward of the fire, bursting into flames where they landed. He could feel the heat of the fires scorching his back; he knew the end was near. The horses were beginning to stumble, they were floundering with exhaustion. None of them could go on much longer.

Suddenly the wind dropped away to nothing and it became oppressively hot and airless. It was as though the vast unburnt expanse of grassland – the earth, the sky – they were all holding their breath. The crackling roar of the flames seemed to fill the sudden silence as they drew ever closer. Kyot urged Sprint forwards to take him to Eventine and Fairlight but as he rode ahead he heard what seemed to be a low rumble of thunder. He looked up. A flash of brilliant lightning burned across the darkness and three large, ice cold raindrops struck his upturned face. At that moment the Border Runners began to bark furiously, their voices mingling with another long peel of thunder. Rockspray stooped to Kyot's shoulder and sought refuge beneath his cloak.

'I knew the shepherds' warning meant that the weather would change,' cried out Eventine. 'There's going to be a storm. Draw in closely together, everybody, and keep going: we are not out of danger yet.'

Her voice was drowned out by continuous peels of thunder rumbling in the sky above. Stark flashes of lightning cracked across the black bellies of the thunderclouds that were boiling above their heads. Then everything seemed to stop. A heavy moment of silence descended on the grasslands. It was soon broken with anxious shouts and the pounding of horses' hoofbeats as they gathered together. The grasslands ahead of them seemed to vanish in a misty haze and an icy wind touched their faces. Then there was a clap of thunder and lightning seemed to touch the ground all around them. A fierce rain squall swept over them and in seconds they were soaked to the skin, engulfed in a deluge.

'Ride on! Ride on!' Kyot shouted as the rainstorm lashed at them and beat down the tall grasses, filling the ditches, turning them into seething streams.

The advancing wall of fire wavered, exploding into balls of sparks, and then it stopped as the full force of the deluge struck. The greedy, devouring flames hissed and crackled before collapsing, extinguished by the lashing rain and turning in moments into billowing clouds of dense, yellow smoke and scalding spouts of steam that rose to briefly fog the air with their choking fumes before the rainstorm swept them away.

One of the women called out to Elionbel, attracting her attention above the roar of the pouring rain. 'Surely we can stop awhile now. We must try to make a shelter, the children are soaked to the skin, they'll catch their deaths if we don't stop.'

'We'll stop soon, I'm sure we will once Eventine has found us somewhere safe,' Elionbel tried to reassure her as she reached across to tighten Krann's cloak in a hopeless attempt to keep out the weather.

Kyot knew they could not keep up such a pace, but he had glanced back and caught a glimpse of their pursuers through the clearing smoke and he knew they dare not stop. He eased the company back to a trot however, and ordered the Archers to move in on either side of the children and use their shields as best they could to keep the worst of the downpour from them. Eventine rode in beside him.

'We must try to reach the Weir Pike Ford before this deluge turns the river into a raging torrent. We will never be able to cross once the level of the water has risen above the banks and it could be daylights before the river subsides.'

'If that happens all is lost, we must cross before darkness falls or perish.'

Eventine was about to add something, but then Kyot sent Rockspray ahead to lead the company. Then he drew her away and they cantered to the top of a small hillock for him to point back silently the way they had come. Her heart seemed to sink with despair. Now that the deluge had extinguished the fires and the smoke had been dispersed she could see quite clearly the monstrous hordes swarming forward through the smouldering heaps of wet ash. It would not be very long before they reached the place where the storm had brought the fire to a halt.

'Who are those vile creatures who can run so tirelessly? What evil is it that gives them their strength? They never seem to tire; even if we reach the ford they'll still be there, only a footstep behind us . . .'

Eventine grasped his arm. 'Look! Look over there, away to the right, I don't believe it – it can't be – look!'

Kyot blinked the raindrops from his eyes and stood in his stirrups. He stared in disbelief across the blackened, charred grasslands at what looked like a strange, ragged line of ancient trees, a hundred or more, gnarled and bent and carrying huge spears, advancing, converging unseen with giant strides on their pursuers. The trees were surrounded by a host of mounted Archers, but from the shapes of their bows and the clothes they wore Kyot could not recognize them. Behind the horsemen he could see from their small stature orderly ranks of Tunnellers running forwards, all fully armed. Kyot and Eventine sat watching, mesmerized as the strange army of trees and mounted warriors attacked. The element of surprise was theirs: they swept through the unsuspecting creatures with ease. Kyot could hear the shriek of arrows, the ring and clash of steel mingled with the shouts and screams of battle. The dark, shadowy cloud of the Eretch rose into the air above the creatures, for an instant it hung in the sky and then it was swept away by the storm. It was all over so quickly. In moments the bulk of their pursuers were lying dead amongst the ashes of the fires and the few that escaped were fleeing back in the direction of Stumble Hill with the carrion birds.

'We must ride after them and find out who they are. We must thank them for saving us,' Kyot urged, but it was too late. The trees and warriors were already moving away, vanishing as mysteriously as they had appeared, hidden by the drifting curtain of rain.

One of the trees paused and turned, lifting a knobbly arm and holding a blood-stained spear high into the air.

Kyot could just make out a deep, resonant voice booming out through the dull, steady roar of the deluge:

'King Thane is siege-locked. He is trapped in Candlebane Hall. Gather every loyal warrior you can and hurry to the Granite City.'

'Thane is siege-locked? But how can that be? Has the city fallen?' Kyot cried out in dismay as he spurred Sprint forwards, but the tree was already turning, striding away through the rain.

'We will be there, I pledge my word on it. We will be there with every Marcher, Archer and galloper we can gather!' Kyot shouted, hoping that he could be heard above the roar of the weather.

Kyot looked troubled as he rode back to where Eventine was waiting on Tanglecrown. 'Well what do you make of those strange warriors – and all the Tunnellers who were with them? Trees that can move on their own – I don't like it. And how did the one who stopped to call out to us know that Thane was siege-locked in Candlebane Hall? If you ask me there is more than a sniff of magic about all this, there is something very odd going on. I wish they had waited for a moment to explain themselves, I wish they had told us who they were.'

'They were going in a northerly direction, towards the Granite City. It must be that they are hurrying to help Thane. I think the trees may be some of the warriors that Nevian once cast a spell over. Remember, he turned thousands of them into trees on the Causeway Fields as a punishment for refusing to pledge their loyalty to Thane.'

'No, that's impossible, Nevian's magic came to an end when he faded and vanished into thin air moments after our great victory at the Battle of the Rising. The spell over the trees was broken forever when Thane forgave them.'

'Well whoever you think those trees and warriors are they can't be evil can they? Not after killing those monstrous creatures who were chasing us from Stumble Hill. And they did warn us that Thane is in grave danger and in need of our help. Come on, we had better catch up with the others and try to get over the Weir Pike Ford before the waters become impossible to cross. We must get to Clatterford and out of this atrocious weather as quickly as we can and re-arm before we ride on to the Granite City. I'm sure we'll learn all about those warriors once we get there.'

Lightning flashed and crackled across the low thunderclouds and the rain fell in a steady, hissing roar as they cantered forward, their heads bent low against the weather. 'What are we going to tell Elionbel of the news about Thane being siege-locked in the Candlehall?' Kyot asked.

Eventine rode on in silence for a moment and then shouted back against the storm, 'Nothing. Tell her nothing, she already spends her nights sleepless with worry for Thane, it would serve no purpose to distress her further.'

It was still raining hard, causing night to cast its mantle early beneath the thick stormclouds by the time they reached the river. The waters had risen dangerously high and were beginning to wash over the tops of the wide flat stepping stones of the Weir Pike Ford. The riverbank was crowded with people from the grassland villages who were jostling and pushing to get across. Many were leaping into the water with impatience and trying to use the places that the carts had been driven across, only to flounder, waist-deep in the swift current. They had to cling desperately to the ropes that had been hastily stretched across the river in an effort to prevent themselves from being swept away. The Archers who had brought the people to the ford rejoined the company full of dire warnings to Kyot and Eventine that they would never be able to get across if they waited for their turn so patiently. Kyot looked from them to the milling crowds and shook his head.

'We can hardly force a passage through them can we?'

'There is no need,' Eventine cried, remembering that there may be another place to cross further downriver – a wide, rocky shelf where her father's wagons used to cross when they were loaded down with crystal bowls, plates and window panes destined for the Granite City. It would, she knew, be far too deep to cross on foot there, but they might manage it mounted on horseback.

Leading the company along the riverbank she brought Tanglecrown to a halt on the edge above the drovers' ford. The river was wider here and swirling with white ripples and twisting eddies, clearly showing her how fast the current ran, but she knew she dare not hesitate. Tightening her grip on Tanglecrown's reins she spurred him down the slippery bank. The water surged and frothed around his legs, quickly rising to touch his belly, covering her boots. Tanglecrown roared and held his head high as Eventine felt him slip and scramble, often losing his footing, but step by step he forced his way across.

Once she had safely reached the other side the rest of the company followed, the children's ponies safely sandwiched between strong, sure-footed horses and once they had all reached the far bank Eventine insisted that she should first ride back to the Weir Pike Ford to rally the grassland people before setting out towards Clatterford.

'There will be shelter,' she shouted, 'warm, dry clothes and food for every one of you who will come with us to the Granite City and rally for the King. For those of you who can bear arms we will give you weapons if you will pledge to use them under Thane's standard and fight against the creatures who set the grasslands alight and destroyed your houses.'

As the grassland people shouted out promises against the wind she turned to lead the company into the rain-swept darkness to cover the last few leagues of their journey to Clatterford.

VII

A Meeting of
Old Friends

NIGHT DREW its velvet shrouds of dreams across the forests and the vast, undulating grasslands of Elundium that seemed to stretch away to the very edge of sight below the Emerald Mountains. But in some places the soft colours of dusk still lingered and birds sang amongst the tall whispering pine trees, hoary beeches and gnarled old oaks that peopled the steep heather meadows at the head of the pass that zig-zagged its way down across the sheer mountain wall and disappeared into the thickly-wooded valleys below. Nightshapes were slowly weaving indigo shadows and the still quiet of evening as Eider and Largg's huntsmen, their swords and daggers drawn, moved stealthily through the heather, passing between the gnarled old trees, careful not to make a sound as they closed in around the encampment that one of their scouts had spotted from a stony ridge hidden amongst the trees on the edge of the heather meadows.

The scout had ridden back with such haste that his sweating horse had skidded and slipped on the steep, rocky slope and he had barely been able to draw enough breath to describe the camp full of monsters of the type that Eider had seen attacking Cawdor. It lay just ahead of them, guarding the pass that led down into Elundium and in his opinion there was no way they could get around it. Lowering his voice to a fearful whisper he described everything he had seen. The first instant he had realized that they were not alone on the roof of the world was when he had heard quite ordinary voices and laughter and had seen thin blue spirals of smoke rising from the cooking fires. He dismounted and began to creep closer in an effort to get a better look when he suddenly heard deep booming sounds and felt the ground shake beneath his feet; evil creatures howled and he glimpsed huge, knobbly creatures moving slowly through the trees and out into the heather meadows. They had appeared to be moving towards his hiding place.

Eider did not know what to make of the scout's report. They had all heard the howl of what everyone else had insisted were wolves but still to him they sounded like Border Runners. And as for the description of huge, knobbly creatures he had seen through the trees they didn't sound at all like the scaly, clawed, half-human beasts who had attacked Cawdor. He could not imagine there being an ordinary voice or any laughter amongst those evil, shadowy monsters. But who were they if they were not these creatures?

Ayeshe had stayed with them, journeying far further than she should have done, and she had only returned to her father after a tearful farewell, extracting a promise from Eider that he would return as soon as it was possible. She had left them when the distant high pass that would take them down into Elundium was in sight. Eider felt alone without her and her knowledge of these wild, rugged mountains. Few of the other huntsmen accompanying him had ever journeyed this far beyond the borders of Largg's hunting grounds and they whispered to each other about two-headed giants and scaly serpents, savage beasts that they feared must inhabit every dark ravine and gully that they had to ride through. The closer they came to the borders of Elundium the more they looked to Eider as their leader.

Now, crouching in the heather in readiness for attack, as the thickening shadows of night swirled around a gnarled old, black ebony tree Eider wished that Drib was with him. He really missed the incessant, optimistic chatter that seemed to fill the boy and he had come to realize that he was the best friend he had ever had. In any case at that moment he had a very real need of Silkstone, the owl who had befriended Drib when they were both prisoners in the cellar beneath Candlebane Hall. Silkstone cold have flown silently over the encampment and he would have used his sharp eyes to see if it was full of friends, or foe. He could have even counted exactly how many there were camping there. Eider was in a quandary. He didn't want to attack if they were friends but he couldn't afford to squander the element of surprise if they were enemies.

The huntsmen closest to him crouched beside an ancient beech clothed in flowering vines. One of them put his hands to his mouth and made a soft, cooing owl's call. The sound was repeated amongst the other huntsmen as they told Eider that they were all in position and ready to attack.

As Eider waited for his men to take their positions he found himself wishing that they had found Berioss and the rest of the Tunnellers on their long journey from Largg's tower through the petrified forest. They had come upon more than one deserted camp site, usually beside hidden ponds or waterfalls, but the ashes of their fires had long gown cold and they had left no trace of who had camped there. Berioss, Eider knew, would have known exactly what to do in his situation. He began to lift his hand to his mouth to give the signal to rush forward when he heard a soft rustle of evening breeze in the hitherto still air combing its fingers through the sparse leaves of the black ebony above his head. He took no notice of this warning and rose slightly, pursing his lips to give the signal, but before he uttered a sound or even realized the danger he was in, a mass of sinuous branches snaked down and wrapped themselves around him, covering his mouth and smothering his scream of panic. The knobbly, twig-like fingers held him still and grabbed his arms in a painful, vice-like grip.

At that very moment all the gnarled old trees that had been standing so still, their feet buried in the heather meadows, rustled and came to life, seizing the huntsmen who were crouched, hiding in their shadows. Branches creaked and groaned as they disarmed the men and held them prisoner. Eider struggled violently, trying to break free, trying to shout out a warning but it was no good: the more he fought, the tighter the branches gripped him. He felt himself being lifted up off the ground as he tried to kick out at the trunk of the tree but the branches shook him and a deep, resonant voice boomed out, almost deafening him.

'Be still! We are not enemies. Come with me.'

In the next instant he found himself being carried forward into the encampment. Fires suddenly flared up in the centre of the camp and in the light of the flames he caught a glimpse of the other huntsmen, trapped like him and being carried to the centre of the encampment. Behind them amongst the pine trees he thought he could see a ring of people and the pale, luminous eyes of many Border Runners, but he could not be sure. He didn't have the time to look more closely before he was put down none too gently and found himself in front of a sturdy old beech tree. In the uncertain light of the fires he felt that it had the look of an ancient warrior about it, almost as though it had stepped out of one of those stories that Loremaster Grout used to tell them in the Learning Hall. He remembered how he had learned about the time when Nevian, the Master of Magic, had cast a spell over the disobedient warriors and turned them all into trees. He had never believed all that nonsense before but now he realized that he had been wrong to doubt the legends.

He stared up at the strange old figure and the hairs on the nape of his neck prickled as two of its upper branches, which definitely had the shape of muscular arms with broad, leathery hands, moved to demonstrate how one carried a spear. The lower part of the trunk was split into two massive legs and the large feet splayed out into thick, root-like toes. Thick vines and trailing flowerheads crowned its head and through the strips of bark Eider could just make out a face with sea-grey eyes looking straight down at him. The tree swayed slightly and a hand reached out its twig-like fingers to grip his chin. Eider felt his head being turned from side to side as the tree bent forward and the mouth split into a grin. Then he could feel the air fill with a deep rumble of laughter.

'Well, Eidergoose. I thought I had trained you to be a better warrior than this: you have allowed yourself and your men to be caught very easily, and it was such a simple trap.'

Eider blinked and stared, speechless as he searched the old tree. It had spoken his name in a voice so familiar. He used to know the voice well but it could not be, it was not possible.

'Berioss? Is that you, Berioss?'

'Yes, it really is me, Marcher Berioss. Despite my strange appearance I am still the same man, Eider.'

Berioss laughed as he embraced the startled Archer, easily lifting him up off his feet.

Dozens of familiar voices seemed to call out to him at once, all wishing him well and expressing concern and soon he was surrounded by a crowd of his old friends. There was Oaktangle, Mistletoe, Blackthorn, Quencher and all of the rest of the company who had survived the rout and destruction at Cawdor. There were also many faces he did not recognize and they were all milling around him with the rest. Border Runners barked and howled greetings, horses neighed, hands grasped his and arms embraced him, everybody seemed to be talking at once until Berioss clapped his hands together and in a deep, booming voice called for order.

'I know there are a host of questions to be asked and answered, and a hundred tales to be told by the fireside tonight, but should we not first greet those who travel with Eider and make them feel welcome amongst us? Come, surely we have not all forgotten our manners. Let there be food and drink and a warm place at the fireside as he introduces them all to us.'

Eider had been completely overcome with the surprise of seeing Berioss in the shape of a gnarled old tree. But then to be surrounded by all the friends who he had given up hope of ever seeing again . . . he had completely forgotten about the huntsmen. Looking around him he caught sight of them all huddled together, suspiciously watching the ring of trees who had just released them from their branches. Hurrying across he urged them to come forward.

'There is nothing for us to fear, these trees are really

warriors. Berioss will explain everything, he will tell you who they are once we are all settled around the camp-fire. Most of the others you see are Tunnellers and the loyal kingsfolk who journeyed through the depths of winter to join us at Cawdor. They are the ones we have been searching for as we travelled through the petrified forest.'

Reluctantly, and still sticking close together, the huntsmen followed Eider into the centre of the camp. Eider looked at the silent, expectant faces of his friends as they waited in the firelight for him to speak and tell them what had happened to him. He felt his face blush hotly with shame and he could not hold their gaze. The awful memories of how he deserted them in their moment of greatest need flooded back and filled his mind with the sights and terrible sounds of those hideous, half-human creatures who had attacked them at Cawdor. He remembered the strangling fear that had seized him, overwhelming him and freezing his fingers on the bowstring, preventing him from riding Nightshade forward; the horse had reared up, spinning round as he became infected by the same terror that had possessed the man. And yet as the memory of his cowardice welled up to haunt him so too did all that he had learned about discovering his real strength and he knew the depth of courage that dwelt within him. Slowly he lifted his head and looked from face to face around the expectant circle.

'Fear stole my courage as we galloped together across the Causeway. When I first saw those monsters who had attacked the citadel I deserted you all and I ran away. I know I can never ask for your forgiveness and I would not expect it.'

There, he had said it, and with a voice loud enough for everyone to hear.

'Many of the bravest warriors quail at their first sight of the enemy . . .' Berioss began, only to have one of the huntsmen hotly interrupt him.

'Eider is the very bravest of warriors, and he is one of the greatest Archers ever known. He saved the Lady Ayeshe's life when all alone: he stood his ground as a ferocious dragma beast charged at her out of a dark cavern.'

'Enough. I thank you Kussak for the faith you have in me, and I am grateful for you wishing to tell them that I have found my courage, but they must judge me as they know me and they know me for that one moment of cowardice.'

Eider spoke softly, struggling to hold his head high. Somehow having found what he had lost made the losing of it all the more awful to bear.

'I saw nothing of the battle because Berioss had sent me to look after the people who had managed to escape, so I do not know if I would have had the courage to face those hideous creatures,' Oaktangle said quietly.

'Damask and I were seized by the same terror as you, Eider, only we were thrown to the ground when our horses reared up before they crossed the Causeway to gallop through the gate arch towards those monsters. If it had not been for Berioss leaping to the ground and standing over us wielding his double-edged Marcher's sword we would never have been able to crawl to safety,' Mistletoe added.

'None of us fared much better than you, Eider – it was Berioss who took the full brunt of the attack when those monsters swarmed towards us and he kept them back so that we could all escape one way or another. Except, of course, for Drib who charged headlong into the citadel to try to rescue Sloeberry but he was driven off, gravely injured, and Sloeberry was taken prisoner. Look what happened to Berioss after those evil creatures drove him backwards over the crumbling cliff edge: he would have plunged to his death on the cliffs below if he had not changed into the shape of a tree. I, for one, have nothing to forgive you for, and I only feel joy that you have found us,' Blackthorn grinned as he gripped Eider's hand in his.

'If it had not been for those forgotten threads of Nevian's magic changing my shape like that I would have fallen to my death, there is no question,' Berioss laughed, but then his face became very serious. 'You have shown real courage today, Eider. Telling us the truth about what happened to you at Cawdor was no easy matter, I doubt if the words came easily. There are few of us who could have been that brutally honest about our weaknesses.'

'You mean you are not angry with me? You don't hate me for running away?' Eider asked as he looked around from face to face. An overwhelming sense of relief flooded over him as he saw the laughter and smiles surrounding him in the firelight and he took a moment or two to catch his breath.

'You said Nevian changed you into a tree – but how? Was he there at Cawdor? Did he make all those other trees move? I have never seen anything so strange before.'

The old Marcher laughed, causing the thick bark that encased him to creak and groan. 'It is a long story, Eider, and we don't have enough time for the telling just now but yes, in a way, Nevian was there at Cawdor, or at least some of the threads of his magic were there in me and it seems that these same threads have been dwelling deep down in all the other warriors he once cast a spell over. It may be that because King Thane has great need of us again, the magic has re-awakened. I don't know, but we have been coming upon more and more of us the closer we journey towards Elundium and we are all eager to fight for him again, if only to shed these uncomfortable shapes.'

'Berioss will talk to you all night about these tree warrior friends of his if you let him, and sometimes the creaking of their bark or their deep, whispering voices will keep you awake for hours but you have not told us how you met these huntsmen, or who they are.' Mistletoe's voice was full of curiosity as he interrupted the old Marcher. 'And who is this Lady Ayeshe whose life you saved? And please tell us what a dragma beast looks like, we are all longing to know, it sounds so very frightening.'

'You ask who my companions are? Why these are the very best of Largg's huntsmen, the bravest in the kingdom. Largg rules the realm that occupies the mountain peaks, all the way from the petrified forest to the borders of Elundium and it was his daughter, Ayeshe, who found me when I was overwhelmed with despair at knowing how I deserted you all. If it had not been for her kindness . . .' and here Eider blushed hotly, clearing his throat before continuing, '. . . if it had not been for her father's patience and the warmth and friendship of his people I may never have found my courage again. But let me tell you about the strangest thing that happened in the middle of a feast we had to celebrate my slaying of the dragma beast: it is because of it that we are here. Drib appeared, suddenly, out of thin air. I know, I know it sounds odd but that is what happened. At first I thought it was his ghost but it wasn't, really. He told me that he is with Nevian, the Master of Magic, and that most of you had escaped from that terrible attack, he told me that Sloeberry had been taken a prisoner and he warned me that the Chancellors have siege-locked our King in Candlebane Hall. He told me that Elundium teeters on the brink of black ruin. Largg took Drib's warning seriously because he fears for the safety of the whole world if the Chancellors seize power in Elundium, that is why this company of huntsmen are accompanying me to fight for King Thane.'

If Eider had expected the news to cause a stir amongst his friends he was disappointed; there was not a flicker of surprise to be seen as he looked around their faces.

'We know how badly it goes for King Thane because Nevian found Berioss in the ruins of Cawdor, the magician was just standing there waiting when he managed to clamber back to the top of the cliff. He urged Berioss to find us, that is why we are hurrying to reach the Granite City. Nevian wants us there by mid-winter's day but Berioss thinks we'll need to be there long before that. It is taking so long to rally everyone still loyal to the King – it is slowing us down. But you have not told us about Ayeshe yet, and we sense that she is very important to you,' Blackthorn grinned.

Eider smiled back as his eyes momentarily filled with a misty, far-away look. 'What can I tell you – she is Largg's daughter, and she is very beautiful.' He looked out beyond the firelight to the distant mountain peaks which shone out in the silvered starlight.

'I'll wager that there is more to this than you are telling us. Come on, we want to know everything, we won't let you rest until you have.' Damask was insistent and the others crowded closer in anticipation.

Eider laughed. It was good to be back amongst his friends again, but here was no hiding secrets from them. 'All right, but these stories really deserve a minstrel.'

Somebody at the back of the crowd began to play a soft lullaby and he grinned, leaned forward and began to tell them everything that had happened to him from the moment Nightshade reared up and bolted, carrying him away into the safety of the forest, to when the tree warriors had so unexpectedly grabbed hold of him and his hunting party. When Eider finished he looked quizzically around to his friends and asked, 'What I really don't understand is how you knew we were creeping up on you. These are the very best, the most experienced huntsmen in the Emerald Mountains and they can track the wariest quarry, they can get close enough to reach out and touch the creature without it even being aware of their presence. I thought we had moved so stealthily you could not possibly have known we were there when we encircled you.'

'You were good, my boy, you certainly know your skill. At times you melted so perfectly into the shadows that it was almost impossible to see how close you had approached. You would have all been very difficult to catch if you had not crept into the trap we had set. You used the old trees for cover, you crouched down beside them and now you know who they are you will understand why that was your one mistake.'

Berioss laughed as he explained to the huntsmen how the Border Runners had cast a wide, protective circle around them while they travelled, keeping a constant lookout for those creatures who had attacked Cawdor. They had no intention of being caught unawares a second time.

'The dogs brought us word that there was a large company of mounted warriors on the road behind us, catching us up at every footstep, so we set a careful watch and we became troubled as you drew closer. None of us could recognize the clothes you are wearing or the type of weapons you carry. You did not seem to be like the monsters, you seemed even from that distance to be fair rather than dark, but we could not afford to take any chances – that is why we set our trap,' Berioss concluded in his deep, booming voice.

'Well, I am glad we are all together again and the sooner we get ourselves back to the Granite City and put those evil Chancellors to the sword the better it will be for everyone,' Eider replied, stifling a yawn.

'I wish we really were all together,' Damask murmured.

'You need not worry yourself about Drib – he'll be all right, he has an uncanny knack for landing on his feet no matter what misfortunes befall him. You watch, he'll rescue Sloeberry and he'll be back with us all safe and sound in no time. He told me that is what he was going to do when he appeared so mysteriously at the feast. He said he had already set out with Nevian to do just that. Why, with the Master of Magic's help he has probably already rescued her.'

'Nevian's magic doesn't seem to be up to much these days. From what Berioss has told us of his futile attempts to return him to his proper shape we don't hold out much hope. We fear it might already be too late for Sloeberry: she was being cruelly tortured, we are all so worried about her.' Oaktangle's voice was low and full of tears.

'The worst of it is that there is nothing we can do about it. Nevian expressly told Berioss that we are to proceed to the Granite City in the utmost secrecy. He insisted that to reveal our purpose too soon would be to squander our chances of ever defeating the might of the Chancellors. But we would love to be able to rescue Sloeberry, I can't see how we would harm the master plan if we do that, can you?' Blackthorn stared accusingly at the old Marcher as he spoke.

'It is all a matter of strategy, you know that. If we do anything rash, if we reveal ourselves then we are finished. There are not enough of us yet to openly challenge the Chancellors in battle, you must be able to see that. There is nothing I would like better than to rescue Sloeberry but we don't even know where they are keeping her a prisoner.'

'But tell me this, what will happen if we come upon some of those black Chancellors' men who destroyed our home at Cawdor? Will we just slink away and hide? Will we just let them march on past?' Eider asked.

Before Berioss could answer a deep murmuring rose from amongst the trees and one voice spoke out. 'No, no, by root and branch we could not let that happen. We are warriors. We will lower our spears and sweep through them, we will trample out their evil.'

Dozens of deep voices murmured their agreement from amongst the gnarled old trees as they stood before the firelight.

'We must move with caution. We must not attack unless it is absolutely necessary,' Berioss cried out. But the rustling of the leaves and the creaking of the ancient boughs drowned out his voice.

Eider felt the ground tremble beneath him and he leaned towards Oaktangle. 'Well I, for one, would certainly not want to see that lot charging towards me.'

A smile hovered on Oaktangle's lips and he nodded in agreement. 'Nor would I, and hopefully there will soon be hundreds of Tunnellers marching with us. It has been decided that once we have descended into Elundium we will head first for the Rising to rally my people. I think Lord Willow will look upon those crimes we were falsely accused of in a very different light now, don't you?'

'I should certainly hope so, he must realize by now that it was the Chancellors who were behind it all the time. But forgive me, is it very far from here to the Rising?' Eider asked.

'Well nobody is quite sure,' Mistletoe interrupted. 'Some say it is only two daylights' journey, others say it is at least six, but at least all those old warriors seem to agree that it is in a north-westerly direction and somewhere along the edge of the grasslands. But I really wish we had a proper map instead of having to rely on other people's memory all the time.'

Berioss' booming voice suddenly brought their talk to a halt. 'It is time that everybody took some rest. We will break camp and be on our way as the first light of dawn touches the sky. Eider and the huntsmen will need warm, comfortable places to sleep. It is late, the night already draws towards morning. Come on now.'

It wasn't until late into the second daylight after they had descended the steep and often treacherous, zig-zagged pass out of the Emerald Mountains and followed the road through the thickly wooded foothills that they caught sight of the Rising. For all of the next day it was no more than a distant, hazy mound that occasionally showed itself above the trees, but gradually, with each hurrying footstep, it grew until it finally seemed to fill the landscape. As they drew near it could be seen for what it was: a huge, dark fortress of earth and bones that glittered and reflected the early evening sunlight. Eider shivered as he looked up at the Rising and remembered the stories that the elders had told him, stories of how it had been built. Stories of the time when Lord Willow's people had been bound in chains by the first Granite Kings and made to raise the bones of Elundium and build great cities. How they had been enslaved and passed on from King to King, his race knowing nothing of freedom, always building for others.

Then, as Krulshards' darkness came to smother the world, they were forced to build the Rising. They had been chained together as they trampled the soft earth, layer by layer, dying in their thousands until it rose high above the shadows. Eider stood and looked up in awe as he remembered the whispers he had heard when they had spent that winter together in Cawdor. He had heard tales of how Krulshards had captured the Tunnellers and condemned them to live in his darkness, tunnelling and enlarging the City of Night as a punishment for building such an impenetrable fortress for the Granite Kings. He had heard Mistletoe tell how the Rising had become a place of great beauty and peace, its sides thick with flowers, after King Thane had released them from bondage and given them the fortress as their own. But it was no place of beauty now, as he looked up at it he could see that its sides were stripped bare and fenced with jagged, razor-sharp spikes. It was ready for war.

'This place has changed much since we were here last,' Berioss muttered, drawing the company into close rank behind him.

The village of Wood Rising looked deserted, the thatch was broken and many of the roofs had collapsed through neglect.

'I wonder where everyone has gone,' Damask asked anxiously.

The company halted behind Berioss in front of the locked gates that prevented them from crossing the Causeway Bridge which spanned the dyke and led to the steep spiralling ramp and up to the broad plateau on its summit where Lord Willow had built his long hall.

'Look! Look up there, I can see a movement at the top of the ramp,' Oaktangle cried, hurrying forwards to where Berioss stood at the head of the company.

'It is Lord Willow and Lady Oakapple, they are surrounded by many of our people and they are all armed with spears and bows,' Blackthorn called out, hurrying forward to join Oaktangle.

'Perhaps they think we are going to attack them. I would be pretty frightened if a forest of old trees suddenly appeared on my doorstep – and look at the rest of us, what do you think we look like?' Eider warned, spurring Nightshade to stand close beside Berioss.

'Put down your weapons all of you. Oaktangle, Damask, Mistletoe, all of you Tunnellers, come forward, show yourselves, stand here.'

'We come in peace!' Berioss' voice boomed out as the Tunnellers hurried to show themselves but nobody moved; in fact a few seemed to be nocking arrows onto their bow strings.

'I fear we are going to have a difficult job convincing them who we are,' Quencher muttered as many of the company shuffled back out of bow-shot.

'Have faith and stand still, all of you. Even in these troubled times my people will not loose their arrows on those who are unarmed. Give them a moment so that they may see who we are,' Oaktangle called as he walked out alone in front of the others, lifting his empty hands.

When he knew he could be seen clearly he called out, 'It is I, Oaktangle, and with me are Mistletoe, Blackthorn,

Damask and all the Tunnellers who were falsely accused of beginning these troubles that have now brought Elundium to the brink of ruin. Despite all the hardships we have endured, we are loyal to King Thane and we are marching back to the Granite City to fight for him, to help rid the world of the treacherous Chancellors who are behind all this misery. You must not fear the trees. These trees you see with us are also loyal to King Thane, they are the warriors who once vanished into the wilderness. They are still loyal to the King and are bound by their old pledges. It is the thread of Nevian's magic that you see in them. Will you open the gates for us? Will you not let us in? Surely you have not forgotten us?'

As Oaktangle's voice faded into the evening shadows silence fell and for a long moment the world seemed to be holding its breath. Then Lord Willow called out Oaktangle's name and a cheer welled up on the summit of the Rising and with a rush of footsteps the gates were flung open. Lord Willow was first onto the Causeway Bridge and grasped first Oaktangle's hands in greeting and then each one of the other Tunnellers who he had once accused of betraying their pledges to King Thane. He apologized for doubting them and for believing that they had jeopardized their people's safety and friendships with the folk of Elundium. As they reached the top of the steep ramp he turned and spoke loudly so that all those who crowded the plateau could hear him.

'I judged you all over-harshly. I blindly chose to believe those wild rumours that were being spread falsely and I looked too eagerly for fault when clearly there was none to find. I know differently now, we all know that none of the troubles were of your making and we are truly sorry for all the suffering you have been forced to endure. I am sure the King would have realized your innocence all the quicker if only I had spoken up for you.'

Willow hesitated and the ground shook beneath his feet as Berioss, surrounded by many of the other tree warriors, strode to the top of the ramp and stopped behind Oaktangle. Willow frowned as he looked up to the gnarled old beech tree who stood slightly in front of the others. There was something familiar about the weatherworn features of its face, the steady, sea-grey eyes that looked down at him. Suddenly he remembered who it reminded him of.

'You are Berioss! You are one of the two Marchers who risked their lives to protect those of my people who had been falsely accused! You are a true and loyal kingsman and yet I refused to listen to you when you protested their innocence. There are not words enough to express the wrong I did to you.'

Berioss looked down and a smile crinkled the bark that covered his lips as he heard Lord Willow restore his integrity and honour. 'It is not words of apology that I seek, my Lord, we have always known our innocence. Words will not help us now but a strong company of your people, as many as you can spare, armed and willing to march with us to fight to free the King. That much I will ask of you.'

Willow stepped forward and reached up to grip the old Marcher's knobbly, twig-like hand. 'King Thane has a good and loyal friend in you, Marcher Berioss, and in all who march with you. Yes, you shall have what you ask for, and more. Every one of my people will march from here, every man and woman, every child big enough to carry a spear or wield a sword, every one of us who can bend a bow shall swell your ranks.'

'That is indeed more than I asked for and it will greatly strengthen our battle crescent, but we must hurry or I fear we will arrive too late – we still have so far to travel. We must march at first light to cross the endless grasslands,' Berioss cried as his branches shook and a crisp shower of late-autumnal leaves floated down onto the ground around his huge feet.

Willow smiled and looked out for a moment, gazing at the distant horizon line where the sunset was wreathed in misty fire and the mantle of night was darkening the sky.

'I have not forgotten the gift of freedom that King Thane gave my people after he released us from Krulshards' enslavement in the City of Night. We shall march with you for the love of your King but there is much to organize if we are to set out at daybreak. Summon everyone who waits beyond our gates and tell them there is a welcome here for them and room enough in our great hall for all those loyal to the King. There will be such a feast tonight and we will hear stories of battles, old and new around the firelight.'

VIII

Eavesdropping

'WHEN ARE WE EVER going to see an end to these trees and get to Stumble Hill? I will never get there in time to rescue Sloeberry if we carry on at this speed!' Drib muttered under his breath. He was feeling wretched. It was getting much too dark to see what lay ahead and Nevian had told him a good hour earlier to find somewhere to stop for the night and make camp, but still he urged the horses on a little further. The circus wagon creaked and jolted so very slowly over the unseen ruts in the Greenway they were following through Meremire Forest that it seemed to Drib they would never reach Stumble Hill.

Everything seemed to have gone wrong lately. Events seemed to have conspired to slow them down at every moment since they left Underfall. The journey was much longer than he had imagined it would be and Nevian had insisted that they reinforce the illusion that they really were a travelling circus. To that end they stopped and performed in every village they came to along the road. The magician felt that they must take every opportunity to spread secret doubts in the people's hearts and warn them of the Chancellors' cruel tyranny, urging them to rise up against it, but it was causing their journey to take forever. Then in Muddlewich Sparkfire had cast a shoe and it had taken ages to find a blacksmith whose forge was still alight and who could make them another, and then another age seemed to go by while they waited for it to be fitted.

And another thing, they were constantly being stopped and searched by the roving bands of Snatchpurse's men who were specifically searching for a small crippled boy. On more than one occasion Drib had had to vanish in a blink to avoid being caught. Nevian had had little sympathy and was none too gentle when he pointed out that it was all his own fault and that Snatchpurse would not be searching for him at all if he had not drawn attention to his presence by using the crystal Eye of Arabra to transport himself into the centre of the victory feast just as the creatures were celebrating. Drib knew it had been a rash thing to do, to appear out of thin air in front of Snatchpurse and grab his whip, but at least he had caught a glimpse of Sloeberry, and he thought it possible that she had seen him too. And it may not have been a complete disaster: he had eavesdropped on two of the villains who had been ransacking their wagon close to the village of Sourweed and he had learned that she was still alive – he had overheard them cursing her for causing so much trouble. He had also heard that the other creatures had their doubts as to whether Drib was alive at all so their searches were never very thorough, but they always slowed them down even more.

Drib had breathed a huge sigh of relief when he had heard them discussing Sloeberry. She was alive now but how long could she survive? Time was their enemy and just when he had thought they were moving on a little faster they had reached the Deepling Gorge and found the bridge destroyed. Snatchpurse's men must have done it as they advanced through the forest. It was still possible to reach the bottom of the gorge on horseback by following a steep, treacherous track, and there was a ford of sorts at the bottom that crossed the Eversparkle between jagged rocks, but it would have been impossible for the large circus wagon to cross there. Drib had been all for riding on alone to try to rescue Sloeberry but Nevian was dead against it, forbidding him to do any such thing. They had no other choice but to keep to their side of the valley and follow the gorge on the old road through the forest and over wild heathlands until they could ford the river further down. Then they had to ride back along the other side to rejoin the Greenway and follow it to Stumble Hill, which, to Nevian's reckoning, should be just beyond the village of Deepling.

Drib was almost bursting with impatience at this point and Nevian, sensing the boy's frustration, had tried to console him – but to no avail. He felt that it was the long hand of fate working to their advantage since their enforced detour would take them through many isolated villages that they would otherwise have missed. In each village they had stopped and recruited more loyal kingsfolk who were all sick of the reign of terror that the Chancellors' men were forcing upon them. They had secretly joined the Kindred Spirit the moment Snatchpurse's spies had turned their backs. They had disguised themselves in all manner of wonderful garments, all performing different, colourful acts and the string of carts and rickety wagons now stretched out behind them in the thickening gloom of evening.

There were carts and wagons of every shape and size following them now, all brightly painted in the colours of the circus. Battle Owls by the stoop had answered Orundus' call and they had silently flown to join them, many of them hovering motionless disguised as kites above the slow-moving procession. Grannog, the Lord of Dogs, had drawn many Border Runners from the depths of the forest and Equestrius, the Lord of Horses, had summoned the Warhorses who had been disguised with mud and briars and were even now harnessed to the carts or secretly keeping pace with them hidden by the dense undergrowth from the evil flocks of carrion birds who constantly watched them during daylight hours, wheeling and soaring above their heads.

They had reached the other side of the remains of the burned out bridge, rejoining the Greenway and leaving the sourfaced inhabitants of Deepling behind them two daylights ago but even though Nevian was constantly reassuring him that they would reach Stumble Hill very soon now Drib did not altogether believe him. The old magician's calculations and attempts at magic seemed to have become more and more erratic the further they ventured into Elundium. Drib's fears for Sloeberry's safety were intensifying by the minute, and the thought that they would arrive too late to save her life was almost more than he could bear. It was late autumn already and the trees were almost stripped bare of their green leaves. The smell of the coming winter hung in the air.

Drib blinked as he realized that he had let his mind wander back over their interminable journey through the forest instead of looking for somewhere to make camp for the night. He looked around and saw that the ground rose sharply ahead of them and he could quite clearly see lights ahead through the trees.

'Nevian, come quickly, look here, there is a village or some sort of settlement just a little way ahead on the top of the hill. Shall we go on and stop there?'

Nevian had been sitting huddled in the back of the

wagon engrossed by an ancient parchment showing a map of the Granite City and filling his mind with various strategies for freeing the King. Drib's voice broke through his thoughts and he stuck his head out through the awning. 'Stop, you fool, stop!' he hissed. 'Quickly, bring the wagon over here, hide it under the trees. There should be enough cover. Let us hope nobody's seen us.'

Drib recognized the urgency in the magician's voice and he steered the wagon into the deep drifts of autumn leaves that had piled up beneath the trees, bringing the wagon to a juddering halt out of sight of anyone using the road. Behind them the rest of the circus carts vanished into the trees and stopped, their inhabitants worried by the sudden halt and arming themselves before hurrying forward and crowding around Nevian's wagon.

'What place is this?' Drib frowned, standing on the seat of the wagon and peering ahead through the swirling nightshapes. He could just make out a tall, granite ruin silhouetted against the darkening sky. It had flickering lights burning in some of the broken windows.

'That, Drib, is the tower on Stumble Hill,' the magician muttered grimly, 'and by the look of it it did not fall easily to the Chancellors.'

An uncertain murmur rose through those who had gathered around the wagon as they learned that they were so close to their enemy's camp, but Drib felt his heartbeat quicken and he reached for the hilt of his dagger which he had secretly sewn into the lining of his acrobat's jacket as he stared at the distant flickering lights in the tower while Nevian spoke. Sloeberry, he knew beyond any doubt, was being held prisoner in that ruined tower. He was so close to her, so close. All he could think about was leaping to the ground and running as fast as his crooked legs would carry him until he found her and brought her to safety. Nothing else mattered, not the King, not the fate of Elundium, not even the people around him; all that mattered was that she should be safe again. Memories of her gentle voice came to him and he remembered how it held the echo of skylarks flying high on the wind above summer fields. He could almost feel the warmth of her touch, see the laughter in her eyes – it all came flooding back and he could hardly wait another moment to be with her once again. Even as Nevian was warning the others to be on their guard and not in any way reveal their true purpose, he moved to jump to the ground from the wagon only to feel Nevian's restraining hand upon his shoulder.

'Let me go! I must rescue Sloeberry. I can't bear to do nothing now that we are so close. Let me go!'

He struggled to break free from the magician's firm grasp. His head was full of the images of the terrible suffering that Sloeberry had been forced to endure and he had to reach her. He had to save her.

'To act impulsively, Drib, might – no will, I am sure – endanger her life even further. Rushing headlong into that tower is exactly what Snatchpurse wants you to do. Be patient and tomorrowlight the circus will visit Stumble Hill and you will use your cloak of invisibility to search out the Chancellors' weaknesses and after you have done that I will work out a plan to rescue her.'

Drib nodded bleakly. He knew that the old man was right but it didn't stop tears of helpless frustration well up in his eyes. A rumble of thunder suddenly split the air and lightning crackled across the treetops, momentarily lighting up the tower. A chill wind moaned and whipped through the branches above their heads and stirred up the leaves that carpeted the Greenway. Nevian frowned and looked up. He sniffed the air with his beak-sharp nose and smelled the change in the weather, laughing as another peel of thunder rent the air and forks of lightning flashed and crackled all around them.

'If I am not mistaken the weather is turning to our advantage. A savage storm is just breaking and if it rains hard enough it should hide us, keeping us safe from prying eyes tonight. Quickly, all of you, secure your carts and get under cover. Drib see to the horses and be as quick as you can.'

Umm, who had been standing close to the wagon, his head tipped to one side as he listened, gave a deep musical wail and ducked down, crawling into a tiny space beneath the cart and covering his ears with his large hairy, seven-fingered hands.

'It will have to be a cold supper for everyone tonight I'm afraid – we dare not risk lighting a fire lest any of Snatchpurse's watchmen spot us,' Nevian called out to the dispersing crowd.

Drib had been watching the dark, threatening storm clouds all day as they built up in the distance away beyond the eaves of the forest. He had heard the faint rumbling of thunder and seen the occasional flash of lightning and thought no more about it. The storm had not seemed to be moving in their direction and now suddenly it was breaking right above their heads and he barely had the time to jump to the ground to unharness the horses and throw weather sheets across their backs before the first rain squalls swept across the forest, drenching him before he could picket the horses in the safety of trees. Turning round he ran back to the wagon, climbed in and pulled the awning tightly shut behind him. The sound of a deep, dull roar that was getting louder broke through the clouds. The next moment the deluge struck, bending the stoutest branches and snapping the small twigs. Large raindrops beat on the top of the wagon and filled the drainage ditches in an instant. The roaring sound grew louder and louder and he felt Nevian's hand upon his arm, his lips were close to his ear.

'You had better get some rest, there is nothing else we can do while this storm rampages around us.'

Gradually the thunder and lightning moved away across the forest and the ferocity of the tempest eased into a steady, monotonous downpour. Drib yawned and snuggled down beneath his cloak, feeling grateful that he was dry and warm. Nevian was right, there was nothing he could do tonight, but he could use the time to riddle out a way to rescue Sloeberry. He was determined not to sleep, but the steady drumming of the rain on the roof of the wagon soon lulled him and dreams of happier times swept over him. The beating of the rain blended and merged in his head to become the sound of horseshoes clattering over sun-dappled cobbles. In the distance he could hear the sigh and whisper of the sea breaking against the black marble cliffs of Cawdor and the cry of seabirds as they wheeled and circled in the air. The clatter of the hoofbeats grew louder and then he could hear Sloeberry singing as she led Sparkfire out through an archway that was festooned with hanging vines and perfumed orchids. He whispered her name in his sleep and she seemed to come close to him. She looked so beautiful, her slender face surrounded by the strands of her dark, silken hair and her large, round eyes that always seemed to hold so much warmth and laughter. Drib smiled in his sleep, his hands twitching as he moved them beneath the cloak. It seemed as though their hands met and their fingers began to entwine. He tried to pull her close to him, to speak her name, but no words would come. He tried to pull harder but her image began to melt through his fingers.

'Drib! Drib! Wake up, Drib!'

A voice hissed in his ear. Blinking, he started awake as he felt someone shaking his arm. He was disoriented and confused as he stared into the darkness that was filled with the sound of drumming rain as it battered the roof above his head.

'Drib, wake up, listen! There is something going on out there, on the Greenway. Listen. Drib, are you awake?'

Drib sat up as he suddenly realized where he was and recognized Nevian's voice. 'What is it? What's the matter?'

'Be quiet and listen. There are voices, a lot of swearing and cursing going on. They are passing by us on the Greenway. I have seen lights through the trees so some of them must be carrying lanterns. Luckily we are hidden from them by the trees but who are they? At first I thought they must be one of those patrols that are always stopping and searching us, I thought they must have been caught out in the storm and were returning to the tower but there are far too many of them for that. Listen, they are still going past now. Can you hear them? Can you make out what they are saying?'

Drib crawled as quietly as he could to the front of the wagon and opened the flap a little, pressing his ear to the gap. The voices seemed louder now and he could pick out the occasional word and hear the strings of curses against the weather but they were passing by too far away and too quickly for him to catch more than fragmented snatches of what they were saying.

'I'm not sure that I can hear enough,' he whispered

after ducking back inside the wagon and blinking the raindrops from his eyelashes. 'But it sounds as though they were suddenly attacked somewhere. I am sure they said they had suffered heavy casualties and they seem to be hurrying back to report to Snatchpurse. They certainly seem to be very upset by what has happened to them. They are not looking forward to the reception they are likely to receive.'

'That must mean that we have some unsuspected allies out there somewhere. But where are they? And who are they? Clearly it cannot have been Berioss. Even if he has managed to find Eider and the rest of your friends there would never be enough of them to attack the number of those creatures that are hurrying past now, and it couldn't have been Thunderstone – he would not have more than a squadron of Gallopers siege-locked in Underfall. Kyot and the Archers must still be in disarray after fleeing from the tower before it fell. Who could it have been?'

Nevian paused and then muttered to himself. 'If only my magic had not faded so much I would dearly love to be in that tower to listen to what they will be telling Snatchpurse at this moment.'

'I can do that! I can make myself invisible and follow them in. I'll listen to everything and while I'm there I'll just have a look round.'

'You could, my boy, you could indeed,' Nevian chuckled softly in the darkness, but as soon as the laughter had risen to his lips so it died away, and his voice became very serious. He crackled a spark alight with slow deliberation, shielding it with the tail of his ragged hessian cloak and held Drib's gaze as he looked deeply into his soul.

'Before you contemplate such a venture I want you to promise me that no matter how desperate Sloeberry's plight might be should you see her you will not attempt to rescue her on your own. No matter how much you are tempted through anger you will not reveal yourself. You will not give Snatchpurse the slightest hint of our presence here. Can you promise me this, Drib?'

Drib so wanted to get inside the tower. He had so wished to rescue Sloeberry from the first moment that the magician had told him that they had reached Stumble Hill and here was the perfect opportunity, and yet much as a voice cried out inside him to do it he could not lie or make a promise to Nevian that he would not keep.

'I . . . I . . . I don't know. I am afraid my heart may lead my head,' he mumbled, looking away.

Nevian looked down at the small crippled boy and in the feeble light of the spark he smiled. Drib would not let him down, he was sure of that. 'Go now, go quickly or the doors of the tower will be shut in your face, but beware of the dangers you face. Do nothing rash, tread softly and leave not a single foot print, do not breathe hard enough to stir the candle flames. Just listen, listen and find out everything you can, and then hurry back.'

Drib did not need telling twice. He called out to Silkstone, begging him to keep a lookout from the trees as he pulled his boots on, threw his cloak around his shoulders, and without another sound he slipped through the gap in the canvas flap and jumped lightly to the ground. He then vanished into the night, splashing through the mud and puddles between the trees and catching up with the stragglers of the column who were just passing through the doors of the tower. Hanging back for a moment while he whispered the necessary words of magic, he snapped his fingers and abruptly disappeared from sight and in a moment he was slipping between the last two lumbering creatures as the doors swung shut, scraping across the wet cobbles.

Drib paused for a moment and pressed himself into the shadows beneath an archway on the edge of the outer courtyard as he watched which doorway the creatures went through. He thought it better if he allowed his eyes to grow accustomed to the livid, flickering, smoky light cast by the crude, tar-dipped reed torches that hissed and spluttered in the rain where they had been forced into the broken lamp brackets along the outer walls. Everywhere he looked fallen masonry and the debris of Snatchpurse's brutal attack still littered the ground, giving the tower a forlorn air of devastation and ruin far worse than its outward appearance hinted at. Drib cautiously picked his way across the courtyard to where the villains had disappeared and as he reached the doorway he stepped into a dimly-lit, low-vaulted passageway. He hesitated as the dark air was rent by Snatchpurse's voice as he screamed and cursed at the three captains that he had sent in pursuit of the Archers who had fled from the tower only moments before it fell.

It wasn't difficult to follow the harsh sound of Snatchpurse's curses along the vaulted passageway but Drib had to keep his wits about him to avoid colliding with the stream of shady figures who were fleeing in the opposite direction, trying to get as far from their master's murderous wrath as they possibly could. Ahead of him Drib could see a crowded archway and from the volume of the curses and the way the creatures shuffled and cowered, moving uncertainly from one clawed foot to the other, there was no doubt that Snatch was inside. Drib moved closer and waited his chance. The moment the door opened and a small gap appeared between two of the creatures, Drib slipped inside, weaving and twisting soundlessly past them. He worked his way into the gloomy, low-beamed, crowded chamber until he was close enough to hear everything that was said. There were piles of filth and rubbish with broken pieces of furniture lying everywhere but nothing he could use to hide himself in. Drib continued to creep carefully forwards between the creatures' clawed feet. Suddenly two creatures moved aside in front of him and he caught sight of Snatchpurse towering over the three of his captains who were sent in pursuit of the Archers and who were now kneeling in front of him.

Drib had never intended to try and get this close to the man and he froze, stifling a gasp of horror as he looked up into his scaly, hideous face. He was close enough to see the raw, suppurating wounds that Silkstone's talons had gouged into his cheek when he had accidentally drawn Snatchpurse back with him through the Eye of Arabra. His face was a tight, snarling mask of hatred, his eyes glittering slits, the pupils shrunk into murderous pinpoints of light as he reached back with a clawed hand for his battle mace that lay amongst the evil-smelling raw bone ends and mouldy scraps of half-eaten food that littered the table behind him.

'There can be no excuses for failure, you miserable cowards!'

Snatchpurse's voice was laden with malice as he hissed at the trembling men and lifted his battle mace high above his head. 'You have betrayed the trust I put in you when I sent you to catch and kill those wretched Archers. You have betrayed me!'

'Betrayed me! Betrayed me! Har, har, har!' a harsh voice mocked from somewhere above Drib's head. Flinching, he looked up and searched the smoky rafters for the source and caught sight of the white magpie, Squark, shrieking and mocking from where he had perched on the king post beam.

'Please, great Lord and Master, spare us . . .' one of the captains pleaded, reaching out to touch Snatch's feet. 'We did exactly as you ordered. We pursued the Archers relentlessly, we set alight everything that lay in our path, we burned everything. The fires were just about to overwhelm the Archers when a sudden and unexpected storm came from the Emerald Mountains and broke right over us. There was a deluge the likes of which we have never seen before. Please believe us, master, the waters were so great they quenched the fires instantly. We have never seen anything like it.'

Snatchpurse seemed to hesitate, the mace poised, about to strike, when another of the captains seized the opportunity to cry out. 'Even though the storm put out the fires we were about to charge through the hot, smouldering ash with no concern for our safety, we were about to butcher those Archers when we were suddenly attacked. We were caught off our guard by a strange forest of moving trees. With the trees were hundreds of mounted Archers from a tribe we have never seen and there was a host of those cursed Tunnellers all armed to the teeth and travelling with them. We stood no chance.'

'Yes, master, we did our best, but these warriors suddenly appeared from the west emerging through the smoke, slashing and stabbing with a ferocity we could not withstand. They pursued us for leagues but we managed to escape them and come back here.'

Snatchpurse slowly lowered the mace a fraction and a whispered murmur of cautious relief ran around the room. Nobody dared to move, they hardly drew breath, every one of the men crowded in that room knew how ruthless their master could be, how his moods could change so suddenly, especially when he doubted someone's loyalty. And they all knew to what lengths he would go to exact his revenge. He would not hesitate to smash their skulls or slit their throats: killing pleased him – he was always looking for the excuse to hand out a death sentence.

'Trees that move? Tunnellers armed to the teeth?' Snatch hissed suspiciously. 'Now that is a ridiculous story, quite improbable. You will have to do a lot better than that if you want to stay alive.'

'But it is true, every word of it, master. Upon our lives we would not lie to you, none of us would dare to. It was as though some of those old warriors appeared suddenly from the direction of the Emerald Mountains, you know which ones, the ones who refused to pledge their allegiance to King Thane after the Battle of the Rising. You remember, the magician, Nevian, turned them into trees an age ago on the Causeway Fields. It had to be them, there is no other explanation. They looked exactly like them with their huge trunks all twisted and gnarled, their fingers a mass of twigs and their skin had the texture of rough, age-cracked bark. It was so thick and strong that our spears just glanced harmlessly off them.'

'Magic? Magic?!' Snatch was growing angry again and threw his mace aside, unsheathing his dagger as he grasped the closest of his captains by the throat and lifted him up off his feet. 'Don't you dare suggest that the Thronestealer was blessed by Nevian and that those times were beguiled by magic. Those trees were not magic. All the so-called magic that ever existed in Elundium has vanished; it disappeared along with that treacherous, meddling magician after the Battle of the Rising. All those trees he cast his

243

spell over were changed back into men an age ago. The magic is gone I say. Now tell me the truth of what really happened. Tell me how you failed me or do I have to cut it out of each one of you in turn?'

The men swallowed nervously and wrung their hands together in despair. Sweat was beading on their faces and running down between the scales that covered their heads. As the dagger pricked the captain's skin he knew that no matter how he told it his master didn't want to hear.

'The . . . the . . . the warriors were huge, my Lord, and they looked like trees to us, covered in smoke as they were. But we did see the mounted Archers and the Tunnellers much more clearly. The Archers were dressed in fur-lined cloaks and their breeches and tunics looked as though they were fashioned from many different animal skins. They wore helms emblazoned with the heads of eagles and all manner of winged serpents. Their arrows were tipped with vicious steel blades that sheared through our thick, armoured skin, cutting us to the bone. We were defenceless against them.'

Snatch laughed harshly and savagely shook the man. 'What of the power of the Eretch? What of that black power that is infused into your armoured hides? Are you now trying to tell me that it did not protect you?' he hissed in fury as his clawed hands tightened around the man's throat.

'The Eretch deserted us the moment we were attacked. They vanished into the smoke.'

'Lies! All lies! Trees do not move on their own, there are no warriors like the ones you tell me of and the Eretch would not have deserted you like that! I should slit your throats this instant for daring to utter such untruths.'

But still Snatchpurse hesitated as he stared down at the

three men and let his gaze pass slowly over the others who were crowded nervously in his chamber. There was some truth in the men's stories; all their bodies had lost their shadowy strength to some degree, their spines and ridges of scaly armour had become pale and brittle where the evil had oozed out of them. A cold shiver of fear made the jagged spines on his back rattle. It was one thing removing the hold that the Eretch exerted over his men but quite another having the Eretch desert them, leaving them helpless and vulnerable at the first sight of real danger.

'There must be some truth in what these captains are saying. Take a look at this arrow.' Thorograsp's voice broke into Snatch's thoughts and he looked down at the broken, bloodied arrow with its steel-bound blade that Thorograsp was holding out.

'What direction did this force ride off in?'

'They rode to the north, my Lord. After they gave up chasing us they rode towards the Granite City.'

For a moment Snatchpurse stood perfectly still as those words brought the awful realization that the warriors who had attacked and almost destroyed his men were even now heading towards the Granite City to break the siege and rescue the Thronestealer from Candlebane Hall.

All this time Drib had been creeping closer to Snatchpurse, listening intently, trying to ensure that he heard every word that was spoken when, from the corner of his eye, a movement caught his attention and he heard the clink and rattle of a chain. Turning his head he saw a heavy iron-linked chain lying upon the floor; it moved slightly between the clawed feet of the crowd. Drib frowned and followed it with his eyes as it snaked between the scaly legs before disappearing into a gloomy corner of the room. Something was moving in the shadows beneath a pile of broken furniture and it was slowly emerging from its hiding place. Drib suddenly gave a shallow gasp of surprise and felt his heart quicken as he saw that the tiny, fragile figure, crouching and moving slowly forwards into the light was Sloeberry. He gasped and, forgetting all else, he moved a step towards her. Something inside him warned him to stop and he fought down the impulse to rush across the chamber and throw his arms around her. She looked pitifully thin, almost emaciated as she crept to the edge of her hiding place, clutching a single wayside flower to her bosom. It had faded and its leaves were crumpled, faded and yellow, but it was obviously precious to her. She seemed to be trying to listen to what was being said and as one of the captains described the ranks of armed Tunnellers who charged them Drib thought he saw a flash of hope and defiance light up her bruised eyes.

Drib had not expected to find Sloeberry so easily and seeing her crouched there in the shadows distracted him for a moment – he almost forgot the danger of the task he was involved in and would, if he had not acted quickly, have revealed his presence. As Drib still stared across at Sloeberry, Snatchpurse, having decided not to slit the throats of his captains, roughly cast them aside, shouting, 'There is not a moment to lose. We must march on the Granite City tomorrowlight and we will kill that Throne-stealer, we will set his head upon a spike above the Stumble Gate so that all traitors may look and quake. We must set off immediately before those warriors who are advancing through the grasslands have the chance to free him. Go! Go! Go all of you and make ready!'

The captains, released from Snatchpurse's grasp, stumbled backwards straight towards where Drib was standing, cloaked by his invisibility. He looked round at the last moment and recognized the danger just in time to sidestep one and, bending his knees he sprang into the air, somersaulting over the other's scaly head. But to his horror, and far too late to stop himself, he realized that he was about to land so close to Snatchpurse that he could touch him, so close that he was about to land squarely on Snatchpurse's shadow. He remembered that Thunderstone had said something about the creatures not being able to bear the pain of their shadows being trampled upon. Gritting his teeth Drib tensed – there was no way to avoid the shadow but he was ready to leap again the moment his toes touched it. His feet vanished into the dark, distorted blackness. Touching the shadow made his toes tingle unpleasantly and sent a shudder of revulsion up his spine. Drib rose into the air again immediately, his jaw and hands clenched tightly, and he turned towards the door, searching desperately amongst the milling creatures for somewhere to land.

Suddenly Snatchpurse gave a howl of pain as the Eretch who dwelt within him clawed at the inside of his skull and screamed in his ears. The creatures stopped to look at him. Snatchpurse spun round towards them, snarling and cursing, slashing wildly with his dagger, expecting the razor sharp blade to cut into the scaly hide of whoever had dared to come that close to him. The crowd froze in terror as they heard their leader shout out, 'Who has dared to touch my shadow?'

For an instant his scaly skin prickled, the spines rising along his back as the same sensation that he had felt on the night of the feast flooded over him. It was as though somebody had been there. Somebody he could not see had been near him, watching over him.

'Crooked Drib! Crooked Drib is here, I know he is,' he hissed with raw hatred boiling in his brain. His eyes narrowed to murderous slits as he hunted the room in search of him.

Drib heard Snatchpurse's threatening snarl right behind him as he landed lightly on his feet and began to run for the door. He knew he had to get out of there as fast as he could – to stay another moment would be madness – but he stopped. He could not help himself. He turned around to look at Sloeberry. He knew he could not rescue her, and that even if he did manage to release her from the chains they would never reach the door alive, but he could not leave her without letting her know that he had been there. But how would he do that? Then he remembered the fragile flower she was clutching and he whispered the words of magic that he had learned in the Runesgate Tower.

'change the colour, change the hue,
perfume the petals,
bring flower and leaf back to summer beauty.
incarnadine. opera. opera.'

He smiled as he saw a look of startled surprise come into Sloeberry's eyes and the tiny wayside flower swelled up into its summer beauty. She brought it up to her nose, savouring its delightful perfume, and he saw her lips silently whisper his name before she shrunk back into the shadows, shielding the tiny flower with her hands. He knew then that she was aware of his presence and that had to be enough for now.

Without another moment's hesitation Drib ducked and dodged from left to right between the half-human creatures as he fled into the darkness, leaving Snatchpurse to snarl and curse with hatred behind him. He found his way out of the fortress and into the pouring rain, back to where the circus wagon was hidden amongst the trees.

'You bring me both good and troubling news, my boy, and in each there is much to riddle out. To act foolishly on what we now know could lead to certain disaster.' Nevian's brow was furrowed by worry by the time he had finished listening to Drib's account of everything he had overheard in the Archers' ruined tower.

'Could one of those gnarled old trees really have been Berioss? Do you think Oaktangle and the others were amongst those Tunnellers? And what about . . . ?' Drib began to ask.

'Enough of your questions, Drib, give me time to think.' The old man frowned the boy into silence as he drew his hessian cloak tightly around his shoulders and sat hunched, deep in thought, mulling over everything that the boy had told him.

The only sound in the darkness was the steady drumming of the rain on the roof of the wagon and it seemed to Drib to be a long time before Nevian spoke again. 'Yes,' he muttered at length, 'there can be little doubt that Berioss is one of those gnarled old trees who attacked Snatchpurse's men in the grasslands – but what about the other trees? The only reason I can think of to explain them away is that they are more of those warriors that I once cast a spell over an age ago on the Causeway Fields. But why and how the threads of magic have dwelt in them for so long and how I will ever find an antidote to break the spell and free them all defeats me for the moment. As for those strangely dressed, mounted Archers – well, who knows? My guess is that they are a company of Largg's huntsmen. Drib, do you remember when you glimpsed Eider in Largg's tower high up amongst the Emerald Mountains beside a frozen lake, well somehow I think that Eider must have convinced Largg to send his huntsmen out to Candlebane Hall to help to break the siege. As for the Tunnellers, well it wouldn't surprise me in the least to discover that Oaktangle and the rest of your friends are amongst them, and that bit is the good news; there seems to be a great company rallying to help the King. The worrying thing is that I have told Berioss to spread the word as he travels that all those loyal to the King must be at the doors of Candlebane Hall by midwinter's day and I fear that if Snatchpurse sets out for the Granite City tomorrowlight then Berioss, and everybody else, will arrive too late. Unless . . .'

'Unless? Unless what?' Drib cried, breaking into the old man's thoughts as he crackled his spark alight.

'Well unless they are warned they will arrive too late, surely even you can see that. Somehow we have to alert them, we have to tell them that Snatchpurse intends to march upon the city immediately. I feared this would happen, I knew that if Snatchpurse got wind that those loyal to the King were gathering he would act quickly. That is why I counselled secrecy and caution but it is too late now, no point in fretting, we still have the advantage of knowing what that treacherous Chancellor's son is intending to do and to be forewarned is to be forearmed. Now we must pass on that knowledge to the kingsmen – but how? That is the riddle. Elundium is a vast place and my powers of second sight have all but faded: I cannot divine where they are. And even if I could I couldn't reach them in time, not if I'm still going to bring the Kindred Spirit to the Granite City on Snatchpurse's heels. Now don't look at me like that, you certainly cannot even think of trying, it's one thing hiding here in the circus but I doubt you would get very far on Sparkfire with every one of Snatchpurse's men watching out for you. But there must be a way, if only I could think of it.'

'There is!' Drib interrupted, making the magician look sharply at him. 'Or at least I think there is. Surely some of those men who have joined the Kindred Spirit while we were travelling through Méremire Forest used to be dispatch riders or Gallopers once? Couldn't a few of them mount the Warhorses and ride out to warn Berioss and the Archers? Surely if some of the Border Runners and Battle Owls could be persuaded to go with them they could go on ahead and find all the kingsmen in plenty of time to . . .'

'Yes, Drib, you are right, they might well reach them in time; at least they must try. Now go quickly and wake all those who once rode for the King and bring them to me right away. They will have a long ride ahead of them and they will need to be as far away from here as possible, away from the prying eyes of those evil carrion birds before the new daylight dawns. Now hurry boy, hurry.'

Drib had barely pulled the wet hood of his cloak down over his head to keep out the foul weather before he heard Nevian calling softly for Equestrius and asking him to gather the Warhorses. As he jumped down out of the wagon the Lord of Warhorses splashed past him in the dark as he ran from cart to cart in search of the riders.

'Well we've done the best we can to alert those loyal to the King of the changing situation – let us hope that luck rides with our horsemen,' Nevian murmured as he listened to the last of their hoofbeats fade into the stormy darkness before he let the canvas flap of the wagon fall back into place.

As he turned to Drib he smiled. 'You have done well tonight, my boy, now get some sleep, we will have a very busy day tomorrowlight.'

Drib snuggled down beneath his cloak but he couldn't sleep. One thing had been troubling him, gnawing away inside his mind ever since he had arrived back from eavesdropping. How on earth were they to rescue Sloeberry? Now that Snatchpurse was marching on the city they would never be able to get close to her again. The last thing he had heard Snatchpurse shout at his men just before he had slipped out of the door of the chamber was that her guards were to be doubled and that she was to be watched constantly.

'Wearing yourself out with worry won't achieve anything, Drib. I haven't forgotten: at the first opportunity we will rescue Sloeberry, I give you my word on it. If anything it might be easier once Snatchpurse's men are on the move, despite the orders you overheard as you slipped out of the chamber.'

Nevian's voice made Drib start and he blushed in the darkness. During all his time with Nevian in the Runesgate Tower he had never got used to the magician's ability to read his thoughts so openly. 'But how can we keep close to her if they are marching on the city?'

Nevian laughed softly. 'That, Drib, will be the easiest part. Marching men will need entertainment each time they stop to rest. It shouldn't be too difficult to convince Snatchpurse – after all I have a letter written in the hand of that creature Unsnark, who was in charge of the siege of Underfall, extolling our virtues and praising the excellence of our circus. He has given us the right to perform in every village along the greenways' edge on our way to Stumble Hill where we are to present ourselves to the Lord Chancellor, the Honourable Snatchpurse.'

'Letter? I didn't know that creature had written a letter about us!'

'He didn't!' Nevian chuckled, touching the rolled, yellowing parchment that was concealed in his inner pocket and bore a perfect forgery of the Chancellors' seal. 'My powers have not entirely deserted me yet, you see. But before you go to sleep I have a question for you. Think back, Drib, do you remember shutting all the windows and locking the door of the Runesgate Tower when you left? And most importantly did you extinguish the lamps? I know you ran back into the tower to make those kites to disguise the owls, but did you clear everything up after you made them?'

Drib cast his mind back. They seemed to have left in such a hurry, but now he thought about it he remembered he had not emptied the bucket of water that he had used to mix the paint, neither had he extinguished the lamps or shut the windows. He couldn't remember even shutting the door; beginning the journey had seemed so much more important at the time. 'No, I'm sorry, I must have forgotten, I hope it doesn't come to any harm. But why do you ask me that now? We have been gone from the tower for ages.'

'It's the storm, Drib. I had been watching it gather over the Emerald Mountains for days before it broke and there is something very different about it. The clouds seem to have boiled so angrily, the lightning is so bright, the deluge so fierce, I have a feeling the storm might well have had its beginnings in my storm engine.'

'But how could that be?' asked Drib with an awful, sinking feeling in his stomach.

'It could happen easily enough. It would not take much more than a gust of wind blown in through a half-open doorway. It would start the sails, and then a spark from a forgotten lamp would only need to fly at an opportune moment, and then there was that bucket of water . . .' Nevian laughed again. 'Don't worry, Drib, fate sometimes works in the strangest ways and I think this may have been to our advantage. If you had not been so forgetful there would have been no deluge to quench that grassland fire and then Kyot and all the people who escaped from the tower would have perished. And this foul weather has hidden us up so successfully tonight, there will be no prying eyes around until it lets up, and so much rain is bound to slow down Snatchpurse's march on the Granite City. You have done just the right thing, quite by accident, but I would not normally approve of such forgetfulness. Now you go to sleep and leave the worrying to me.'

Drib sighed and pulled his cloak up to his chin as he listened to the rain beating down on the roof of the wagon and heard the distant rumbles of thunder.

'Just think of it, I made this storm,' he murmured to himself as his eyelids fluttered and he drifted off to sleep.

IX

Circus of Deceptions

LATE IN THE NIGHT the steady downpour stopped and the morning dawned cold, dull and grey. A fine, soaking drizzle drifted across the greenway and dripped from the branches of the trees. Everything glistened and smelled of damp and wet leaf mould. The ground quickly turned to sticky mud beneath the feet of the Kindred Spirit as they quietly made ready to finish the journey to the tower on Stumble Hill. Weather sheets were stripped off the horses' backs, shaken and stowed away, their brass and leather harness was fitted and they were positioned between the shafts of the carts and wagons; collar chains and breeching straps were checked and tightened and attached to the tugs on the shafts. Once everybody was ready and dressed in their circus clothes the drop chains were released. The horses snorted and threw their weight into their collars and the heavy vehicles shuddered and swayed before they slowly moved forward through the trees to the edge of the greenway and came to a halt. Nevian stood up onto the high seat of his wagon and lifted his hands to appeal for silence. When he was sure that all the people were watching him he called out to them in a soft voice.

'Now remember all of you, be on your guard and keep your wits about you because once we leave the shelter of these trees we will be in full sight of our enemy. From this moment until we have freed our King from Candle-bane Hall, until we have defeated these treacherous

Chancellors, we will be right beneath their noses. Our performances as circus artistes must be foot-perfect and beyond suspicion.'

Nevian suddenly laughed and delved beneath the voluminous folds of his cloak, pulling out a leather pouch sealed with wax to keep the air out.

'Perhaps today we will add a little sparkle to our acts – something to distract prying eyes!'

Breaking the seal, he quickly drew out a small pinch of sulphur and saltpetre and put them in the palm of his hand so that everybody could see.

'Watch carefully,' he instructed, spitting on the mixture and mixing it together into a sticky ball.

Before it had a chance to glow or burn his hand he stopped it coming into contact with the air by clenching his fist tightly shut. The company held its breath, watching, wondering what he was going to do next. None of them really believed all the talk they had heard about his ailing powers and they all still thought he had the ability to do real magic. With a sweep of his hand Nevian tossed the tiny ball of quickfire up into the air above their heads, where it fizzed and sparkled as brightly as a newborn star, before landing in the wet grass where it spluttered and hopped about erratically before vanishing in a shower of hot sparks.

'It's magic! It's real magic – what did I tell you? Nevian's powers haven't faded, we all knew that!' One of the company could not control his excitement.

Nevian merely smiled and shook his head as he gave the pouch to Drib, who began to distribute a pinch to each of the clowns and tumbling men.

'Quickfire is not magic: do not be so easily fooled, any of you,' Nevian frowned. 'It is nothing more than two compounds that those who may sometimes pretend to be a magician may use to their purpose, or lazy alchemists sometimes use to bring a pot or crucible quickly to the boil. I have given it to you to use to impress Snatchpurse's men, so that they will marvel at our performance and clamour to see more. But be warned. Mix it exactly as I have just shown you and make sure you keep your hands tightly shut until the moment you throw it into the air, otherwise it will burn you. Use it wisely and use it when I give the signal which I will do as we draw close to the tower. Are you all ready?'

Heads nodded and a murmur of agreement rose amongst the company. The stilt-walkers bent and moved slowly through the trees, the clowns and jugglers, each with a hand tightly holding their still ball of quickfire, took their places in the head of the procession. Umm picked up the thick iron bar that he was to bend and twist into many different shapes in his role as the strongest man in the world, but he kept very close to the wagon, fighting down the urge to slip away into the forest. He was truly afraid of what lay before them and it was only his promise to Drib that kept him there.

'It will be all right, nothing terrible is going to happen. Don't worry, I will keep an eye on you,' Drib whispered to him as he took his place amongst the acrobats.

'Keep a sharp look out!' Drib called up to Silkstone and all the other owls who were disguised as kites. They waited, their painted wings outstretched as they perched awkwardly on the tops of the carts and wagons, ready to rise up into the air above the circus the moment they emerged from beneath the trees.

The musicians quickly found their places, shielding their instruments as best they could from the water dripping from the trees. Nevian cast a last, quick, critical eye over the Kindred Spirit and nodded with satisfaction.

'Musicians – play a rousing tune. It is time for the circus to begin!'

He gathered up the reins and released the brake, giving Equestrius the signal to move forward. The wagon jolted, its wheels cutting deeply into the wet ground as Sparkfire and Equestrius threw their weight into the harness and strode out onto the greenway. The owls rose into the air with barely a sound and hung noiselessly as the drifting drizzle made their brightly painted disguise glisten. No sooner had the musicians played their first notes and the clowns and jugglers begun their routine of foolery and pantomime than they were spotted approaching the tower. The milling crowds of Snatchpurse's army were forming into noisy, unruly columns outside the tower and they stopped and fell silent, staring as the circus approached. The sky suddenly darkened above them.

'Beware the carrion birds!' Nevian warned instinctively, but he need never have uttered a word: the people of the Kindred Spirit had long grown used to the flocks of evil birds swooping down unexpectedly and flying in and out amongst them, searching and prying with their sharp eyes.

The birds found nothing more than the usual ragged circus troupe that they spied upon daily and upon whose slow progress through Meremire Forest they had regularly reported back to Squark, their leader. They soon returned to their roosts in the tower.

'Now comes the moment of truth. Will he recognize me?' Drib muttered, suddenly overcome with panic as he reached the pinnacle of a double somersault and caught a glimpse of Snatchpurse striding out of the tower and coming towards them through the ranks of his men. Fear made Drib's heart pound – his tumbling skills seemed to desert him as he landed awkwardly on his feet and ducked down to hide amongst the other acrobats and clowns.

'You can't stay crouching in the mud like that, somebody's bound to see you. Make yourself invisible. Keep moving. Now do something quickly.' One of the other acrobats pushed Drib forward as he tumbled away, leaving him exposed.

They had come to the end of the greenway and passed through a mass of tangled thorns thick with a heady scent before entering an area where the ground had been trampled into a sea of mud by the forming ranks of Snatchpurse's army. There was nowhere Drib could hide. Masses of the half-human creatures and hundreds of Snatchpurse's men were staring suspiciously at the circus procession: they were less than five paces away. Drib was paralysed with fear. It felt as though every one of those hideous creatures was staring directly at his crooked legs. He tried to whisper the words of magic that would render him invisible but he could not snap his fingers, he could not move and no sound would come. The front ranks of the creatures stirred and suddenly burst apart as Snatchpurse, with Squark perched on his shoulder and surrounded by his most trusted captains, strode through his army and stopped. He was so close to Drib that the boy could see the mud oozing up between the claws on his feet.

Nevian realized that something had gone wrong. Silkstone gave a low warning hoot that was disguised by the music of the pipes and drums but Nevian could hear it and half-rising in his seat he saw Drib's dreadful predicament. He had always secretly worried about this confrontation and wondered if Drib would have the courage and the faith in his own abilities to face it.

'The quickfire – use it now! Create a diversion and get Drib back into the wagon and out of sight!' he called out urgently.

Instantly the word was passed through the procession. Bright, fizzing arcs of fire rose up out of the clowns' hands and a dazzling fountain of light briefly lit up the grey shrouds of mist that were drifting around the tower. It lasted but a moment before it spluttered out into the mud between the startled creatures' feet, but it was long enough. Just long enough for Drib to gather his thoughts together and summon his frightened wits. He felt strong hands grasp his arms and lift him onto his feet as one of the jugglers whispered to him to run for the cover of the wagon.

'No, no, it's all right. I'm all right now. I'll make myself vanish by standing perfectly still amongst the musicians. I'll be safe there.'

He knew Snatchpurse had sensed his presence in the chamber the night before when he had accidentally landed on his shadow. He had heard his curse, and he didn't want the cruel beast sensing him again – especially the moment the circus arrived. He had practised blending in often enough and he knew he could vanish into his surroundings, but this time he would have to rely on his tumbling skills to reach the musicians. Everything, but everything depended on him not being recognized.

Taking a deep breath, he sprang into the air at the very moment the quickfire vanished in puffs of sparks. His confidence and courage had returned and nobody noticed him work his way into the centre of the musicians just as Nevian brought the procession to a halt and stopped his wagon directly in front of Snatchpurse. Snatchpurse's cruel face split into a sneer of distaste as he approached the wizened old man sitting upon the high seat of the rickety circus wagon. He glanced up at the mass of brightly-coloured kites that hung, swaying as they rode high on the wet breeze above the ragged band of no-good gypsies and he dismissed them as nothing more than foolish toys. But he still had suspicions: he didn't trust this so-called circus.

'How dare you trespass here in the grounds of my tower without permission! How dare you distract and delay my army from its triumphant march on the Granite City with your miserable circus tricks. Your pretty lights don't impress me!'

'But please, great Lord Chancellor Snatchpurse. I beg you – please. Give us a moment's indulgence,' Nevian pleaded in a conciliatory voice. 'We are only poor circus folk following the greenway, we did not mean to trespass but as we have travelled we have heard so many stories of the wondrous things you have done to free the people of Elundium from the tyrannical reign of that wicked King Thanehand that we have hurried here as fast as we could to seek the privilege and the honour of entertaining you and your men. What you saw just now was but a meagre shadow of our real talents. Please give us the chance to perform properly. Let us travel with you and set up our circus tents wherever you stop to rest. We seek no reward but to please you. I promise you will not be disappointed.'

'Entertainment! You call that crude tomfoolery entertainment?' Snatchpurse threw back his head in mocking laughter. His men misunderstood his mirth and a roar of laughter went up from his army and shouts of encouragement erupted from the ranks as many voices called out to see more of the circus.

'Shut up you fools!' he hissed, suddenly serious, and

their laughter died away into an uncertain silence as they saw their master's eyes narrow and bright bubbles of spittle froth at the corners of his snarling mouth, a sure sign that he was in the worst of tempers.

All at once he tensed and grabbed at the frail old man's arm, shaking him violently. 'I don't hold with circuses, or the likes of the wandering, no-good gypsies who perform in them. And I will have none of them in my Elundium. Why I have a good mind to show you the sort of entertainment that I enjoy right now by slitting your throats one by one. Firstly, for wasting my valuable time and secondly, for not obtaining the proper authority to travel on the greenways. That, above all things, is a serious crime now that the Chancellors control the roads. Nobody travels without permission, do you understand?'

Drib and many of the warriors disguised as the Kindred Spirit were watching closely. They saw the murderous intent in Snatchpurse's eyes and watched the glint of the steel blade as his dagger was unsheathed and brought menacingly up towards Nevian's throat. The owls unhooked their talons ready to stoop whilst Grannog and the Border Runners crouched in the shadows beneath the carts, snarling silently as they made ready to leap out in Nevian's defence. All the warriors felt for the weapons they had concealed beneath their circus costumes. They knew they were helplessly outnumbered but would not see one drop of the magician's blood spilt needlessly. They would make these half-human creatures pay dearly for any harm that may befall him.

'But we do have written permission. It is stamped with the seal of authority to travel these greenways that you gave to Captain Unsnark, my Lord. Look, here it is, clearly written in his own hand.'

With so quick and deft a movement that few saw the magician's hand move, Nevian reached into his inner pocket and withdrew the parchment scroll, gravely offering it to Snatchpurse.

'Permission to travel ... har ... har ... har,' Squark shrieked. Snatchpurse scowled the magpie into silence as he muttered under his breath.

'How dare Unsnark be so free with my seal of authority. I'll flay him alive for such insolence.'

But the proffered parchment stayed the Chancellor's dagger hand and he hesitated before lowering the blade and seizing the scroll from the magician's hand.

'Authority to travel, indeed. I'll give Unsnark more than he bargained for when he cares to show his face around here again,' he hissed as he read each word carefully.

Nevian was quick to use the moment of indecision to his advantage. 'Captain Unsnark was so pleased with our humble circus and with our eagerness for our talents to serve your cause in whatever way we could, great Lord, that he gave us not only the authority to journey here but the permission to perform in every village we came upon along the greenway's edge. We have joyfully carried out his wishes to the letter, singing your praises for making the world a better place now that the Chancellors rule again. Wherever we have stopped people have joined us and now we are all eager to serve you.'

Snatchpurse stared hard with hooded, suspicious eyes, glaring at the old man in the cart. He screwed up the parchment, crumpling it into a tight ball before dropping it on the ground and trampling it beneath his feet. 'Your permission has been revoked!' he hissed through tight, thin lips.

He had known about this ragtail band of gypsies, thieves and vagabonds the lot of them, he had known about them from the moment they had wandered out of the woods on the westerly edge of Notley Marsh and set up their wretched circus upon the Causeway Fields in the shadow of the fortress of Underfall. Now that he had risen to power, nobody moved in Elundium without him knowing about it. Squark and the flocks of carrion birds made sure of that. Snatch had had his suspicions about this so-called circus – this Kindred Spirit as they called themselves – from the first moment they had appeared. There was something about them, something that didn't ring true, something he couldn't quite put his finger upon. He had instructed his roving patrols to search them thoroughly, looking specially for any sign of that wretched cripple boy or the owl that had scarred his face, but they had found nothing. The circus folk appeared to be exactly what they said they were. They didn't cheat or steal, they gave excellent entertainment and they didn't start any trouble. It all made him even more suspicious.

'You are nothing but a band of wandering gypsies!' he suddenly sneered, raising his dagger again. 'I don't have the time to waste on doubts about the likes of you. No, it is far better that I make an example of you and then my Honourable band of Murderers can march all the quicker for the killing. Elundium will be better off without your kind.'

'But, great Lord, we have hurried here to serve you,' Nevian cried, shrinking back.

A murmur of disquiet arose and spread through the ranks of Snatchpurse's men as he stepped forwards, intent on slitting the frail old man's throat. At any moment they expected him to call them forward to murder the rest of the circus. Many of them had enjoyed watching the Kind-red Spirit approach – the bright, fizzing arcs of light, the colourful costumes and all the joyful music – and they had been hoping that their master would let the circus stay with them as they marched.

Thorograsp felt the mood of their men and realized the stupidity of the senseless act their leader was about to commit – and for what? A moment of power. He reached out and, despite the risk to his life, he grabbed Snatch-purse's arm.

'Wait, Snatch, wait. Don't act too hastily, listen to me first.' He whispered softly so that no one else could hear.

Snatchpurse spun round, his face a mask of fury that anyone had dared to intervene and steal his moment of pure pleasure.

'Listen to me,' Thorograsp insisted, raising his voice a little. 'I know these circus folk are nothing better than wandering gypsies but we could use their loyal support. Think of the benefit they might be to us. They could entertain our men at the end of a long daylight's march, they could sing our praises to the people in all the villages we pass through, surely that would be of more use than making an example of them here?'

Much as Snatchpurse hated hearing Thorograsp's ad-vice something deep down inside him told him that his friend was right. 'But how do we know we can trust them?' he muttered sulkily as he resheathed his dagger.

'What harm can they possibly do to us? Look at them, they are only circus folk, they are all unarmed,' Thorograsp laughed, relieved that Snatchpurse had obviously decided to spare their lives. But would he allow them to follow their army?

Snatchpurse turned around slowly to stare at Nevian.

'And what do you play in the circus, old man?' he demanded. Somewhere in the back of his mind a forgotten memory had been stirred. He was sure he had seen him somewhere before, but he couldn't quite remember where.

'I am only a humble soothsayer, a teller of small fortunes, my Lord, nothing more.'

'So you are a fortune teller. Then tell me who is the most powerful man in all Elundium?'

'Why you will be, Lord Chancellor Snatchpurse, you will be when you have the King's crown upon your head.'

Snatchpurse suddenly laughed out loud and almost patted Nevian's arm in affection. 'That, my good fortune teller, is going to happen sooner than you think. Your circus may accompany us but keep well back out of our way and do not interfere with our advance. When we stop each night you may perform your tricks.'

Without another word Snatchpurse turned on his heel and strode away, impatient for the march to begin. His captains gave hurried orders to burn the tower and amidst a lot of noise and confusion, snarling and cursing, the massed ranks of the Honourable Company of Murderers, marching beneath their black banners, began to move forward slowly, tramping through the mud, filing out past the burning tower onto the greenway and heading in the direction of the Granite City. To the passing soldiers, the old man sitting on the driving seat of the circus wagon appeared to be half asleep, huddled in his tattered hessian cloak, his head bent against the drifting drizzle, but Nevian's hawk sharp eyes missed nothing. He counted every one of Snatchpurse's warriors, noting which ones had scaly, armoured skin and which had acquired the grotesque features that he had come to realize meant they were the host of the Eretch. He also noted which ones were ordinary village folk pressed into serving the Chancellors' cause. He counted their weapons and assessed their strength and once the last of them had vanished into the shrouds of mist that hung amongst the trees he signalled to the Kindred Spirit to follow.

Once he saw the wagon moving Drib jumped up to sit beside the magician at the first opportunity. 'That was a close shave. For a moment there we all thought that the ugly brute was going to slit your throat.'

Nevian laughed. 'You need not have worried. It will take more than that treacherous Chancellor's blade to put an end to me, Drib, but . . .'

The old man frowned and glanced anxiously around him as he grew very serious. 'But all of you must learn to tread more carefully if or when there is another confrontation. And I have no doubt that time will come. We need to be very circumspect if we are to free the King from Candlebane Hall.'

'More careful – but how? We all played our parts perfectly. Unless you mean when I . . .'

'No, no, you mastered that moment of fear quite well. It was after that, when Snatchpurse drew his dagger. Had he or any of those standing close by cared to watch you all they would have seen each one of you reaching for the weapons you have hidden inside your costumes. I will never know how they missed it. Think yourselves lucky this time but in future be on your guard!'

'But when we saw that monster threaten you, and knowing all the terrible things he has made Sloeberry endure, it made my blood boil. I so wanted to slash and stab at his vile, scaly skin, I wanted to tear his eyes out, put my hands around his throat and slowly strangle the life out of him. I think we all wanted to make him suffer, we all wanted to make him pay for what he has done!' Drib replied angrily, clenching his fists so tightly that his knuckles went white.

'Those are dangerous words, Drib, and they sound more likely to have spilled from Snatchpurse's mouth than your own. Be careful that your anger does not cause you to sink to the same level as the Company of Murderers. Remember, there can be nothing honourable in murder, it will be through law – through justice – that Snatchpurse will be held accountable for his crimes. He will have to pay for them soon enough.'

Drib looked away, struggling to control his fury. He knew that the magician was right about these sort of things, but he was sick of not being able to strike back, especially now that Sloeberry was so close. He knew that she was somewhere ahead of him, no more than a league away – maybe only half a league – trapped amongst those hideous creatures, being beaten and jostled along, unable to defend herself as the lash cut cruelly across her back. And he could do nothing to rescue her. Pulling his hood down against the worsening weather he sunk down into himself and listened to the creak of the wagon and the squelch of its wheels in the sodden ground and thought of Sloeberry as the hours passed. There was really nothing he could do but wait.

'Did you see her earlier today?' Nevian asked softly as the gloom of evening set in. He had sensed the pain and frustration, had felt the pent-up anger welling up inside Drib all day.

Drib nodded bleakly and told the old man how he had caught a glimpse of her being driven out of the tower by a tall, thin-faced creature, the same one who had been in charge of her on the night of the feast when he had travelled through the Eye of Arabra. He did not tell Nevian how he had watched as the sallow-faced creature had dragged her through the mud and all the time she was clutching the crumpled wayside flower that he had secretly brought back to life in that dreadful chamber the night before. The stem of the flower had been broken but still she shielded its fragile petals as best she could as she stumbled forward and struggled to stay on her feet. She had managed to glance quickly across towards the Kindred Spirit as the guards drove her forward and out of sight but the look of hope, the light that shone in her eyes, told him that she knew he was close by. Nevian, he was sure, would never know how much self-control it had taken at that moment not to call out her name. He would never understand how difficult it had been for him to stay perfectly still, hidden amongst the musicians rather than rush to the wagon and grab at one of the hidden swords. Every cell in his body wanted to cut a path through those vile brutes and free her.

'Have patience, Drib, have patience. The moment to free her is close at hand,' Nevian whispered.

'But how? She is surrounded by a solid ring of those creatures, we will never be able to get close to her.'

'Yes we will,' the old man insisted. 'But you must be brave, Drib. An opportunity is bound to arise when we get closer to the Granite City. Even these half-human creatures must rest and sleep some time. Watch them carefully and be ready, they're bound to stop soon before it gets too dark to see: they will make camp for the night and we will begin our circus performance. I want you to slip unseen amongst our enemies and search out those who have not been infected by the evil of the Eretch while we keep them occupied. I counted a number of ordinary village folk as they marched past us this morning who, by the miserable look on their faces, have been unwillingly pressed into serving the Chancellors. Go secretly amongst them and sow the whispers of freedom in their ears. Make them believe that they can be rid of the heavy yoke of the Chancellors' tyranny, but counsel caution, and warn them to await the signal before they cast the seeds of revolt. Let them know that the King, unlike the Chancellors, is a just and fair man who will forgive all those who dare to rally beneath his standard when it is unfurled before the doors of Candlebane Hall. Tell them that whatever they do they must await the signal.'

'But won't that be rather risky? What if I accidentally whisper to the wrong person and they go straight to Snatchpurse and reveal everything I said?'

Nevian thought for a moment and then shook his head. 'I think it highly unlikely you will choose unwisely. I have seen the way Snatchpurse behaves towards his men and there is little love lost there, and he appears to have little or no regard at all for the ordinary folk. They have simply been forced to serve his treacherous cause. I doubt if there are many among them who would dare to speak openly in his presence, especially about voices they think they might have heard in the dark, voices that whisper about rising up against him. They will be in too much fear of having their throats slit on the spot. But that doesn't mean you are to be careless. Choose carefully who you whisper to and remember there is quite a difference between subtle suggestion and blurting out everything I have just said. Use your head, boy, listen for disgruntled voices and if I am not mistaken you will hear plenty of them. Plant the idea of revolt in their minds, suggest what they might do when the right moment comes, but go gently amongst them, because they are living in daily fear of being punished for their innermost thoughts. Whisper to them the way you did at Underfall when Unsnark grew suspicious about the existence of the road I told him we had used to reach the Causeway Fields. Remember how you moved through the guards whispering softly in their ears, stirring them with promises of freedom from the Chancellors' tyranny if only they would say that they knew of the road. It worked then didn't it?'

Drib nodded slowly, although he wasn't at all sure he could do it again. Nevian was asking him to suggest a lot more this time.

'And use your imagination while you are in the heart of the encampment, use your eyes and ears to find out . . .' Nevian stopped abruptly and frowned. There was something ahead of them, black, indistinct shapes were looming out of the gloom blocking the greenway.

'Look sharp, Drib, make yourself scarce. The Honourable Company of Murderers has finally made camp.'

Nevian took hold of the reins and drove the wagon in under the trees at the edge of the road. Drib whispered the words to make himself invisible and slipped soundlessly out of sight before the wagon came to a halt. He pulled the hood of his warm, waterproof cloak down over his head and slipped out into the rainy darkness, leaving the music and noise, the laughter and dancing lights of the circus behind him as he passed unseen and unchallenged into the heart of their enemy's camp. Slowly and cautiously he began to work his way through the hundreds of crude shelters that they had erected hastily to keep themselves out of the worst of the weather, pausing for a moment beneath each leaking sack roof he crouched under, listening to the men who were huddled together. He smiled to himself as he realized how right the magician had been about them as he heard them muttering and cursing in their furtive, grumbling voices, complaining about the wretched conditions they were forced to endure as they tried to keep the smouldering fires of wet wood they had gathered alight and heat the meagre portions of evil smelling broth that they had been issued with. Drib chose his words well and sowed the smoky darkness with whispers of promises for the future, and the beginnings of a revolt.

'What was that? What did you say about the King?' one of them hissed to the fellow sitting next to him, his eyes watering from the smoke of the fire he was sitting over as Drib finished whispering between them and began moving silently backwards towards the opening.

'I didn't say anything, but I thought I heard you say that you think the King would forgive us.'

'That's odd, I swear that it's almost exactly what I thought you said just now.'

They glanced anxiously around them, lowering their voices and whispering to each other.

'I don't know who is putting these ideas into our heads but I wish they were true. I'm sick to death of these Chancellors.'

'Well I don't know if the King will ever forgive us but I'll tell you one thing for sure: I'm willing to take the chance and throw myself at his mercy if the opportunity ever arises.'

'Well I'm with you on that, but keep it to yourself, you never know who is out there listening to us, spying on us in the dark.'

Late in the night Drib finally reached the furthest edge

of the vast encampment. He was worried that he had not caught even a glimpse of Sloeberry and he chose to take a different way back in the hope of coming across where they were keeping her. It wasn't long before he arrived at a large pavilion made from strong, weatherproof canvas. There were lamps alight inside and heavily armed guards patrolled in front of its entrance flap. From the raised voices he could hear, he realized that it must be Snatch-purse's tent – he was cursing and snarling at somebody. Drib crept closer, moving around to the back of the tent, intent upon gathering as much information as he could for Nevian, when he almost blundered into one of Sloeberry's guards who cursed and stared wildly around him when Drib trod on his shadow. A stake had been driven into the ground and Sloeberry was chained to it, left to suffer without any protection at all from the weather. The ground around her had been trampled into a sea of mud and then smoothed out so that the footprints of anyone attempting to approach her could be seen in the light of a dozen, tar-dipped, reed torches that hissed and spluttered in the rain. A circle of guards stood, statue-still, watching her constantly, and just inside this circle, sheltering beneath a piece of hessian sacking, was the tall, thin creature who had driven her out of the tower at Stumble Hill.

Drib felt his anger rising and it took all his self control not to rush forwards and attack her guards, especially the one who he had seen beat her. He stood, calmed his pounding heart and moved forward. He went as close as he dared, edging forward between the towering monsters until the tips of his toes where on the edge of the smoothed circle of mud.

'Sloeberry, Sloeberry,' he whispered. 'Sloeberry, it's me,

Drib. Don't move, don't let your guards know I am here, just blink your eyes if you can hear me.'

Sloeberry was huddled on the ground and didn't move a muscle except to shiver and tremble from the rain that was soaking through her rags and freezing her body.

'Sloeberry,' he whispered again as loudly as he dared, willing her with all his heart to hear him.

Slowly her head rose a fraction and her long eyelashes fluttered. She had heard him. She was searching amongst her guards, looking for where the sound of his voice could have come from.

'Be still, my love, don't move, you won't be able to see me no matter how hard you look but I am here, I'm really here and I am going to rescue you soon . . .'

Suddenly he realized he had said too much. The guards on either side of where she was standing had become restless. They snarled and growled, turning from side to side to see what had disturbed them, to find where the unfamiliar sound had come from on such a night. Drib stepped back quickly out of their way and ducked down as their spears stabbed the air above his head. He stayed low and crawled to the back of Snatchpurse's tent. There was nothing he could do; with all his magic there was nothing he could possibly do to help her that wouldn't alert those monsters to his presence. He was about to slip away when he saw something very strange happen. The creature who seemed to be Sloeberry's gaoler emerged from his shelter and spoke urgently to the guards, warning them that their master would not look too kindly on them if she died of exposure during the night. He then dragged his shelter through the mud and positioned it to keep the worst of the weather off her before retreating to the outer edge of the circle.

Drib moved slowly along the back of the tent when he heard Snatchpurse's raised voice coming from inside as he talked to his captain. He stopped and heard him say, 'Squark has brought me news of that wayhouse at Woodsedge. He has warned me that a small company of those miserable Marchers have barricaded the greenway against us.'

'We'll slaughter them all. We will burn their wayhouse to the ground.' Drib heard Thorograsp laugh as they began planning their assault on Woodsedge, delighting in the mayhem they would cause when they caught the Marchers by surprise. Armed with this disturbing news, Drib hurried back to Nevian.

'We can't allow them to massacre Woodsedge. We just can't allow it to happen. Somehow we have to get there and warn them.'

'Those Marchers would do better to hurry with all speed to the Granite City, we will have to get word to them.'

'Somebody could ride ahead, couldn't they? Somebody could warn the Marchers. I know it's late and there are only a few hours until dawn but if they left now and rode hard – they would have to hide during the daylight hours of course but surely . . .'

'No, no, it's impossible,' Nevian interrupted brusquely. 'The swiftest horses and the best riders have already ridden to warn Berioss and Kyot, they are already raising the alarm throughout Elundium. There is nobody left for such a journey.'

'But Sparkfire could do it, he is one of the nighthorses . . . or Equestrius . . . surely the Lord of Warhorses would have the heart and courage for such a journey?'

'They would be able to do it, but who would pull the wagon in their place? Neither of them could do it on their

277

own, it's too heavy, especially now the ground is so wet. Remember that Snatchpurse's men are suspicious enough about us, they're sure to smell a rat if one of the horses suddenly disappears.'

Nevian paused for a moment. 'Of course, there is a horse who could easily cover such a distance.'

'But who, who is there?'

'I have caught an occasional glimpse of Esteron, the King's horse, keeping pace with us in the forest. He must have escaped from the Granite City before Candlebane Hall became siege-locked. But Esteron is a Warhorse and has only ever allowed the King on his back. There is nobody in the Kindred Spirit who could ride him, even if we could bring him close enough. Now let me think for a moment.'

'I once rode upon Esteron's back,' Drib suggested in a small voice. 'The King found me lying in the gutter after the boys had beaten me in the Learning Hall, he sat me on Esteron and I rode him to the end of the lane and back. Perhaps he would let me ride him again if he knew how important it was. I've still got that special saddle that Flock made for me at Cawdor so that despite my crooked legs I could always ride Sparkfire – and it would fit Esteron I think.'

Nevian looked across at the boy, seeing him in the feeble light of the single lamp that he had left burning to guide him back from the encampment, and he smiled. Drib, for all his disability, lacked nothing in courage. But why, the old man wondered, was he offering to ride to Woodsedge rather than stay here close to Sloeberry? Surely he would rather be watching, waiting for that golden opportunity to rescue her. There was something odd here, something Drib wasn't telling him. Drib felt the magician's eyes boring into him and he tried to look away, but found that he couldn't.

'The truth, Drib, what is it you are trying to hide? Out with it now.'

Nevian saw tears fill Drib's eyes. 'If I stay here much longer I am bound to give us away. I won't be able to help myself. I can't bear seeing Sloeberry chained up and so cruelly beaten. I can't stand by and do nothing any longer, I just can't. All the time I was in the camp sowing the idea of revolt, I was really looking for Sloeberry. I know I promised not to do anything foolish but I found her and I tried to speak to her. The guards nearly caught me. Another time I might not be able to get away and I will be putting all our lives at risk. I know I will let you down and I don't want to, but I can't help myself.'

Nevian reached out and comforted Drib. 'You have never let me down, Drib, and you will never do that; I know you better than you know yourself. You will ride to Woodsedge on Esteron if he will permit it and you will tell Marcher Tombel, and any other loyal kingsman you meet upon the road, to make their way with all speed to Candlebane Hall.'

Drib blinked away his tears as Nevian rose and called out softly into the darkness, sending Orundus and Silkstone into the forest to search for Esteron.

'Keep watch over Sloeberry for me. It breaks my heart to go but I know I must.'

'No harm will come to her, Drib, no harm that I can prevent, you have my promise,' the old man answered as he threw open a secret compartment in the floor of the wagon.

'Isn't that my helm and my riding clothes? That's what I was wearing when Umm brought me to the Runesgate Tower. I didn't know you had hidden them here!'

Drib picked up his knee-length riding boots and his soft, leather breeches and looked over them in amazement. Outside he heard Silkstone hoot and then the squelch and splash of a horse approaching across the muddy ground.

'There is much you don't know, my boy. Indeed there are all manner of things stowed away in this wagon, things you would never know about, things that may just come in useful one day – here, catch, you might need it on the road.' Nevian threw his sword to him, laughing. 'Now go quickly, get dressed, you have a long, hard ride ahead of you.'

The magician's face had turned serious as he opened the flap of the wagon and climbed down stiffly, carrying Drib's saddle and bridle. In moments Drib was dressed and ready for the road and he jumped out to find Esteron tacked and waiting.

'This is a great honour,' Drib began, running his hand across the horse's powerful shoulder but Esteron snorted and brushed his muzzle across the boy's cheek impatiently. He had not forgotten the small, ragged boy who had once spent a moment on his back and, in thanks, had given him a fragment of sugar crystal.

'There is no time for idle chatter, Drib. You must reach Woodsedge ahead of this Company of Murderers so you had better get going. Here, put this dispatch for Tombel somewhere safe inside your jerkin. And here is a proclamation for any loyal Kingsman to read, it has my mark upon it should they doubt your word, it urges them to make all speed to Candlebane Hall. Silkstone will be with you, he will be your eyes in the dark. Now ride on a loose rein, leave the finding of the way to Esteron. Go, ride faster than the wind and keep an eye open for those evil birds, Snatchpurse must not know you have ridden ahead.'

Esteron arched his neck and with flared nostrils he pirouetted and strode away towards a gap in the trees. Before Drib had a moment to call out they were in the forest, cantering hard through the dead, dark hours of the night, heading towards the first, faint glimmer of dawn.

X

Candlebane Hall

NEVIAN SHIVERED and pulled his cloak tighter around his frail shoulders in an effort to keep the foul weather out but still it numbed his bones. He peered ahead from the high seat of the wagon as it bumped and lurched slowly forward over the deeply rutted, muddy ground before finally breasting the top of the last of the rolling hills and began the long descent towards the Granite City. Somewhere not far ahead of them, hidden by the shifting curtain of mist and rain that blew across the greenway, lay journey's end, but it brought little comfort to the old man as dawn broke around their slow procession and cast its bleary, grey light across the ruin and devastation that lay on either side of the greenway in the wake of Snatchpurse's advance. Nevian feared that they would arrive too late and find defeat staring them in the face.

A knot of anxiety had been growing, tightening in his stomach, since the middle of the second daylight after Drib had ridden ahead on Esteron. There had been a sudden commotion amongst the flocks of carrion birds who constantly patrolled the countryside far and wide. The air above Snatchpurse had darkened with their shrieking cries and he had immediately increased the pace of the advance. He had doubled the men pulling the siege engines and battering rams and had refused all pleas to stop and rest. He had driven them hard beneath the sharp cutting edge of the lash, marching them late into each night, and forcing them onto the road again before dawn broke. Nevian had feared that Drib might have been spotted by the birds and that Snatchpurse now knew both who he was and the purpose of his desperate ride. But as the day wore on he realized that if that had been the case Snatchpurse would have butchered the Kindred Spirit immediately, and yet he had taken no more notice of them than to curse them as a band of no-good wastrels. True he had cancelled all future performances on the road, but he had promised his men that they would be entertained when the Chancellors' black pennant flew from the spire above Candlebane Hall.

Nevian sat alone late into the grey hours worrying what news the carrion birds had brought to Snatchpurse. What had they seen that had made him drive his army forward at such a breakneck pace, hurrying them towards the Granite City? How Nevian missed the daylights of his real magic when, with a mere snap of his fingers and the quick turn of his head, he could have seen and heard everything that moved the threads of destiny. How he regretted the fading of his talent and the blind, stumbling ignorance with the constant worrying that his present circumstances forced him to endure. Privately he had sent word through the Kindred Spirit telling them to drop back a little further behind the last of the siege engines that were being dragged along the greenway ploughing deep, muddy ruts into the wet ground. He had cautioned each warrior to keep well out of Snatchpurse's way, to arm themselves but to keep their weapons hidden beneath their circus clothes as they drew closer to Woodsedge.

Nevian breathed a silent sigh of relief when they reached the remnants of the barricades that had been erected to block the advance of Snatchpurse's army. They had been torn up and trampled into the mud but he could see no evidence that the barricades had ever been manned or had stood the force of a battle. The wayhouse at Woodsedge stood empty and derelict, its doors and windows smashed and the area was totally deserted of any sign of life. Nevian realized that Drib must have reached the Marchers in time to warn them, but what, the magician worried, had happened to the boy since then? He had been expecting him to return immediately but the previous night had been his last chance to slip unnoticed back into the company of the Kindred Spirit under cover of darkness. They would soon be reaching the gates of the city and still he had not reappeared. Nevian urgently needed Drib with him to report news of Marcher Tombel and he needed to know how many loyal kingsmen he had managed to rally, but more importantly he needed his ability to become invisible. He wanted to find out all about Snatchpurse's plans and how he intended to assault Candlebane Hall. Without Drib they would all just be guessing in the dark.

The old man's worries were suddenly interrupted as the wagon jolted and slewed sideways. He had to grab at the seat to prevent himself from being thrown off the wagon as it veered towards the crumbling edge of the drainage ditch that rang along beside the road and one of the rear wheels slipped into a deep rut. The horses snorted and tossed their heads as Nevian cried out. They threw their weight against the harness and managed to stop the wagon sliding but it rocked violently before it lurched forwards and the wheel tore free of the muddy rut. Nevian had barely settled himself on the seat again and picked up the reins when the wet, shifting mist that had descended to shroud the dreary landscape drifted apart and the new-found shaft of sunlight briefly revealed the city. Nevian gave a cry of dismay as he hauled on the reins and called out to the company, bringing them all to an abrupt halt.

A stone's throw ahead of them lay the grey, granite walls and beyond them he could see the soaring spires and the thousands of steep, weather-bleached roofs of the city that rose sheer and imposing out of the mist. They were much closer to journey's end than he had realized. With hurrying footsteps, their swords drawn, the Kindred Spirit crowded around the wagon, and all voices were demanding of Nevian what they should do next. The old man slowly stood up and looked about him.

'That's odd,' he murmured, peering ahead, his head slightly tilted to one side as he listened and looked through the great, gloomy archway of the Stumble Gate that stood open and unguarded. 'Hush, all of you. Now look and tell me what you see – and listen, what do you hear?'

For a long moment the company stood utterly silent.

'Why, there is nothing to see save the walls of the city,' one voice piped up. 'And I can hear nothing but the hiss and roar of the rainwater as it pours out of the swollen gutters and runs into the culverts to empty into the great ditch. The city is silent except for the sounds of this foul weather. And worse, we are all alone out here. What has happened to all those loyal kingsmen who were supposed to be flocking towards the city? Are we the only ones here? I don't like it.'

Nevian nodded grimly. 'Nor do I. The silence is wrong, I would almost prefer to hear the roar and snarls of Snatch-purse's army or the thunder of the siege engines as they battered against the walls of Candlebane Hall. I expected to hear the slow drag and creak of those engines, the thumping of the battering rams and the scraping of the ladders as they were being hauled up through the narrow, winding, cobbled streets of the city: I did not expect this unnerving silence. It is as though the battle were finished before it had time to begin. This silence baffles me.'

'Snatchpurse must have driven his men faster than we realized,' one of the tumblers replied. 'They must have forged ahead once we lost sight of them in the drifting mists during the night. We have arrived too late, the siege is over and the King and all those still loyal to him must be lying dead amongst the rubble of Candlebane Hall.'

'Why don't we release the owls from their disguises?' an impatient clown called out, reaching beneath his cloak to unsheath a dagger. 'Kites are no good to us now and they could fly over the city and tell us what is happening.'

Nevian tilted his head back and looked up through the crowded roofs that from where he sat seemed to climb on top of one another, forming precipitous cliffs of slippery tiles topped with tall, blackened chimney pots. He looked around to the sheer walls and then the spires of Candlebane Hall that crowned the highest circle of the city and then he smiled as he shook his head.

'No, we must do nothing hasty. We might squander our element of surprise. What may have happened to the Chancellors' murderous mob is, as yet, a mystery but one thing I can tell you is that the King is not dead. I know that for certain. And I know one other thing, he is not yet defeated. The siege is far from over. Look, raise your eyes, the emblem of the owl in blue upon a field of gold still flies above Candlebane Hall. All is not yet lost.'

'But what are we to do now?'

'Do whatever it is you do as the Kindred Spirit. Surely there is only one thing left to be done after journeying so far,' Nevian laughed as he gathered up the reins and prepared to drive the wagon through the Stumble Gate. 'We must hurry with all speed and travel up through the streets of the city. The circus has one last great performance and we will act it out before the doors of Candlebane Hall. Musicians play, acrobats tumble and jump, clowns begin your mummery. Let the joyous sounds of the Kindred Spirit draw out the city folk so that they may witness the Chancellors' defeat and the triumphant return of King Thane!'

The drums rolled slowly, the cymbals crashed and the whistles, pipes and fiddles joined to swell the rousing march as the Kindred Spirit passed beneath the shadowy archway of the Stumble Gate and began their long, winding climb up through the narrow streets of the city.

Change, it was always said, was for the worst, and the majority of the city folk, unsure about many of King Thane's sweeping changes and dubious that those changes would have the ability to improve their lives, had been easily beguiled by the sweet lies and false promises of better times under the Chancellors. All they had to do, they were told, was to depose the Thronestealer and then the rightful rulers of the kingdom could be reinstated. Those lies and falsehoods had fuelled revolt but the people had quickly learned what stupid fools they had been once the Honourable Company of Murderers had seized power. They had seige-locked the King in Candlebane Hall and the people walked in fear of their lives. They had to keep well-hidden, crouching in the shadows lest they catch the eye of their oppressors, and few of them had bothered to watch the engines of the King's final destruction as they were dragged past their houses and up into the higher circles of the city. The cursing shouts and the whistles of the cracking flails that drove the men forward were enough to make even the bravest city man creep away and slink back out of sight.

But suddenly there was a different sound in the streets. They could hear joyful bursts of music, shouts and laughter, clowns and tumblers, and when they looked out they saw tall, angular men on stilts who rapped on their shutters and tapped on their doors, beckoning them out into the streets. No one had heard such sounds for so long that curiosity began to get the better of them and doors and windows were silently opened a crack as startled faces peered out to look at the brightly coloured circus procession making its way past. Word was quickly passed from house to house and people were slowly drawn out. One by one they began to fill the streets and the crowds rapidly swelled as they followed the circus up towards Candlebane Hall.

The closer Snatchpurse came to the city the more he was haunted by black doubt. He found himself filled with a nagging worry that those warriors who had attacked his men in the grasslands must have rallied all the ragged peasants – the nobodies and the beggars that they had foolishly left alive when they had burned and looted their villages on their triumphant advance across Elundium. Somehow, he feared, they had got ahead of him and broken the siege to free the Thronestealer. His nightmares told him that the city was already held against him, its walls and battlements bristling with spearmen and Archers.

'We should have killed every one of those kinglovers

– we should have cut their throats while we had the chance. We should have made sure that the King would never have any allies, not a single one.'

Despite the constant assurances of his most trusted captains that there were not enough loyal kingsmen left in all Elundium to defend even the doors of Candlebane Hall, let alone break the siege, he still was fuelled by doubts. Even the daily reports brought in by the carrion birds telling him that all the roads leading towards the Granite City were empty did little to allay his fears. The spectre of defeat was waiting, biding its time, ready to strike. He knew it was there in the shadows and black news did, indeed, arrive long before they reached Woodsedge, heralding an altogether unexpected disaster.

The carrion birds had spotted Ironpurse, Snatchpurse's father, and all the other old, disgraced Chancellors on the greenway hurrying in the direction of the Granite City. These were the same Chancellors who had brought disgrace and humiliation upon their families for being caught treacherously letting the Nightbeasts into the city when they had attacked during the last, glorious daylights of King Holbian's reign. These were the same spineless Chancellors who had compounded their crimes by fleeing with anything of value they could lay their hands upon instead of using the art of cunning and the deception of good government to turn the situation to their advantage. Snatchpurse had never forgiven them for that and as far as he was concerned they had lost the right to call themselves Chancellors from the moment they had fled in disgrace. Yet now it appeared that as soon as word had reached them of his triumphant advance into the city they were hurrying to sieze the prize he had worked so hard to achieve.

'They shall have none of my glory!' he had seethed, sending his carrion birds to spy on their every movement and driving his men on even harder to ensure that they would arrive in the city first.

Girrolt was waiting in the flickering light of the lamps of the Stumble Gate, anxious to greet Snatchpurse the moment he and their army reached the city, weary and soaked through from the long nights of forced marching. He greeted them with the dire news that Ironpurse and the grand council of their fathers had reached the gates ahead of them, just before darkness fell. They had stripped all Snatchpurse's men of their rank and they had gone straight to the Learning Hall, letting it be known that they were the rightful rulers of Elundium and that they were taking command of the siege.

'You . . . you . . . you let those spineless weaklings dare to challenge my authority? You just stood there and let them seize command? You did nothing . . . nothing to stop them?' Snatchpurse raged, his lips thinning and his eyes narrowing into murderous slits as he grabbed at Girrolt's neck with a clawed hand.

'We . . . we . . . I could do nothing. My own father was amongst them. They were all so forceful, they were dressed in their ancient robes of office and they demanded that we acknowledged their hereditary right as the Chancellors of Elundium. They issued orders to everybody.'

But Snatchpurse was deaf to his arguments and pushed him roughly aside. 'I'll teach them all about hereditary rights. I'll show them who has the authority to rule. The only argument they'll hear from me is the cutting edge of my dagger drawn across their treacherous throats for daring to try and steal what is rightfully mine. Come on, Thorograsp, Kush, Girrolt, Huxort, Uxort, come on all of you, bring your most ruthless men – no, bring *everybody* with you and follow me. The Honourable Company of Murderers has a small matter to settle in the Learning Hall. Come with your daggers drawn – we have old scores to settle before we kill the Thronestealer.'

'But what about the seige? Some of those loyal kingsmen might reach the Candlehall while we are in the Learning Hall. Surely we shouldn't leave all those siege engines and battering rams lying unattended beside the ladders in front of the gates of the city? Anybody might steal them. Don't forget that those performing gypsies are right behind us on the road.' Thorograsp was reluctant to follow Snatchpurse into the Learning Hall. He didn't have much respect for his father or for the way all their fathers had brought dishonour and exile down on them but he didn't want to have a hand in their murder. He knew he could not dissuade Snatchpurse from such a bloody act and he didn't have the courage to openly oppose him, but he felt if he could just be somewhere else while it took place he could live with his conscience.

Snatchpurse threw back his head and laughed. It was a cruel and pitiless sound. 'You worry yourself over trifles, Thorograsp. We are within sight of victory. Those ragtail circus folk can do us no harm, and, rest assured, the carrion birds have not reported any sight of a single kingsman within ten leagues of this city. There is nothing out there save some gnarled, old trees and miles of empty roads. But to stop you worrying I shall have all our engines of war dragged up and positioned ready for the final assault on Candlebane Hall. There will be no need to guard these gates so the rest of you can come with me.'

Without further argument Snatchpurse turned on his heel and strode into the city. But on reaching the bottom of the steps which led up to the Learning Hall Snatchpurse stopped and stepped back into the shadows. The steps were heavily guarded by men dressed in the uniforms of the Chancellors' guard, uniforms that belonged to the times when their fathers had ruled Elundium.

Girrolt slipped into the shadows beside Snatch and whispered, 'Those are not our men, they arrived last night with our fathers. They search everyone seeking an audience with the Chancellors. I think it is because they fear your arrival.'

'Do they indeed,' Snatchpurse muttered. The ghost of a smile thinned his lips. 'Well there is more than one way into that place. Let us see if we can't give our benevolent fathers a little surprise.'

Dividing his men, and leaving enough of them to overpower the guards when he gave the word from within the Learning Hall, he took the others and kept them to the shadows, slipping quietly into Blackbone Alley that ran along the back of the Learning Hall and leading them to a little-used scullery door. Putting a finger to his scaly lips he motioned to those who crowded behind him to proceed silently.

'Remember, anyone wearing the uniform of the Chancellors' guard is a traitor. Kill them swiftly and silently: do not leave a single one of them alive.'

Lifting the rusty latch he let the scullery door creak and swing open, beckoning his men to stay close behind him. He unsheathed his dagger and wet the blade with his tongue, tasting and savouring the dry, congealed blood that spotted it. 'Now let us show our fathers who the true rulers of Elundium are,' he sneered as he moved soundlessly through the warren of darkened rooms and cubby holes at the back of the hall and stepping carefully over the bodies of the majority of their father's guard who were sleeping wrapped in their cloaks after their long, exhausting journey from the Meremire Forest.

Loremaster Grout had never liked Sweepscuttle, the evil-smelling Master Chimney Sweep who had found himself a position of prominence the moment the King was siege-locked in the Candlehall and at that moment he was quite happy to lay the blame at Sweepscuttle's feet to save his own skin but the Grand Council would have none of it. They were threatening to deal with the Sweep the moment they had finished with him. It wasn't his part in deposing the King they were finding fault with, they wanted the King dead as much, if not more, than he did, it was the way their sons had set about achieving it that he was being held culpable for.

'I ... I ... I really did my best, great Lords,' Grout stuttered. 'I tried hard to teach your children the ways of government. I toiled tirelessly to make them understand all the cunning and deception it would take, all the trick-ery of politics, but they would not listen. They were all for seizing power through mayhem and murder. I tried to stop them. I tried urging caution and told them of the more subtle ways of bringing about the King's demise but they threatened to show King Thane those letters I wrote to you just after the Battle of the Rising where I offered to help you to overthrow the King. I had no other choice but to help them in any way I could, you must understand that.'

'How can you expect us to believe that, you lying crea-ture,' Chancellor Grasp shouted, half-rising from his chair in his anger. 'We know you have been responsible from the very beginning, putting ideas into their heads. Where, if not here, would they have seized on the thought that there could be any good, any honour, in cold-blooded murder? Where, if not here in the Learning Hall, would they have heard such an idea? Whose lips but yours would have voiced it? Judicial hanging following the letter of the law, to take a life in the benefit of profit is good government. Greed and envy both have their place in law. But this wholesale slaughter that they have indulged in cannot be right. It is you, Grout, we hold accountable for turning our sons into these monsters that they have become. Why we have even received reports that their physical appearances have changed and . . .'

A harsh cackle of laughter erupted from beneath the low archway. 'So you would dare to steal what others have made available.'

Snatchpurse, followed reluctantly by all the original conspirators of the Honourable Company of Murderers strode into the hall and headed directly towards his father's chair. Grasp stared open-mouthed in horror at his son: he barely recognized him and saw only the monster he had become. His face was all covered in scales and the top of his head had been disfigured by a bony ridge of vicious spines. Ironpurse rose to his feet as he saw his son coming for him with dagger in hand. Only a moment before he had been so self-assured, but now his face was blanched a deathly white and his mouth seemed to be soundlessly begging for mercy.

'Guards! Quickly, guards, help me, we are under attack. Help!' At last he managed to cry out, lifting his fists in a futile attempt to protect himself as Snatchpurse towered over him.

Sneering down at his father he gave the signal and

those of his men who had hidden themselves in the shadows outside the Learning Hall attacked the guards. There was a muffled commotion on the steps beyond the closed doors of the hall. They could hear shouts and screams and the brief clash of steel but then nothing save the rush and gurgle of rainwater emptying out of the gutter spouts and the frightened, rasping breaths of the grand council as their sons approached.

Ironpurse gave a cry of pain as Snatchpurse roughly prodded him with his blade. Its needle-sharp point pierced the rich weave of his ceremonial robe and pricked his skin, making him gasp as he shrank back, trapped in his chair.

'Call yourselves Chancellors, proud men – the rightful rulers of Elundium? You are nothing but weak fools, scavenging thieves who do not deserve to creep on your bellies in the shadow of my triumph. To think you had the audacity to walk in here and try to seize my power.'

As he raised the blade towards his father's throat his face hardened with contempt. 'You shall have nothing, you deserve nothing.'

'But ... but ... surely you see the sense in using our knowledge and all our experience. That is why we hurried to the city. We were not trying to steal anything from you, we are here to help you to restore proper order ...' Grasp began, only to fall silent and cower away as Snatchpurse glared at him, his face darkening with rage.

'You dare to try and silvertongue me? If it was not for what we have done you would still be hiding in exile. We don't need your help. Thorograsp, slit his throat. All of you, silence them immediately. Put an end to this Council of Chancellors.'

Thorograsp took a step towards his father and hesitated.

'What are you all waiting for? Do I have to do everything myself?' Snatchpurse snarled, turning towards Grasp, but before he could raise his dagger Thorograsp grabbed his arm.

'No! I have had enough of all this senseless killing. Elundium is ours, we don't need . . .'

His words were cut off by Snatchpurse's blade as he jerked it upwards, shearing through his armoured hide and piercing his heart. Thorograsp shuddered, his eyes full of pain as the Eretch who had dwelt inside him oozed out through the pores of his skin. His scaly, armoured hide lost its vivid indigo colour, turning a dull shade of grey as he fell towards the floor.

'Run, father, run for your life.'

He crumpled to his knees and the spines and ridges of Nightbeast armour that had infused into his skin to protect him began to peel off and flake away. In the moment of confusion the old Chancellors fled, shedding their robes as they ran for the doors. Snatchpurse stood in the centre of the hall shouting and cursing, stabbing wildly into thin air until he brought them all to order. Anxious eyes were turned towards him as the rush of their fathers' footsteps faded down the empty corridors. Their fear made them shuffle backwards as they expected his rage to be turned against them for disobeying him, but instead he unexpectedly threw back his head and howled with laughter.

'Let them go, let them go. They will not get very far. There is nowhere for them to hide now that we rule Elundium.'

Turning, he bent his bloody blade to sever the thongs binding Grout's wrists and hauled the Loremaster to his feet. 'You weren't on the point of betraying us just a moment ago, were you, Grout?'

'No, oh no my great Lord. Betray you? I was trying to tell the grand council that I was not clever enough to have thought up the idea of forming the Honourable Company of Murderers and that all I have ever done was to help you win back what was stolen from you. As the Loremaster it is my duty to record the true history and Lore of Elundium and report it as it happens.'

Snatchpurse looked coldly at Grout. His men's disobedience had left a sour taste in his mouth. He would deal with them all at a later date, but he needed some satisfaction; Thorograsp's death was not nearly enough. He had intended to kill Grout just to make an example of him but he hesitated, his lips thinning into a calculating smile.

'You, Grout, shall be rewarded for your loyalty. You shall stand beside me at my right hand as we break the siege. You shall be in clear view of everybody so that you can write down the true account of our glorious victory.'

Snatchpurse glanced up at the tall, rain-streaked window as a shaft of sunlight broke through the clouds. 'Look, even the weather turns to our advantage. Come, Loremaster, bring parchment and quill and let us hurry up to Candlebane Hall. It is time to break the siege and set the Thronestealer's head upon a spike.'

The rain suddenly slowed and the clouds began to break apart; shafts of bright sunlight burst through the gloom and cast strong shadows of the hurrying circus procession across the wet cobbles as they passed noisily through the high, stone archway of the upper circle of the city. Ahead of them the centre of the square was crowded with the siege engines and battering rams that they had been following along the greenway. Now they were drawn up in lines, ready for the final assault on Candlebane Hall that stood at the far end of the tree-lined square bathed in sunlight.

'The weather breaks to our advantage,' Nevian began, only to frown as the circus procession slowed and bunched uncertainly together. Their music faltered as anxious eyes searched the broken doorways and windows of the merchants' houses surrounding the square. They looked at the mounds of rubble and the piles of debris that reflected a long and bitter siege, searching for the sight of the loyal kingsmen they had hoped would rally to the King. But there were none. The square was crowded with the men who had been forced to pull the war engines and they were resting wherever they could find a place to squat or sit. They were too weary to do more than glance up as the circus approached.

'What shall we do now? There are too few of us to stand and fight, and the doors of Candlebane Hall are locked against us.'

There were many voices in the Kindred Spirit whispering together in alarm as they gathered around the wagon. Nevian half-rose from his seat as perplexed as the rest of them as he, too, quickly searched the square. He had hoped all along that either Berioss or Tombel, both seasoned warriors, would have reached the city ahead of them strengthened by all those still loyal to King Thane and at least have fortified the upper circle. That hope faded as they drew closer to the city but now they faced a different and baffling dilemma. He had expected to be stopped at every turn on their journey up from the Stumble Gate and yet they had proceeded unchallenged. He had expected to find Candlebane Hall under attack and yet the siege engines stood silent. Snatchpurse and his evil monsters were nowhere to be seen. What, he wondered, were they up to now?

The men resting in the square were beginning to stare suspiciously at them. He knew they must do something quickly. 'We must try and cross the square, we must get as close as we can to the doors of Candlebane Hall.'

'What's the point in that?' muttered a warrior standing close to the wagon. 'Any fool can see that those siege engines have been positioned so close to it that they will destroy it in moments and then we'll be directly in the line of fire.'

Nevian glanced at the rows of war machines and laughed as a plan began to form. He leaned forwards and whispered, 'Remember, we still hold the element of surprise. Those men still believe we are circus folk. We must use our disguise to disable those engines of war as we cross the square and at the same time we will alert those inside the hall with our music of freedom and let them know we are here. Musicians, upon my signal you must play your most rousing tune and as we pass by those infernal machines you must use your concealed weapons to cut their ropes, jam their cogs and render them entirely useless. Now move forwards all of you and we will make this our greatest performance. We will reform before the doors of Candlebane Hall ready to make our last, defiant stand. Forward! The Kindred Spirit moves on!'

With a sudden joyful burst of music the circus surged ahead between the rows of machines. The foolery and antics of the clowns, the high somersaults and leaps of the acrobats, the daring juggling acts and the roar of the flames pouring out of the fire-eaters mouths caused such a stir amongst Snatchpurse's weary men that they roused themselves, cheering and laughing, calling for encores. They were so easily distracted by the colour and pageantry, the magic of the circus, that they were blind to the true purpose of the Kindred Spirit as they slowly and methodically wove their way through the long lines of siege engines. Umm, the seven-figured Yerrak, joined the strongest men in the company and they set about bending the iron-bound, throwing arms off the catapults, snapping off the releasing levers. Hidden knives severed ropes and pulleys, axle grease from the buckets that hung beneath was used to smear the rungs of the siege ladders and the pull handles of the battering rams, while sharp stones and broken shards of wood and metal were carefully pushed in amongst the giant cogs and winding wheels. It was all done in an instant and so surreptitiously that nothing looked out of place after the circus had passed and crossed the square.

Nevian steered his wagon in close to the wall beside the doors of Candlebane Hall and the Kindred Spirit, grim-faced and ready to make their stand, closed ranks around him as their music died away. The old man reached into the wagon and pulled out a tightly furled standard. 'Do not reveal yourselves just yet,' he warned, 'but unharness the horses and be ready to release the owls the moment I cut the thongs that bind this King's emblem. When it flies that shall be your signal.'

Grannog and the Border Runners who had been moving hidden beneath the carts and wagons, began moving slowly forwards, their hackles raised, their fangs bared in silent snarls. Orundus and the owls unhooked their talons in readiness to stoop from where they floated in the air above their unsuspecting enemies. A ripple of movement, no more than a breath of wind that might stir in the summer corn, passed through the Kindred Spirit as they gripped the hilts of their swords or reached for the spears that were hidden beneath the floors of their carts. As the music died away the city folk who had dared to venture out of their houses to follow the circus up through the city reached the archway that led into the upper circle. The Honourable Company of Murderers had forbidden them to go anywhere near Candlebane Hall since the siege began. They had been threatened on pain of death and the fear of this punishment made them hesitate, full of fear. As they wondered what to do they heard Snatchpurse's army approaching, filling the lanes behind them. Too late they realized that there was no escape – they were cut off with nowhere to hide.

Nevian saw their dilemma and heard them cry out in panic. He quickly urged them to run across the square, telling them that there was space enough for all of them behind the wagons and carts. The air darkened and the sun vanished behind the clouds as though it heralded doom; the sounds of flocks of carrion birds wheeling overhead with bloodcurdling shrieks, and armoured boots scraping over wet cobbles grew louder and louder. The Kindred Spirit instinctively drew closer together, bracing themselves as Snatchpurse, brandishing his battle mace, burst through the archway at the head of his army with the Loremaster creeping alongside him. His army spilled through into the square, the hideous creatures running to their places at the seige engines and battering rams or hurrying to grab at one of the forest of siege ladders. The rest formed themselves into dense ranks ready to storm the Candlehall the moment its walls were breached, eager to see the doors riven and splintered upon the ground.

Snatchpurse was anxious to break the siege and started ordering his men to their places, unaware of the circus' presence. He had reached the centre of the square before Grout brought them to his attention by commenting on the pleasure it would be to have such a colourful gathering to witness his victory. The Loremaster's words brought Snatch to an abrupt halt and he cursed, spitting at the ground between his feet when he saw them.

'They are not witnesses, you fool! They are nothing but a raggedy, no-good band of gypsies who have plagued me with their unsavoury presence all the way from Stumble Hill!'

He turned, furious, and snarled at his captain, 'Who told them they could trespass here before the doors of my Candlehall? Who gave these beggars and vagrants permission even to enter the upper circle of the city? I want them all out of here, do you hear, out of this square immediately! From now on all gypsies and vagrants, all beggars are to be murdered on sight.'

'Why don't we let them stay, Snatch, they'll give us good sport,' Kush laughed. 'They'll die like squashed flies beneath the rubble once our siege engines are set in motion. And if they try to make a run for it then we cut them down. They are trapped here, they'll never get through the archway.'

Snatchpurse nodded, almost smiling at the thought, it would be the perfect way to be rid of them once and for all. He lifted his hand to give the signal for the assault to begin but then hesitated. His mouth tightened into a sour line of hatred as he caught sight of Crimp coming through the archway dragging Sloeberry by the heavy chains that shackled her.

'Crimp, bring that creature over here. I want her beside

me to witness the final moment of my triumph. Hurry, boy, hurry.'

Snatchpurse was impatient to begin and as soon as he was close enough he struck Crimp a hard blow across the top of his head for dawdling and sneered when he saw the girl stumble and trip as the line slaked out and cut into her bleeding ankles.

'Nobody is ever going to rescue you. Even that cripple's ghost won't be able to help you now. There is nobody to save you or the Thronestealer, they are all dead! Come on, let us move closer to the doors of Candlebane Hall, the view of the Thronestealer's final defeat will be much better from there.'

As he walked away he tugged viciously on her chains, pulling her through the lines of the siege engines.

'Well, old man, you were right when you foretold that I would be the most powerful man in all Elundium; it is a pity that you were not clever enough to foretell your own death,' Snatch gloated as he saw Nevian stand up and support himself on the seat of the wagon, holding onto a rough wooden slat bound with a ragged old piece of embroidered cloth.

'Do not be so sure. Power can be as elusive as quicksand, and as difficult as mercury to hold onto. Remember, the crown is not yet yours.'

Nevian spoke softly as he broke the first of the three thongs that bound and hid the King's standard. He had caught a glimpse of the faces crowding the windows high up in the Candlehall and he knew they had watched the Kindred Spirit as they crossed the square. He also thought he had seen movement – figures hiding in the shadows around the derelict houses that bordered the streets. The sight of them had rekindled the hope that they were not alone, that those figures belonged to loyal kingsmen who had reached the city in time. But that hope hung by such a slender thread and he held his breath as he broke the second thong.

In the silence he thought he heard the faint sounds of the siege locks being released from the thick, ironwood doors of Candlebane Hall. He listened as he made out the sound of rusty bolts and latches being slowly drawn back. Doubt flickered momentarily in Snatchpurse's eyes and he glanced behind him at the dark mass of his army who were poised and ready, waiting only for the signal to attack. He threw his head back and laughed at his fears.

'And who is going to stop me now? Who will stop me seizing the crown – you, you frail old man? Will you stop me, you and your ragged band of gypsies?'

With a swift tug at the final cord Nevian raised the King's standard and the picture of the owl upon a field of gold spread out beside him. 'We are not quite what we would seem,' he cried out, casting aside the ragged, hessian cloak to reveal his rainbow cloak. When Nevian had unfurled the King's standard the Kindred Spirit had taken it as a signal to release the owls and they had shed their disguise to immediately attack the flocks of unsuspecting carrion birds and drive them out of the city.

All around him the Kindred Spirit cried out defiantly, calling for the King and casting back their cloaks to reveal their weapons. Snatchpurse was taken completely by surprise and cursed himself for not following his instincts and murdering the treacherous circus folk from the moment he first saw them. As he stared at them in shock the doors of Candlebane Hall were flung open and King Thane, pale and wasted, yet still proud and armed ready for battle stood, surrounded by many of the city folk who had weathered the siege with him, all armed with swords and spears, all crowding round, pushing forwards and standing on the steps of the Candlehall.

Snatchpurse rapidly regained his composure and sneered at them as he raised his hand to give the signal for his men to attack. 'You fools, you stupid fools, there are not enough of you to hold that doorway against me.' His laugh echoed around the square. 'If you think you can stop me with this futile gesture of defiance then you must be blind. Don't you realize? You will all be dead in a few moments.'

He dropped his hand, motioning for the attack to begin. The Kingsmen standing on the steps shrank back. The huge siege engines rattled and groaned as the men working them wound the pullies and loaded the massive boulders and cauldrons of boiling oil in their cradles, preparing to hurl the contents. They creaked and shook and suddenly the wood began to splinter and the iron bands binding them sheared apart. Ropes snapped and cogs jammed and one by one the engines of destruction began to break apart as their mechanisms exploded making them sway and topple onto their sides.

Snatchpurse spun round, white-faced and livid, watching helplessly as his precious war engines smashed themselves to pieces. Many of his men were screaming, trapped beneath them, boiling oil scalding their skin as it poured out of the upturned cauldrons and spread out across the cobbles. The sight of the devastation and ruin sent a ripple of fear through the solid mass of men who were waiting to storm Candlebane Hall. As the thunder of the last engine toppling over onto its side faded, they heard another sound that put terror into their hearts. It was the sound of hoofbeats echoing in the narrow lanes that led up through the city and the rush of armoured boots coming from beyond the high archway. It was getting louder by the moment and with it came the roar of a thousand voices calling out the King's name.

Suddenly the Marchers and Gallopers were streaming through the archway and pouring out of hundreds of hiding places around the square, lowering their spears as they advanced. The gnarled old trees that lined the square suddenly came to life and began to stride forward as they reached out with their strong, knobbly hands, grabbing at the frightened men. Armed Tunnellers were running through the archway led by Lord Willow, Tombel and a company of Marchers who were close in behind them. Drib suddenly appeared, galloping through the archway on Esteron, sword in hand and Silkstone flying, talons out, above him. He was standing high in his stirrups, frantically trying to catch sight of Sloeberry.

'Attack! Attack!' Snatchpurse screamed as he saw victory slipping through his fingers, but his vast army of pressed men hesitated. They remembered the whispers they had heard in the dark on their long journey along the greenway and wondered if the King really would forgive them if they surrendered.

'Attack you scum! What's keeping you, attack them now!'

Kush, Huxort and all of Snatchpurse's captains who had been infected by the evil of the Eretch shouted and raised their iron-tipped flails in an effort to drive the men forwards, but one by one those who remembered Drib's words began to throw down their weapons and drop to their knees, their voices joining together as they called out to the King for mercy and forgiveness.

Snatchpurse seethed with fury as he raised his battle

mace. He was about to stride in amongst his men and force them forward when a movement seen from the corner of his eye caught his attention and he spun round just in time to see Nevian jump down from his wagon and reach out to pull Sloeberry to safety. With a snarl of pure hatred he hurled his mace at the magician. It spun once in the air and struck the old man hard in the centre of his chest sending him crashing backwards against the wheel of the wagon, his breath knocked out of him. Snatchpurse grabbed at Sloeberry's chains and as he brutally pulled her closer to him he unsheathed his dagger.

'You ugly little goblin, you will not escape, I will cut out your heart and hold it up for all to see. I will slit your throat in full sight of all those cowards before you take another step!' He grabbed at her chains and brutally pulled her closer to him as he unsheathed his dagger.

Silkstone hooted a shrill warning, flying down to Drib's shoulder and pressing his talons through the weave of his doublet, making him look across the square. 'No! No!' Drib cried out in horror as he suddenly spotted Sloeberry struggling to get away from Snatchpurse who had already raised his dagger for the killing blow.

The owl rose into the air and Esteron forced a path through the crush of men, rearing and plunging, leaping over everything that lay in their way. Eider had just ridden in beneath the archway at the head of the company of Largg's huntsmen and he heard Drib's desperate cry. Looking across the square he saw Snatchpurse raise his dagger and he reached back into his quiver, finding a steel-bladed barbed arrow which he quickly nocked onto the great hunting bow that Largg had given him. Snatchpurse was almost out of bowshot, but he knew he could not afford to miss.

'Stand!' he whispered to Nightshade as he pressed his knees against the rolls of the saddle as he drew the arrow back until its feathered flight touched his cheek lightly. Nightshade stood perfectly still, neck arched and breathing hard as the huntsmen surged by on either side. Eider could hear the pounding of his own heart as he carefully took aim and waited for a clear shot.

Berioss and the other tree warriors had been waiting in the upper circle of the city for Nevian to arrive before they revealed themselves; he had not realized that the magician had been leading the circus until he had watched him unfurl the King's standard and cast off his disguise. He had hurried forwards when Snatchpurse struck the old man with his mace, hurling his spear which had glanced off the wagon to fall harmlessly to the ground. Looking around, eager to find something else to help him save Sloeberry he caught sight of a double-handed battle axe that lay discarded on the ground and he reached down, grasping it with both of his knobbly hands. Suitably armed he strode forward towards Snatchpurse.

Crimp thought he could do no more to protect Sloeberry when he saw the magician jump down to pull her to safety, and he thought to use the moment of confusion to creep away and save his own skin. He heard Sloeberry cry out. Looking back he saw the flash of sunlight on Snatchpurse's dagger as he raised it above the frightened girl's head. At that moment something snapped inside Crimp. This time he would find his courage, this time he would not let that monster harm anybody else. He would do something, he would stop him – but how? Crimp grabbed the hilt of his dagger and brandished it but he was too far away.

'Here, boy, use this,' and the handle of Snatchpurse's

iron-tailed whip was pressed into his empty hand by the breathless magician.

Crimp grasped the handle and lifted the flail high into the air as he rose to his feet. All the rage, the anger, the hatred of the terrible things he had been forced to do came together and focused on that creature who stood towering over Sloeberry. He struck out with all his strength and the lash sang through the air, its razor-sharp iron tails wrapping and knotting themselves tightly around Snatchpurse's throat, cutting into his scaly skin, choking him and freezing his stabbing arm. Snatchpurse gave a cry of pain as Crimp jerked hard on the handle of the whip and the flails began to cut deeper, strangling him. He staggered as he gasped for air, dropping Sloeberry's chain and clawing at his bloodied neck. His eyes began to bulge, not with pain but with blind fury. His mouth snarled and frothed as he lunged savagely at Crimp, slashing and stabbing at him, trying to murder him as much as he was trying to save himself.

Crimp tried to jump back out of his way but it was too late, Snatch's blade jerked viciously upwards, piercing his chest, splintering the bone. Hot blood gurgled in his throat as he was lifted up off the ground and for a moment everything seemed to be frozen in a blur of pain. Then he could see clearly. He could see an owl stooping out of the sky and flying towards Snatchpurse's snarling face, he could hear the thunder of approaching hoofbeats and the sweet sound of arrows shrieking through the air. With his last ounce of strength, before his life-blood completely seeped away, Crimp tried to plunge his own dagger into Snatchpurse's heart. His strength was failing, the blade barely scraped the skin of the toughened hide and Snatchpurse snarled and spat in the dying boy's face. He was about to hurl him aside when a carefully aimed arrow struck Crimp's hand as it held the dagger, forcing the knife through the scales and into Snatchpurse's chest.

The Chancellor's son shuddered as he looked at the killing thrust and watched his black heart pump out his life's blood. He sank to his knees and as his strength ebbed so the Eretch began to ooze out of him, wailing as they vanished into the sky. Crimp looked up towards Sloeberry and saw her cradled in Nevian's arms with Berioss about to bring the battle-axe down on the chains that bound her. She was safe, released from that tortuous misery; there was no more he could do. With a soft sigh Crimp's head sank forwards onto his chest and he welcomed the darkness of death as it closed in around him.

At that moment Drib appeared, galloping hard across the square. He had heard her call out his name, he had seen the tears of joy in her eyes and as she reached up he leaned down out of the saddle, gathering her up in his arms. She was safe, at last! She was with him and the evil torturer was dead. A great shout of victory rose up from all those loyal kingsmen who had watched Snatchpurse's body collapse onto the cobbles while it was abandoned by its evil allies, then they saw all the other creatures still possessed by the Eretch close ranks around their leader's body. The black wraiths were whispering to their hosts, scratching inside their heads, warning them they could expect no mercy for the crimes they had committed and telling them to fight, telling them there was no other escape.

With snarls and curses the Honourable Company of Murderers raised their weapons. Kyot signalled to his Archers and all the warriors that surrounded the square lowered their spears. They all waited on the King's command.

'Fire!'

The arrows sang as they shrieked across the square and every one of the Honourable Company of Murderers fell writhing to the ground as vile ghostly shapes and pools of shadows seemed to make their evil bodies take on another life.

'Their shadows! Tread on their shadows! We must drive the evil out!' called out Errant from the steps of the Candlehall.

Lord Willow led the Tunnellers in amongst the creatures and before the Eretch had a chance to react they ran amongst the bodies and began to stamp on their shadows. The dark evil of Eretch was driven out of the bodies – it seeped out through their armoured, scaly skins, flowed through their eyes and gurgled out of their mouths. The air above Candlebane Hall darkened as the cloud of their ghostly shapes rose, but with the next breath of wind they were blown away. Gone forever.

The ranks of the Kindred Spirit cheered Drib on as he gathered up Sloeberry and they opened their ranks to let him through. He reined Esteron to a halt at the bottom of the steps of Candlebane Hall and stood in front of the King where he gently lowered Sloeberry to the ground. Immediately a crowd gathered and a locksmith picked the locks, throwing the shackles to one side as healers bathed her raw wounds with oiled cottons. Drib dismounted and knelt to offer the hilt of his sword up to King Thane as he handed him the reins of the proud Warhorse, behind them the roars of victory rose to new heights as the evil shadows of the Eretch melted away.

'Lord, I know it was wrong of me but I borrowed Esteron without your permission.'

King Thane silenced him with a smile and a shake of

his head. 'Esteron is a Lord of Horses, Drib, it is he who decides who shall sit upon his back, and he alone. But come with me, both of you, there are more important matters to put right.'

Leading Drib and Sloeberry to the top step of the Candlehall he held their hands for all to see and then summoned Nevian to read out the names of all the Tunnellers who had been falsely accused of starting all the troubles that had brought Elundium to the brink of ruin. Then he called to Eidergoose and Marcher Berioss who stood awkwardly with him at the top of the steps.

'People of Elundium,' Thane gently called to all the people in the square, 'we owe a great debt of gratitude to these who I have summoned here before you, for they alone held the fate of Elundium in their hands. Their courage never faltered and to them all honour is given. The freedom of this city and the free passage in all Elundium is theirs, and they shall want for nothing for the rest of their lives.'

The cheers of the crowds rose to a deafening roar of approval and then Loremaster Grout and Sweepscuttle were brought forward to answer for their crimes and the cheers fell away into an uneasy silence, for many of them knew how they had aided and abetted Grout and Sweepscuttle in those first heady daylights when the Chancellors' sons had seized power. They held their breath, fearing that either of the accused may single them out, detail their part in bringing the King to his knees. King Thane swept his eyes over the silent crowd. He knew full well how they had betrayed him and yet if he wished to rebuild his kingdom he had to find the strength to forgive them.

'Well, Drib?' he said, turning to the small crippled boy and away from the two men who were crying out for mercy and trying to lay the blame on one another. 'Neither of them treated you too kindly in the past, what would you have me do with them?'

'I . . . I . . . I don't know. I don't want you to hurt them but they must make some amends for their crimes I suppose.'

'I think, my lord, I have the perfect solution,' Nevian called out. 'Sweepscuttle should be reduced in rank to a humble journeyman sweep who will travel the length and breadth of Elundium to clean the chimneys of the peasant folk, his only reward being the food that the people choose to give him; while Grout should journey back with us to my tower in the Runesgate where I believe there is enough copying and sorting of my books of magic to keep him busy for a very long time. Drib will need a good scribe if he is to fathom out an antidote to break the spell that I once cast over Berioss and all these other warriors. I don't doubt they are growing very impatient and would wish to be turned back to their own shapes.'

'Do you mean that I am to return to the Runesgate? But what about Sloeberry?' Drib frowned, putting a protective arm around her shoulders.

'Sloeberry will come with you, of course. Have you not realized yet, boy, that your destiny is to follow in my footsteps? If you are to become a Master of Magic you will have to come back with me and finish your apprenticeship.'

Smiles and murmurs of approval rippled through the crowd, mixed with relief that the King had let them off so lightly. But he had not finished with them yet.

'There shall be a shadow-treading ceremony on each mid-winter's day that you are all commanded to attend. It will be a pilgrimage of many days: you will be marching in the worst of weathers and it will serve to remind you how close your actions brought Elundium to the brink of ruin.'

'This shadow-treading ceremony should be held at the Rising,' Lord Willow announced, and the King quickly agreed.

Nevian laughed and lifted his arms high into the air, shaking out the shimmering folds of his rainbow cloak so that it caught all the glory of the low winter's sunlight. 'Tonight!' he called out to the hushed, expectant crowd, 'Tonight there shall be a great feast. There will be music and laughter ringing around Candlebane Hall once more and in the firelight we will hear the brave stories told of how the victory was won.'

'No, Nevian, no. Much as I would dearly wish it – and I would share my last crust with these people – there is no food in the city, not enough for a great feast such as this. Surely you have not forgotten that the Chancellors have brought us to the brink of ruin – they have almost starved us.' Thane was frowning anxiously as he tried to prevent the magician promising the impossible, but it was already too late, the words had slipped out and talk of the great victory feast was spreading faster than quickfire through the crowd.

Nevian looked out into the far distance, his head tilted slightly to one side as he chuckled. 'Have faith, my Lord, the food for this feast will be provided, and more besides. Order the servers and the cooks and scullions to prepare the banqueting hall, have fires lit beneath the empty roasting spits and lay the tables with the best crystal goblets and china plates. There are unknown friends on the road and they are near journey's end.' The old man smiled and held Thane's bewildered gaze for a moment before he slipped into the crowd and disappeared.

'Unknown friends? But who can they be? Every friend a man could ask for, and more, is already here. Nevian, wait . . .' Thane began, but his anxiety turned to a shout of joy when he saw Elionbel with Eventine and the children surrounded by a strike of Archers riding beneath the archway into the inner city. Many of the crowd had already turned and a great welcoming cheer began to echo around the walls as the people drew back and left a clear path across the square.

Stumble, weary from such a long journey but still proud, arched his neck and with bit rings jangling he forged his way ahead of the others to lead them towards Candlebane Hall. There were tears of joy in Thane's eyes as he ran down the steps to meet his wife. He reached up and embraced Elionbel as she threw herself from Stumble's saddle into his arms.

'You were my one hope through every dark daylight. Oh how I have prayed for this moment, my love,' he whispered lifting her up off the ground and holding her tightly, his heart too full for more words. Mulcade stooped silently down to Thane's shoulder, his wings outspread as a shield of privacy from the eyes of the crowd and he alone saw the moment their lips met and it was some moments before Thane led his wife into Candlebane Hall amidst applause and laughter.

Time slipped quickly through the hour glass in the aftermath of such a victory and there was much to do as the people cleared away the debris of the siege. But everyone lent a hand, and with much hustle and bustle Candlebane Hall and all the tables in the banqueting hall were prepared for the evening. Soft candlelight reflected from the hundreds of rows of empty plates and crystal goblets as the sun set in a blaze of fire beyond the distant horizon line. Thane stood with his wife close beside him to look out of the high windows across the city and watch the nightshapes as they began to swirl and drift slowly up over the granite walls and weather-bleached roofs, filling the steep winding lanes and blind alleyways with the colour of night. Thane was worried, what was he to do? Nevian had assured him that food for the feast would be provided but the people were even now beginning to make their way up through the city and the tables were empty.

'Lord, there are lights upon the road – thousands of them – and they are approaching the city,' a watchman shouted from the top of the towers of granite.

Thane frowned as he peered out into the thickening gloom and he saw a slow moving procession of heavily laden wagons and carts surrounded by horsemen dressed in clothes that appeared to be fashioned entirely from animal skins. As the procession reached the lamps that illuminated the Stumble Gate and passed beneath the archway Thane caught glimpses of dozens of Nightboars and all manner of wild game that had been killed and gutted to make them ready for the roasting spits. They were piled up in the carts and there seemed no end to them.

'There must be food enough for the victory feast and enough for the people of Elundium to fill their stores to keep them through the winter. It is a miracle. But who has brought it all here?' Thane cried, trying to see who had come to lead the procession through his city and up the narrow streets.

'Come, we must greet our guests, whoever they are. We must give them thanks for what they are so bounteously providing,' Elionbel laughed as she squeezed Thane's hand and hurried down the narrow stairway into the hall.

By the time they reached the gallery above the banqueting hall the first of the Nightboar carcasses was being positioned over the roasting pits and a young lad was basting it with hot fat. The halls were filling rapidly as the people from the city came to celebrate their freedom and all those loyal kingsmen who had gathered to fight with King Thane were helping to unload the heavy wagons and carrying in barrels of mead and flagons of wine. The women were carrying great rounds of cheese, baskets of wholesome forest fruits, sweetmeats of every kind imaginable and freshly baked breads and they were setting them down on the tables before finding themselves places for the feast. The noise and the hubbub subsided as Thane and Elionbel's presence was felt and by the time they reached the last stair the King was none the wiser as to who had just arrived in his hall. The crowd thronged around the threshold but they moved respectfully aside as Nevian, accompanied by Thunderstone, brought into the hall an elderly huntsman cloaked entirely in a cape of pure ermine with a beautiful young woman walking at his side.

Nevian looked up and frowned as he realized that Thane would not know of Largg. He opened his mouth to introduce him but before he could utter a word Eider, bow in hand, burst into the hall, blushing with embarrassment as everybody turned to stare at him while he threw himself down to kneel in front of the King. He was ashamed of himself for forgetting to deliver the letter that Largg, Lord of the high peaks of the Emerald Mountains, had entrusted with him on the morning that he had left the tower beside the azure lake.

'Lord, Lord, I must apologize for not giving you this important dispatch. It was entrusted to me but I completely forgot about it, there was so much to do, we had to secure the city when the Chancellors were defeated . . .' he stuttered, breathless, and turned to fumble for the crumpled parchment that was hidden inside his tunic.

'There is no excuse for forgetfulness, Eider, but the letter is not needed now.' Nevian smiled. 'In fact the lack of it has made the surprise of Largg's arrival with the provisions all the better. Get up, boy, the King doesn't want you grovelling at his feet, this feast is a time for celebration. Now get up.'

The old magician bent stiffly to offer the young Archer a hand but Largg was quicker and he firmly gripped Eider's arm as he pulled him to his feet. Eider felt such a fool for forgetting the letter but his colour deepened as he caught sight of Ayeshe standing beside her father. She stepped forward, her eyes gentle, and took his hand to bring him closer.

Greygoose, Eider's father, had just ushered his family to their rightful place amongst the other Archers of the city when he caught sight of his son as he burst into the hall with such disrespect and he watched in horror as the boy tried to plead for the King's forgiveness. He was too far away to hear what was being said, or what was being discussed between Largg and the King, but he watched as his son was brought to his feet and held by the hunters; he had no doubts that whatever his son had done it would bring shame and more disgrace on his family's name. Much as the Captain of the Archers had wanted to believe otherwise throughout the long siege, and despite the King praising Eider and all the others who had helped to defeat the Chancellors, there was no escaping the fact that the boy had sunk into bad company. One look at the wild clothes he was wearing and at the way he carried his bow was enough to tell him that. Pale faced, Greygoose took a step forward, lifting his hands towards his son in the hope of catching his eye and stopping him thrusting himself forward where he did not belong. Good manners should have told him to wait at least until the feast was over.

The delicious smells of roasting meats were beginning to waft through the hall as Elionbel escorted Largg towards the high table. Thane hesitated, turning to Nevian to ask, 'What do you think has happened to Drib, Sloeberry and Berioss – and what about the rest of the Tunnellers and all the warriors who are still trapped by your magic? What of them? Surely we cannot begin before they arrive?'

The old magician lifted his head and tilted it slightly to one side as though he were listening, catching at sounds that originated beyond the noisy talk and laughter that filled the smoky halls. After a moment he chuckled softly, 'They are just beyond the threshold and it will be but a moment before they are with us, my Lord.'

Thane turned to glance towards the entrance where the last of the city folk were hurrying through to their places when he caught sight of Greygoose trying to catch his son's attention. He knew something of the distress Eider's sudden disappearance had caused for his father and he knew that his Chief Archer blamed himself for the boy running away from the city. 'Eider,' he called out sharply, 'I think that before you take your place at table, young man, you had better go and see your family, they deserve an explanation – they have been distraught with worry since your disappearance.'

'Perhaps, my Lord,' Nevian intervened, signalling towards the minstrels' gallery, 'we should ask Largg's minstrels to entertain the company while we wait to start the feast. There is one particular ballad that Greygoose should hear.'

Three of Largg's musicians began to sing and Greygoose's eyes brimmed with tears of pride as he listened to the ballad of how his son had found the courage to stand his ground and alone, with just one carefully-aimed arrow, slew the huge, winged dragma beast and saved Ayeshe's life. The vast company in the hall fell silent as they heard the song and there was silence amongst them as the verses unfolded and it became clear that Eider was held in great esteem amongst Largg's people. Greygoose realized, as he looked across to his son, that he had wrongly misjudged him. The wild boy had, indeed, grown into a fine young man.

A movement at the entrance of the hall made the King turn and he smiled as he saw Drib and Sloeberry, hand in hand hurrying into the hall. He then gave the long-awaited signal for the feast to begin. Before his hand had lowered his eyes widened with surprise as he saw Berioss following a few footsteps behind them.

'By all the magic that once dwelt in my rainbow cloak what has happened to you?' Nevian exclaimed in astonishment.

His shouted surprise stopped the musicians' song and all eyes turned towards the old Marcher. He looked almost like his old self. Gone were the knobbly branches that had once served as arms. Gone were his twig-like fingers, his thick legs and the mass of roots that once had protruded from his toes. Everything had shrunk back to its normal size: his feet were once more encased in boots and the age-cracked bark that had covered his body had vanished. He looked, well he looked almost like the old Marcher Berioss, except, if possible, he looked younger.

But how had this come about? With raised eyebrows Nevian turned his gaze towards Drib, but try as he might he could not disguise the smile of delight as he asked, 'Well, Drib, what have you been up to? It looks as though you could hardly wait until my back was turned.'

Drib felt his face flush hotly. 'I ... I ... I didn't mean any harm, honestly, but you did say I was to try to discover an antidote to that spell you once cast over Berioss once we got back to the Runesgate – don't you remember? Well I read some and remembered a few from the last time I was in the tower and I thought if I put them together and spoke them out loud just before the sun set – well the next moment Berioss was changing back into his old self. You're not cross are you? I haven't done the wrong thing again have I?'

'Cross? No, my boy, I'm not cross at all. In fact I am delighted, yes, quite delighted to discover that you have such a talent, and you must develop it, you really must. Now you have to tell me exactly how you wove the spells together, and you must record it, it is really most intriguing.'

'Now enough, the food is spoiling,' Thane called out. 'Minstrels play and let tales of great valour be told in the firelight as we eat.' He gently put his hands upon Drib and Sloeberry's shoulders to guide them into their places on the high table.

At a signal from the King everyone in the banqueting hall rose to their feet as they reached their places and the people lifted their crystal cups and silver goblets. Thane waited for silence and then with a loud, clear voice he called out, 'Once, while riding through this city, I came upon a small, crippled boy who lay bleeding and hurt in the gutter. He had been cruelly treated, beaten by his peers, taunted for daring to dream. And what was his dream? He dreamt that one day he would ride a great Warhorse. When I heard that I lifted him up out of the gutter and set him upon Esteron's saddle. I told him that it was no crime to dream, I also said that sometimes it was our dreams that helped us to achieve more than we ever thought possible. I now know that if Drib had not held onto his dreams, that if he had faltered in the face of adversity, if he had once allowed doubts to take a hold, then we would not all be here to celebrate the victory with this feast tonight. Good people of Elundium, let us all give thanks to Drib.'

Drib didn't know where to look and he felt his face flush scarlet as the crowd all gave a great shout of thanks. The sound rose and echoed through the smoky rafters of Candlebane Hall. The King leaned across to him and said softly, 'Now we can say that we truly stand on the threshold of a new Elundium and it is because of everything you and the Knights of Cawdor achieved.'

Magician
Raymond E. Feist
New Revised Edition

Raymond E. Feist has prepared a new, revised edition, to incorporate over 15,000 words of text omitted from previous editions so that, in his own words, 'it is essentially the book I would have written had I the skills I possess today'.

At Crydee, a frontier outpost in the tranquil Kingdom of the Isles, an orphan boy, Pug is apprenticed to a master magician – and the destinies of two worlds are changed forever. Suddenly the peace of the Kingdom is destroyed as mysterious alien invaders swarm through the land. Pug is swept up into the conflict but for him and his warrior friend, Tomas, an odyssey into the unknown has only just begun. Tomas will inherit a legacy of savage power from an ancient civilisation. Pug's destiny is to lead him through a rift in the fabric of space and time to the mastery of the unimaginable powers of a strange new magic. . .

'Epic scope . . . fast-moving action . . . vivid imagination'
Washington Post

'Tons of intrigue and action'   *Publishers Weekly*

ISBN 0 586 21783 3

Weaveworld
Clive Barker

Weaveworld is an epic adventure of the imagination. It begins with a carpet in which a world of rapture and enchantment is hiding; a world which comes back to life, alerting the dark forces from which it was hiding, and beginning a desperate battle to preserve the last vestiges of magic which Humankind still has access to.

Mysteriously drawn by the carpet and into the world it represents are Cal Mooney and Suzanna Parrish, two young people with no knowledge of what they are about to live through and confront. For the final conflict between the forces of good – the Seerkind – and of evil, embodied by the terrible Immacolata and her ravening twin wraith sisters, is about to take place.

Weaveworld is a book of visions and horrors, as real as the world we live and breathe in, yet opening doors to experiences, places and people that we all dream of, but daren't hope are real. It is a story of quest, of titanic struggles, of love and of hope. It is a triumph of imagination and storytelling, an adventure, a nightmare, a promise . . .

'Graphic, grotesque, and yet compellingly readable . . . its energy is unstoppable.'   *Washington Post*

'A powerful and fascinating writer with a brilliant imagination. *Weaveworld* reveals Clive Barker as an outstanding storyteller.'   J. G. Ballard

ISBN 0 00 617489 2